THERE WAS NO AVOIDING IT . . .

He was here, and she would have to confront him. Reminding herself that her children's future rested on the next few minutes, she squared her shoulders and stepped forward with her hand outstretched.

"My lord, I am pleased to make your acquaintance," she said, a polite smile of welcome pasted on her lips. "I often heard my dear husband speak of you, and it is a great honor to meet you."

Stephen stared at her hand as if he'd never before seen such an object, and then he slowly reached out to take it in his. "Lady Brockton," he said, his voice hoarse as he struggled to master the emotions raging inside of him. Just what the hell was going on? he wondered, his lips thinning with suppressed fury.

Cat saw the fury in his dark eyes and suppressed a tiny sigh. This was going to be difficult.

Lady Cat

Joan Overfield

Zebra Books
Kensington Publishing Corp.
http://www.zebrabooks.com

To my beloved grandniece, JC Thrall

ZEBRA BOOKS are published by

Kensington Publishing Corp.
850 Third Avenue
New York, NY 10022

First Printing: January, 1999
10 9 8 7 6 5 4 3 2 1

Printed in the United States of America

Prologue

Keswick, England 1810

"Please, Catheryn, say you will do it."

"Hush, Edward, you know you must not say such things," Lady Catheryn Brockton implored, her tone gentle as she laid a cool cloth against her husband's forehead. She'd been performing the repetitive task since early afternoon, and her hands were chapped and cold from the constant immersion in water. She knew one of the servants could easily have done the same thing, but she refused to leave Edward's side.

"Why shouldn't I say it?" Edward, the seventh Viscount Brockton, demanded in the peevish tone of the invalid. "It is the truth."

"I know, but I don't want you to agitate yourself," Cat said, her voice trembling with emotion. "You know Dr. McGwen said that you—"

"The devil with the doctor!" Edward's eyes glittered in his wasted face. "I am dying, blast it! What difference does it make whether I am agitated or not?"

Cat's dark green eyes grew misty, and she quickly lowered them lest Edward see the tears. She knew he was only speaking the truth, but still the knowledge was painful.

"Catheryn . . ." As if sensing her misery the viscount stretched out a thin hand and laid it on her arm. "I know what I am asking of you is difficult," he said, his voice soft, "but you must know I would never do such a thing if there was any other way."

Despite her unhappiness, Cat could not help but smile at his words. "Difficult," she repeated, shaking her head as she lifted her eyes to meet his. "Oh, Edward, you always were the master of the understatement."

An answering smile touched the viscount's lips as he gazed up at his young wife. "And you were often the only one to catch my little witticisms," he remembered. "I recall when you first came here as governess, I'd catch you hiding a smile even as my fine guests failed to get the joke. You were always too sharp by half."

This reminder of her original position at Larks Hall drove the smile from Cat's lips, and she glanced uneasily away. "I know you are worried about the succession," she said, her hands twisting in her lap. "And given the alternative, I can not say that I blame you. But you must see that what you are suggesting is wrong."

"Why?"

The simple question brought her eyes flashing back to his face. "*Why?* Edward, you are asking me to commit adultery!"

Edward flushed at her bluntness. "You are refining too much on petty morality," he muttered, pleating his sheets between his fingers. "Besides, how can it possibly be adultery when I have given you my permission?"

"But—"

"No, hear me out," he interrupted, his voice surprisingly firm. "I know what you are going to say, but you are wrong. Granted what I am suggesting is a crime in the eyes of the law, but I refuse to believe God would condemn either of us for it. Not when we are doing it for the sake of the children."

The thought of Edward's delightful daughters melted Cat's heart, as it always did. Elizabeth had been eight when Cat had first come to Larks Hall, and Lydia three years younger. From the moment she'd clapped eyes on them her heart had gone out to the two girls, and she adored them as if they were her own. That was why she had agreed to marry Edward when he had asked it of her. She loved her girls, and there was nothing she wouldn't do to insure their happiness. But this. . . .

"Even if what you are saying is true, you still must see the difficulties," she said, forcing herself to be practical. "I am not even acquainted with Lord Rockholme, and from the little I have heard of him I can not say that I should care to change that. The man is a shocking rake."

"Which can only work to our advantage," Edward replied wisely. "A virtuous man would never be tempted to stray from the fold."

"And that is another thing." Cat's creamy skin took on a rosy hue. "What makes you think his lordship would be attracted to me? I am hardly the sort of high flyer he is said to favor."

Her husband gave her a sagacious look. "You will forgive my bluntness, my dear, but to a man like my cousin all cats are alike in the dark. So long as they purr when he strokes them, he has little care as to their appearance."

There seemed to be no proper way to respond to this, and so Cat took refuge in a modest silence. The thought of being in bed with a man . . . any man . . . was still enough to disconcert her. Although she and Edward had been married for over three years, her knowledge of such matters was quite limited. Given the precarious state of his health and his aesthetic nature, she supposed it wasn't surprising she had yet to conceive the son he so desperately craved. But mayhap the problem lay with her, and not with him. She was brooding over the best way to broach the delicate matter when she became aware he was speaking to her.

"I am sorry, sir," she said, sending him an apologetic smile, "but I fear I was not attending. What did you say?"

"I was saying that as for the matter of your not knowing the earl, that can be easily remedied. Open my stationery box."

Puzzled, Cat did as she was bid, opening the red leather case that was always kept at Edward's bedside. Inside she found a letter inviting him to a hunting party to be held the following weekend at the home of Lady Exter, which explained, she supposed, why she had not also received an invitation. The *ton* had yet to forgive the upstart governess for her audacity in marrying a wealthy viscount.

"Lord Exter is one of Stephen's old classmates," Edward explained at her puzzled expression. "The last letter I had from him mentioned he was planning to attend, and that he hoped to see me there."

"Yes, but I fail to see how this will do us any good," Cat pointed out as she returned the card to the box. "The invitation is for *you,* not me."

"Already taken care of, my dear. I have written Lady Exter a letter explaining that while I can not attend, my late wife's younger sister is paying us a visit, and that I would like her to go in my place."

"I wasn't aware Lady Brockton had a younger sister," Cat protested, frowning at memory of the vain, amoral lady who had been her predecessor.

"Few are. Louisa married a man her family considered beneath her touch, and her name was never spoken again," Edward explained, covering his mouth as a cough shook him. When he recovered he continued in a rough voice. "I learned some years ago that her husband had died, so you see, she is perfect for our needs. You will attend the party as Mrs. Frederick Thurston, a lively young widow not adverse to a bit of casual lovemaking."

"Edward!"

"I am sorry, my dear." He had the grace to look ashamed. "But for our sakes that is how you must appear. Granted Stephen is a bit of a rogue, but he's not an out-and-out scoundrel like Jeremey. He would never approach a lady he didn't think would return his attentions."

The mention of her husband's nephew and heir presumptive was enough to make Cat's blood run cold. The man was a brutal, drunken swine, and the memory of the way he had attempted to force himself upon her still gave her nightmares. If Edward hadn't heard her cries . . . She shuddered in horror.

"But . . . but what if I . . . I do not conceive?" she asked, pushing the ugly memories from her mind. "Or what if I have a girl? Mr. Sedgewood would still be your heir, and we would still be beneath his thumb. All of this would have been for naught."

"But we would have tried," Edward corrected gently, covering her hand again with his. "If nothing else we can say we tried. Besides, the Rockholmes have always bred sons; I do not think you will have a worry on that score. Do you really wish to see Larks Hall or the girls in that bastard's hands?" he pressed when she remained silent.

Cat's stomach lurched with nausea at the very thought. Already Jeremey was borrowing against his inheritance, and she knew he'd have the estate bled dry within a matter of years once he was the viscount. Then there were the girls to consider. The last time he'd imposed himself upon them she'd caught him watching Elizabeth, an evil smile on his sallow face.

Because of the rules of inheritance Edward had no choice but to pass his estate on to his nearest surviving male relative. And without a son that heir was the despicable Jeremey Sedgewood. Only a son could protect the home and stepdaughters she loved. A son . . . .

"Very well, Edward," she said at last, knowing in her heart that she had no other choice. "I will do as you ask."

One

Exter Manor, Kent

His last night as a free man. Lord Stephen Jonathan Wrexley, the Earl of Rockholme, allowed the thought to roll about in his mind as he lifted his glass of champagne to his lips. Tomorrow morning he would leave for Portsmouth to meet up with his regiment, and from there depart at once for the peninsula. After that . . . who knew? This could well be his last opportunity to taste the sweet life on this earth, and Stephen knew exactly how he meant to spend it. In bed, with the prettiest and most accomplished lady he could find. Fortunately, for him, that did not present a very great problem.

He glanced casually about him, his midnight-dark eyes, which one of his mistresses had once likened to jet drops, resting on the attractively gowned women gathered in the parlor. He had intimate knowledge of many of them, and had at least flirted with the rest. No challenge there, he decided, his eyes moving on to the group of women gathered in front of the fireplace.

The first woman to catch his eye was a pretty redhead, Lady Davinia Dewhurst, or the Divine Davinia, as the wags insisted upon calling her. She'd been his mistress for a few weeks last year, but he'd cut it off when rumors her elderly husband was threatening a divorce reached his ears.

His gaze lingered thoughtfully on her stunning face as he weighed the dangers against the pleasures, but in the end he decided not to risk it. There was no love so cold as an old love, he thought cynically, and in any case he was in the mood for something new and exciting. Then he saw her.

She was sitting with the other ladies, her glorious black hair caught in an artful arrangement of curls, and her slender body displayed by a stylish gown of green satin. Her features were lovely enough, he supposed, although of course they paled in comparison to Davinia's. Her skin was the color of cream and roses, and he wondered idly if it felt as soft as it looked. He was debating whether it would be worth the trouble to find out when she suddenly glanced up, and eyes as green as the most exquisite emeralds met his.

The breath caught in Stephen's throat, his body tightening in response to the bold appraisal he read in those shimmering green depths. He saw something else as well, but he was too intent upon the way his heart was racing to dwell on some nebulous emotion. Now here, indeed, was a possibility, he decided, his lips curving in a smile of anticipation.

"Fetching little thing, ain't she?" a voice asked at his elbow, and he turned to find Albert, the Marquess of Exter, standing at his side.

"An exquisite," Stephen agreed, his eyes still holding hers. "Who is she?"

"Mrs. Louisa Thurston," Lord Exter provided, taking a sip of champagne. "A relation of sorts to your cousin, Brockton."

"Of sorts?" The woman had glanced away and appeared to be deep in conversation with the lady at her right, but Stephen was too practiced in the sweet games of seduction to be put off by her seeming indifference.

"Mrs. Thurston is the sister of his first wife," his host explained, trying not to grin at the wolfish expression on Stephen's face. "She is apparently a widow who has only recently come out of mourning, and has been staying with Brockton. He wrote Anne to decline her invitation, and then asked if she would invite Mrs. Thurston in his stead. Apparently there is a bit of tension between her and the new wife."

"I can imagine," Stephen drawled, temporarily diverted by the thought of his bookish cousin. He'd forgotten Edward had been invited, and he felt a moment's regret that he wouldn't be seeing him. Of all his far-flung relations Edward was the only one he could tolerate above half an hour's time.

"Yes, well, bound to be some resentment, what? People were properly shocked when Brockton married his children's governess with Marie scarce cold in her grave. Can't say as I blame Mrs. Thurston for getting her pretty nose out of joint."

"It is hard to think of Marie as ever being cold," Stephen observed with a cool laugh. "Not when she is in a horizontal position, at any rate. From the gossip that reached my ears I gather she was as loose as an opera dancer, and would bed down with any man who caught her fancy." His gaze flicked back to Mrs. Thurston. "Is it a family failing, do you think?"

"I wouldn't know, old boy," Lord Exter said with a chuckle. "But if you mean to find out, kindly do me the favor of being discreet. Anne will have my lights and liver if you create a scandal . . . another scandal, that is," he added with a friendly poke in the ribs.

"I will, of course, do all within my power to spare my lovely hostess a moment's discomfiture," Stephen assured him drolly. "Now do your hostly duties and introduce me to the lady fair. Judging from the way Waterville is leering after her, I had best be fast to put in my claim to her affections."

"Since when has a bit of competition bothered you?" Exter demanded, even as he was guiding Stephen across the parlor to where the ladies were sitting. A few seconds later Stephen gave a formal bow as Albert presented him to the object of his desire.

"Mrs. Thurston," he drawled, his eyes meeting hers as he carried her hand to his lips. "May I say what a delight it is to make your acquaintance? You are every bit as lovely as your dear sister."

Those green eyes narrowed fractionally, and for a moment Stephen thought he saw displeasure there; but the expression was quickly gone as she gave him a languid smile. "It is very kind of you to say so, my lord," she said, her voice surprisingly musical. "But most people say Marie and I look nothing alike."

"A scurrilous lie, ma'am," he replied, struggling to recall what his cousin's former wife had looked like. Her hair had been dark if memory served, and he eagerly seized upon the image. "You both are blessed with dark hair, although yours, I think, is a trifle darker. It puts me in mind of black satin."

Her cheeks grew even rosier, and he was enchanted by the sight. He couldn't recollect when he had last seen a blush . . . a genuine blush adorning a lovely woman's cheeks. Deciding he'd played propriety long enough he held out his arm and offered to show her the rose garden. She hesitated fractionally, and he thought she was going to refuse him; but in the end she rose gracefully to her feet, accepting his arm with a smile.

"Exter mentioned you are a widow," he commented as they strolled up and down the moonlit path. "Pray accept my condolences."

"Thank you, sir, but it has been some time now, and I have learned to accept my tragic loss," she replied, her eyes fixed firmly ahead of her. "It was the fever."

"Ah." He gave a wise nod, and they continued in silence for another few feet before he asked. "How are my young cousins doing, by the by? They were snotty-nosed brats the last I saw of them."

To his surprise a smile of genuine delight lit his companion's face. "Well, they aren't snotty-nosed brats now, " she said with a chuckle. "Elizabeth—or Beth, as she informs us she wishes to be called—is going on thirteen, and she is turning into quite the young lady. When I was packing to come here she asked me to pay most specific attention to the ladies' gowns so that I might apprise her of the latest fashions."

"And what of Lydia?" Stephen was secretly pleased that he was able to recall the younger girl's name. "She is . . . what? Seven these days?"

"Nine, and horse-mad as can be. I was adjured to make a thorough study of his lordship's hunters as they are, and I am quoting, 'prime bits of blood.' Her burning ambition at the moment is to be a jockey, and we live in constant fear that she will run off and join a circus troupe or some other such thing."

Again Stephen was surprised both by her apparent fondness of her nieces and by the casual way she spoke of the family. Perhaps relationships between them were not so strained as Exter believed, and for a moment Stephen wondered if he had misread her character.

"And how do they like having their former governess as their new mama?" he asked, drawing his arm slightly down so that she must perforce move closer. If she was as virtuous as he was glumly beginning to suspect she was, she would naturally step away. "I recall my governess, Miss Dicks, and I can think of no fate worse than having her as my mother. She was a hatchet-faced harridan, who was fond of pinching me and locking me in closets when I misbehaved, which, admittedly, was a daily occurrence."

"Miss Elliot . . . that is, Lady Brockton, is nothing like that." She remained at his side. "She is rather nice as a matter of fact, and I certainly would not call her 'hatchet-faced.' "

"Indeed not." Stephen moved so that his thigh brushed against her. "I daresay she must be a diamond of the first water to have tempted my bookish cousin into marriage so quickly after Marie's death."

"Edward is not bookish, and they waited the full twelve months of mourning before taking their vows!"

Her vehemence startled him, and he turned to her with an amazed look. "I beg your pardon," he said, "I meant no offense. I was given to understand you did not approve of the match."

In the moonlight Mrs. Thurston's face showed a variety of emotions, but in the end she assumed a look of polite indifference. "It is none of my business to either approve or disapprove," she said, her voice subdued as she glanced away. "But I do think Society is being rather hard on m—on Lady Brockton. Edward only married her for the sake of the girls, you know. They took their mother's death quite hard, despite the little they saw of her, and he wanted only to provide them with some measure of security."

"That may be, but what of the governess, hmm?" Stephen gave a cynical laugh. "She must have been more than happy to exchange her caps for a coronet."

"She married Edward because she is devoted to the girls, and would do anything for them," he was informed coolly. "Monetary considerations never once crossed her mind."

Stephen studied the proud tilt of her chin before giving a slow smile. "Now I have offended you," he murmured, reaching out to stroke her jaw. "Will it help if I cast myself at your feet and beg forgiveness?"

She flinched at his touch, but did nothing to end it. "I do not think Miss Dicks pinched you nearly enough," she complained with a light laugh. "You are still misbehaving most shamefully."

"That is so," he murmured, turning his casual touch into a caress. "But if you think it will do any good, you may feel free to pinch me anywhere you please. I am putty in a woman's hands."

"Are you?" Her hand stole up to touch his face. "Why do I believe it is the other way around?"

Stephen was about to respond when he heard the tinkling of the dinner bell. Much as he would like to continue this intriguing conversation, he knew he didn't dare risk offending his hostess. Besides, he'd learned that anticipation only made things that much sweeter. With that thought firmly in mind, he took a reluctant step back. "I suppose we had ought to be returning," he said, his eyes lingering on her lips.

"Yes, I-I suppose we had ought to," she agreed, her voice slightly breathless. "I am sure they must be wondering what we are up to out here amongst the pinks and peonies."

"I am sure they have a fair idea," he returned wryly, hoping no one would notice the unmistakable evidence straining the front of his breeches. He gave her mouth another look, and then decided the devil with propriety. If he didn't have at least a taste of those luscious lips, he would go mad. His arms stole about her, and he drew her boldly against him.

"My lord!" Her hands went to his chest as if to push him away, but he would have none of her coyness now. He moved against her until he knew she could not help but be aware of his arousal.

"Ah, my sweeting, you would not be so cruel as to deny a starving man a morsel, would you?" he murmured, bending his head to nip playfully at her lip. "Just one kiss, that is all I ask of you. One small kiss, hmm?" His mouth closed over hers in hungry demand.

The feel of her lips beneath his inflamed Stephen's already heightened senses. Her mouth was honey-sweet, and although her response was somewhat untutored, it was still enough to make him groan with pleasure. By exerting a slight pressure he was able to pry her lips apart, and his tongue slid inside in search of further delights. Her gasp of surprise only made things easier for him, and he deepened the kiss with increasing fervor.

"Ah, God, my dove," he muttered, when at last he raised his head. "But you make my senses swim. Say you will come to my bed tonight. I will die if I can not have you."

"I . . . I . . . Lady Exter . . . she will think me fast," she stammered, her cheeks flushed, and her green eyes dazed. He'd felt her hesitancy when he'd rubbed his tongue against hers, and the knowledge that she wasn't a jaded flirt had filled him with fierce pleasure. Her words that she still considered she had a reputation to protect added to that conviction, and he gave her another kiss.

"Lady Exter, for all she can be rather high in the instep, is no fool," he said, when he could breathe again. "She knows these things happen, and so long as we are discreet, she will have no objection. Now come, say you will join me in my lonely bed. Or I could always join you in yours," he added when she did not answer.

She gave a sudden start. "No! That is . . . I . . . I can come to yours. If you are certain that is what you wish."

Her reply baffled him for a moment, and then he was laughing in eager delight. "Having just been in my arms, dearest one, do you really have any reservations on *that* score?"

To his delight she grew even rosier, and he gave a complacent nod. "Just so, my sweet. Now, if you will give me your arm, I shall escort you back to the house. Much as I would like to ravish you here among the blooms, I am afraid I do not dare. I can wait." He stole another look at his body. "I think."

* * *

Dinner seemed interminable to Stephen. He was forced to sit and eat course after course when his whole body was throbbing with painful anticipation. Because of the seating arrangements, he was placed far up the table from Louisa, but by turning his head he could keep her in sight. He noticed that she only picked at her food, and it pleased him to think she was suffering as much as he was. He also noted she was imbibing rather freely of the excellent wine his host was serving, and he found that less pleasing. Making love to a lady who was jug-bitten was seldom satisfactory to either partner.

"You are frowning, dearest," a soft voice purred in his ear as Lady Dewhurst lay her hand on his arm. "Is your pursuit of the little widow not going as you had hoped?"

He gazed down into her dark blue eyes, trying to remember what he had ever seen in her. She was beautiful, yes, and God knew she was accomplished in bed; but it had been a skill honed in the beds of a dozen men before she had consented to grace his. He decided he preferred a slight bit of shyness in his conquests.

"I was not aware I was pursuing her," he returned in a cool voice. "We spent most of our walk discussing my cousin's young daughters."

Davinia's russet eyebrows arched in affected amusement. "That must have been a disappointment for you," she murmured with a provocative laugh. "But I do not think you spent all your time discussing domestic matters. I know you well enough to know what you look like when you have been . . . shall we say . . . encouraged? What happened? Did Mrs. Thurston suddenly remember her virtue at an inconvenient moment?"

Stephen's face stiffened in disapproval. In the past he would have responded to Davinia's cattiness with a laugh, and perhaps a word or two about the lady he was currently pursuing, but for some reason he could not define, he was reluctant to do the same with Louisa. His dark eyes grew frosty as he picked up his wineglass. "Mrs. Thurston is an exceptional lady," he said dampeningly. "And I think that is all to be said on the matter."

"Got cold feet, did she?" Davinia gave a husky laugh. "Well, I can not say that I am surprised. I was listening to her speak earlier, and really, she is so depressingly *nice.* All she spoke of were her little nieces, and what is worse, I fear she may be a bluestocking. She actually admits to having read Wordsworth." She gave a shudder as if discussing some heinous perversion.

Stephen was tempted to say that he had also read Wordsworth, but decided it was not worth the effort. It was obvious Davinia was but jealous, and he had no desire to make Louisa the target of her displeasure once this night was over. If only he hadn't enlisted, he thought, feeling a twinge of regret for the first time. He would have enjoyed instructing the shy widow in the amorous arts.

Fortunately for his temper, Davinia soon turned her attention elsewhere, and he was free to study Louisa at his leisure. She seemed nervous, and he wondered if he would be her first lover outside of her husband. The realization had a heady effect upon him, and he vowed to take his time in pleasuring her.

There was whist and music after dinner, a punishment Stephen endured with quiet stoicism. Finally the guests began drifting off to their beds, and he waited a full half hour after Louisa had retired before taking his own leave. In his room he made quick use of his basin and razor, not wishing to mark her soft flesh with his beard. He also turned back the sheets, setting the scene for seduction as he had done countless times before. That this might be the last time he made love to a woman in this life added a certain piquancy to the occasion, and his heart was already hammering in excitement.

Time dragged, and he was beginning to think his dove had lost her backbone when the door handle slowly turned. A few seconds later a pair of wide green eyes peered at him from around the door. He gave a welcome smile and started forward.

"There you are, darling," he said, reaching out to draw her into the room. "I was beginning to think you had changed your mind, and that I would have to seek you out."

"I . . . I didn't know how to find your room," she stammered, her eyes growing even wider at the sight of the dark hair peeping through the front of his silk dressing robe. "I didn't want to ask any of the servants, but I didn't know what else to do."

"Which servant did you ask?" he queried, his blood racing

at the sight of her black hair falling to her shoulders in a tangle of ebony curls. He caught some of them in his hand, enjoying the feel of them trailing through his fingers.

"The maid they assigned me," she answered, her breath catching at his touch. "M-Mary, I think she is called."

"Then I must be sure to leave Mary a very nice bonus to see that she develops amnesia," he said, using his grip in her hair to draw her against him. "I would not have you made the object of servants' tattle."

"That is very nice of you, my lord," she replied, giving a soft gasp as he bent his head to press a gentle kiss to her neck.

"I am a nice man." He was smiling as he raised his head. "And you, my love, are entirely too nervous. You've never done this before . . . have you?"

Her face went pale and then a fiery rose. "Nonsense," she denied, dropping her eyes from his intense scrutiny. "I have been . . . I mean, I was married for three years, and my husband was hardly a eunuch."

"But I am your first lover since then," he said, capturing her chin in his hand and turning her face up to his. "Aren't I?"

She licked her lips, a gesture he found highly erotic. "Yes," she admitted quietly, "you are."

He ducked his head and placed a kiss on her mouth. "Thank you," he murmured, butting his nose affectionately against her. "It is a rare gift you are offering me, and you may rest assured that I will treat it and you accordingly."

She looked as if she wanted to say something, but in the end she held her tongue. Her eyes seemed almost sad as they gazed up into his, and he wondered what was going on in her mind. He reached out to draw her closer, but she was already moving of her own volition, her soft body pressing tantalizingly against his. Her hands went to his chest, and when they began caressing the soft hair that grew there he groaned in pleasure.

"Ah, your hands burn me like a flame," he murmured, his hands clenching in her hair. "Touch me, angel. Let me feel your hands everywhere."

She hesitated; then he felt her hands fumbling with the knot on his robe, tugging at it until it fell open, exposing his naked body to her. His vow to take it slow dissolved under the heat of his passion, and he captured her hand in a rough grip, carrying it down to his throbbing hardness.

"God, like that," he implored fervently, moving against her fingers. "You make me wild!"

Her touch was unskilled, but still so sweet he feared he would surely explode. He kept his hand tangled in her hair, using the pressure to raise her head to his. His mouth was urgent as he pried her lips apart, his tongue flicking insistently against hers until he felt her response.

He kissed her hungrily, his demand increasing as both his arms stole about her to lift her up against him. He could feel the heat of her thighs beneath her silk dressing gown, and he knew that if he did not get inside her, he wouldn't last another minute. Holding her close he carried her to the bed, his eyes moving over her as he laid her on the cover.

"That is a very fetching night robe you are wearing," he said thickly, his hands skimming over the silk and untying ribbons along the way. "But if you do not remove it this instant, I fear I will have to rip it from you."

Her face was flushed, but she did as he asked, sitting up slightly as she fumbled with the ribbons. He watched for a few seconds and then gently brushed her hands aside.

"No, let me," he implored, disposing of the troublesome ties with an experienced flick of his wrist. He parted the violet-colored silk, and then leaned back to study the tantalizing sight of her in her thin negligee. Her breasts were small but delightfully rounded, and he could see the dusky rose of her nipples pressing against the delicate material. This small but unmistakable sign of her pleasure added to his urgency even as it made him realize he had been rushing her. Determined to give her even greater pleasure, he circled one sweet bud with the tip of his finger.

"When I am ready, I am going to take this in my mouth," he said softly, his eyes intent upon her breast. "I am going to kiss you until you are writhing in pleasure, and then when you cry out, I shall start with the other one. Will you like that, my sweet?"

"C-cat," she stuttered, her eyes closing as he continued the tantalizing caress.

"Hmm?" He was only half attending, intrigued at the way her breasts were rising and falling as her breathing deepened.

"I . . . I am called Cat," she said, her hands going to the back of his head.

He shot her a quick glance of surprise. "I thought your name was Louisa," he said, momentarily distracted.

She shook her head. "My given name is Louisa Catheryn, but I prefer to be called Cat."

He considered the matter; then the corners of his mouth kicked up in a boyish grin. "Cat," he repeated, smoothing one of her gleaming dark curls over the curve of her breast. "The name suits you. Will you purr and scratch my back when I pleasure you, my sleek, green-eyed Cat?"

"I . . . I do not know," she admitted, then arched her back as he lightly pinched her nipple. "I wish you would not do that."

"What?"

"That!" Her nails dug in his back as he repeated the caress.

"Do you not like it?"

"I don't . . . I'm not . . . my husband never . . ."

"Never touched you like this?" He had peeled the robe from her shoulders and was now baring the rest of her body.

She shook her head. "No. Never."

"Then the more fool he," he declared, delighting at the sight of her breasts gleaming in the glow of the scented candles he'd had the foresight to light. "A woman like you was meant to be savored slowly, and not devoured in a single gulp."

"Actually, I think I would prefer it if you did devour me," she managed, gasping as he cupped her breasts in his hands.

He gave her a wicked smile. "And so I intend to, Cat, but later. This comes first." He bent his head, drawing the point of her breast into his mouth, his cheeks flexing as he drew on her flesh with consummate skill.

She did cry out in pleasure then, her head tilting back and her hips arching against his. He moved his hands down the satiny expanse of her back until he was cupping her buttocks, squeezing them even as his mouth was tugging at her breast.

"Stephen!" She panted, moving helplessly. "Oh God, Stephen!"

"Cat!" He nipped at her breast, then soothed the wound with a swirl of his tongue. "I want you!"

"Yes!" Her hands slid down his neck to his back, and she held on to him with surprising strength. "Yes, Stephen!"

He lowered her to the bed, his hands pulling the rest of her clothes from her. He was so hard he was in agony; but even in the fire of his passion he remembered her inexperience, and he forced himself to go slow. "Did your husband ever kiss you here?" he demanded, branding a damp kiss on her stomach. "Or here?"

"No, he never . . . Stephen?" Her voice grew shaky as he slid a finger inside her. "Stephen, what are you doing?"

"Something that fool you married should have done years ago," he answered, adding a second finger and moving it in and out. "You are a woman of passion, Cat, and this is what you were made to experience."

He could tell she did not know what he meant, but he was more than willing to show her as he moved his thumb over the swollen bud of feminine passion he could feel was already throbbing against him. When he touched it more firmly she arched her hips, and out of the corner of his eye he saw her teeth sinking into her bottom lip as her eyes squeezed shut.

"Don't hold back," he urged, his fingers moving faster. "I want to hear your cries, Cat. I want to know I please you."

"You do," she assured him, her voice almost nonexistent. "I never knew it could be like this."

Her words made him swell with masculine pride. "It can be even better," he promised, sensing she was approaching her peak. "It can be a pleasure so sweet you scream from it. And it will be like that for you, my darling, I give you my word."

"I don't understand . . . oh God, Stephen . . . what—" Her voice broke off, her back arching as the spasms tore through her. He felt her sweet shudders and he couldn't hold back another moment. She was still shaking when he slid into her, his hips rocking against hers as he joined his body to hers.

"Cat, oh God, Cat, you are mine!" he gasped, his whole body trembling as he moved against her. He couldn't seem to get deep enough, so great was his hunger. He bowed his back, going in as far as he could and then drawing back until he was almost out, and then thrusting back even deeper. The bed shook beneath his onslaught, and he could hear the rhythmic squeaking of the frame. It made him want to go faster, harder, and when he did he could hear her cries rising in unison.

He could feel his own completion approaching, and he moved his hands to grasp her hips. "Wrap your legs around my waist," he ordered, lost in passion as he continued thrusting. "Like that . . . yes . . . hold me tighter, Cat. Tighter. Yes . . ."

"Stephen!" Her voice was broken, and through half-opened eyes he could see the dazed pleasure on her face. The sight was all it took to send him over the edge, his body slamming against hers in a frenzy of passion. He gave a low, harsh cry as he went still, squeezing his eyes shut as his body shook and quivered beneath the force of his climax. When it was over he collapsed against her, his heart thundering in his chest.

The trembling continued, leaving him drained and yet eager for more. He waited until he was certain he could breathe before raising his head. "Are you all right?" he asked, his arms holding her in a tender embrace. "I didn't hurt you, did I?"

She shook her head. "You didn't," she assured him, her fingers brushing back the strand of sweat-dampened hair that had fallen across his forehead.

"You're certain?" He was frowning down at her, realizing for the first time how very small and delicate she was. "I was rather rough . . . much rougher than I meant to be. You're such a little thing."

Her green eyes flicked away from his. "Yes, quite certain," she said, her voice as polite and remote as if she were at a country tea. "But perhaps I ought to return to my rooms. It is late, and I wouldn't wish the servants—"

"Cat, it's a little too late to be embarrassed, don't you think?"

Stephen interrupted gently, touched by her shyness. "There is nothing to be ashamed of, you know."

"Isn't there?"

Stephen realized she was thinking of her late husband, and the knowledge infuriated him. The stupid sot hadn't deserved Cat, he decided with a flash of possessiveness, and he was damned if he'd let her continue mourning the man while she was in his bed. He tightened his hold on her, aware of his body stirring to life.

"Are you sure you're all right?" he asked, moving teasingly against her so that she could feel him in the most intimate part of her.

She gave a small gasp, her fingers flexing on his shoulders. "I . . . yes . . . I am f-fine," she stuttered, her cheeks blooming with color.

"Good." He bent to nip playfully at her throat. "Because I find I am also fine. Hold me, my Cat. Hold me."

The rest of the night passed in a sensual whirl as Stephen aroused and then satisfied his sweet Cat again and again. His hunger for her never seemed to be sated, and he grew almost desperate to feast his fill. In his saner moments he told himself it was because he was leaving for the battlefield on the morrow, and that he was only storing up memories against what looked to be a long famine of celibacy. But when he felt Cat moving against him, her beautiful eyes closing in abandon, reasons and explanations ceased to matter. All that mattered was Cat, and when he finally fell asleep, it was in her arms.

The room was still in darkness when something awoke him. He opened one eye, his arm automatically reaching for Cat. When he found her gone, his other eye flew open, and he sat up.

"Cat?"

"I was just leaving," her voice came from near the door, and he turned his head to see her standing in the doorway, her violet robe once again wrapped about her.

The tightness in his chest relaxed, and he patted the bed beside him. "Come back," he said, his voice soft and inviting.

"I really shouldn't," she protested, her hands twisting nervously as she gazed at him. "It is growing light, and there is a chance I could be seen leaving your room."

"Anyone you encounter will be sneaking back from their own tryst," he said, tossing back the covers and advancing toward her with a purposeful stride. "They won't care."

"I . . . I hadn't thought of that," she admitted, her eyes growing dark as they studied his naked form.

"Don't go," he implored, reaching out to stroke her face. "I want you to stay with me."

He heard the breath catch in her throat, saw her eyes flutter shut. "I really shouldn't . . . ," she protested, tilting back her head as his hands boldly caressed her breasts.

"Yes, you really should," he contradicted, his voice thickening with awakening desire. He continued touching her, smoothing away her clothes as he kissed and stroked every inch of her. Only when she was clinging to him, her knees too weak to hold her, did he finally sweep her up in his arms and carry her to the waiting bed.

He laid her down tenderly, but when he would have slipped inside of her, she stayed him by laying her hand on his chest. "No, Stephen . . . wait."

He stilled at once, his eyes flashing to her face. "What is it, my love?" he asked, concerned despite his passion. "Are you, too sore?"

She blushed at his bluntness. "It isn't that."

"Then what is it?" He nudged her with the tip of his sex. "I am about to die from wanting you."

She grew even rosier, but her green eyes were unwavering as she gazed up at him. "You have given me so much pleasure, she whispered softly, touching the side of his face. "Now I want to please you. Show me how, Stephen."

Oh God, his breath lodged in his throat at her soft plea. He could feel himself growing even harder, his heart pounding as impossibly erotic images filled his mind. "You have already pleased me, more than any woman ever has," he said, too aroused to realize he meant every word.

"Then, I want to do more." She moved until she was kneeling beside him on the bed. "I want to . . . to touch you as you have touched me." Her hands skimmed down his hair-roughened chest. "Kiss you the way you have kissed me." Her head tipped forward as her tongue found the tip of his nipple.

"Cat!" Stephen's hands closed convulsively in her hair, and he tipped his head back, straining to fill his lungs with air.

"Show me, Stephen," she repeated, her hair brushing his thighs as her mouth ventured lower. "Show me what to do."

He groaned again, his control shattering as he showed her what he wanted . . . what he needed. Her lips kissed every part of him, and when he felt the tip of her tongue sweetly exploring the cleft of his sex, he thought he would lose his mind. His hips bucked, and he knew he wouldn't be able to stand much more. He fell back on the bed, pulling her on top of him.

She looked startled at first, and then her eyes grew smoky as he thrust inside her. He cupped her breasts in his hands, squeezing them in time to his thrusts until he felt her tightening around him.

"Stephen!" She flung her head back, her hands resting on his chest as she moved with him.

"Do you want it faster, Cat?" he demanded, controlling her movements with his strong hands. "Harder? Tell me what you want!"

"Harder," she managed, her voice breaking as a climax shook her. "Harder!"

He moved again, not breaking momentum as he reversed their positions. He grabbed her legs and placed them high on his back as he continued thrusting. When he felt a second climax grab her he finally allowed his own release to take place, his back arching as he emptied himself into her sweet body. Through the red mists filling his head, he could hear her sobs of satiation, and the sound filled him with savage satisfaction.

"Cat," he murmured her name with a shaky breath, too weary to open his eyes. "Don't leave me."

He felt her fingers curl about his ears. "I won't," she promised softly, "not yet."

Her answer was less than satisfactory, but he was in no shape to debate the matter with her. He settled himself more comfortably against her, his head nestling against her breasts as he fell into an exhausted slumber.

The room was half-filled with light when he awoke to find Cat bending over him. "Thank you," she said simply, her eyes filled with tears as she gazed down at him. "I shall never forget you."

"Cat?" His voice was slurred with sleep, and he fought to stay awake. "What is it?"

"Good-bye," she replied, already moving away from him. "Please do not try to see me again."

"Cat." He sat up in bed, shaking his head as if to clear it. "Wait . . ." But he was too late. The door closed behind her with a soft click, leaving him alone in the dawn-lit room.

Two

London, 1815

"God save the king!"

"God save the Duke of Wellington!"

"God bless the Prince of Wales!"

The sounds of jubilation rang through the streets, penetrating even the staid corners of Hanover square. Servant mingled freely with master as the occupants spilled out of the great houses to join in the impromptu celebration of Wellington's glorious victory at Waterloo. From his vantage point at the library window Stephen watched the joyous crowd with an odd sense of detachment. His lips thinned derisively, and he wondered if the throng below would be nearly so happy if they'd had to endure even a quarter of the pain suffered by the soldiers who had fought and died to bring them this glorious victory.

"The mob must indeed be happy if they are willing to bless Prinny," Lord Exter observed wryly as he joined Stephen at his post. "The last time the streets were like this they were screaming for his head."

Stephen let the heavy crimson drape drop back into place as he turned away from the window. "Yes, wars have the effect of bringing out the best in those not obliged to fight them," he replied with a cynical laugh. "I suppose we might as well forget about joining Hadley at his club. There's no way in Hades we'll make it through that crowd tonight."

"Not unless we walk, and even then it would be a chancy thing," the marquess agreed, watching in concern as Stephen limped across the room to help himself to the contents of the brandy decanter.

"Especially with this leg of mine," Stephen added, rubbing his thigh. A musket ball had glanced off the bone, and the wound had become badly infected. He'd been damned lucky not to lose his leg, and he considered an occasional limp a small price to pay.

Exter's face was red with mortification as he rushed to Stephen's side. "Stephen, you mustn't think I was referring to . . . that is, I never meant to imply that you—"

"Relax, Albert, I know what you meant," he interrupted his friend's apology with a wave of his hand. "And I quite agree with you. The thought of venturing out in that crush is decidedly disconcerting. We'll dine in instead."

"Not unless we mean to prepare the meal ourselves," Exter returned, relieved Stephen hadn't taken offense. "If I am not mistaken, I believe that was your butler and cook I saw slipping from the house to join in the celebration."

The thought of his plump cook and rigidly proper butler mingling with the revelers brought a genuine smile to Stephen's face. "Then, we'll have to fend for ourselves," he said with a laugh. "God knows it won't be the first time I've had to forage for something to eat, and I'm damned sure my larder can provide us with more than a scrawny chicken and a half-rotten potato."

"So one would hope," Exter drawled, his blue eyes solemn as he considered Stephen's words. Since his friend had returned to England some three weeks earlier, he'd adamantly refused to discuss his experiences in the war, but from the little he'd let slip, Exter could only imagine that it had been pure hell. God knew it had changed Stephen beyond all recognition, and there were times when Albert couldn't believe the grim-faced stranger standing before him was the lighthearted rake of his youth.

"Blast it, Stephen, why the devil did you do it?" he demanded, unable to hold the words back. "What could you have been thinking of when you bought that damned commission?"

Stephen looked startled at the marquess's outburst, and then his face settled into the familiar harsh lines. "As I recall I was bored," he said, his eyes shadowed as he studied the contents of his glass. "Lovemaking had grown rather pallid, and I was hoping battle might prove a trifle more diverting."

"Curse you, Stephen, I am serious!"

"So am I." Stephen raised cold brown eyes. "I bought my commission as a lark, thinking to ride off to battle like one of the knights in Scott's tiresome poems. I thought it would be a glorious adventure to remember in my dotage. Ah youth." His lips twisted in a bitter smile.

"But what about your title?" Exter pressed, struggling to understand Stephen's reasoning. "What if you had been killed?"

"Then the title would have passed to my brother Jason," Stephen replied with an indifferent shrug. "He's four years younger than I, but he'd make a far better earl. Before posting for the peninsula I signed over one of my lesser titles and estates to him, and he's made remarkable improvements. Besides"—he gave a harsh laugh—"I didn't really believe I could be killed. Of course, that was before I realized there could be some fates worse than dying."

There was an uncomfortable silence, and then Stephen gave another laugh. "But enough of such boring reminiscences," he said, clapping a friendly hand on Exter's shoulders. "Tell me of your lovely lady. Did you leave her at home, or is she out somewhere in this mob?"

"Not if she knows what is good for her," Albert replied darkly. "When the first real news began making the rounds, I left strict orders that she was not to venture beyond the front doorstep. I knew how it would be, and there was no way I was going to risk her going out into the streets."

"And do you really think she will obey you?"

"I can only hope. Speaking of Anne, I am commissioned by her to bring you to the Billingtons' soiree on Friday. She has missed you quite dreadfully, and she is all puffed up at the thought of showing you off to her London friends."

"I would be delighted to oblige the lady," Stephen drawled, smiling at the image of his friend being bear-led by his pretty minx of a wife. "What time shall I make my appearance?"

"Ten o'clock," Exter said with a grin. "Do you know, if we

weren't such good friends, I daresay I would find my wife's preference for your company somewhat alarming."

"Pistols at ten paces?" Stephen queried politely.

"Against you? Never." Exter gave a bark of laughter. "I have no desire to let you put a bullet through my heart and leave Anne a widow. She's too dashed pretty to leave alone."

The mention of pretty widows dimmed the amusement in Stephen's eyes. "Yes, she does look rather well in black," he agreed absently, his mind drifting back to Cat. Since his return to England he'd toyed with the idea of attempting to see her, but so far he'd yet to work up sufficient nerve.

In the five years since that night, he'd relived those sweet moments in her arms a thousand times. Sometimes the hot memories were all that kept him sane, and he'd clung to them with almost desperate determination. He'd even written her a letter, sending it to his cousin's house in the hopes it would somehow reach her. His only answer had been a prim note from Brockton's governess-wife, informing him that Cat had returned to her own home. He'd written again requesting further information, but Lady Brockton had denied any knowledge of Cat's exact location.

Perhaps he'd venture up to Keswick, he thought, his interest piquing. He'd heard Edward had died some eighteen months ago, and so he had already been planning a duty call. He was one of the guardians for Edward's children, and he supposed that if nothing else he could peek in on them. Yes, he decided, feeling more alert than he had in days. Perhaps that was what he'd do. . . .

"Mama, do come quickly, Demetria has had her foal!" Miss Lydia Brockton exclaimed, her dark eyes shining with excitement as she dashed into her stepmama's study. "Oh, you must come at once, he is the prettiest little thing!"

"In one moment, Lydia," Cat responded calmly, folding the letter she had been reading and tucking it into the desk drawer. It was early afternoon, but she'd been at the accounts since breakfast, and some of the strain was obvious in the green eyes she turned on Lydia. "Now tell me more of Demetria's foal," she offered, smiling at the sight of the straw clinging to the girl's fly-away dark hair.

"He is a bay, just like her, and he has a blaze on his face like his papa," Lydia obliged, tugging at Cat's arm. "Only you can see him so much better if you come to the stables. Do hurry!"

Cat allowed herself to be pulled to her feet, her hand held easily in Lydia's as they walked out of the house and down the flower-edged path to the stables. It was late June, and the scent of the delicate blooms was heavy in the soft air. Closing her eyes Cat could smell the pinks and roses, and in that moment she was transported back to another garden and another time and place.

Stephen. In the five years since that magical night she had been unable to put him from her mind. He had been the lover of her dreams— had she ever been able to imagine even half of the things he'd shared with her that night—and she knew she'd die remembering every moment of their embrace. There were countless nights since then when she'd awaken trembling, her heart pounding and her body aching with want, and she'd reach out for the man who was never there. Thank God Edward had died never knowing her shameful secret, she thought gratefully. She felt guilty enough as it was.

The foal was just as delightful as Lydia assured her it would be, and after a thoughtful discussion they decided upon the name of Wellington for the little fellow. After admiring the foal and praising its dam for a job well done, Cat went to have a private word with the head groom. The letter she'd been studying was from Jeremey, demanding a larger advance and his choice of horses from the stables. He was even threatening court action, and she wanted to make it clear to the grizzled groom that regardless of what any servant of Jeremey's might claim, he was not to give them any horses.

That done, she turned and made her way back to the manor house, her mind on Jeremey and his machinations. Since the moment the courts had declared Edward's will to be valid, he'd done everything within his power to make her life a misery.

Having her appointed the children's principal guardian over him had infuriated him, and she shivered as she remembered the hatred in his eyes as he'd vowed to make her pay for foiling his plans. If he should ever learn the truth. . . . She shuddered again, pushing the thought from her mind.

Back at the house she went up to Elizabeth's rooms to check on her progress. A new governess had been working with the girl, and she was anxious to see the results. She found her hard at work learning her sums; a task she seemed to be enjoying with surprising relish. When Cat praised the governess, Miss Blakely, for her success, the younger woman gave a sheepish grin.

"I must admit I was at my wit's end trying to get Beth interested, but then I hit upon the perfect scheme."

"Really? And what was that?" Cat smiled at her own memories of trying to interest a much younger Beth in her studies. "I thought she didn't care for anything other than fashion."

"Precisely so," Miss Blakely agreed with a laugh. "I ordered up some gazettes from London, and have sat her down with the books and a budget, and she has been happily adding, dividing, and subtracting all morning! She is doing quite well, although her future husband may not care for her more creative bookkeeping practices."

"I applaud your resourcefulness," Cat said, casting the pretty girl a fond look. "A pity you can't devise similar stratagems for her other subjects."

"Ah, but I have. Our French lessons shall consist of all the terms for fashion and clothing, while history shall be devoted to a study of ladies' court dresses through the years."

"And geography?" Cat's green eyes were sparkling with laughter at the governess's inventiveness.

"Learning the origins of silk and cotton. Science still has me somewhat baffled, but I am working on it."

Cat burst out laughing at that. The sound brought Beth's head up, and she gave Cat a warm smile. "Good afternoon, Mama," she said in the cultured accent she had spent hours perfecting. "I trust you are well?"

"Quite well, dearest," Cat assured her with a fond smile.

"Miss Blakely was just telling me of your prowess at arithmetic."

"Oh, there is nothing to it once you get the hang of it," Beth replied airily, glancing down at the column of figures she had been laboring over. "But really, you would not believe how dear the price of silk has become! Perhaps now that Napoleon is finally conquered, the price will settle down."

"An excellent observation." Despite the fact it had been many years since she'd taught, Cat was unable to resist praising a pupil for quickness. "You would be surprised at how political events can influence such things as fashion and the price of silk."

"Really?" Beth looked much struck by this before saying, "I daresay you are right, Mama. Only recall how everyone went mad for the Russian style last year when the czar and his sister visited London."

"That is so, dearest." Once again the girl's astuteness pleased Cat. "And I remember a grand lady of my acquaintance telling me that at the time of the Terror they wore red ribbons about their necks as memorials to those who had been guillotined."

"Ugh!" Beth wrinkled her nose in distaste. "I don't think I'd care to ape *that* particular fashion!"

"You would if everyone else was wearing it," Miss Blakely ventured a gentle tease. "You know you couldn't bear it if you weren't dressed in the first stare of fashion."

"Well, perhaps if it was in the *very* first stare of fashion," the girl conceded, and then gave a dreamy sigh. "I wonder what all the crack will be when I make my bows."

Cat lingered in the schoolroom another quarter hour, advising Miss Blakely on the curriculum and listening to Beth read from Shakespeare. Satisfied as to Beth's progress, she then took her leave, her expression troubled as she returned to her study.

Beth's artless words had brought to mind the problems they would face when Beth would be old enough to take her place in the Fashionable World. As the daughter of a viscount it would be expected of her, and certainly Cat couldn't fault her for wanting what was only her right; but how could she arrange such a thing when she herself had never been presented?

There was no help for it, she decided with a dejected sigh. She would have to begin contacting Edward's relations in the hopes one of them could be persuaded to sponsor Beth. Or if that failed, she supposed she might try writing Beth's mother's family. There was an aunt as she recalled, and if the lady was still out in Society, perhaps she might be persuaded to help. Feeling somewhat better now that she had something constructive to do, she sat at her desk and began composing letters.

She was finishing her first such letter when there was a tap on the door and one of the maids entered. "Excuse me, my lady," she said with a low curtsy. "But a gentleman has called and is asking to speak with you."

"Did he say who he is?" Cat asked, wondering if Jeremey had sent one of his loathsome friends to plague her. If so, she would soon make short work of him. She was in no mood to tolerate his mischief-making today.

"It's one of his lordship's relatives, mum," the maid said, her expression eager as she recalled the gossip in the servants' hall. "Lord Stephen Wrexley, the earl of Rockholme."

Stephen sat in the sunny parlor enjoying a cool glass of lemonade as he waited for his hostess to join him. He'd ridden up from London on a whim, eschewing his elegant travelling coach for horseback, and the ride had left him pleasantly exhausted. The journey had been a long and at times painful one, but any discomfort he felt had been more than compensated by the unexpected peace he'd found. After the long years of seeing nothing but death and destruction, he'd needed the gentle green hills of England to heal the wounds on his soul.

Perhaps he'd ride down to Oxfordshire and visit Jason, he thought, turning the plan over in his mind. Or he might even ride to Kent and have a look at his own neglected estates; Lord knew it had been years since he had last seen them. Of course, he amended with a hungry grin, much would depend on what he found once he succeeded in locating Cat.

He'd spent the long ride from London formulating various strategies for dealing with Lady Brockton. She was the key, his one link to Cat, and he was determined to wrest Cat's whereabouts from her. He'd successfully interrogated dozens of prisoners while on the peninsula, and he didn't think he'd prove any less successful with a simple country governess, although he'd hardly be employing the same methods of persuasion. He was, after all, a gentleman.

The sound of the door being thrown open interrupted his reverie, and he glanced up as a gangly young girl in a rather dirty blue dress came dashing into the room. She skidded to a halt in front of him, her brown eyes shining with excitement as she demanded, "Is that your horse outside? The black with the white star on his forehead?"

"It is indeed," he replied, smiling as he realized this was the horse-mad Lydia Cat had once described so lovingly.

"He's a real prime goer," the young lady assured, sidling closer. "Sound as a brick, Jemm says, and Jemm knows *everything* about horses. What are his lines?"

"I am ashamed to say I don't know," Stephen confessed with an apologetic shrug. "I had my agent purchase him at Tatts, and that is all I know of him."

"You bought a horse sight unseen?" She was clearly scandalized. "How do you know you wasn't gulled?"

Stephen's smile grew frosty. "Because I am the earl of Rockholme," he said calmly, "and no one gulls me."

At the mention of his name the girl took a step back. "You're the earl?" she asked, her tone as suspicious as only moments before it had been friendly.

"Yes, I am," he said, hiding his surprise at her sudden animosity. "And you're the Honorable Miss Lydia Brockton."

If he meant to discomfit her, he was soon disappointed, for if anything her expression became more hostile than ever. "You're not to bother my mama," she warned, her grubby hands closing into fists. "We don't need any more guardians to look after us. We can look after ourselves."

"That is quite enough, Lydia," a cool voice came from the doorway as a dark-haired woman entered the room. Stephen stared at her, his heart constricting in his throat as he gazed at her. "My God," he managed in a strangled voice. *"Cat!"*

* * *

When she'd first heard Stephen was awaiting belowstairs, Cat's first impulse had been to swoon. She knew a meeting between them was inevitable given the fact Edward had named him one of the children's guardians, but she'd always pushed the thought from her mind. Now there was no avoiding it. He was here, and unless she meant to take to her rooms like some silly heroine in a novel, she would have to confront him. Reminding herself that her children's future rested on the next few minutes, she squared her shoulders and stepped forward with her hand outstretched.

"My lord, I am pleased to make your acquaintance," she said, a polite smile of welcome pasted on her lips. "I often heard my dear husband speak of you, and it is a great honor to meet you."

Stephen stared at her hand as if he'd never before seen such an object, and then he slowly reached out to take it in his. "Lady Brockton," he said, his voice hoarse as he struggled to master the emotions raging inside of him. Just what the hell was going on? he wondered, his lips thinning with suppressed fury.

Cat saw the fury in his dark eyes and held back a tiny sigh. This was indeed going to be difficult, she thought, turning to Lydia with a smile.

"Lydia, I think it best that you go to your rooms," she said in a firm voice. "But first you will apologize to our guest for your poor behavior. I will not have him thinking you are so shockingly ill-bred."

"But, Mama, he—"

"I am waiting."

Lydia subsided with a scowl, knowing that when her mama used that soft tone it was best to do as she said. "My apologies, my lord," she grumbled, dropping a half curtsey. "I meant no offense. Although I still say we don't need another guardian," she added, flashing Cat a defiant look.

"Your objections have been duly noted," Cat said, giving the girl's unruly hair a gentle tug. "Now you may go. And Lydia," she added as the young girl reached the door.

"Yes, Mama?"

"Two rows, I think."

Lydia opened her mouth as if to object, and then closed it again. "Yes, Mama," she repeated, her shoulders drooping as she shuffled from the room.

There was a heavy silence as both Cat and Stephen eyed each other warily. Deciding it was safest to continue as she had started, she turned to him with an apologetic smile.

"I trust you will forgive Lydia," she said, taking quiet pride in her cool poise. "I fear she is something of a hoyden at times, and her experience with guardians has not always been—"

"Devil take it, Cat, what is going on here?" Stephen demanded, unable to bear the pretense another moment. "Just what sort of rig are you running?"

Cat paled at the raw anger in his voice. Could she do it? she wondered. Could she really brazen her way through the next few minutes? Then she reminded herself of the consequences should she fail.

"I beg your pardon, my lord," she said, drawing herself up with cold pride, "but I have no notion as to what you may mean. I am running no sort of rig, and I resent your implying that I am."

"You know full well what I mean," he snarled, glaring at her in furious disbelief. That she could stand there regarding him as if he were no more than a distant stranger filled him with an icy rage, and it was all he could do not to take her in his arms and shake her. Surely she didn't mean to pretend as if they had never met? he wondered savagely, and then stiffened as he realized that was precisely what she did intend.

"No, I do not," Cat insisted, ignoring the insidious trembling in her knees. "And furthermore, I will not have you address me in that tone of voice. If you can not treat me with the respect accorded my station, then I am afraid I shall have to ask you to leave."

"Your station!" The words burst from Stephen's lips before he could control himself. My God, he thought incredulously, but the woman was a bold-faced bitch. How could he have been so mistaken as to her true character?

The contempt in his voice made Cat flinch, but she resolutely stood her ground. "Precisely, sir, my station," she replied with the hauteur worthy of a duchess. "And that station if I need remind you is mistress of this house. I am Lady Brockton, Viscountess Brockton, and you may either treat me as such, or you may leave. The choice is yours."

For a moment Stephen feared he would strike her, so great was his anger. Only his natural reluctance to harm a woman kept him from acting on his impulse, and he fought to master his fury. "Very well, *Lady* Brockton," he spat out, clenching his hands so tightly his knuckles turned white. "If that is the way you wish it. But do not think this is the end of it. You may have won the opening skirmish, but the war is just beginning. And war, my dear, is something at which I am a master. You will do well to remember that." And with that he turned and stormed from the room, slamming the door behind him.

Three

The sound of the door slamming shut echoed in the parlor like a pistol shot, breaking the temporary paralysis holding Cat in its coils. The walls were still reverberating with the noise when she collapsed onto a chair, her face buried in her hands as she fought to control the tremors racking her body.

"What am I going to do?" she asked aloud, her eyes filling with tears. "Dear God, what am I going to do?"

She had known the encounter would be difficult, but she'd never anticipated it would be quite this bad. The memory of his contempt and anger made her stomach churn, and his parting words filled her with dread. With Jeremey snapping at her heels like a rabid dog, the very last thing she needed was another enemy, and her instincts warned her Stephen would prove even more dangerous than Jeremey. Jeremey at least confined his animosity to threats and crude insults while Stephen . . . she shivered as she remembered his claim at being a master of war. Stephen would make the most implacable enemy of them all.

She spent another several minutes lost in misery before her sense of duty recalled her to her responsibilities. What was she doing sitting here and crying like a pea-goose? she wondered crossly, swiping at the tears staining her cheeks. She had her family to think of, and the sooner she set about protecting them, the better.

Now that the initial confrontation was over, it was time to begin planning for the next. She'd been caught unawares this time, but should Stephen—*Lord Rockholme*, she corrected herself sternly—pay her another visit he would find her ready for him. Let him hurl whatever ugly accusations he chose, she thought with a grim smile. She had only to stand there and calmly deny everything, and there was nothing in Hades he could do about it.

A quick glance at the anniversary clock on the mantel brought her scrambling to her feet. It was almost three o'clock, time for Eddie's tea. The thought of her small son brought a warm glow to Cat's heart, filling her with love even as it filled her with a fierce resolve. She would do everything within her power to guard her son and daughters, she vowed silently, and if the earl got in her way, then so be it. He might think the French and their allies made formidable foes, but that was because he had yet to go up against her. He might be a master at war, but she was a mother fighting for her family. They would just see who emerged as the victor from the next battle.

After storming out of the house Stephen leapt up on his horse, his one thought to put as much distance between himself and Larks Hall as possible. He'd ridden less than a mile from the house when his temper cooled enough to allow him to think. If he left now, then it was the same thing as granting her the victory. The thought of how happy that would make her was enough to have him turning his mount around; his face set as he rode into the small town of Keswick in search of lodging.

The innkeeper at The Silver Lion was almost speechless with gratitude at having so noble a patron in his establishment, and personally escorted Stephen to his best set of rooms. Once settled in his temporary quarters he began sending out messages, notifying others of his change in plans. He'd made arrangements to stay with an old army friend at his home in Glennridding and wrote to inform Richard he had been "unavoidably detained." He also wrote his solicitor in London, arranging for funds to be advanced to him and for his valet to journey north to join him.

Once that was done he ordered a bottle of the innkeeper's finest and set about getting foxed with studied determination. When he remembered how he'd mooned over Cat, dreaming of her embrace until he couldn't bear to touch any of the prostitutes that followed the army, he felt like getting sick. He'd been a fool, he acknowledged bitterly, and the admission was almost as painful as the bullet that had shattered his leg.

Equally as hurtful was the realization that he had cuckolded Edward. Granted he and his cousin had never been close, but he'd always liked and respected the man. The notion that he had betrayed him, however innocently, cut his pride to the quick, and he cursed himself almost as roundly as he cursed Cat. Thank God Edward was already dead, he thought sourly, for he'd never be able to meet his eyes knowing how thoroughly he had bedded his cousin's adulterous wife.

Images of that night tormented him, and no amount of brandy could dull their impact on his senses. God, she had been sweet, he groaned silently, his eyes closing as the memories washed over him. She'd been as untutored as a virgin, her touch shy as she responded to his hoarsely whispered pleas. And to think it had all been a lie, he thought bitterly, a skillful charade that had managed to fool even him.

He would make her pay, he vowed, taking another sip of brandy. As he'd told Lydia, no one made a gudgeon of him and walked away unscathed, and if it was the last thing he did, he would see that Cat regretted using him to betray her husband. But first he would need to learn what sort of game she was playing.

If the last years had taught him anything, it was the need for coolness in battle and the importance of preparation. He acknowledged he'd already committed a serious tactical error in confronting her directly, which meant he would now be forced to employ other, less obvious strategies. The irony of the situation was not lost upon him, and a hard smile touched his lips at the pleasure it would give him to deceive the woman who had so badly deceived him.

He would play the penitent courtier, he decided, propping his booted feet on the hassock as he tipped back in his chair. He'd return to Larks Hall bearing flowers and sweet apologies, pretending to dance to her tune while the entire time he would be scheming to expose her. Pleased with his plan he poured himself another glass of brandy, savoring its potent heat even as he savored his plans for revenge.

Beth was crushed at having missed her first opportunity to meet a real earl, and Cat was hard-pressed to placate her. A shopping trip to Keswick was proposed by Miss Blakely, and the following day the ladies of the house set out for the small village in their travelling coach. The coach was a recent purchase, and although she had decried the expense at the time, Cat was now grateful she had bowed to Beth's pleading. The girl would soon be old enough to go about in Society, and it would not do for her to be seen in the ancient, poorly sprung relic Cat had inherited from Edward.

A disgruntled Lydia accompanied them, uncomfortable and resentful in the new gown of yellow cambric Cat had insisted she wear. "I still don't see why I had to come," she grumbled, plucking at her azure ribbon. *"I* met the earl."

"So you did, dearest." Cat gave her tumbled curls a playful tug. "But we thought you would enjoy shopping with the rest of us ladies."

The expression on Lydia's face grew even more pained. "Shopping," she said, in the tones of one discussing a visit to the tooth drawer's. "I hate shopping. Beth will only sigh and moon over a bunch of silly drawings in a book, and roll her eyes at any boy that she sees."

"I will not, you hateful toad!" Beth forgot her pose as a dignified young lady long enough to cast her younger sister a threatening scowl. "I have never rolled my eyes at any boy."

"You rolled them at Squire Grisby's oldest boy at church last Sunday," Lydia pointed out in the smug manner of younger sisters everywhere. "Like this." She rolled her eyes outrageously, batting her lashes so vigorously that even Beth had to laugh.

"I most assuredly did *not* behave like that, you odious brat," she said, giving her sister a poke with her silk parasol. "I did acknowledge him when he raised his hat to me, but that was all. He is quite handsome though, is he not?" she added with a heartfelt sigh.

"Not as handsome as the earl." Lydia was not yet finished plaguing her sister. "Of course, you don't know that because you didn't get to see him."

The conversation would have doubtlessly disintegrated into a squabble if Lydia hadn't suddenly cried out, "Look! There is the earl's horse!"

Cat's heart stopped, then started again with a painful lurch. "I'm sure you are mistaken, Lydia," she said, moistening her lips as she struggled for composure. "What would his lordship be doing in Keswick?"

"I don't know, Mama, but that is his horse." She pointed to the black stallion tethered to a post outside of an inn. "He bought it at Tattersalls, you know."

When it came to horseflesh Cat was more than willing to bow to her stepdaughter's expertise. If she said the large black with the star on its forehead was Stephen's, then it was. She'd suspected, of course, that he was still in the area, but she'd been hoping for a brief respite before confronting him again.

"Should we stop, do you think?" Beth was already adjusting her bonnet. "He is our guardian, and we wouldn't wish to snub him."

"The earl is at a public inn, Lydia," Cat reminded her, forcing herself to keep her tone controlled. "It would not be at all the thing for us to visit him there."

"Oh." Beth accepted her mama's dictum with a sigh. She considered the matter and then brightened. "Well, if he is our guardian, should he not be staying with us? Mr. Sedgewood stays with us whenever he comes for a visit, and I am sure I would prefer the earl's company to his."

Much as Cat knew she should reprimand Beth for talking ill of an elder, she couldn't bring herself to be so hypocritical. On the other hand, she couldn't foster her fancy that Stephen should take up residence with them. She cringed at the thought of the young girl artlessly inviting him to stay at Larks Hall.

"His lordship is a gentleman, Beth," she said in her most dampening manner. "And unlike Mr. Sedgewood he understands that it would invite the most unfavorable comment were he to stay with us when we have no male relation at home."

"And besides, I don't want him there," Lydia declared, her bottom lip thrusting forward in a pout. "He yelled at Mama."

"Mama!"

"Your ladyship, you should have sent for the servants," Miss Blakely spoke in unison with Beth's cry, their faces wearing identical expressions of concern.

"He . . . he didn't forget himself with you, did he, my lady?" Miss Blakely added, casting Cat a worried look. Although she was now a governess, she was of very good family and had been privy to a great deal of Society gossip. "I believe his reputation is not all that it should be."

Tempting as it was to paint Stephen in the blackest light possible, Cat knew she could not. "No, it was nothing like that," she said quietly, her eyes fixed on her gloved hands. "We . . . I suppose you might say we did not get along. He seemed to take me into dislike upon sight, and I naturally objected to his rather high-handed manner."

"I hate him," Lydia declared stoutly, her small chin coming up in determination. "And so I mean to tell him, even if I have to embroider a hundred rows!"

"Should you ever encounter his lordship again, young lady, you will treat him with proper respect or you will find yourself embroidering a thousand rows," Cat corrected her sternly. "Regardless of your feelings, the earl is your papa's relation, and I will not have you treating him with contempt. Am I understood?"

The threat of a thousand rows had its desired effect, and Lydia hunched her shoulders. "Yes, Mama," she said, lowering her eyes to the tips of her patent slippers. "But in my heart, I shan't ever like him."

"In your heart you may think as you please," Cat returned gently, "but I mean what I say. You wouldn't wish to disappoint your father, would you?"

"No." Lydia chewed her lip.

"Good, then that is the end of it, I think. With the exception of the twenty rows, that is."

"What twenty rows?" Lydia's head came up in alarm.

"The twenty rows you owe me for listening at keyholes and remaining downstairs after being told to go to your rooms," Cat replied, determined not to shirk her parental responsibilities. "And you are not to go near the stables until Monday."

Lydia's lips opened in automatic protest, but the look in her mama's green eyes had her closing them again. "Yes, Mama," she said in a tone that indicated she considered herself to be much put-upon. "I will do as you say."

"See that you do." Cat resisted giving her a reassuring hug. "And you, too, Beth," she added, giving the older girl a speaking look. "Should we meet the earl, I want your word you will mind your manners."

"I hope I may know what is expected of a viscount's daughter," Beth said with the chilling pride of a seventeen-year-old. "You needn't worry that I shall bring disgrace upon the family name."

"Good." Cat sat back in her seat, her head beginning to throb from tension. The day which had started with such high spirits now seemed sadly overshadowed, and if it weren't for her fear of tempting fate, she would have wondered glumly what else could possibly go wrong.

Stephen saw the coach pass just as he was stepping out onto the street. Even if he hadn't recognized the emblem painted on the door of the black coach, the man standing next to him was more than willing to identify the occupants for him.

"Ah, there is Lady Brockton now," said Mr. Framham, Cat's solicitor, nodding his gray head in approval as the carriage rumbled past them. "I own I was a trifle skeptical when the late viscount first drew up his will, but as I was just telling you, no three children could ask for a better, more level-headed mother."

"That is reassuring to hear," Stephen replied, following the coach with narrowed eyes. "Given the terms of my cousin's will, it would have been most unfortunate to have allowed her such an unusual degree of power."

"Indeed," Mr. Framham agreed, relieved his lordship was

taking news of the will so well. When he'd received the earl's summons to call upon him, he'd dreaded another uncomfortable interview such as he had suffered with Mr. Sedgewood, but the harsh-faced young lord had surprised him. Rather than demanding the will be overturned or accusing him of being in collusion with Lady Brockton, he seemed only interested in assuring himself his young nephew and nieces were receiving the best of care.

"I still find it interesting that Edward should choose to award trusteeship of the estate to Lady Brockton rather than to Sedgewood or myself," Stephen continued, concentrating on the details of the will he had just learned. "One may understand my cousin's reluctance to entrust a child to a man of Sedgewood's stamp, but I had no idea he held me in similar contempt."

"Nothing of the sort, my lord!" Mr. Framham was properly shocked. "Indeed, both your cousin and Lady Brockton spoke of you in terms of the utmost respect. But you were a soldier in combat, and there was always a chance you would be killed."

That was so, Stephen thought, recalling the many times when he had come perilously close to such a fate. Still, the wording of the will puzzled him. He and Sedgewood were nominally the guardians of Edward's young son and daughters, and yet it was Cat as the estate's executrix who held the real power. Perhaps that was why she was pretending not to recognize him, he brooded. Any hint of scandal attached to her name could give Sedgewood the edge he needed to have the will overturned, something he had been trying to do since Edward's death, according to Cat's rather pompous solicitor.

The realization gave him pause, and for a moment he was tempted to put aside his plans for vengeance. It was one thing to make Cat pay for her treachery, but quite another to allow innocent children to suffer because of it. Although he and Sedgewood scarce knew one another, he was sufficiently acquainted with the other man's reputation as to regard him with loathing, and the thought of his gaining any control over the children was an anathema to him. Still, he could not allow Cat to escape some form of retribution.

There had to be some way he could satisfy both his conscience and his pride, he mused, his dark eyes thoughtful. Some way he could repay Cat for playing him for a fool without placing Edward's children in jeopardy. Meanwhile he would proceed with his original plan of dancing attendance upon Cat. The thought of how that would discomfit her brought a cold gleam to his eyes, and he took his leave of Mr. Framham, his lips set in a calculating smile as he set off after Cat's carriage.

The rest of the morning passed in an exhausting blur for Cat. The headache she'd developed earlier had blossomed into a full-blown migraine, and by the time they left the milliner's shop she was ready to collapse. The girls and Miss Blakely were walking slightly ahead of her, and Cat was wondering how to broach the subject of returning home when someone jostled her from behind. She turned around, the apology on her lips dissolving as she found herself staring into a pair of familiar dark eyes.

"Lady Brockton," Stephen drawled, his smile in place as he doffed his hat to her. "We meet again."

Cat managed to hide her dismay behind a cool smile. From the moment Lydia had pointed out his horse to her, she'd known such a meeting was inevitable, and she'd been unconsciously steeling herself for it. "Lord Rockholme," she replied in chilling, polite accents, her chin held high as she fixed him with her most aloof gaze. "How delightful to see you again."

"Is it?" He was unable to resist the taunt. "And here I was fearing you would deny ever having clapped eyes on me . . . as you have before."

Cat turned a deathly white, but before she could respond the girls and Miss Blakely had rushed back to her side, closing ranks about her as she faced Stephen.

"And, Miss Lydia, how are you this day?" Stephen turned to the younger girl, who was regarding him with marked hostility. "I trust you are well today?"

"Yes, my lord."

He raised an eyebrow at her clipped words, but said nothing. Now that he knew more of the situation *vis-à-vis* the will, he couldn't fault her for her distrust of him, although he meant to reassure her at the earliest possible opportunity. Regardless of the enmity between him and Cat, he was determined to do what he could for the children. With that thought in mind he turned to the older girl, who was standing protectively beside Cat.

"And you must be Miss Brockton," he said, flashing her a smile designed to melt the heart of any young girl. "You have the look of your mother about you, if you don't mind my saying."

"Not at all, sir." Beth's chin came up in perfect imitation of her stepmother. "Although I fear you are being overly generous in your praise. Mama was quite the beauty."

Another bridge to mend, Stephen winced, although his smile did not waver. "Great beauty would seem to be a family trait, then," he drawled, his eyes flicking to Cat. "Her sister was also an Incomparable. Have you ever met your Aunt Louisa?"

Beth's dark brows knitted at the unfamiliar name. "I can not say as I have, my lord," she admitted, her proud pose forgotten.

So much for that lie, he gloated, keeping his gaze fixed on Cat. "A charming young lady, and a most elusive one," he said, keeping his tone light. "She stole my poor heart some years ago, and I have been searching for her ever since, but all to no avail, I fear. Perhaps *you* might be persuaded to help me in my quest, Lady Brockton."

Her fury over the cruel way he was taunting her was all that kept Cat from collapsing. Not for anything would she grant him the satisfaction of terrorizing her, she decided, squaring her shoulders as she returned his mocking gaze. "Had I any notion as to the lady's location, I should be only too happy to share that information with you, my lord," she said, her green eyes silently damning him. "However, as I do not, I think that is all that needs to be said on the matter. Would you not agree?"

Had he not been so furious with her for her duplicity, Stephen would have applauded her courage. She was actually daring him to reveal the truth, he realized, concealing his amazement behind a carefully blank facade. Evidently there was more bottom to her than he first realized, and he chided himself for underestimating his enemy.

"Certainly, Lady Brockton," he said with a low bow. "We shall consider the matter closed."

"Good."

"Not that I intend abandoning my quest, of course." He added the thrust with the deadly skill of a swordsman. "In fact, I am quite resolved to find the lady. And I shall find her, make no doubt of that."

"I beg your pardon, my lady"—Miss Blakely stepped closer to Cat—"but if we don't hurry, we'll miss our appointment with Mrs. Pearsall. You know how cross she gets when we are late."

Cat made a mental note to increase the girl's salary on the spot. "You are right, Miss Blakely, thank you for reminding me," she said, a credible smile on her lips as she held her hand out to Stephen. "If you will pardon us, your lordship, I fear we must be on our way. Here in the wilds one learns not to annoy one's modiste by keeping her waiting overly long. Good day."

Stephen accepted her hand with a low bow. "Good day, Lady Brockton," he said, seething because he knew he had no choice but to let her leave. He could see his boast had rocked her, and he'd hoped to press the attack; now he would have to wait. Still, he was determined that he not quit the field totally bested.

He carried her hand to his lips, his eyes holding her wary gaze as he pressed a warm kiss to the back of it. He saw the color seep into her face, and knew she was remembering the last time he had touched her so intimately. "I shall look forward to seeing you again, my lady," he murmured, his voice as soft and provocative as his dark eyes were cold and challenging. "May I hope you will be home to me?"

Cat cursed him for his clever machinations. After her stern lecture to the girls, she knew she could not snub him without some sort of explanation. Freeing her hand with a discreet tug, she gave him a cool nod. "We are usually home to callers on Thursday afternoons, Lord Rockholme," she said in the tone she had often used as a governess when faced with a misbehaving pupil. "You may call upon us then."

"Ah, but I am not precisely a casual caller, am I?" Stephen reminded her suavely. He had no intention of allowing another two days to pass before seeing her again. "Your late husband was my second cousin, and the terms of his will appoint me your children's guardian. Why, we are practically brother and sister! Shall we say tomorrow afternoon?"

The mention of the will called to mind the power he held over them, and Cat bit back her harsh retort with visible effort. "Tomorrow would be fine, my lord," she said stiffly, hating him more than she had any other person, save Jeremey. "We shall see you then."

Four

The following afternoon Stephen presented himself at Larks Hall at five minutes before one of the clock. He'd learned from a footman he'd taken the care to bribe that the Brocktons ate their midday meal at precisely this time each day, and he'd timed his arrival to insure an invitation to join them. He knew no hostess worthy of the name would keep a guest cooling his heels while she dined, and he wasn't in the least discomfited when instead of conducting him to a drawing room, the butler led him to the dining room where the family was already gathered.

"Ma'am," he greeted her with a polite bow, feigning an expression of chagrin as he glanced about the elegantly appointed room. "I hadn't meant to intrude upon your family's meal. Pray accept my apologies. I shall wait for you in the drawing room." He turned as if to leave. Cat didn't disappoint him.

"No, please, my lord, will you not join us?" she said, the angry sparkle in her green eyes belying her civil tones. He knew she was aware she had been maneuvered, and the smile he sent her told her he gloated in the fact.

"Thank you, Lady Brockton," he said, settling onto the chair the butler had pulled out for him. "It is kind of you to invite a hungry soldier to break his bread with you. I appreciate it."

There was a strained silence, and then the servants began passing the plates of food. He sampled some of the excellent mutton broth being offered as the first course before turning to Elizabeth, who was seated at his right.

"Miss Brockton, I learned from your solicitor that you are

soon to be eighteen years of age," he said, offering her the smile that had never failed to set the debs' hearts to fluttering. "Is that correct?"

The young girl shifted on her chair, obviously torn between delight at having been singled out and the lingering hostility he had sensed in her yesterday. Delight won out, and she gave him a wary nod in response. "Yes, my lord," she told him, her cool tones mimicking Cat's. "My birthday is in October."

"Ah, my congratulations, then," he said, nodding pleasantly. "You will be making your bows soon after, I've no doubt. I must remember to write my sister and ask if she would be so good as to sponsor you once your Season starts."

"Your sister, sir?" This from Cat, who was still watching him with a marked degree of suspicion.

"Lady Barton, the marchioness of Barton," he provided with a bland look, playing the first of his many trump cards. "She is quite the power in London, or so I have heard. Although I must own I find it difficult to think of Charlotte as anything other than a troublesome brat," he added, giving a deliberately disarming chuckle. "But that is how it is with brothers and sisters. I am sure she thinks of me still as that ogre of a big brother who delighted in putting snakes on her nursery chair."

"You put a snake on your sister's chair?" Lydia demanded, looking much struck at the notion. "I never thought of that."

"I'd forgotten your lordship was Lady Barton's brother," Cat said, shooting Lydia a censorious look. "But I would be most grateful if you would write her on Elizabeth's behalf. I was at my wit's end trying to think of who might sponsor her."

He took a sip of the ale the footman had just set before him. "I shall be delighted to do so," he assured her, all innocence. "But I fail to see why you should be so eager to find a sponsor for Miss Brockton when that is something you could manage yourself. Now that you are out of mourning, I am certain there would be no impropriety attached to it."

There was another silence, this one more hostile, and Stephen made a mental note to mind the little barbs he cast at Cat. It was obvious her stepdaughters were devoted to her and wouldn't countenance any attack upon her. Since winning the children to his side was vital to his mission, it was a mistake he was determined not to repeat.

"I was never presented, my lord," Cat replied with quiet dignity. "That makes it impossible for me to sponsor Elizabeth."

"I see," he replied, pulling at his ear and looking sheepish. "My apologies, ma'am, if I have given offense. It hadn't occurred to me you hadn't been granted a Season. But I see no great problem," he added calmly. "Charlotte can sponsor you as well."

"Mama! Oh, what fun!" Elizabeth cried, clapping her hands with delight. "We shall make our bows together!"

Cat sent him a furious glare before responding. "We shall discuss this later, Elizabeth," she replied in what he was certain was her best governess tones. "The luncheon table is hardly the place to plan one's Season.

"Miss Lydia." Stephen abandoned Elizabeth and was next pouring his charm on the scowling fourteen-year-old. "What was the name of the groom you mentioned to me the other day, the one so knowledgeable about horses? I may have need of his services."

At first he didn't think the young lady would answer, but after Cat cleared her throat rather loudly, she complied. "His name is Jemm," she muttered sullenly. "But I don't see why *you* should need to speak with him. "He's *our* groom."

"Lydia!" Cat set her spoon down, clearly appalled at the young girl's behavior. "That was very ill-mannered of you!"

"No." Stephen surprised her by holding up one well-shaped hand. "It is quite all right, Lady Brockton. I think I understand her objections. My first day here it was I who behaved with a singular want of manners, and she rightly resents me for having given offense. Is that not so, Miss Lydia?" He fixed the girl with a look that was surprisingly adult to adult.

Lydia's scowl remained firmly in place. "You shouted at Mama," she accused Stephen defiantly. "You upset her, the way *he* does whenever he comes nosing about."

He was obviously Sedgewood, Stephen realized, suppressing a fastidious shudder at being compared to his repellent cousin. "I realize that," he said, not above playing the penitent to achieve his goals. "That is why I wished to call upon you all. I know my behavior that day is not something in which I can take any pride, and I am most heartily sorry for it. I was cross and tired when I arrived, but that didn't give me the right to take out my temper upon your mama. It was wrong of me, and I can only hope she, and you, of course, will forgive me."

Lydia remained silent for several moments, her gaze searching his face. "You won't yell anymore?" she demanded, clearly skeptical. "You won't upset Mama again?"

Again it was obvious Cat felt duty-bound to correct her charge's boldness. "Lydia, I do not think—"

"No, Lady Brockton," Stephen interrupted, silencing her with a look. "She has the right to ask." He glanced back at Lydia.

"I have no intention of making you a promise I may not be able to keep," he told her bluntly. "I am a soldier. I am accustomed to giving orders, and having those orders carried out without question. Sometimes I shout; sometimes I am short-tempered and say and do things I later regret. That is the way I am, and I make no apologies for it. The only thing I will promise, is that I will do nothing to bring disgrace upon my name, or my honor. Is that acceptable to you?"

Lydia mulled over his answer before replying. "All right," she said, giving a decisive nod. "But," she warned with a threatening glare, "if you hurt Mama, I shall make you sorry. Jemm has been teaching me to shoot, and he says I am as good as any boy. If you make her cry, I shall take Papa's pistols and shoot you in the leg. See if I do not."

The rest of the meal passed without incident, and after making their curtseys to Stephen, the girls went off with Miss Blakely for their afternoon lessons. Any hopes Cat might have harbored that Stephen would continue his gentlemanly charade and take his leave were dashed when he rose to his feet and fixed her with an implacable stare.

"I have my copy of Edward's will with me," he said without preamble, the warmth he'd shown the girls replaced by cool disdain. "If you've no objections, there are several clauses I should like to discuss with you. It shouldn't take very long."

With the butler and other servants looking on there was no way she could refuse, and Cat forced herself to swallow her simmering fury. "Of course, Lord Rockholme," she said, folding her napkin and rising to her feet. "This way." She guided him to her study at the back of the house.

She was annoyed, but not surprised, when instead of taking the chair in front of the desk as befitted a guest, Stephen moved behind her desk and lowered himself onto her chair. It was evident he was attempting to put her at a disadvantage, and her lips tightened at the obviousness of the ploy. Vowing he would not succeed, she settled on the remaining chair.

"What is it you wish to discuss?" she inquired, her expression carefully blank as she faced him. "Is there a particular clause which concerns you?"

Instead of answering, he leaned back in his chair. "You are to be commended for the excellent job you have done raising Edward's daughters," he told her, regarding her coolly. "They are both charming young ladies; if a trifle too spirited, in Lydia's case. And it is obvious they are devoted to you."

So he meant to fence, did he? Cat thought, mentally squaring her shoulders. Very well, she would oblige him.

"The fact seems to surprise you," she replied, her chin lifting in unconscious challenge.

She knew she had erred the moment the edges of his hard mouth curled in a feral smile. "Not really," he drawled, his gaze holding hers. "You forget I have experience of the devotion you inspire in others. It was weeks before I was interested in bedding another woman after our night together."

Cat's cheeks fired with fury. "If you are going to be offensive, sir, then you may leave," she informed him freezingly. "I have already warned you I will not tolerate such insolence."

He dipped his head in mocking acquiescence. "Of course, my lady," he murmured, his dark eyes sparkling with derision. "Now, let us discuss my meeting my ward."

The abrupt change of topic had Cat scowling in confusion. "What are you talking about? You have already met the girls."

"I was referring to your son, Edward's heir," he replied, his air of ennui replaced by a familiar hardness. "I have yet to meet him, and I mean to remedy the situation. Kindly have him brought down."

Eddie! Oh God, he wished to see Eddie! Panic filled Cat's heart, and for a moment sheer terror blanked out all thought. She fought it back, inch by painful inch, her mind racing as she tried desperately to think of some way of protecting her son without arousing Stephen's suspicions.

"I'm afraid that isn't possible at the moment," she said, careful not to sound too reluctant. "He is napping, and I don't wish to disturb him. It is vital children his age be kept to a strict routine, you know. Would you like to see him tomorrow?"

He looked as if he meant to object, but after a moment he nodded his head. "If it is convenient," he said, and much to her relief removed the packet of papers from his pocket and spread them out on the desk.

"I have a question regarding the payments made to you as executrix of Edward's will," he said, flipping open the papers.

As this was a battle she had oft fought with Jeremey, Cat did not have to fumble for a reply. "The money is for the upkeep of Larks Hall, and is perfectly within the law," she said, disappointed Stephen should prove to be as greedy as his cousin.

He looked up at her in surprise. "It is not the payment I object to," he said, his tone reproachful. "Rather it is the paltry amount you are being given I find troubling. It can not possibly be enough to support you and your family."

Cat lowered her eyes to hide her astonishment. "Our needs are simple," she said, annoyed he should prove her wrong yet again. "We lack for nothing, I assure you."

"Perhaps not," he conceded, sounding far from convinced. "But with Elizabeth to make her bows in a year, I fear you may find yourself lacking the necessary. I'll speak to your solicitor about having the amount increased by next quarter."

His unexpected generosity had Cat squirming with resentment. In truth, she'd been thinking of asking for a small increase, but had put it off for dislike of the dust Jeremey would doubtlessly raise. Now it seemed the problem had been solved for her, and much as it galled her pride, she knew she had no choice but to thank the man responsible. Drawing a deep breath, she lifted her head and met his watchful gaze.

"That is good of you, sir," she said stiffly. "Thank you."

Now it was his turn to look startled. He hesitated a moment, and then slowly inclined his head. "Not at all," he said, his tone matching hers for wariness. "Whatever you may think of me, you must believe I mean to do my duty by Edward's children."

Despite the antipathy she bore him, Cat didn't doubt his quiet claim for a moment. The ardent lover who haunted her dreams was a man of conviction, and it was obvious she had underestimated the strength of his resolve. And more was the pity, she mused with an unhappy sigh. Things would have been a great deal easier for her had Stephen been the pleasure-loving rake she'd once called him.

"Speaking of my duty to the children, there is something else I wish to discuss with you." Stephen's cool voice cut into Cat's dark thoughts, and she looked up to find him studying her with that same watchful air.

"And what might that be?" she asked, wondering what was going on behind his implacable facade.

"Why do the girls hate Jeremey?"

"I beg your pardon?"

"Why do the girls hate Jeremey?" he repeated. "And don't try telling me they do not. I would have to be the greatest simpleton to draw breath not to remark upon the dislike they bear him. Is it merely they resent his position as their guardian? Or have they cause for their aversion?"

Cat thought of the dreadful scene Jeremey had subjected them to on his last visit less than a month ago. He'd been foxed, as usual, and demanding an advance of his annuity. When she'd refused, he'd become ugly, and it had taken two footmen to eject him from the house. She shuddered in memory of threats and abuse he had screamed from the front doorstep.

"They have cause," she said at last. "I fear Mr. Sedgewood has given them a very poor impression of guardians."

"Has he attempted to force his attentions upon either you or Elizabeth?" he asked, and then gave a cold smile at her startled expression. "You needn't look so surprised. I may have been out of the country for a number of years, but tales of Jeremey's perversions reached me even in France. I am aware of my cousin's unsavory reputation, I promise you."

Cat clenched her jaw, recalling the night Jeremey had forced his way into her bedchamber. There had been no overt attempts since then, but the way he spoke to her, and the filthy way he looked at her, made it plain he was but biding his time. That was why she took such extraordinary care never to be alone with him longer than absolutely necessary. She wasn't about to make the mistake of placing herself at his dubious mercy.

"Cat." Stephen leaned forward, commanding her attention. "Answer my question," he ordered, his dark eyes stormy as they met hers. "Has Jeremey ever importuned you or Elizabeth?"

Cat drew herself up, banishing the awful memories with an impatient toss of her head. "He has never touched Elizabeth," she told him with cold certainty. "Else I would have put a bullet through his black heart."

"But he has touched you?" Stephen pressed, and there was something hard and dangerous in his tone that had her squirming in discomfort.

"Not of late," she admitted, glancing uneasily away. "But when I was governess he made it plain he considered me as nothing more than a parlor maid he could make free with as he pleased. One night he broke into my room, and if Edward hadn't heard me screaming and come to my aid, he would have raped me."

"And since then?"

"Since then I have taken care whenever I am forced to be alone with him. You may also be certain he is never allowed anywhere near the girls unless I am with them. There is nothing I would put beyond that beast," she added darkly. "Nothing."

There was a stiff silence, and when she glanced back at Stephen, the muscle in his lean jaw was ticking. It was several moments before he spoke. "I can see Jeremey and I shall have to have a little chat," he said finally, leaning back in his chair. "I will make it plain what behavior will be expected of him if he wants to continue visiting here."

Cat wasn't sure she cared for the sound of that. She knew

Jeremey well enough to know he would vociferously deny any wrongdoing. Indeed, he would undoubtedly insist she had invited his attentions with her wanton behavior. And given Stephen's experience of her, she brooded, frowning in worry, could she honestly blame him if he chose to believe Jeremey? Worse, if he believed his cousin's tales, might he not be tempted to brag as well? To boast of their night together? And if Jeremey learned of that night and put two and two together—

"No!" she said quickly, too quickly, if the way he was scowling at her was any indication. She could see the objections he was about to utter reflected on his hard countenance, and she tried to think of some explanation that would placate him.

"You may speak to him certainly, if that is your wish," she said, managing an indifferent shrug. "But I much doubt it will do any good. Jeremey is not the sort of man to take kindly to criticism. Were you to take him to task, I can guarantee it would have the exact opposite effect, and his behavior will be twice as objectionable. Not a pleasant prospect, I assure you."

He opened his mouth and then closed it again, obviously displeased with her response. She recalled what he'd told Lydia about being accustomed to giving orders, and decided it was nothing less than the truth. He looked as if there was nothing he'd like more than to order her to do his bidding, and it clearly frustrated him he could not. She took childish delight in the knowledge.

"Very well," he said, annoyance dripping from every word. "I promise not to speak with him so long as he keeps his distance. But," he added with a warning scowl, "I make no promises if he comes here. I won't allow the sot near the girls."

Since this was a sentiment she more than shared, she had no trouble agreeing. "If he comes to Larks Hall, you may say and do whatever you please," she told him. "But until then, I want your word you will make no attempt to contact him. Please, Stephen," she added, his given name slipping unbidden from her lips when he remained silent. "For the girls' sake, promise me you will not write Jeremey."

There was another silence, longer, more intense, and then he gave a slow, deliberate nod. "As you wish, Cat," he agreed, his tone betraying nothing of his thoughts. "For the girls' sake."

After leaving Larks Hall, Stephen went for a long ride to blow the cobwebs from his mind. Spending the afternoon in Cat's company affected him more than he was comfortable admitting, and he was furious with both Cat and himself. Devil take it, he castigated himself sternly, he was no better than the greenest country lad mooning over some winsome milkmaid. If he didn't watch his step, he'd soon be believing whatever sweet lies fell from those provocative lips of hers.

Perhaps that was the problem, he brooded, giving his horse its head as they thundered across the countryside. He did believe her. Or at least, he believed she loved her family and Larks Hall, and would do whatever was needed to keep them safe. It was also plain she loathed and feared Jeremey Sedgewood, and given what she'd told him, he didn't fault her for it. The thought of Jeremey touching Cat in any manner filled him with a deadly rage, and for one moment he violently wished his cousin back from London so he could have the pleasure of killing him.

He continued brooding for the rest of the ride, and by the time he returned to the inn he was aching with exhaustion. After seeing to his horse, he limped up to his room and collapsed on his bed. The next morning he awoke feverish and in great pain, and grimly accepted there would be no riding out to Larks Hall that day. The hours he'd spent attempting to outride his frustration had aggravated his injured leg, and in this condition, even a carriage ride was beyond his meager powers.

Perhaps it was for the best, he thought, penning a polite excuse to be sent to the Hall. Being near Cat had a deleterious effect upon his senses, and if he was to succeed in exacting his revenge, he would need all his wits about him.

He slept fitfully on and off through the day, pain and fever gnawing at his weary body. At one point he thought he could feel cool cloths being applied to his forehead, and decided he must be dreaming. He had to be dreaming, he mused, groaning in relief at the soothing touches. He'd ridden to Keswick alone, and even half-mad from fever, he couldn't imagine the officious innkeeper ministering so personally to a guest. He was almost asleep again when the feel of a cold, wet rag plopping on his forehead brought his eyes flying open, and he found himself staring up into the face of an old woman he'd never seen before.

"Who the devil are you?" he demanded, clutching the blanket to his chest and scowling up at her.

"I am Nurse," the old woman informed him curtly. "Lady Brockton sent me to have care of you. Now lie still, mind, and let me be about my duties."

Stephen stirred restlessly on the sheets, disliking the notion of being indebted to Cat. "There is no reason for her ladyship to trouble herself with me," he grumbled, a flush that had little to do with fever staining his bewhiskered cheeks. "I am fine, only a bit weary."

"Hmph!" Nurse shot back, clearly unimpressed. "You're weak as a cat, and not half so sensible. But now that you're awake, you might as well have some of the broth I brought with me. It'll set you on your pins right enough." She heaved herself to her feet and padded over to the fireplace where a cooking pot was warming in the coals.

Stephen watched through narrowed eyes as she dished up the steaming soup. He hadn't gone through five years of war without having learned something of the nature of leadership, and it was obvious the old nurse thought herself to be firmly in command of the situation and him. Well, he brooded, his pride rebelling, they would just see about that! Fighting nausea and weakness, he managed to lever himself up onto one elbow.

"I have told you, I am fine," he said, drawing on a shallow pool of strength to force an edge of authority into his voice. "You may return to Larks Hall. I have no need of your services."

Nurse regarded him with a mixture of annoyance and resignation. "Men are twice the work of a child, I do say," she murmured, sighing as she rose stiffly and walked back to him. She regarded him for a brief moment, and then reached out a gnarled hand and shoved him back flat against the pillows.

"Fine, are you, my lord?" she asked, and then gave a brisk nod as he glared furiously up at her. "Good. Now, finish your broth, and go back to sleep. If you are feeling better when you wake up again, I shall let you have a dram of whiskey."

Stephen wanted to shout and rail his fury at the old woman, but his years in the army had taught him something else as well: the intelligence to know when to quit the field. He pulled his blankets up to his chin and gathered the remnants of his dignity about him.

"Yes, Nurse."

The old woman stayed at Stephen's side for the next two days as the fever stormed through him. The wound in his leg had never healed properly, and now it became infected. On the third day he awoke to find his valet from London at his side, and he blinked up at the older man in confusion. "George?" he asked, wondering if the fever had affected his mind.

"Aye, sir," his valet said, regarding Stephen down the considerable length of his nose. " 'Tis me."

"What the devil are you doing here?" Stephen demanded. Had he sent for him? he wondered. He'd meant to, but damned if he could recall writing the note.

"You sent for me," the older man reminded him. "I arrived days ago, but the old biddy what was nursing you wouldn't let me in. 'Twas only when the fever was at its worst, that she consented to accepting my help. A right proper tartar, she were," he added, a note of reluctant respect in his voice.

Stephen had vague memories of the old nurse seeing to some of his more personal needs, and squirmed like an embarrassed schoolboy. "Well, I am most happy to see you," he muttered with relief. "I daresay I stand in sore need of your services."

"Aye, my lord, that you do," George replied with the easy familiarity of an old retainer. "But I'll soon have you looking as fine as a sixpence."

After a long bath and a thorough shave, Stephen was feeling much more the thing. His appetite was painfully sharp, and he tucked hungrily into the food his valet brought him. He was either ravenously hungry, or the inn's cooking had improved beyond measure. He said as much to George and was surprised when the older man gave a wry chuckle.

"Aye, if such fare came from this place, 'twould be a miracle. A beggar's hut would put the larder here to shame."

Stephen stared down at the remains of the beefsteak he had just devoured. "Then where did it come from?" he asked, an uncomfortable suspicion growing inside him.

"Larks Hall," George confirmed cheerfully. "Her ladyship had a fresh basket sent over for you every day. A sweet creature, she must be, to be so caring to a stranger."

An image of Cat, shivering in his arms, flashed in Stephen's mind. How the devil was he supposed to avenge himself against her when it now appeared he was in her debt?

"Aye," he muttered, his jaw hardening in savage frustration. "A sweet creature indeed."

Five

Cat spent the four days' respite granted by Stephen's illness shoring up her defenses, and plotting her strategy. Her first response was to send Eddie as far from Larks Hall as possible, but upon reflection, she decided against it. Not only could she not bear the notion of being parted from her son for so much as a day, but she feared such a step could only serve to pique Stephen's curiosity.

A woman with nothing to hide would have no cause to deny his request to meet his ward, she reasoned, and the last thing she wanted was for him to begin wondering if she *did* have such a cause. And even if he did notice any resemblance between himself and Eddie, it was unlikely he would remark upon it. Dark hair and eyes were a trait shared by both the Brocktons and the Wrexleys, so Eddie's coloring was hardly exceptional. She had nothing to worry about.

She was still telling herself the same thing two days later, as she sat nervously in the parlor awaiting Stephen's arrival. He'd sent 'round a note earlier that morning announcing his intention to call upon her, and she decided to make use of his visit to introduce him to Eddie. The sooner she got their initial meeting behind her, the sooner she could relax.

"Who is this man, Mama?" Eddie asked, dark eyes bright with curiosity as he squirmed in his chair.

"A friend of your father's, dearest," Cat told him, not for the first time. "His lordship was your papa's distant cousin."

"He is a soldier," Eddie said, and Cat hid a smile as she

noted her son's inquisitive mind had retained the one fact of importance to him. "Does he have medals? May I see them?"

"I am sure he must have several," Cat replied, recalling the anxious days after a battle when she'd searched the papers for any mention of Stephen. "But I fear he shan't be wearing them. This is a social call, and he won't wear his uniform for that."

"I would," Eddie said, with the cool certainty of his young years. "And a sword, too." He leapt off his chair and began swinging his arm in lusty imitation of a soldier swinging a saber. "Kill the Frogs! Kill the Frogs!"

"A sentiment I heartily agree with, lad."

A wry voice sounded from the doorway, and Cat turned in surprise to find Stephen standing there. He was dressed to the nines in a riding jacket of black serge, a pair of doeskin breeches tucked into a pair of glossy black Hessians. She thought he looked every bit as arrogant and dangerous as he had the first time he had come to Larks Hall, until she saw the pallor on his face and the lines pain and exhaustion had carved into his lean cheeks. Despite the mistrust and fear she bore him, her animosity melted in compassion.

"My lord, I didn't know you had arrived," she said, studying him with worried eyes. "How are you feeling?"

"Better, thank you," he replied, his limp pronounced as he walked into the room. "And as for not knowing I was here, I asked the butler not to announce me. After the past few years in the army, I find I've lost all patience for protocol. I trust I haven't given offense?"

"Not at all, sir," she began, but before she could say anything else, Eddie ran up to Stephen, his tiny face filled with lively curiosity as he looked up at him.

"You are a soldier," he informed Stephen solemnly. "And an earl." He cocked his head to one side, frowning in childish confusion. "What's 'an earl'?"

To Cat, it was as if time stood still. Father and son, each so like the other it was painful to see, gazed at one another, and for an agonizing moment Cat feared her heart would break. How could Stephen look down into Eddie's face and not see himself? she wondered, blinking back tears. And, God help her, what would she do if he did?

An eternity passed as Stephen continued staring down at Eddie, and just as Cat was certain the suspense would kill her, he reached down and brushed back a lock of dark hair that had fallen across Eddie's forehead.

"Nothing so important as being a soldier," he said, smiling. "Have I the honor of addressing Lord Brockton?"

"No, I am Eddie," her son corrected, his tone faintly chiding as he continued studying Stephen. "Edward Jonathan Brockton."

Stephen's smile widened. "I stand corrected," he said, inclining his head in apology. "And I am Stephen."

Cat was still struggling for composure when there was a tap on the door, and a maid appeared bearing a tray.

"Cakes!" Eddie abandoned Stephen and rushed over to the table where the maid was arranging the food. He was reaching greedily for the nearest tart when Cat managed to find her voice.

"Only one, Eddie," she said, seeking solace in the mundane duties of motherhood. "And since Lord Rockholme is our guest, you must allow him to select first."

"Stephen," Eddie reminded her, casting her a roguish grin that was similar to the one on Stephen's face.

How she got through the next half hour without going mad, Cat knew not. With Eddie pestering their guest with an endless stream of questions, there was no need for her to make idle conversation, and she was coward enough to be grateful for the fact. She poured out tea and prepared plates, every inch the attentive hostess even as she struggled for the control that had always served her in good stead.

Finally the thirty minutes she'd allotted for the visit were up, and with a silent sigh of relief, she rose to her feet. "It was very good of you to call upon us, my lord," she said, dismissal in her voice as she placed a protective hand on Eddie's shoulder. "Thank you for coming."

Stephen also rose to his feet, albeit somewhat awkwardly, and offered her a low bow. "You are most welcome, Lady Brockton," he replied, his dark eyes meeting hers with cool challenge. "But before I take my leave, I was hoping for a walk in the gardens. They were quite lovely, as I recall. And, of course, I wouldn't dream of going without saying hello to Miss Brockton and Miss Lydia. Are they at home?"

The words were polite enough, but Cat was clever enough to hear the command and the determination behind them. Since refusal was out of the question, she gave in with what good grace she could muster. "They are in their rooms," she said, imagining how delighted the girls would be for any excuse to escape their lessons. "If you will excuse me, I will let them know you are—"

"I'll go!" Eddie interrupted, wriggling free and dashing for the door before Cat could stop him. He'd almost reached the door when he skidded to a halt and cast Stephen a glance over his shoulder. "You will stay here?" he demanded with a suspicious scowl. "Right here?"

"Right here," Stephen promised, then chuckled as Eddie dashed out of the room, calling out for his sisters in a voice that echoed through the large stone hall.

"I would give my entire fortune to have even half his energy," he said, still chuckling as he turned to Cat. "Is he always so . . . exuberant?"

The rueful observation brought a smile to Cat's lips. "He is almost five, my lord," she told him with a mother's fond pride. "He has the fortitude of a battalion."

Stephen nodded. "And it would take a battalion, I'm thinking, to keep up with the little devil. However do you manage, ma'am?"

Surprised at his friendliness, Cat answered without hesitating. "I have an excellent staff, but even then it takes both of his sisters and myself to keep a watchful eye on him when we are outside, or heaven only knows what mischief he might do."

Stephen chuckled again. "That I can readily believe, for I have never been so ruthlessly interrogated. I vow, had he asked me 'Why?' one more time, I should have surrendered on the spot." Then he shook his head.

"Do you know, I can not recall seeing Edward as a young boy, and yet I must have done, for there is something so familiar about Eddie. The eyes, perhaps. Edward's eyes were brown, weren't they?" He sought Cat's gaze.

Cat fought back the urge to swoon. "Yes, as are the girls'." *And yours,* she thought silently, and then added, "Nurse vows Eddie is the image of his father at the same age."

Although distracting Stephen hadn't been her objective, it was obvious that was precisely what she had done. He turned to her, his expression abruptly serious. He straightened his shoulders, assuming a rigid military posture as he once more met her gaze.

"Speaking of Nurse, I wish to thank you for sending her to me," he said, his voice every bit as stiff as his stance. "It was very good of you, and I thank you for your kindness."

Uncertain how to respond to such grudging gratitude, Cat fell back on the cold manners she'd learned to affect since becoming Lady Brockton. "That is quite all right, Lord Rockholme," she informed him with a cool lift of her chin. "I am happy to—"

"No," he interrupted, cutting through the air with an impatient gesture. "Save your graces and airs for another time. I *am* grateful, even if it doesn't sound like it. I know I could well have died if you hadn't sent that impossible old woman to bully and care for me. And I want to know why you did it. Considering the way we've brangled since my coming to Larks Hall, it can not be because of any affection you bear me."

Cat didn't answer; not out of defiance, but because she didn't know what to say. When she'd received his message, crying off on his visit, she'd assumed him to be jug-bitten and dismissed him as being little better than Jeremey. But when a note from the frantic innkeeper arrived detailing how ill he truly was, she'd reacted out of a confusing whirl of emotions she didn't care to examine too closely. She only knew she couldn't bear it if he were to die, and so she'd sent Nurse to him, knowing it would tangle matters between them even further.

"Cat?" Stephen's insistent voice shattered her reverie, and she glanced up to find him watching her. "I am waiting."

"You are Edward's cousin," she said at last, deliberately

avoiding his gaze. "He spoke of you with great fondness, and I know it is what he would wish me to do."

There was a long silence as Stephen continued regarding her. "And that is the only reason?" he pressed, taking a hesitant step toward her. "There was no other motive involved?"

She knew he was alluding to their night together. The intimate knowledge they had shared with each other was there in his voice, but for the first time since his unexpected reappearance in her life, there was no anger or bitterness underlying his deep tones. He was simply asking for the truth, a truth she dared not give.

"No," she said, forcing herself to meet his hooded gaze. "There was no other motive involved. How could there be?"

At first she thought he would dispute her refusal, but in the end he merely inclined his head, his manner as icy and remote as her own. "Very well, Lady Brockton. In that case, I pray you will accept my thanks. I am in your debt."

The arrival of the children, chattering in noisy excitement, spared her the necessity of an answer. Settling behind the tea cart, she dispensed sweets with a calm smile, but even as she chatted with the girls and Miss Blakely, she was painfully aware of her guest's every movement. He was sitting on one of the gilded chairs with Eddie on his lap, solemnly responding to the boy's eager questions. It was a domestic scene straight from her most secret fantasy, and the embodiment of her worst nightmare. Father and son, so close, and yet unaware of each other's true identities. Her heart broke at the sight, and she wondered how long she could endure the pain of it before losing her mind.

Stephen spent the next several days wrestling with his conscience and his pride. While recovering from his illness he'd had a great deal of time to consider the matter between Cat and himself, and he decided that whatever debt he thought she owed him, she had more than repaid him with her unexpected kindness. But while he might be willing to forgo his revenge, he wasn't yet ready to let the truth of that night drop. For reasons he couldn't understand, it had become vital to his pride that she admit they had been lovers. He would never use the knowledge to hurt her as he'd once schemed, but he had to know she'd been as moved by that night as he had. Once he had that, he would go back to London and pick up the threads of his life once more.

The first problem, as he saw it, was learning what he could of Cat. Since he couldn't very well go to her for answers, he decided his next best bet lay with the children. To that end he spent the days insinuating himself into the daily routine of the Hall. It was appallingly easy, as both the girls and Edward welcomed him into their midst with surprising enthusiasm.

Lydia was friendly enough so long as he restricted the conversation to her beloved horses, but she grew closemouthed and wary the moment he tried drawing her out on the subject of Cat. It was the same with Elizabeth. she would chat freely with him for hours about fashion, his sister, and what the patronesses of Almacks were *really* like, but a single mention of her stepmama had her suddenly remembering her presence was required elsewhere. Only young Edward remained at ease with him, but Stephen soon learned it was dashed hard prying information from a child.

"No, I do not want to hear the fishes talk, Edward. I was asking you about your mama," Stephen said, striving valiantly for fortitude. At Edward's suggestion he had taken the lad out to the estate's fish pond, hoping to use the situation to learn more of Cat. But so far the only thing he had learned was that four-year-old boys were inveterate chatterboxes.

"Mama doesn't hear the fishes," Edward told him, his look clearly reproachful. "They're boy fishes. They only talk to me."

"But there must be girl fishes if there are boy fishes," Stephen said, trying to think of some way to guide the conversation in another direction. "Perhaps the girl fishes talk to your mother."

Edward gave a weary sigh. "Only boy fishes talk," he informed Stephen with studied patience. "Girl fishes just swim."

Despite his frustration, such masculine logic brought a reluctant grin to Stephen's lips. Until the age of fifteen when a worldly-wise maid introduced him to the sweet wonders of the boudoir, he'd also held females in similar disdain.

"What are you gentlemen discussing so earnestly?" Cat asked, a gentle smile on her face as she joined them. She was dressed in a simple gown of green-and-white-striped cambric, a Lavinia bonnet of chipped straw covering her dark curls, and Stephen took a moment to appreciate her before responding.

"The linguistic abilities of fish," he told her, his gaze moving approvingly over her. "I had no idea the little creatures were so very clever. I see I shall have to treat my trout *almandine* with greater respect."

The quip won him a musical laugh, and he realized with a start he'd never heard Cat laugh before. The sound sent a thrill of delight through him, and he was momentarily nonplused. Luckily for his *sang-froid,* Edward was there to make up for his lack of conversation. The boy began pelting him with question after question, pausing in the interrogation only when a colorful butterfly fluttering nearby caught his attention, and he went dashing after it with a squeal of delight.

"He's a lively lad," he commented, watching as Edward darted up and down the path in pursuit of the butterfly. "Does he never stop asking questions?"

A rueful glow darkened Cat's green eyes. "When he is sleeping, or when he is eating. Although that usually doesn't prove a very successful deterrent. Nurse and I are forever scolding him not to talk with his mouth full, but he is always forgetting. The girls are naturally appalled, and think him quite the savage. I remind them they doubtlessly did the same thing when they were but four."

"I keep forgetting he is so young," Stephen observed. He recalled both Cat and her solicitor had told him Edward's age, but the lad was so bright, he'd somehow formed the opinion he was older. "Then I am doubly surprised he speaks so well. My brother's son was about that age the last I saw of him, and he could scarce say but a few words."

"Nurse says it's different with each child," Cat replied, pulling at the crocheted gloves covering her slender fingers. "It is hardly fair to compare the one with the other."

Stephen considered this for a brief moment. Now that he thought of it, he recalled his mother once mentioning he had started talking at the age of two, while his two brothers were nearer to three. His sister, he was certain, must have sprang from the womb chattering like a magpie.

"I suppose you are right," he allowed, and then decided he'd had enough of discussing Edward. For the first time in days he had Cat to himself, and he meant to make good use of the opportunity. Feigning nonchalance, he gave a languid sigh.

"It's very restful here; so peaceful and so green. Lord, how I longed for the like of it when I was in the heat and dust of Spain."

"Yes, Larks Hall is lovely," Cat agreed, and he could feel the puzzled gaze she cast him from beneath her thick lashes. "But I am sure your estate must be even more beautiful."

Stephen let his thoughts drift to the huge, elegant mansion that had been his family's ancestral seat for the past two hundred years. "It's beautiful, to be sure," he said, a faint sense of nostalgia tugging at him. "I left my youngest brother, James, in charge while I was away. I have another brother, Jason, who manages one of my other estates."

"Jason, I remember him," Cat said unexpectedly. "He came to Edward's funeral. He-he was very kind."

Stephen noted the way her voice faltered, and felt an unexpected flash of jealousy. His younger brother was most handsome, and before his marriage, nearly as successful with the ladies as was he. Had he comforted Cat? he wondered darkly. And precisely what form did that "comfort" take?

"Your brother looks much like you," Cat continued, not seeming to notice his simmering silence. "When I first saw him standing in the church, I thought it was you."

It took but a moment for the import of Cat's artless confession to penetrate Stephen's brooding anger. "Did you?" he asked, stretching out his leg with a bored yawn. "I don't know if I should be flattered or insulted at such a comparison. Jason was an overdressed dandy with a penchant for the most appalling waistcoats in his youth."

"Well, he was very properly attired in mourning black when

I met him," Cat assured him. "And his conduct was all that it should be. He was very much the gentleman."

"But you thought he looked like me?" Stephen slid into the opening with the cunning of a skilled warrior.

"At first glance. His hair is dark, like yours, but his eyes are blue, and he's not nearly as tall."

"I daresay you are right," he said, moving coldly in for the kill. "But I am still puzzled you should mistake Jason for me."

Edward had disappeared from sight, and he could tell her attention was focused on that, rather than on him. "Why should that be so remarkable?" she asked, searching for some sign of her son. "You are brothers, after all."

Stephen allowed himself a brief moment to savor his victory before speaking. "That is so, but it is still puzzling you should see me in him. Because according to you, *Lady Brockton,"* he all but spat her title at her, "we never met until the day I rode into Larks Hall. Explain that, if you can."

There was a brittle silence as a look of horror froze Cat's expression. It was obvious she only now realized what she had let slip, and more obvious still how bitterly she was wishing those words unsaid. But it was too late. Perhaps it had been too late from the moment he'd seen her walking into the drawing room. She closed her eyes for a brief second, and when she opened them again, they were as cold and empty as death.

"Very well, my lord," she said quietly, turning to meet his gaze with icy aplomb, "you have trapped me. It was very cunning of you, and I applaud you for your unquestioned skill. You are indeed a master of the art of war. How foolish of me to forget."

To his amazement, he could feel himself flushing. "Damn it, Cat!" he exclaimed, scowling in discomfort. "It doesn't have to be a war between us! All I want is the truth."

"The truth." She gave a harsh laugh. "As you wish, sir, the truth you shall have. It *was* me that night. I came to the house party at Lord Exter's. I let you seduce me. I lay with you. I let you use me like the most common of whores. I betrayed my husband and our vows. There is your truth, your lordship, may you savor it and be damned." And with that she turned and walked away, leaving him to stare after her in helpless frustration.

After retrieving her errant son and returning him to his nanny, Cat went up to her rooms to indulge in a bout of angry tears. She wept from fury, from fear, and from a sorrow that was threatening to tear her apart. That night in Stephen's arms had been her most cherished possession, a beloved treasure to take out and examine in the long, lonely hours of the night. It had helped her survive after Edward's death, but now instead of warming her, it made her skin crawl with revulsion, and it was for that reason she hated him most.

If she thought it would have helped wash the memory of that night from her mind, she would gladly have bathed in boiling water. But it was much too late for that, and she didn't think a thousand baths would be enough to make her feel clean again. The realization prompted another fresh flow of tears.

Dinner that evening was subdued. It was the first time in many nights they dined without Stephen in attendance, and it was plain his absence was keenly felt.

"But his lordship promised to help me with my dancing," Beth said, her lips protruding in a sulky pout that was too studied to be genuine. "He was even going to demonstrate the waltz!"

"Young ladies making their bows do not waltz, Elizabeth," Miss Blakely said, albeit in a kindly tone. "And pray do not pout like that in London. You will he taken for a green country miss if you do."

The pout vanished as if by magic, but before the young girl could think of anything else to say, Lydia spoke up.

"*I* waited forever in the stable for his lordship to come," she said, with a dramatic toss of her head. "Jemm waited, too, even though he was supposed to be exercising the horses. And then when the earl did come he scarce said two words to us before mounting his horse and riding off. I thought it exceedingly rude of him, and so I shall tell him tomorrow when he comes to call."

Cat shifted uncomfortably on her chair. Although she hadn't asked Stephen to leave Larks Hall and never return, she realized she was counting on his sense of honor and discretion to do just that. Just as she was relying on his sense of honor to remain silent about that long-ago night.

"Perhaps Lord Rockholme won't be coming back," she said, hoping to soften the blow as best she could. "Today he spoke of going down to Kent to visit his estates."

"He'll come," Lydia said with surprising certainty. "He promised me I could ride his horse, and since I haven't had a chance as yet, I know he will be back."

"And he said he would show me how the London ladies use their fans to flirt with the beaus," Beth added, smiling. "He says no beauty is considered truly accomplished until she has mastered the art."

Lydia shot her a smug look. "What makes you think *you'd* be considered a beauty, frog face?"

A heated quarrel quickly ensued, but Cat listened with only half an ear. She was aware the girls had been spending much of their time in Stephen's company, but she hadn't known they would become so attached to him in so short a while. Although upon reflection, she supposed she shouldn't be surprised. She knew only too well how charming he could be, and it was no wonder both Beth and Lydia should succumb. Still, it troubled her.

Since their father's death they'd had no real masculine presence in their lives, except for Jeremey, of course, and he hardly counted. If Stephen did leave, as she hoped he would, would they be hurt by it? And if they were hurt, how could she make it up to them? It was a question that kept her awake long into the night.

When she awoke the following morning with heavy eyes and a pounding head, she was no closer to resolving the conundrum of Stephen and what she should do about him. On the one hand it was best for all if she kept him at a distance, never allowing him close enough to guess her most carefully guarded secret. But on the other hand, his presence could prove beneficial to the girls. Beth most expressly would benefit from such an association, especially if Stephen made good on his promise to have his sister arrange her coming out. In the end it was that argument that proved the most compelling, and she decided she had no choice other than to encourage him to spend as much time as he wished with her daughters.

With that thought in mind she sat at her desk and penned him a note, inviting him to join them for a picnic that afternoon. She was about to ring for a footman and have the note delivered to him at the inn, when a maid arrived with the message that Stephen had called and was awaiting her in the drawing room. Pausing only long enough to dash some cool water on her face, she squared her shoulders and went down to face the enemy.

Six

In the drawing room an exhausted Stephen awaited Cat's arrival with mounting apprehension. He'd been awake most of the night, and the more he reflected upon it, the more he came to realize he'd had no right forcing Cat to admit they had been lovers. However badly he might have needed to hear the words, they had accomplished nothing, other than causing her pain. That was why he'd returned to Larks Hall. Even if it meant grovelling, he was determined to do whatever it took to win her forgiveness. He was mentally composing various apologies when the door opened, and Cat stepped into the room.

"Lord Rockholme, how kind of you to call," she said, gliding forward with that delicate grace he so admired. "I was just about to send a note inviting you to join us for a picnic."

"Were you?" He regarded her solemnly. "After yesterday I should think I'm the last person on earth you would wish to see."

She flushed, and her gaze skittered away from his. She walked over to the mullioned window and stood gazing out at the gardens. "I think we are agreed that yesterday and what we discussed are best forgotten," she said, keeping her back to him.

"All right," Stephen agreed, watching her with hooded eyes. "But first there is something I must say to you, and to do that, I need you to look at me. Look at me, Cat. Please."

She hesitated, and for a moment he feared she wouldn't comply. But at last she turned around, and the misery he saw etched on her delicate features added to the feelings of guilt and self-loathing weighing him down. Seeing the fear on her face and knowing he was responsible dealt him a stinging blow, and it took every ounce of courage he possessed to keep from breaking rank and fleeing like a coward. Instead he stood his ground doggedly, meeting her gaze with what ragged pride he could muster.

"Forcing you to admit to something you obviously wished forgotten was wrong, and I am most heartily sorry for it," he said quietly, noting her surprised start with grim remorse. "I behaved like the worst sort of villain, and although I know I have no claims upon your generosity, I am asking that you find it in your heart to forgive me."

He was horrified when the jewel-colored eyes which had haunted him for the past five years began filling with tears.

"My lord, I—"

"No!" he interrupted, taking a halting step toward her. "Hear me out, I beg of you. The night we met I knew I would be leaving the following morning to join my regiment. I knew I was riding off to war, to my own death, perhaps, and I wanted a memory, a sweet memory, to take with me. You were that memory, Cat, and I thank you for it. It kept me sane through all the madness, all the horror that is war. When I saw you again and you acted as if we'd never met, it struck me on the raw. Like any mindless beast I lashed out without thought or care for the hurt I might cause, and I did hurt you, Cat . . . didn't I?"

The tears which filled her eyes were now spilling down her cheeks, but she never once glanced away. "No more than I hurt you, it would seem," she replied, her voice not quite steady.

"I wasn't hurt, not really," he denied, more to spare her feelings than his own. "It was more sheer male vanity than anything else. We men are prideful creatures when it comes to such matters, and I wanted to know that you remembered that night. That you remembered me. When you pretended you did not, it was an affront to my very manhood. That's a poor excuse, I know, but it's the only one I can offer. I pray it is enough."

Cat wiped at her cheeks, her lips forming a shaky smile as she regarded him. "It is enough."

"Then you forgive me?" He wasn't quite ready yet to believe in his good fortune.

"I forgive you," she assured him. "And more than that I-I . . ." Her voice trailed off.

"You what, Cat?" He edged closer, unable to resist the impulse to touch her cheek. He had to touch her, even in the smallest way, or he feared he would surely explode.

She raised tear-dampened eyes to his. "I remember," she whispered brokenly, reaching up to cover his fingers with her own so that in that one heartbeat of time they were once more flesh to flesh. "I remember that night. I remember you. I've never forgotten a single moment of it." And then before he could speak, she turned and fled toward the door. He expected her to open it and dash out, and was unprepared when she stopped and turned once more to face him.

"The-the children are hoping you will join us," she said, her gaze fixed firmly to the right of him. "You won't disappoint them, will you?"

So, she was seeking his company for her children's behalf rather than her own, Stephen thought. The realization shouldn't have hurt, but somehow it did. "I wouldn't dream of it," he replied, his hands clenching at his sides. "Thank you, Cat."

She looked as if there was more she wanted to say, but in the end she gave a jerky nod. "I'll let them know you're here," she said, and then slipped quietly from the room.

Days turned effortlessly into weeks, and still Stephen lingered in Keswick. Each morning when he rode out to Larks Hall he'd tell himself this would be the day he'd say his good-byes, and yet each night before he rode back to his rooms at the inn he'd find himself making excuses why he couldn't leave. There were the children, of course, especially Eddie, who had become his lively, chattering shadow. The lad had become so adept at slipping out of his nursery to follow him that in the interest of the child's safety, Stephen simply took him with him, putting the boy up on the saddle in front of him so he could keep a better eye on him.

Cat never objected to the arrangement . . . precisely, but Stephen was aware of how often she would watch him, an expression of fear and sadness in her eyes. The fear baffled him almost as much as did the sadness, for he would sooner die than bring harm to the child. He tried reassuring Cat on this score, but the more he declared his fondness for her son, the more apprehensive she seemed to become. It was a puzzle he couldn't solve, and so he pushed it from his mind, refusing to let it darken the halcyon days he spent at Larks Hall with Cat and her family.

He'd been recovered for almost a fortnight when Cat asked him to ride out to one of the farms to help supervise the draining of a field. Delighted to be of assistance he rode out at once, with Eddie perched on the saddle before him. The men had barely begun the back-breaking task when a rider galloping hell-bent for leather toward them caught his attention. He'd just recognized the horse as one of Cat's hunters, when he realized who was riding the beast.

"Lydia! What the devil do you think you're doing? Come down from there at once!" he demanded, his heart in his throat as he strode over to where the huge stallion had plunged to a halt.

"Cousin Stephen! You must come at once!" the young girl cried, tumbling from the saddle into Stephen's outstretched arms. *"He's* at the house, and he's shouting at Mama, and calling her a jade, and—"

"Who's calling Cat a jade?" Stephen interrupted, a deadly anger firing his blood.

"Jeremey Sedgewood, of course!" Lydia exclaimed impatiently, dancing from one foot to another and tugging at his hand. "He rode up just now with a group of his cronies, and they're all as drunk as wheelbarrows. When Mama said they couldn't stay, he called her a jade and told her he'd damned well stay in his own house if he damned well pleased. And the other men *laughed,* Cousin Stephen! They laughed at Mama."

Stephen turned to one of the laborers standing behind him. "Watch Lord Brockton," he ordered the man curtly. "And make certain Miss Lydia stays as well."

"But Cousin Stephen—"

"You will remain here, Lydia, and that is an order!" Stephen told her, bending down to fix her with a stern look. "Have I your word you will obey?"

Lydia's dark brown eyes reflected a grudging trust. "You'll make them leave?" she asked hesitantly.

Stephen lightly tapped her dust-streaked face. "I will make them leave," he promised. "Now mind you stay here and keep an eye on Eddie. I'll be back for you as soon as I can."

"Shall I send some men with ye, me lord?" the tenant whose field was being drained asked, eyeing Stephen warily. "Things are like to get a bit . . . awkward."

A hard smile touched Stephen's lips. "Oh, things will get awkward, all right," he promised softly. "Things will get damned awkward by the time I've finished." He turned and strode over to where his horse was tethered, vaulting into the saddle and riding off before anyone could stop him.

A heavily laden travelling coach was pulled up in front of the house when Stephen came galloping up. The door to the house was open, and he could hear the sound of voices raised in anger.

"I will not tell you again, Mr. Sedgewood, I won't have you in this house while you are in this condition." He recognized Cat's voice at once. "You and your friends will leave."

"And I told you I won't be thrown from my rightful property by a presumptuous doxy." The sneering insult in Jeremey's voice had the blood roaring in Stephen's ears, but he brought himself under ruthless control before dismounting and walking into the front hall. The tableau that greeted him had his temper flaring out of control again in less than a heartbeat.

Cat was standing in front of the staircase, the upper servants huddled uncertainly behind her. A quartet of men were standing in front of her, and although it had been over five years since he'd last clamped eyes on him, Stephen had no difficulty recognizing his distant cousin as the overfed, overdressed dandy in the dishevelled coat. He even recognized one of the three men standing beside Sedgewood, smirks on their faces, as they watched the unfolding drama. Dismissing them as of no importance, he strode up to Sedgewood, concentrating the full brunt of his fury on his cousin.

"What the devil is going on here?" he demanded, eyeing the other man with icy contempt.

Jeremey turned, something unpleasant flickering in his eyes before he managed a drunken bow. "Well, well, if it isn't my esteemed cousin," he said mockingly. "Welcome, my lord. I heard you was back from the wars. Damned Frenchies can't do anything right, 'twould seem."

Stephen stared at Jeremy's flushed, plump face, imagining the pleasure it would give him to plant his fist in the center of it. "You are a disgrace to whatever good name you once possessed," he told the other man, making no effort to soften the disgust he felt. "Lady Brockton has asked that you leave, and I suggest you do so while you are still in one piece."

Instead of being cowed by the not-so-subtle violence in Stephen's warning, Sedgewood seemed amused. "Ah, like that, is it?" he sneered, his lips twisting in an ugly smile. "Are you worried we shall ruin your sport with the lovely widow? Never fear, cousin. You may keep bedding the wench as often as you please, so long as you let us have our turn, eh, lads?" He turned to give his companions a lecherous wink.

"Too tart for my taste," one of the men opined, studying Cat through his quizzing glass. "Puts me in mind of my old nanny."

Stephen's hands clenched into fists, and he took an impulsive step forward, only to be brought up short when Jeremey produced a sword from the cane he had been holding.

"Ah, ah, my lord," he warned, deftly swirling the tip of the sword inches from Stephen's face. "No sudden moves, mind. It would be a shame to scar that handsome phiz of yours."

Stephen froze, more furious than seriously alarmed. He'd faced and killed better swordsmen than Sedgewood a hundred times in battle, but he wasn't so foolish as to provoke a drunken man with a naked blade. He took a calming breath and made one last stab at reasoning with a man he now regarded as a monster.

"Lady Brockton is our cousin's widow," he said, his voice one that would have had a smarter man fleeing for his life. "I can not allow you to insult her. Perhaps you've forgotten your manners, as your friends have obviously forgotten theirs, but I've not forgotten mine. If you don't do as her ladyship requests and leave at once, I have no qualms of calling you out. Of calling any of you out," he added, shooting the other three men a look of deadly warning.

"A duel?" Sedgewood gave a mocking laugh. "Yes, you'd do that, wouldn't you? You were ever the gentleman. When you weren't busy bedding every woman in sight, that is. The ladies still sigh for you, you know. Why don't you run off to London and oblige them, eh? I will tend to her ladyship."

Stephen didn't need further goading. He simply brought his hand up in a violent arc, backhanding Jeremey and sending him sprawling onto the polished marble floor. As he fell Stephen easily ripped the pretty sword from his hand and lithe as a cat had the deadly point resting against Sedgewood's throat.

"Guard well your tongue, *cousin,*" he warned coldly. "Unlike you, I know what to do with a sword, and I'll kill you before you draw your next breath if you dare insult Lady Brockton again."

Sedgewood's pale eyes bulged in his florid face. "Now see here, Rockholme," he sputtered, blustering and bullying to the end. "This is no concern of yours!"

Stephen remained silent, sweating as he fought to control his warrior instincts. More than anything he wanted to kill Sedgewood; not just because of what he'd said about Cat, but because of what he had tried to do to her all those years ago. Any man who would attempt to force himself upon a woman didn't deserve to live. It would be so easy to take Sedgewood out, to slaughter him like the pig he was. All he had to do was apply the slightest bit of pressure and. . . .

"I say, my lord, no need for bloodshed, what?" said one of the men who had accompanied Sedgewood, inching cautiously forward. "Old Jeremey was just having a bit of sport, and—" He broke off in terror when Stephen's implacable gaze swung in his direction.

"A bit of sport?" Stephen repeated in low fury, taking care to keep the blade of the sword poised on Sedgewood's throat.

"Is that what you call forcing your way into a lady's home and offering her every manner of insult?"

"Oh, be quiet, Lester, do, before you get the lot of us killed," one of the other men ordered, dabbing at his forehead with a shaking hand. "And pray accept our apologies, my lady," he added, offering Cat a hasty bow. "This is all an unfortunate misapprehension. We were made to understand our company would be welcome." He shot Sedgewood a look of undisguised loathing.

"Then you were made to understand wrong," Stephen said before Cat had the chance to answer. "Now get out, and take this piece of dung with you."

There were no arguments. The three men stumbled forward, all but falling over each other in their haste to do as Stephen had ordered. Sedgewood protested vociferously, struggling angrily in his friends' grip; but they were clearly more frightened of Stephen than they were of Jeremey, and they hustled him out the door and into the carriage. Stephen followed, waiting until they were inside before speaking.

"I know you, Claibourne," he said, addressing the oldest of the men. "And it will be a small matter for me to learn the rest of your names as well. If I hear of any of you so much as mentioning Lady Brockton's name with other than the greatest respect, I will track you down and kill you."

"You won't get away with this, Rockholme!" Jeremey, more flushed and dishevelled than ever, threatened furiously. "You'll pay for interfering with me, do you hear? You'll pay!"

Stephen did no more than look at him, but it was enough to end the sputtering tirade. "I hear," he said, then transferred his attention to the other men. "Let this be a lesson to you," he told them coldly. "And in future, take better care who you call friend. Next time you may not escape so lightly. Go back to London, and pray we never have cause to meet again."

He slammed the door closed and stood back, keeping watch until the carriage had rumbled out of sight. When he walked back into the house the staff was still clustered on the stairs, but of Cat there was no trace. He turned to the butler.

"Where is Lady Brockton?"

"She left, my lord," the older man said, offering Stephen a tentative smile. "Like as not, she has gone out to the gardens. That is where she usually goes whenever she is upset."

It took Stephen several minutes of searching before he managed to find Cat. He'd expected she would be tearful, perhaps even frightened, but to his amusement she was neither. His sweet Cat was in a spitting fury, and she was none too shy who knew it.

"That fat, odious, monstrous beast!" she raged, pacing up and down the stone pathway. "I hope he gets the pox and dies drowning in his own puke! I hope he gets gangrene and swells up like a pig's bladder! If he comes back again, I vow I'll kill him with my bare hands and throw the pieces down the privy!"

Stephen's lips twitched at such unladylike ferocity, but he was wise enough to keep his amusement well-hidden as he stepped forward to confront her. "I trust you're not speaking of me, my lady," he drawled, smiling at the look of chagrin on her face when she spun around to glare at him. "I'd hoped we had placed such enmity behind us weeks ago."

"Stephen!" She raced to his side in a flurry of ruffled silk. "Are you all right?" she demanded anxiously, her worried gaze moving over him. "He didn't hurt you, did he?"

Stephen was so stunned by her show of concern and her use of his Christian name, it was several seconds before he managed to find his voice. "No," he said faintly, staring down at her in astonishment. "He didn't hurt me."

"That filthy swine!" she muttered, her eyes once more flashing with outrage. "I can't believe he had the effrontery to threaten you! You ought to have run him through with that ridiculous sword of his instead of just knocking him flat."

"Indeed," Stephen agreed, and then unable to contain himself any longer, he threw back his head and gave a shout of laughter.

"Well, I'm happy you find this so amusing!" Cat retorted, sending him an indignant scowl. "For myself, I've never been more humiliated in my life. That a guest of mine should be treated so shabbily in my own home is beyond all bearing!"

Her righteous pose had him chuckling anew. "Then place the fault where it lies, Cat, with that bastard Sedgewood," he said, reaching out to tug a strand of black hair that had worked its way free from her chignon. "You can't hold yourself accountable for his repellent behavior."

"I couldn't believe it when I was told he'd arrived," Cat grumbled, obviously not yet ready to let go of her ire. "I was in the middle of my books, and—" She stopped talking and cast him a confused frown. "How did you know he was here? I thought you were helping Mr. Oswald drain his field."

"I was. Lydia came to get me. Something you should have done, instead of attempting to deal with four drunken men on your own," he added, his tone reproachful.

"Lydia!" Cat was instantly diverted. "Oh, the poor child, she and Beth must be frantic by now! And Eddie, too! What am I doing, standing out here and muttering to myself like an idiot? I must go to my children." She would have rushed past him had he not reached out to gently grab her by the arm.

"Lydia is fine, and so is Eddie," he assured her, gazing down into her worried eyes. "I left them with Mr. Oswald and the others; I'll ride back for them in a moment."

"But—"

"My God, Cat, do you never once think of yourself?" he interrupted, suddenly furious with her, and not knowing why.

She blinked up at him in confusion. "What do you mean?"

He gave her a small shake. "I mean, you've just been through an experience vile enough to give any lady the vapors! You should be in your rooms indulging in a fit of hysterics; instead you can think only of the children!"

"Of course I am thinking of the children!" she exclaimed, clearly more perplexed than ever. "I'm their mother!"

Her blind refusal to see the facts infuriated him as much as Sedgewood's insulting behavior. Without stopping to consider the consequences of his actions, he pulled her roughly into his arms.

"You're also a woman, Cat," he said, watching with grim satisfaction as her dark green eyes flared with awareness. "A beautiful, desirable woman. When will you admit that?" He swept her up against him, ducking his head to take her mouth in a kiss of unfettered passion.

Her lips were soft beneath his, and they tasted every bit as sweet as he remembered. It drove him wild, and he deepened the kiss, his tongue seeking hers with urgent hunger. In some distant part of his mind his conscience shouted an urgent warning, but he was too aroused to care. This was the moment he'd been longing for for the past five years, and he was damned if he'd stop now. He kept kissing her, slaking his thirst until the need to breathe had him reluctantly raising his head.

"Cat!" His voice was raw with pleasure as he lifted his mouth from hers long enough to draw a shaky breath. "You're every bit as sweet as I remember."

"Stephen . . ." Cat spoke his name with a soft sigh, her black lashes hiding her eyes from his. "This is wrong . . ."

His answer was to kiss her again, closing his mind to everything but the feel of her back in his arms after so many years. He wanted her with a ferocity bordering on madness, and his body hardened with the strength of his desire. Only the knowledge they were outside where anyone might see kept him from sweeping her up into his arms and making love to her as he longed to do. When he drew back the second time, he was trembling with painful frustration.

"Much more of this, my sweet, and I shall give you cause to think me no better than Sedgewood," he said ruefully, brushing his thumb across her trembling lips. "You enchant me, Cat, as always you have done."

His words brought a distressed flush to her cheeks, and she took a hasty step back. "I-I must go in," she stammered, clutching her shawl about her and hastily averting her eyes. "Beth will be upset, and I must see to her."

"And I must go fetch Lydia and Eddie," Stephen replied, accepting that for the moment, at least, their lovemaking was at an end. Not that he intended letting the matter drop, he told himself silently. He wasn't sure how he and Cat would overcome the many obstacles preventing them from becoming lovers, but overcome them, they would. He'd gone hungry far too long, and now that he'd had another tantalizing taste of her, he wasn't about to let another five years pass before sampling her again.

Somehow it would all work out. It had to. The alternative didn't bear consideration.

Idiot! Fool! Irresponsible hussy! Cat cursed herself roundly as she paced the narrow confines of her study. Stephen might have joked about her thinking him no better than Jeremey, but *she'd* just given him every reason to think her no better than the most wanton of strumpets. Her ardent response to his kisses was undeniable, and it appalled her she should have behaved with such a singular lack of good sense.

"You're a beautiful, desirable woman. Cat. You enchant me."

Stephen's husky voice echoed in her ear, and she shivered at the memory. She knew she ought to have slapped him, perhaps even engaged in the fit of vapors he seemed to think her due; but she had done neither, and it was no use pretending otherwise. She would simply have to retrench, and hope he would continue playing the role of gentleman. And if he didn't. . . . She bit her lip and blinked back tears, suddenly bereft at the thought of never seeing Stephen again. If he didn't, then she would have to do whatever was necessary to keep her family safe.

Hoping to distract herself from such troubling thoughts, she returned to her chair, determined to resume the work interrupted by Jeremey's arrival. She'd barely picked up her quill when the sound of raised voices caught her attention. What on earth? she wondered crossly, rising to her feet and starting toward the door. She was reaching for the handle when the door opened and one of the maids rushed in, bobbing a hasty curtsy.

"It's a young man, my lady, insisting he be allowed to speak with his lordship!" she said, blue eyes wide. "He is the earl's brother, he do say, and says he'll speak with the earl or know the reason why!"

"His lordship's brother!" Cat couldn't have been more amazed if the maid had announced the prince was calling upon them.

"He's in the hallway, madam, and won't budge for love nor money," the maid replied, striving for primness. "Shall I have Mr. Wentworth and the others show him out?"

Cat thought of the frail, elderly butler, who was doubtlessly still recovering from the morning's excitement. "I believe we've had enough of showing people out, Penelope," she said, giving the girl a reproachful look. "Take me to our caller. If he is his lordship's brother, I'm most anxious to bid him welcome."

The young man was still in the hallway, attired in elegant, if somewhat dust-stained, riding clothes, and Cat recognized him at once as being related to Stephen. He might be younger, but she had little difficulty seeing Stephen in his handsome features.

"Mr. Wrexley, how delightful to meet you," she said, smiling as she walked toward him with her hand held out in welcome. "Allow me to welcome you to Larks Hall."

"My lady." He accepted her hand with a bow that managed to be both courteous and impatient at the same time. "Pray forgive me for arriving without warning, but I am looking for my brother and was told I might find him here."

"His lordship has kindly gone to fetch my youngest daughter and son for me," Cat said, smiling at him. His hair might be a few shades lighter than Stephen's, and his eyes were a light, almost startling shade of green rather than jet black, but there was much in him that put her in mind of Stephen on the night they had first met. "He should be back momentarily. Meanwhile, will you not let me offer you a cup of tea? I am sure the ride from town must have been a thirsty one." She walked into the drawing room, leaving him no choice but to follow.

"I am thirsty," he admitted, a sheepish grin on his face as he settled on one of the wing chairs. "And I've ridden a dashed sight farther than from town to see that brother of mine."

"And how far did you ride, sir, if I may ask?" Cat took her customary chair to await the arrival of the tea. She hadn't bothered ringing for refreshments, trusting her well-trained staff to see to the matter without prompting.

"From Rockholme Manor," he said, stretching his long legs out in front of him. "I grew tired of waiting for Stephen to come back on his own, and decided I would ride up and fetch him home where he belongs."

"You have ridden up from Kent?" Cat was horrified.

"Not all in one day," Mr. Wrexley said, looking youthfully

pleased with himself. "Although I have made very good time, if I do say so myself. I'd have been here sooner, but I passed last night in some damned . . . er . . . dashed little town with the most uncomfortable inn in the whole of England, and I got something of a late start this morning."

"Then you must be anxious to have him home again," Cat said, forcing herself to smile even as she was swamped with despair. It seemed the problem of what to do with Stephen had already been solved, she thought, and wondered why she wasn't relieved.

"Anxious? I should say so!" the younger man exclaimed, looking decidedly aggrieved. "He's been in the country for more than a month, and he's not so much as sneezed in my direction! Summer harvest is coming on, and I've better things to do than fight off the matchmaking tabbies swarming around the place. Stephen's the bloody earl; let him be the one to deal with the wretched creatures!"

As if his words had conjured his brother up, Stephen suddenly burst into the room, with Eddie perched on his shoulders. "James!" he exclaimed, pausing only long enough to deposit Eddie in Cat's arms before rushing forward to envelope his brother in a hug of obvious affection.

The embrace was enthusiastically returned before Mr. Wrexley drew back, his eyes suspiciously bright. "Let's have a look at you," he said, his hands cupping Stephen's shoulders as he studied him. "Ugly as ever, I see. I was hoping the French might have done something to pretty you up a trifle."

"They tried, God knows," Stephen said, his laughter sounding so young and carefree Cat's eyes smarted with tears. Realizing the two men most likely needed a few moments of time to be private with one another, she rose to her feet.

"If you gentlemen will excuse me, I believe I shall go see what is taking the tea so long," she said smiling despite her unhappiness. "Mr. Wrexley, may I hope you will honor us with your company for dinner this evening?"

"I should be delighted, my lady," he said, slashing dimples winking in his cheeks as he offered her a courtly bow. "And you needn't put your cook to any trouble. Even a bowl of mutton broth will seem a feast to me after the slop I was forced to endure last night."

Cat was hard-pressed not to chuckle at this. "I am sure our cook can manage something a slight deal more challenging than mutton broth, sir," she said, thinking it obvious the younger man had inherited a great deal of Stephen's charm, along with his good looks. "Please make yourselves at home while I am gone," she added, reaching for Edward's hand. "Come Edward . . ."

"No!" To her surprise he eluded her, dancing out of reach and scowling with indignation. "I want to meet Stephen's brother! He is our cousin, too!"

Cat glared at him in mortification. "Edward Jonathan!" she exclaimed, blushing in distress. "Whatever will Mr. Wrexley think of such rag-mannered behavior!" She reached for him again, only to have him scramble away and dash over to where Stephen and his slack-jawed brother were standing.

"I am Edward," he announced, tilting his head back and staring up at his idol's brother. "And you are James."

James continued gaping down at Edward, and the expression on his face had the blood turning to ice in Cat's veins. It was the expression she had both feared and longed to see on Stephen's own, and yet never saw. Recognition.

"My God," she heard him whisper, his face white as he turned to Stephen. *"That's* why you've tarried here so long! That's why you wouldn't come home even though I begged. For God's sake, Stephen, why didn't you say so?"

"Say what?" Stephen demanded, scowling at his brother as if he feared he'd run mad. "And what do you mean, you begged me to come home? I've had a handful of letters from you since I've been back, and the only thing you mentioned amiss was that the neighbors were badgering you to death about me."

"Blast it, Stephen—" Mr. Wrexley began hotly, only to be interrupted by Cat, who used Edward's absorption with the conversation to catch him up in her arms.

"Edward, you will go to your room this moment and remain there until I tell you you may come out again, or you will not be allowed to dine with us tonight, do you hear me?" she said, determined to spare her son the awful scene she knew she herself could no longer avoid. "Now go."

"But, Mama—"

"I said go, Edward, now!" Desperation made her voice harsher than she intended, and hearing it, Edward burst into noisy tears before turning to flee the room, sobbing as if his heart would break. Stephen stared after him.

"Really, Cat, there was no reason for you to be so hard on the lad," he said, turning to her with a look of disapproval. "He was only excited about meeting my brother, that is all."

Cat tried to find her voice, but she could not. This was her worst nightmare made horrifying reality, and she could do no more than stare up at Stephen in helpless apology.

"You can't mean to deny it," James continued, glowering at his brother. "One has but to look at the lad to know the truth."

"Know what truth?" Stephen was gazing from Cat's frozen countenance to his brother's angry one. "What the devil is going on? If you don't explain yourself, and I mean at once, I am going to toss you into the nearest horse trough!"

James' indignant expression faded into astonishment. "Then you don't know, do you?" he said, slowly shaking his head. "You really don't know."

"I vow, James, you are making less sense than Uncle Clarence, and the poor man is as mad as they come!" Stephen growled, thrusting both his hands through his hair in frustration. "Just say what you mean, damn it, and be done with it."

James hesitated, shooting Cat an apologetic look, and suddenly she knew she couldn't stand by in silence while her life was ruined. If the time for the truth had come, then it was better that the truth come from her. She squared her shoulders, standing in front of James as she met Stephen's troubled gaze.

"He's talking about Edward," she said, raising her chin in quiet defiance. "He's trying to tell you that he is your son."

Seven

"What did you say?" Stephen stared at Cat in disbelief.

Cat was so pale, so still, she might have been carved from purest alabaster. Only her eyes showed any signs of life, sparkling with green fire as she held his gaze. "Edward is your son," she repeated, her soft voice lacking inflection. She might have been announcing tea or discussing the rotation of crops, for all the emotion she showed.

Stephen kept staring at her. He couldn't seem to think or feel. Images kept exploding in his head, like cannon fire in the heat of battle, and their impact staggered him: Cat, shy and sweet in his arms as he made her moan with desire. Cat, proud and defiant, denying ever having met him. And Cat, watching with fear and sadness as he and Edward played. He'd always wondered what she'd been so afraid of, he thought bitterly. Now he knew.

"Stephen?" He felt James' tentative touch on, his elbow. "Are you all right? Here, let me help you to a chair."

Stephen shook him off, his gaze never leaving Cat's face. The ice of shock was melting, and in its place was a rage so deep and so fierce, he shuddered beneath its force. The emotions clawing at him were monstrous, and he feared what he might do if they were to slip free. He had to get out, he thought, sweating as he fought to master himself. He had to leave before he lost any right to call himself a gentleman.

Without saying a word he whirled on his heels and stalked out, ignoring his brother's urgent demand that he return. He walked blindly past the footman holding the door for him, his mind occupied only with flight. His horse had already been taken to the stables by Cat's ever-efficient staff, and although he knew they would have brought him another mount, Stephen was of no mind to wait. He began to walk, and then he began to run, run as if an entire platoon of French dragoons was at his heels. There was no thought in his mind, no emotion in his heart, because he knew if he allowed himself to experience either, he would go mad.

He stumbled several times but never fell, not even when overgrown brambles snatched at his clothes and vicious thorns dug deep into his flesh. He kept running and running, the pounding of his heart and feet muffling the voices screaming in his head. But he couldn't continue his wild flight forever, and at last his lungs and his legs gave out; and he fell to the ground, gasping desperately for air.

"Damn! Damn! Damn!" he raged, pounding the soft ground with his fists. "The bitch! The damned bitch to keep my son from me! I'll ruin her for this! I'll ruin her!"

He would go to London, he thought furiously, rolling onto his back to stare up at a cloudless sky. He would track Sedgewood down and offer him his most profuse apologies. He would tell him that Cat was everything he thought she was, and worse. She was a liar, a thief, a whore, a woman who would deceive her husband and her lover with cold calculation. And to think he was beginning to admire her, he thought, all but choking with bitterness. To like her, to care for her, to—he ruthlessly cut the thought off, refusing to even think the words.

That's what hurt most of all, he decided, facing the truth with cold fury. Despite his initial vow of retribution, he'd forgiven her, magnanimously, in his mind, willing to overlook her deception out of gratitude for the help she'd given when he'd taken so ill. And all the while he was admiring her, she was playing him for a fool, acting the pure and noble widow even as she kept the knowledge of his son from him.

Eddie. An image of the black-haired imp, his dark eyes bright as he asked his endless questions, brought a lump to Stephen's throat. He loved the boy, he realized, moisture stinging his eyes. He was a son any father would be proud of, a son a man could trust to carry his name into the next generation. And he was a son he could never acknowledge without destroying him.

That thought plagued Stephen as he rose to his feet. Much as he longed to expose Cat for the harlot she was, he knew he could not do so without hurting his son as well. As heir to the Brockton name and title, Eddie's position in the world was assured, but as a bastard, even the bastard of an earl, he would have nothing, would be nothing. It was a sobering thought.

After resting several minutes, Stephen glanced around him to get his bearings. His years in the military made it easy for him to discern his location, and realizing he was halfway between Larks Hall and Keswick, he decided to head back for the inn. Given the precarious state of his temper, he judged it best he not face Cat just yet. Later, when he had himself under control, he would decide what to do.

It took him the better part of an hour to reach the village, and by that time his bad leg was giving him hell. If the innkeeper was appalled at his dishevelled condition, he was too discreet to say so, and after ordering hot water for a bath to be sent up to his rooms, Stephen went limping up the stairs. He was annoyed but not surprised to find James waiting for him.

"Stephen! What's happened to you? And where the devil have you been? I was about to mount a rescue party!" James hurried to his side, his face showing both annoyance and concern.

Stephen tugged off his cravat and dropped it onto the floor without answering. His jacket and waistcoat followed suit, and still he remained silent, listening to his younger brother's ravings half attentively.

"Well, here's a fine pickle and make no doubt," James muttered, pacing up and down the room. "Our own cousin's widow! Gad, Stephen, what were you thinking? Or should I say, what were you thinking with? As if I need to ask." He tossed Stephen a reproving glare over his shoulder.

Stephen merely shrugged, and began the arduous task of pulling off his tightly fitting boots. Under ordinary circumstances he would have found the prospect of having a peal rung over his head by his youngest brother both amusing and presumptuous; now it hardly mattered. With the boots off at last, he tugged his shirt over his head and turned to face James.

"Unless you want to wash my back, you'd best leave," he said, flicking his braces off. "I'll meet you in the taproom in an hour. Oh, and if you see George, send him up, will you? I'll want to shave again before going back to Larks Hall."

"You're going back to Larks Hall?" James demanded incredulously. "Why? I should think that is the last place on earth you would wish to go. *She* is there!"

"So is my son," Stephen answered, then took a moment to savor the words. His son. Dear God, he had no idea anything could sound so sweet.

"I wish Jason were here," James said, running a hand through his tousled hair. "He'd know what to do."

For the first time since hearing Cat's stunning declaration, Stephen felt his black mood lifting. "I'm sure he would," he said, smiling at the thought of his steadfast younger brother. "But this has nothing to do with him. Or with you, for that matter," he added, flicking James a mild glance.

"Nothing to do with me?" James appeared properly shocked. "The lad is my nephew! It has everything to do with me!"

Stephen whirled around. "And he's my son," he said, his voice edged with fury. "Stay out of it, James, I am warning you."

James looked as if he meant to argue the matter, but when Stephen took a threatening step forward, he held up his hands in surrender. "Very well, if that's how you wish it," he said, inclining his head coolly. "Just remember you are our father's son, and you have an obligation to our family and to our name. You're the earl, and 'tis past time you remembered that fact. Now, if you'll pardon me, I believe I shall go fetch your valet. Let him scrub your damned back for you."

Cat stood beside the circle of standing stones, her cloak wrapped warmly about her. She'd discovered the circle not long after coming to Larks Hall as governess, and something in the ancient stones called to something deep inside of her. It was to here she came whenever she was troubled, seeking peace in the place many of the locals insisted was haunted by the spirit of a Druid priestess. Usually she dismissed the lurid tales as superstitious nonsense, but today, with a cool rain falling and the wind howling about the massive slabs of gray granite, she found it easy to believe in such things as spirits.

And why should she not? Hadn't she spent the past five years being haunted by Stephen and thoughts of what he could do to her carefully constructed world with a few well-placed words? Perhaps that was why she'd never been afraid of the nether world, she mused, a wry smile touching her mouth. The real world held terrors enough to make even the most hideous of specters seem pale in comparison.

God in heaven, what was she going to do? The smile faded from Cat's lips. She'd seen the look on Stephen's face when she'd told him the truth of Eddie's parentage. He'd been stunned at first, and then so hotly furious she'd taken an automatic step back in fear. But in between those two emotions she'd caught a glimpse of something else, a hurt so wild and deep it had shocked her almost as much as the vicious temper that followed.

Some men might have greeted the unexpected news of fatherhood with indifference or indignation, but not Stephen. However furious he might be with her, she knew there was no way in heaven or in hell he would walk away from his son. And that, she realized, reaching up to brush back a tendril of hair from her rain-dampened cheek, was precisely her problem. She turned to go, freezing when she saw him standing beside her tethered horse.

"We need to talk." His voice was as emotionless as his expression, and just as chilling.

Fear threatened, but Cat ruthlessly brushed it aside. She had a family to protect, and she couldn't afford the luxury of weakness. "What is there to say?" she asked, taking care to keep her tone even. She sensed a core of violence kept tightly under control, and she didn't wish to say anything to precipitate an explosion.

"You had my son," he reminded her, advancing toward her. "I'd say there is a great deal left to discuss."

She stood her ground, refusing to give so much as an inch. "What is it you want to know?"

He studied her for several seconds before speaking. "How can I be certain Eddie is mine, and not some other man's?"

The hateful accusation hurt, although she'd been more or less expecting it. It was a reasonable question, she told herself, and one he was entitled to ask. "You're the only man I ever lay with besides my husband," she told him with as much dignity as she could muster. "And he was incapable of fathering a child."

"How do you know that?"

Again, the question was more than reasonable, but that didn't make her hate him any less for asking it. "Edward was ill, dying in fact, when we were married. We hadn't been together as man and wife for many months before I met you."

"And afterward?" His voice was raw, his eyes burning in his face as he studied her.

"Afterwards he was even more ill. He lived but a few months after Eddie was born."

There was a long, painful silence, and she could see Stephen struggling to find the right way to phrase his next question. "Did he ever suspect the babe was not his?" he asked, the words sounding as if they were being ripped from him.

This was the question she'd most been dreading. The coward in her wanted to remain silent, to let him go on thinking her the type of woman who would deceive her husband with a child that was not his own. It would sting her pride to be sure, but it was a sting she would have willingly endured for her children's sake.

"Cat?" He was regarding her intently. "Did he ever know?"

There was no way to avoid the inevitable, short of lying, and Cat had had enough of lies and half-truths. she turned her back on him, gazing at the silent stones with quiet desperation.

"Edward admired you, you know," she began, her heart pounding in her chest. "He spoke of you often, and when you went into the army, he was sick with worry."

She could feel his quizzical gaze upon her. "I admired him as well," he admitted in a gruff voice. "That's why I was so furious when I learned who you were. I esteemed Edward, and it made me sick to know I'd cuckolded him."

She winced at the blunt words. "I understand that, and it does you credit to feel that way. But if it is any consolation, Edward never blamed you."

"You *told* him about us?" The notion seemed to horrify him.

She closed her eyes, bowing her head in brief prayer. If sleeping with him had required every ounce of courage she possessed, it was nothing compared with what she was now about to do. She gave herself a moment to prepare herself and then began speaking, keeping her back to him the entire time. Only when she was finished did she work up the courage to turn and look at him, and when she did, what she saw staggered her.

Stephen was standing as still and cold as one of the stones, his hands balled in fists at his sides, and his jaw clenched so tightly she wondered it didn't shatter. She thought she'd seen him as angry as it was possible for one man to be, but now she knew she'd seen but a fraction of the fury he was capable of feeling.

"Stephen?" She took a hesitant step toward him.

"A stud," he said, forcing the words through clenched teeth. "You and my cousin used me as a goddamned stud."

Her stomach jolted in fear. "It wasn't like that! I told you, Edward was desperate—"

"I understand that," he interrupted, dismissing her protests with an impatient wave of his hand. "He needed a son to inherit, and so he sent you to my bed to get one."

Even though she'd braced herself for his enmity, Cat couldn't help but resent the scorn in his voice. "You needn't make it sound so cold-blooded," she muttered, trying not to squirm.

"Why? Wasn't that just what it was?" he challenged, his lips twisting in derision. "Although you must allow me to compliment you on your acting abilities, my lady. You had me believing you were as sweetly innocent as you were passionate. Tell me," he added with a bitter laugh, "did you feel anything at all when I was inside you, or was it all just a performance? A means to an end? Was getting your precious babe worth having me pounding into you again and again?"

Something inside of Cat cracked. "Don't . . ."

"Don't? Don't what?" He moved with the suddenness of a snake striking, reaching out to grab her roughly by the shoulders. "Don't speak of it? Don't remember it? Don't make more of it than was intended? What is it you don't want me to do, Cat?"

Tears burned her eyes as she gazed up into his angry face. "Don't regret it," she said, reduced to begging and hating him for it. "Don't regret what we shared . . ."

He started to say something, then stopped, thrusting her away from him as if he couldn't bear the feel of her beneath his hands. "What we shared, madam, was what any animal in rut would have shared," he said, biting out each word with icy revulsion. "You gave my body release, and I gave you the child your loving husband ordered you to conceive."

Loyalty to her late husband had her fighting back her own pain. "Don't speak of Edward like that!" she cried, her eyes flashing with pride. "He was only thinking of the children! He would have done anything to keep the girls from falling into Jeremey's hands!"

Stephen's expression grew mocking. "Something he proved most admirably, as did you, Lady Brockton," he said, inclining his head toward her with insulting politeness. "Did you ever tell him how his son was conceived? Did you tell him how many times I took you that night? How you screamed when I touched you, and how intimately you touched me? Did you tell him that, sweet Cat, or did you let him think you lay there liked some damned virgin, enduring my loathsome touch for the sake of Larks Hall?"

Because it was so close to the truth Cat reacted without thought, lashing out to strike him across the face. His head snapped back from the blow, but other than the temper flaring in his narrowed eyes, he remained unmoved. Time hung suspended in the air as they stood looking at one another, and then he raised the back of his hand to dab at the blood blooming on the side of his mouth where her blow had landed.

"I believe I've had my answer," he drawled, watching her involuntary flinch with grim satisfaction. "That will suffice . . .

for now." He turned and walked back to where he had left his stallion tethered to another tree.

He mounted and sat looking down at her, haughty as a feudal lord eyeing a village maid, she thought, returning his regard with mounting resentment.

"This isn't over," he told her coldly. "You used me. When I come back tomorrow, I'll let you know what that will cost you. And it will cost you, Lady Brockton, that I can promise you." Without another word he whirled his mount around and rode off, leaving Cat alone with the stones and the howling of the wind.

Eddie and the girls were waiting for Cat when she returned from her ride. One look at her drawn face had them swarming around her in concern.

"Mama, are you sick?" Eddie, his finger in his mouth, gaped up at her, his tiny eyebrows meeting over his nose in a scowl that was a perfect replica of his father's intimidating glare.

Lydia dashed up next, worry darkening her eyes. "Did you get lost?" she demanded. "You were gone ever such a long time."

Despite the weariness tugging at her, Cat managed a weak smile. "Since when have you known me to get lost, Little One?" she asked, using her special name for the girl. "I rode out to see the stones, and the ride was farther than I realized. And I'm not sick, Edward," she added with a reassuring smile for her son. "I'm only a little weary, that is all.

"You are wet, Mama." Beth, more sedate but no less concerned, moved forward to lay a gentle hand on Cat's arm. "Come inside and change out of those damp clothes before you catch a chill."

Touched, Cat let them bully her inside and up to her room. While her maid clucked around her, helping her into a warm bath and scolding her for not having a better care of herself, Cat tried to plan what she should next do. So much depended on Stephen and what he would do, but Cat was determined to steel herself against any eventuality. As always Eddie and the girls figured most prominently in those plans, and she tried to think of them and the best way to keep them safe.

"There you go, my lady," said Agnes, her maid, nodding in satisfaction as she helped Cat from the steaming copper tub and into a waiting robe. "Now into bed with you, and mind you stay there 'til morning."

"But the children . . ." Years of duty had Cat protesting even as she was crawling gratefully between the warmed sheets. "Eddie needs to be fed his dinner, and I have to talk to the girls about what happened this morning. They are bound to be upset."

"Nurse can see to the wee lord, and Miss Blakely has already spoken with Miss Elizabeth and Miss Lydia. She told them how his lordship ran off that snake of a Mr. Sedgewood, and they're right as can be. They'll be fine, don't you be worrying. 'Tis you who needs cossetting now."

Cat could think of no rejoinder, and mutely let Agnes tuck her in. After the maid had gone, closing the door firmly behind her, Cat rolled over onto her back to stare up at the ceiling with troubled eyes. In her anguish over Stephen she'd completely forgotten about Jeremey and his equally loathsome friends, an oversight that would have astounded her had she been in any condition to consider the matter.

What would she do if Stephen told Jeremey the truth? That was the heart of her dilemma. Until now Jeremey's rantings, while decidedly unpleasant and embarrassing, had been generally dismissed by the courts and anyone who knew her. An upstart governess she might be, but she was still a lady of good birth with an unblemished reputation. The vicar and several of the local squires had stood in testament of her good character. That and Jeremey's own tarnished name kept his charges from being taken seriously. But it would all change in the wink of an eye if Stephen added his voice to Jeremey's.

She knew she could deny it, and perhaps even succeed, but the damage to Eddie and the girls would be done. They would live their lives with whispers and snickers following them, and it was unlikely they would ever escape the long shadow cast by scandal. Unless she could think of some way of appeasing

Stephen, some way of convincing him to hold his tongue for the children's sake, they were as good as ruined.

Money? She considered and rejected that notion with the same breath. Stephen had ten times the modest income Edward had left, and as an earl, he commanded far more power than she could ever hope to muster. She even thought briefly of offering herself in exchange for his silence, but she doubted that would prove an acceptable coin for him. Even if her pride could stomach such an arrangement, Stephen had made it plain he despised her for her duplicity. He'd like as not prefer cutting off his own hands over ever touching her again. Still there had to be something she could do, and she passed a nearly sleepless night trying to come up with a viable alternative.

She was no closer to succeeding when she awoke the following morning. Her head hurt from lack of sleep, but she bathed and dressed in her finest gown nonetheless. If she was going to the gallows, she decided with a flash of black humor, she was going dressed in a manner befitting the viscountess of Brockton. When she walked downstairs she found the note from Stephen waiting or her. It was brief and to the point.

Meet me at the stones at one of the clock, sharp.

So it was already starting, she thought, tapping the note against the palm of her hand and frowning. His lordship wasn't wasting any time before pressing his advantage. Did he really think he had only to snap his fingers to bring her to heel like a well-trained dog? The notion was almost as great an affront to her pride as was the realization he would be right. For the moment, at least, the power was all Stephen's.

After forcing herself to eat a hearty breakfast, Cat spent the rest of the morning at her books. Because of her prudent management, the estate was in even better shape than it had been when Edward had been alive, and the knowledge pleased her. Even if the worst happened and Jeremey tossed them out of the Hall, she'd managed to set enough aside to keep them comfortably for several months to come. The thought gave her a small measure of confidence, and she was feeling almost optimistic when the time came to go up and change into her riding habit.

"You can't mean to be riding out again, my lady! Not in

that?" Agnes protested, casting a disapproving glance out the window where a steady, gray rain was falling. "You're set to catch your death, it would seem!"

"I won't be gone long, Agnes," Cat soothed, studying her reflection with a critical eye. "There's no need to fret."

"Well, at least take a groom with you," Agnes grumbled, kneeling to straighten the habit's flowing skirts. "There's talk in the village gypsies have been seen in the woods, and I'll not have you traipsing about without proper escort."

"I'll stay out of the woods," Cat promised, blanching in horror at what a servant might overhear. "And as I said, I shan't be gone long. I should be back in time to hear the girl's French lessons, in fact."

"But, my lady—"

Cat had had enough of people telling her what to do. She bid Agnes a hasty good day before snatching her hat off the dressing table and hurrying out the door. Another battle ensued at the stables when the head groom showed a marked reluctance to saddle her mount for her, but by employing a judicious mixture of firmness and cajolery, she managed to convince him to do as she wished. Still, the small battle had delayed her several minutes, and it was a little after one before she reached the circle of stones. Stephen was already there, and if the look on his face was any indication, he was far from pleased.

"You're late," he accused in a stiff voice, moving forward to help her dismount.

If he was looking for an apology, Cat was hanged if she would give it to him. "A few minutes only, sir," she replied, grudgingly accepting his assistance. "The rain delayed me."

He said nothing, his hands hard as they closed around her narrow waist and lifted her out of the saddle. Her own hands fluttered to his shoulders for balance, and the movement brought her flush against his chest. For a brief moment their eyes met and held, and against her will her heart began to race with emotion. She could feel the warmth of his breath on her cheek, and smell the spicy tang of his cologne. The tactile sensations made the breath catch in her throat, and she glanced hastily away, horrified she should be so physically aware of him. His touch lingered for a brief moment as if he was equally aware of her, and then his hands dropped and he took a hasty step back.

"Let's walk for a bit," he said, turning away. "This damp weather is making my leg play up."

She moved to his side, noting he was walking with a pronounced limp. "Were you wounded in battle, sir?" she asked, motivated as much by curiosity as she was by the need to delay the inevitable confrontation for as long as possible.

"Aye, and more than once," he said, his voice taking on a far away note. "I took a bullet in the first hours of Waterloo, and then had to fight on the rest of the day bleeding like a stuck pig. I was lucky not to have lost the damned thing, and luckier still to have survived at all. Thousands did not."

Despite her anger, Cat couldn't help but feel a twinge of pity at the thought of the pain he must have endured. Was it the pain of his injuries and the hell of battle that had hardened him? she wondered. Or had he always been thus, hiding his core of strength behind a rake's careless facade? She sensed somehow this was the case.

The years of warfare might have honed the steel inside of him to a razor's edge, but it had always been there, sharp as death, and waiting to be unsheathed. That she hadn't understood as much was her failure, and she only hoped the cost of that failure wasn't more than she could afford to pay. They walked in silence for several minutes, until they were standing beside the tallest of the stones. He drew her to a halt, then turned to face her.

"This is far enough," he said, his cold gaze meeting hers.

The icy resolve she saw in the ebony depths of his eyes made her stomach sink. "You've decided what you want, haven't you?" she asked, clasping her hands together to hide their trembling.

"I have."

She almost flinched at his unyielding tones. "What is it?"

A cold smile touched his lips. "Soon," he told her. "But first I want you to know that I understand what you and Edward did. I don't approve, mind," he added when she opened her lips to stutter her thanks, "but I understand. To keep Sedgewood from gaining control over those innocent children, I would condone anything short of murder. No, allow me to rephrase. Having reacquainted myself with my dear cousin, I would condone even murder. He is a bastard of the first water, and I can see why Edward was desperate to keep the girls out of his hands."

Cat could scarce believe her ears. She'd been prepared to fight, to plead, to beg in order to gain his silence; now it appeared he was willing to give it to her for gratis. Or was he?

"Then you agree not to tell anyone about Eddie? That he is your son?" she asked, not yet ready to believe she was safely out of danger.

He gave another of those cold smiles. "I agree that making your family pay for your sin is hardly fair," he answered. "And make no mistake, it is they who would pay most grievously for your deception. Therefore I will keep my silence . . . for a price."

Here it is, Cat thought, drawing herself up to meet her fate. "And what price might that be?" she asked with as much coolness as she could muster.

"I have given this a great deal of thought," he said with deadly calm, "and I've decided there's only one way you can repay me for what you have stolen from me. A son. A son to replace the one I love but can never claim. A son to inherit my title when I am dead. Give me that son, Lady Brockton, and I shall let you go."

Eight

Stephen watched Cat grimly, allowing himself a small flash of satisfaction at the stunned expression on her face. So he'd finally succeeded in shocking her, had he? Good. Considering the times she'd rocked him back on his heels, it was only fitting. Taking the revenge he considered his due would be sweet indeed, and he vowed to savor every honeyed moment of it.

When the idea of demanding a son from Cat first occurred to him, he'd rejected it out of hand. He hated her, he'd thought bitterly, and the last thing he wanted was to further entangle himself with her in any way. And yet the thought kept returning, plaguing him in the night like a wound that would not heal. A son for a son. It was the only equitable reparation there could be, the only compensation his pride would allow. Once he'd decided that, he was prepared to do whatever it would take to get what he wanted. What he was *owed*.

"Cat?" He frowned when he realized she still hadn't spoken. "Did you hear me?"

"I heard." Her voice was flat, lacking its usual vibrancy.

His frown deepened, and against his will, he felt a small stab of concern. He'd never thought Cat the type to engage in a fit of the vapors, and wondered what the hell he would do if she swooned. It wasn't a pleasant prospect.

"And?" he prodded, as she remained silent, staring at him with blank-eyed astonishment.

A small shudder shook her slender frame. "You want me to become your mistress?"

He almost smiled at the hopeful note he detected in her voice.

"Nothing so simple as that, Lady Brockton," he drawled. "Sorry to disappoint you. A mistress could never give me what I want: a legitimate heir to inherit my title. Only a wife can do that, and so I'm afraid it must be marriage between us."

She paled so dramatically he feared she really would swoon, and took an involuntary step forward. She took an immediate step back, holding up a hand as if to ward him off. "You can't be serious," she said, her green eyes wide with horror. "You can not possibly wish to marry me!"

He gave a harsh laugh, only too happy to dissuade her of the notion he might be harboring even an echo of the tender feelings he'd once borne her. "Indeed I do not, madam. I'd as lief marry Bonaparte himself, but that is of no moment. You have stolen my son from me, and I demand that you give me another. That is the price of my silence. Will you meet it, or will you not?"

For a moment he feared he may have pushed her too far. Cat looked ready to bolt, panic and terror evident on her face, but after a brief hesitation she seemed to regain control of herself.

"The children," she said slowly, her gaze meeting his with a touching bravado. "What of the children?"

It was shame he felt now, an emotion he ruthlessly ignored. "My *son* will of course stay with us," he said, stressing the word with cool pride. "And because they will become my personal responsibility once we've wed, the girls may come as well. I've grown rather fond of them these past weeks, and should hate to be parted from them."

Her shoulders drooped, and her eyes closed. "Thank you, sir," she murmured, opening her eyes to offer him a hesitant smile. "That is very good of you."

Her gratitude filled him with inexplicable anger. "You mistake me, Cat," he said, annoyed she should construe his actions as weakness. "If I bring Elizabeth and Lydia to Rockholme Manor, it's only because I wish it so. If I wanted it otherwise, arrangements would be made. Do you understand?"

The smile died on her lips, and the blank look was back in her eyes. "Indeed, my lord," she said, turning away from him. "I understand you perfectly."

Something inside of him snapped at her coolness, and he

reached out to grab her by the arm. "Don't make me the villain of this!" he growled, pulling her against him. "From the start you've played me for a fool, so don't act the injured innocent because you were found out and the time has come to pay the piper! I've asked you a question, damn it, and now I'm demanding you give me an answer! Will you marry me, or will you not?"

She opened her lips, but before she could answer a sudden noise had Stephen whirling around, the pistol he carried as a matter of course in his hand. Without thinking he thrust Cat in back of him, shielding her with his body as he scanned the woods for any sign of a horse and rider.

"What is it?" Cat asked, obviously alarmed by his behavior.

He kept scanning the woods, senses trained by years of bloody combat telling him the enemy was still close at hand. "I heard something," he said, his eyes narrowing as he thought he detected a faint movement in the stand of trees to the right.

"It's probably a gypsy," Cat said, trying to peek around him. "Agnes told me they were camped in the woods. They're harmless."

It wasn't a gypsy he'd heard, of that Stephen was certain. The sound that had caught his attention was the rattle of a bridle that was quickly muffled, as if the rider was seeking to avoid notice. If it had been a gypsy and he hadn't wanted them to know he was there, he would never have put a bridle on his horse. Still . . . keeping his weapon trained on the stand of trees, he called out a warning in Rom.

"What was that you said?" Cat asked curiously.

"I told him to show himself or I would fire," Stephen answered curtly. "Wellington often used gypsies to gain information while we were on the Peninsula, and I learned to speak their tongue. If our visitor is Rom, he knows he has precisely five seconds to come out before I start shooting."

To his amazement, Cat grabbed his arm. "No, wait!" she exclaimed. "You can't just shoot when you have no idea who or what you might be shooting at! What if it's one of the girls? Lydia has followed me before."

That did give Stephen pause. He was trying to decide what

next to do when there was a loud rustle of leaves, and a small doe darted out into the clearing and then away. Cat watched it disappear before sending him a satisfied look.

"You see? Nothing more deadly than a defenseless deer, who was doubtlessly more frightened of us than we were of her."

Stephen shrugged, reluctantly returning the pistol to his pocket. He would give a great deal to know what had spooked the deer into bolting, but it would have to wait. At the moment he had more immediate concerns. He took Cat back into his arms, his touch gentle this time as he gazed down at her.

"Never mind that now," he said, studying her solemnly. "What is your decision, Cat? Will you marry me?"

She bit her lip. "Must it truly be marriage?"

He nodded, giving the only answer he could. "Yes, it must."

She hesitated; then when she spoke, her voice was so soft he had to strain to hear. "Very well, Lord Rockholme," she said, her gaze meeting his with quiet courage. "I will marry you."

He expected to feel triumph, or at least a smug sense of satisfaction; instead he felt oddly disappointed. The sensation annoyed him, and he dismissed it with an impatient shrug. Having achieved his objective, he moved next to solidify his position.

"We'll leave tomorrow morning for Kent," he said, thinking quickly. "The earls of Rockholme have always been married in our family's chapel, and that's what we shall do. I've sent James to London to secure a Special License. With luck, we can be married within a fortnight."

He saw her swallow, but to her credit she merely nodded. "I will see to the packing, then," she said. "There is also the problem of Larks Hall and Eddie's succession to his—to Edward's title. Mr. Sedgewood may attempt to make difficulties."

Stephen noted the way she stumbled over the matter of Eddie's paternity, but decided to let it go for the moment. "Mr. Sedgewood is free to try and make all the difficulties he pleases, so long as he understands I will kill him if he so much as opens his mouth," he said, glad to have a target for the restless rage brewing inside him. "Leave him to me."

"Gladly," she agreed, smiling. "But who will tell the children of our marriage? They'll want to know."

He thought about that for a moment. "We shall tell them together," he decided. "It will be better coming from us both."

"As you wish," she agreed, then bit her lip again, her gaze sliding away from his.

He sighed and reached out to gently cup her chin. "What is it, Cat?" he asked, tilting her head up so that he could gaze into her troubled eyes.

"I-I was wondering if I might ask something of you," she began, a hint of blush stealing beneath the soft cream of her cheeks. "I know you feel I have no right to make demands; but as you say, the children are the innocents in all of this, and I don't want them made to be unhappy about our marriage. I want them to think this is a love match."

Stephen wasn't sure what he had expected, but it certainly wasn't this. "You want me to pretend to be in love with you?" he demanded, stunned by her request.

"For the girls' sake," she clarified, her cheeks now bright with color. "They, Elizabeth most especially, are at that age when they see everything in terms of great romance. I don't want them disillusioned by the truth."

He remained silent as he mulled the matter over in his mind. What she was asking of him was shocking, but upon reflection, it wasn't so unreasonable. And in many ways it was precisely the sort of thing he'd come to expect from her. He'd known from the start Cat adored her family, and that she would do whatever she thought best to keep them safe. Hadn't he depended on that unswerving sense of devotion to make her do as he wished?

"I suppose I might be willing to act the ardent suitor," he agreed at last. "For the girls' sake."

The light stole back into Cat's eyes. "Thank you, sir," she said softly. "That means more to me than I can say."

Stephen stared down at her, amazed by the sudden surge of desire heating his blood. Scarce an hour ago he'd been coldly determined to bend her to his will by whatever means necessary; now he found himself aching to make love to her. The dichotomy of emotions confused him, making him question precisely who was in command and who was not. He mentally shook his head, reaching for her and control with the same gesture.

"If we are to convince them ours is a love match, sweeting, perhaps we ought to practice our performance," he drawled, lifting her against him. "Kiss me, Cat. Kiss me like I am the husband you have longed for." He took her mouth in a kiss comprised of passion and frustration.

Her lips were sweet and soft beneath his own, and he devoured them with mounting hunger. Holding her like this, feeling her flesh against his, he could forget her deception, forget his anger and her reluctant sense of duty. There were only the two of them, and a kiss that threatened to flame wildly out of control. When he felt his body hardening with desire he thrust her away from him, knowing if they didn't stop he would likely toss her on the ground and make love to her until they were both too exhausted to move. Savage disappointment clawed at him, and like any wounded animal, he lashed out.

"Once again, madam, you must let me commend you for your acting abilities," he said, clenching his hands into fists to keep from reaching for her. "Almost you convince me ours is indeed a love match. Now come, 'tis time we were returning to Larks Hall to inform our children of our impending marriage."

"Mama! Oh, Mama! You are to be married!" Elizabeth was so delighted by Cat and Stephen's news that she quite forgot her pose as a dignified young lady, and threw herself into Cat's arms. "Oh, I am so happy for you!"

"And I'm happy as well, dearest one," Cat replied, fighting tears as she returned the girl's exuberant hug. "I was afraid you might disapprove."

"Disapprove?" Beth drew back to give Cat a horrified look. "Oh, no, Mama, I should never do that! I adore Lord Rockholme!"

"If you adore me, then you must call me Father," Stephen said, the smile on his face so sincere even Cat believed him.

"In fact, I would deem it a very great honor if you were to do so."

Beth looked startled, and then pleased. "Father," she said, tilting her head as if tasting the word. "Yes, I believe I shall call you Father. We'll all call you Father, won't we, Lydia?" She turned to her younger sister for confirmation.

Cat's heart clenched as she looked at her youngest daughter. While Elizabeth had greeted their news with tears and squeals of delight, Lydia had been less exuberant. Indeed, she'd seemed almost solemn, her brown eyes pensive as she glanced from Stephen to her and then back again. Had she somehow guessed things were not as they should be? Cat prayed not. She'd already sacrificed her dreams of happiness; she didn't want to sacrifice her daughter's dreams as well.

"No, I don't believe I shall call him Father," Lydia said at last, her tone decisive. "Father is far too stuffy. *I* shall call him Papa." And she favored him with a wide grin.

"Papa!" Eddie agreed, racing toward Stephen and tossing his chubby arms about his legs. "Papa! Papa! Papa!" He smiled up at Stephen sweetly. "Papa? May I have my own pony, please?"

The two girls crowed with laughter at such shameless wheedling, but Cat was caught by the expression of undisguised love and longing on Stephen's face as he knelt to his son. "When we get to Rockholme, lad, I shall buy you the finest pony in the whole of Kent," he said, his hand visibly trembling as he brushed back a lock of black hair from Eddie's forehead. "What do you think of that?"

Eddie gazed up at Stephen skeptically. "A *boy* pony?"

Stephen's lips brushed Eddie's hair. "A boy pony," he promised, and Cat wondered if she was the only one to hear the raw emotion in his husky voice.

After the children dashed off to share their news with Miss Blakely, it was time to go down to the kitchens to talk with the staff. This was something Cat assumed she would do alone, but Stephen surprised her by insisting he accompany her.

"You are my fiancée now, ma'am," he informed her, his manner lacking the warmth he'd shown the children. "The sooner everyone understands what that means, the better."

Deciding the outcome wasn't worth the battle, Cat acquiesced, taking the arm he offered as they went down to the kitchens where the staff was enjoying their midday meal. When the butler saw them standing at the door he started to rise, a look of alarm on his face, but Stephen surprised her once again by waving the older man back into his chair.

"As you were, Mr. Wentworth," he said with the easy charm she remembered from their first meeting. "Lady Brockton and I apologize for interrupting your meal, but we have some news we'd like to share with you all. Her ladyship has done me the very great honor of accepting my offer of marriage, and we'll be leaving tomorrow for my home in Kent where we shall be wed."

There was a stunned silence, and then a spatter of polite applause broke out. Mr. Wentworth and Mrs. Livingstone, the housekeeper who had been with the family since before Edward's death, stood to offer a hasty toast to the engaged couple. After accepting their congratulations, Stephen led her back upstairs to her study.

"I need to go back to the inn," he told her briskly. "But I'll be coming back for dinner. Have your butler and housekeeper waiting so that I might speak with them. The rest of the staff will doubtlessly be worried about their situations, and I want them to know they'll be provided for."

Such high-handed behavior scraped Cat's pride on the raw, and she stiffened with resentment. "There's no need for you o trouble yourself, sir," she said, struggling to keep her temper in check. "I'd already planned to do just that. They are my staff, after all." It vexed her beyond all bearing that she felt compelled to remind him of that fact.

He paused in the act of pulling on his riding gloves. "Cat, do you recall I said the sooner everyone understands you'll be my countess, the better?" he asked, giving her a measuring look.

"Yes?"

"That everyone includes you. You're to be my wife, and the first thing you must understand is that I mean to be master in my own home. You're my responsibility now, and I think I've proven to you how I feel about responsibilities. Good day, Cat. I'll see you later tonight."

The rest of the afternoon was taken up with the monumental task of packing up an entire household and dealing with three excited children. Beth seemed intent on taking every item in her wardrobe, while Lydia seemed equally determined to bring every horse, cat, dog, and even a pet chicken with them to Kent. After spending several minutes arguing with her daughter, Cat told her to discuss the matter with Stephen. The arrogant beast had claimed responsibility for them all, she thought, without the smallest twinge of regret. Perhaps it was time he understood precisely what that responsibility would entail.

Miss Blakely also helped out, penning letters to Cat's neighbors and cheerfully performing the myriad tasks that kept cropping up. When Cat tried to thank her, the younger woman gave her a sweet smile.

"It's no trouble at all, my lady," she assured Cat with a light laugh. "I am more than delighted to be of assistance, and please accept my best wishes on your coming marriage. Although I must say I'm not the slightest bit surprised."

Cat glanced up from the ledgers she'd been carefully packing away. "You're not?"

"Oh, no, my lady," Miss Blakely assured her earnestly. "It was obvious his lordship bore you the most tender of feelings, and then yesterday when he drove that dreadful Mr. Sedgewood away, I was certain it was because he was madly in love with you. If-if you do not mind my saying so," she added, her tone growing diffident at the way Cat was staring at her.

"What?" Cat gave her a blank look, and then mentally shook herself. "Oh, no, Miss Blakely, that is quite all right," she said hastily, feeling her cheeks flame with hectic color. "It's just I had no idea Lord Rockholme and I had been so indiscreet."

"Oh, you hadn't! But when he kept coming back day after day, I knew it was more than duty to the children he was feeling."

Cat gave some noncommittal answer, but as she continued working, the image of Stephen, genuinely and truly in love, kept plaguing her. What would it be like if he was marrying her for passion instead of revenge? she wondered wistfully. Would he be the ardent lover she remembered from their one night together, or would he be tender and loving as he gently coached her in the marital arts? In the next moment she was berating herself for such foolishness.

What did she care if he loved her or not? she thought with righteous anger. *She* certainly didn't love him, nor was it likely she would ever do so. He was a hateful, overbearing brute, who cared only for his precious honor and pride. Yes, he had been used and in a most cruel and calculating way, but while she understood his anger, it in no way diluted her own. Hadn't she been used just as much? What of her honor? Her pride? Wasn't she entitled to them as well? The realization made her freeze.

"Lady Brockton? Is something amiss?" Miss Blakely was regarding her curiously.

"No, I was only woolgathering," Cat replied, resuming her packing even as her mind was whirling. She was entitled to her pride, she decided, much struck at the thought. Just because Stephen demanded her body in marriage, it didn't mean he could claim her heart and soul as well. Those were hers to give or to keep as she chose, and she was cursed if she would surrender them along with her person. Let Stephen have what he wanted; she would keep what was important. She would keep herself for herself. Stephen might think he had won, but in the final analysis, she knew the true victory would be hers.

Stephen had marched across the Iberian Peninsula. He had stormed the fortress at Badajoz, defeated the French in the vicious heat of a Spanish summer, and fought his way through the mud and the blood of Waterloo. But not the most dangerous of these adventures had prepared him for the rigors of a cross-country journey in a closed carriage with three high-spirited children.

"No, Lydia, you may not have a turn driving the coach. You are far too young."

"Elizabeth, that is the third time you have changed your bonnet. Chose one and be done with it."

"Eddie, if you don't stop hopping about, I vow I am going to lash you to the top of the baggage cart!"

Stephen's head felt near to bursting before they were even half an hour from Larks Hall. On some idiotic whim he'd graciously consented to ride with the children while Cat followed in another carriage with her maid and Miss Blakely. At the time he'd had the nebulous idea of using the ride to become better acquainted with his son and two soon-to-be stepdaughters. Now he wondered if he'd run quietly mad and no one had bothered telling him about it.

"Poor Papa, is your head bothering you?" Beth stopped playing with the ribbons on her bonnet long enough to cast him a concerned look. "Mama carries laudanum in her medicine case. Shall I have the coach stop so she can give you some?" She raised her frilly parasol to tap on the roof.

Stephen reached out to stay her hand. "Don't bother," he growled, softening the curt words with a grin. "Although if the three of you don't quiet down, I will trouble your mama for laudanum after all, only it won't be my throat I'll be pouring it down. Maybe if the lot of you are snoring peacefully away, I'll have some chance of ending this journey with my sanity still in one piece."

The girls took the threat in the spirit in which it was intended. "Mama doesn't approve of giving laudanum to children," Lydia informed him with a superior look. "She only keeps it in case one of the servants should get a toothache."

"I'm glad to hear it," Stephen said, closing his eyes and wondering if he'd survive the rest of the day without developing a sore tooth. Somehow he doubted it.

The next several hours passed in relative bedlam. He broke up at least five squabbles between Beth and Lydia, kept Eddie from sneaking on the mail coach when they broke for lunch at a posting house near Kendal, and had to issue a sharp warning to a pimple-faced dandy who was ogling Beth quite objectionably when they stopped for tea at an inn. By the time they reached Haworth where they would be passing the night, he was ready to cry peace.

"Tomorrow you and I will ride together," he told Cat as they sat in the inn's private parlor enjoying the fire. "The children may ride with Miss Blakely and your maid, and may God have mercy upon their souls."

Cat hid a smile behind her teacup. "Coward."

"Completely craven," he admitted, without a flicker of embarrassment. "I would as lief face a brace of French cannons as to spend another hour locked up in a coach with those imps."

Cat's smile deepened. "I did offer to trade places after the unfortunate incident at tea," she reminded him, her green eyes dancing with laughter.

He shuddered at the memory of finding Eddie after he'd fallen headfirst into a barrel of the inn's flour. It had cost him more shillings than he cared to remember to keep the outraged cook from boiling his son in oil.

"I was trying to be noble," he replied, a reluctant grin pulling at his mouth. "And I refused to admit I could be bested by two girls who've yet to put up their hair, and a toddler scarce out of leading strings. That will teach me."

They spent another hour discussing the journey they had already made, and how many miles they hoped to make the next day. He'd sent one of the footmen ahead of them to secure rooms and fresh horses at each stop, and he had hopes of making the long trip to Rockholme within a matter of a few days rather than the week or more it would often take. He'd toyed with the idea of stopping in Rowsley to visit Jason, but after careful consideration he decided against it. His brother would be coming to Kent for the wedding, and in any case he was in too much of a hurry to make Cat his bride to tarry so much as a day.

The thought of Cat as his bride had him stealing a furtive glance at her. She was dressed in a travelling gown of maroon-colored velvet, her black hair covered by a prim cap of white lace. The fire had burned low, and the banked flames bathed her in a rich golden light. A sudden memory of her slender body, lit by candlelight as she lay on his bed, flashed in his mind, and his manhood stirred to life in instant hunger.

Take her, his body urged, the need so powerful he clenched his teeth to keep from groaning. They would be wed in less than a week; what matter if they anticipated their vows by a few days? And it wasn't as if they hadn't already known each other as intimately as it was possible for two people to know each other, he reminded himself. She'd already given herself to him once; why not now? He surged to his feet, nearly upsetting the delicate tea table.

"My lord?" Cat blinked up at him. "What is it?" Then as if noting his discomfort, she added, "Is your leg paining you?"

He almost laughed at the irony of her question. "My leg is fine. I was just thinking it was time we were seeking our beds. We've had a long day of it, and I'm sure you must be exhausted."

He knew the moment she became aware of his arousal. Her cheeks flamed bright red, and her eyes widened in astonishment. He walked slowly toward her, his gaze never leaving her face. Her high color had faded somewhat, leaving her cheeks a soft, delicate rose. Her eyes were still wide, and in their emerald depths he saw embarrassment, uncertainty, and the warm glow of a woman's awareness. The one emotion he didn't see was fear, and he kept walking until he was standing directly over her.

She tipped her head back to hold his gaze, and he could see the gentle rise and fall of her breasts as her breath quickened. He remembered the feel of those breasts beneath his hands, the taste of them on his tongue, and his body grew even harder. At that moment their wedding and the confusing tangle of reasons for it was the farthest thing from his mind. He could think only of Cat, and of making love to her on the wide bed in his chambers.

But however much he might burn for her, he knew the ultimate decision must be hers. He'd never used force upon a woman, and he wasn't about to begin now with the woman who was to be his wife. It might kill him, but he wouldn't take more than she would freely give. He held his hand out to her, his heart hammering as he waited for her to make that last move that would send him winging to heaven or plummeting to hell.

Time hung suspended between them as Cat continued gazing up at him. He could hear the crackle of the flames, the monotonous ticking of the clock upon the mantel, but still he waited, his senses humming with anticipation. Slowly, her gaze never leaving his, Cat extended her hand to him. His fingers closed around hers, and he began drawing her to her feet.

There was a tap on the door, and then it swung open. Cat's maid stood on the threshold, her jaw dropping when she saw them standing in near embrace.

"Oh!" She looked momentarily nonplused and began backing out. "I beg pardon, my lord, my lady."

Cat turned to her, whether in relief or annoyance, Stephen knew not. "What is it, Agnes?"

The maid wrung her hands. "It's the young lord, ma'am. Nurse said to tell you the poor thing is sick. She thinks 'tis just the excitement, but he is calling for you."

Cat hesitated and Stephen gave a mental groan, accepting there would be no lovemaking this night.

"Go on up, Cat," he told her gently, raising her hand to his lips. "If you need anything, send for me at once. Otherwise, I will see you in the morning."

She gave him a grateful smile, and then shocked him by standing on tiptoe to press a chaste kiss against his mouth. "Thank you, sir," she said, and for a brief moment he thought he detected a note of regret in her voice. "I shall see you tomorrow, then.

After Cat left, Stephen rang for the innkeeper and requested a bottle of wine be brought in.

"The whole bottle, sir?" The innkeeper looked disapproving.

Stephen considered the matter for a moment. "You had best make it two," he said decisively. "It's going to be a very long night."

Nine

"I now pronounce you husband and wife. What God has joined together, let no man put asunder."

The minister's voice rang through the ancient stone walls of the chapel, sounding in Cat's mind like a magistrate pronouncing final sentence upon the condemned. She was a married woman.

The minister closed his prayer book and beamed at them with every evidence of approval. "You may now kiss the bride," he said, nodding at Stephen.

He turned to her, his face the cold, expressionless mask she'd grown accustomed to in the week they had been at Rockholme Manor. He put his gloved hand beneath her chin, tilting up her face for the brief kiss he brushed over her mouth. When he lifted his head, his jet-colored eyes burned down into hers.

"Mine, Cat," he whispered, his voice so low she was scarce certain she had heard him. Then he turned away, fixing his attention on the vicar as he led the congregation in the final prayers that would solemnize the marriage.

Cat bowed her head as well, wondering if praying for a marriage under such circumstances might be construed as blasphemy. It was one thing to deceive her family and Stephen's, she thought, blinking back tears, but it was quite another to attempt to deceive God. She only hoped the Almighty would forgive her. Having experienced what she considered hell on this earth, she didn't think it fair she should be condemned to it in the hereafter as well.

Finally the ceremony was over, and she and Stephen were

walking up the narrow aisle. There was to be a wedding breakfast held in the huge hall at the Manor, and afterward they would be leaving for the small hunting lodge on the far side of the estate to spend their wedding night alone. The thought had been enough to keep her awake most of last night, and she felt as nervous and uncertain as the most virgin of brides.

"Mama!" Eddie rushed up to them as soon as she and Stephen stepped out into the sunlight.

"Hello, poppet." Mindful of her flowing silk skirts, Cat bent to kiss her son's forehead. "My, aren't you a handsome one in your new suit," she said, heart filling with maternal pride.

Eddie grimaced, as disdainful as any boy at being forced to wear velvet and lace. "It itches," he said, tugging impatiently at the wide collar. He glanced up at Stephen. "Does yours itch, Papa?" he asked, his dark eyes filled with curiosity.

Stephen smiled and brushed his hand over Eddie's head, mussing the curls it had taken Cat and Nurse the better part of an hour to tame. "Terribly," he admitted with a rueful laugh. "But we men must learn to tolerate such discomfort for the ladies' sake. Think of all they endure for us."

Eddie looked more confused than ever, but before he could think of more questions, Beth and Lydia came up to join them, looking like perfect angels in their matching gowns of powder blue silk. The dresses had been Stephen's present to them, and even Lydia had gone into paroxysms of delight at the thought of wearing such an adult gown.

"This chapel is even prettier than our church at home," Beth said, glancing about her with dreamy eyes. "When I am married, may I be wed from here?"

"If you wish," Stephen replied, pressing a kiss to the delighted girl's cheek. "Although I hope that day won't arrive for many years to come. I've only just acquired you as my daughter. I'm not ready to be shed of you so soon."

The teasing remark stayed with Cat through the long breakfast and the endless round of speeches and toasts that followed. He *did* think of himself as the girls' father, she realized, stealing a furtive glance at Stephen. Just as she thought of herself as their mother. Perhaps he didn't love them as she did, at least not yet, but it was plain he cared about them and meant to do his best by them. Considering the reasons behind their marriage, she supposed that was more than she could reasonably have expected.

At that moment Stephen turned his head, his dark eyes enigmatic as they met hers. They were seated side-by-side at a long table, flanked on either side by friends and family, but at that moment it felt as if they were the only ones in the room. Cat could not explain the sudden sense of intimacy—she could only feel it—and her pulses skittered in response. As if sensing her disquiet, he reached out to cover her hand with his own.

"Are you ready to leave?" he asked, brushing his thumb over the back of her hand. "I instructed the grooms to have the gig brought 'round front at one o'clock, and it's nearly that now."

Cat's heartbeat accelerated, but pride kept her from letting it show. "Very well. If you'll pardon me, I'll go up to my rooms to change my gown and—"

He silenced her by doing no more than tightening his fingers around hers. "There's no need for you to change. We'll only be going as far as the lodge." His deep voice was polite, but that didn't make what he said any less of a command. It was there in his eyes and in the proprietary way he was gazing at her. Cat swallowed the fist-sized lump in her throat and managed a smile.

"Then I'll just get my cloak," she said, withdrawing her hand from beneath his. "I'll only be a few minutes." Telling herself retreat wasn't the same thing as running, she picked up her skirts and scurried out of the hall.

Half an hour later she and Stephen were in the open gig driving away with the best wishes of their guests ringing in their ears. It was late July, and the countryside was alive with the sights and smells of an English summer. Despite her nervousness, Cat couldn't help but respond to the beauty around her. She closed her eyes, drawing in the lush fragrance of the roses lining the drive leading to the small lodge.

It's very beautiful here," she said, opening her eyes to cast an appreciative glance about her. "You must have missed it very much while you were in Spain."

"I missed a great many things while I was in Spain," he replied obliquely, taking his eyes off the horse long enough to cast her a cool look. "But you're right, I missed Rockholme in the years I was away. It is good to be back."

It was on the tip of her tongue to ask him why he'd stayed away so long if he loved his home so much, but upon reflection she decided against it. She might now be his wife, but she somehow doubted he would appreciate her asking something so personal. Since that night in the inn when he'd looked at her with such burning hunger, he'd kept his distance from her, touching her only when the children or others were present.

Come to think of it, she realized, frowning slightly, they hadn't been alone for more than a few minutes since arriving in Kent. Granted they had both been busy—she seeing her family settled and attending to the details associated with the hasty wedding, and he with matters pertaining to the estate—but it only this moment struck her how little private time they'd had. An accident? she wondered. Or because he couldn't bear to be in the same room with her? If so, the next twenty-four hours would be most interesting.

The lodge was no more than a cottage, with a low, thatched roof and mullioned windows that winked in the sunlight. Cat had been inside earlier in the week, when she'd stopped by to make certain the lodge was clean and ready for use. Because of its proximity to the Manor the lodge was never meant to house guests, and consisted of little more than the large parlor on the main floor and a single bedchamber on the upper floor. It was the thought of the bedchamber, and the huge tester bed tucked beneath the eaves, that had the breath catching in Cat's throat.

A groom came running as Stephen pulled to a halt in front of the cottage. Stephen tossed him the reins before hopping out and walking around the gig to lift Cat down. His hands lingered on her waist briefly before he turned to the gawking servant.

"Is everything as I ordered?" he asked, his tone clipped.

The groom bobbed his head in eager assent. "Yes, m'lord. Just as you said."

Stephen dug out a coin from his pocket and flipped it to him.

"Thank you, Ned," he said. "You may go now. Oh, and be sure to send someone back for us tomorrow afternoon."

Ned promised to do just that, offering them his cheerful best wishes, before turning the gig around and driving off. Cat watched it disappear from sight, feeling strangely as if she'd been abandoned. Telling herself she was behaving like a foolish chit, she glanced back at Stephen, and every coherent thought she had died at the hard, intent look on his face.

"Are you ready to go inside, Lady Rockholme?" he asked, his burning gaze holding hers.

The time for avoidance was done, Cat realized, fear and anticipation exploding inside her. Once she stepped into that small cottage with Stephen there would be no going back, no avoiding the passion shimmering between them—passion she could now admit burned as brightly on her side as it did on his. Stephen might want her, but it was no more than she wanted him. "Yes," she said, facing him proudly. "I'm ready."

Wordlessly he offered her his arm and after only a moment's hesitation she took it, her fingers curling around the tensed power sheathed in elegant velvet. He led her up the stone steps, pausing when they reached the front door.

"It is the thing, I believe, to carry the bride across the threshold," he said, his cool tone at odds with the hot gleam of his eyes. "All right?"

Cat nodded, not trusting herself to speak. She'd find her voice and her courage in a moment, she thought, but for now the simple act of conversation was beyond her. Fortunately for her, Stephen didn't seem to expect conversation. He simply scooped her up in his arms, shouldering open the door and carrying her inside with the easy strength she'd never forgotten. She half expected him to carry her up the stairs to the waiting bed, and was surprised when he carried her over to the settee instead. She was further surprised when he gently deposited her on the soft cushions without stealing so much as a single kiss. He looked down at her, something not quite tame showing in his eyes, before he took a deliberate step back.

"I need to check something," he said, and then whirled

around and stalked off, leaving her to gape after him in bewilderment.

While he was gone she sat up and glanced around her, confusion turning to amazement as she took stock of her surroundings. The shutters on the windows were closed, and the fire burning in the grate gave the room a warm, inviting glow. The soft flicker of candlelight added to the intimate ambiance, and vases of freshly cut flowers perfumed the air with a heady sweetness. It was a scene set for seduction, and her knees went weak as she realized Stephen was responsible for it all. She was still absorbing that fact when the rattle of crystal heralded his return, and she glanced up as he walked toward her, a tray with glasses of golden champagne held in his hands.

"You scarce touched your champagne at breakfast, and I thought you might be thirsty," he said, handing her a glass before setting the tray down. He picked up a glass of his own and sat casually beside her. He clinked his glass against hers. "To us."

"To us," Cat echoed, lifting the sparkling wine to her lips. She didn't think she could swallow for the lump in her throat, but the champagne slid down easily. The bursting bubbles spread a warm glow in her jittery stomach, and so she took another sip.

"It went rather well, don't you think?" Stephen lounged beside her, as calm as if they had been married for years rather than a few hours.

"Quite well," Cat agreed, trying to imitate his insouciance. But it was hard, very hard, given how aware she was of the warmth of his body, and the familiar scent of his musky cologne tickling her nose. She took a hasty gulp of champagne.

"The vicar was rather long-winded. We'll have to leave Eddie at home the next time we attend services. The little wretch would never stay still for an entire sermon."

"Indeed," Cat said, wondering how he could speak of prosaic things at such a time. Perhaps he'd changed his mind and had no intention of claiming his rights. Perhaps he'd lost interest in her but married her anyway to save his pride. Perhaps—

"Cat?"

"Yes?" She started nervously, then steeled herself to hear his cool words of rejection.

"Will you set down your glass? I fear you'll crush it if you hold it any tighter." Then before she could object, he bent forward and plucked the glass from her nerveless fingers.

"There," he said, his breath wafting over her cheeks as he leaned closer. "That's better."

Was it? Cat's breath quickened at the masculine gleam in his eyes. Apparently her fears that he'd lost interest in her had been unfounded, she thought, her stomach fluttering wildly.

"You looked beautiful this morning," he said, trailing a finger across her cheek. "I thought my heart would stop when I saw you walking down the aisle to me."

Cat didn't know what to say. From her one time with Stephen, she knew him to be an ardent lover: passionate, playful, and full of charm. She supposed she should have known he wouldn't pounce upon her and savage her like a beast, but it hadn't occurred to her he might feel compelled to seduce her. The realization he was doing just that released the tight ball of tension inside her, and her lips curved in a womanly smile.

"Thank you," she said softly, and then taking her courage in both hands, she reached up to caress his cheek. "I also thought you looked most handsome, standing there so stern and correct. Eddie gets that same expression on his face when he's trying his very best not to misbehave."

His eyes took on a devilish sparkle. "Indeed?" he drawled, leaning down to brush his lips over hers. "But as it happens, I am planning to misbehave."

"Are you?" Cat's lashes fluttered closed, the hot, sweet ache she'd never been able to forget gathering deep inside her.

"Mmmm, quite shockingly so, in fact." Stephen's tongue lightly teased the side of her neck. "Have you any objections?"

Cat arched in reaction, her fingers clenching in his dark hair to press him closer. "No," she said, her voice barely audible. "I've no objections."

"Good," he said, then turned his head to cover her mouth with his. The kiss was hot, demanding, and impossibly arousing as he pressed her down against the plump cushions. His tongue flicked against her lips, slipping between them to tangle with hers. It was the kiss that had haunted her dreams, and Cat reveled in the sweetness of it. Past and present merged in an erotic reality that sent her head reeling and her pulses racing.

"Cat!" Stephen groaned her name against her throat, his hands impatient as they slid beneath the smooth silk of her gown. "I want you until I am mad with it!"

She arched as his fingers caught and tormented the sensitive tips of her breasts. "Stephen!" She could scarce speak for the sensations storming through her. "Touch me! Please touch me!"

He complied greedily, pulling the bodice of her gown down to bare her breasts to his searching hands and mouth. He bent his head and took a nipple in his mouth, and the sweet suckling had her crying out with pleasure.

Her hands went to his shoulders, impatiently pulling at the jacket. She wanted to feel his flesh beneath her hands, needed the warm slide of his skin against her skin. He reared back, his eyes glittering wildly in his flushed face as he divested himself of his jacket, waistcoat, and shirt in a few economical jerks. He then leaned down and tugged her gown the rest of the way off, leaving her clad only in her chemise and underthings.

"You are so beautiful," he whispered in a raw voice, cupping her breasts in his hands. "I would dream of you, ache for you, want you until I thought I would go mad. Don't tell me to stop, Cat. For the love of God, don't tell me to stop."

His words moved her beyond anything she thought possible. "No, don't stop, Stephen," she pleaded, pride wilting beneath the heat of her desire. "I don't want you to stop."

He returned to her with a groan, his body pressing her deep into the cushions as he kissed her with wild need. Their mouths fused in hunger, tongues mating as she met him kiss for kiss, touch for touch. That first time she'd been as untried as a virgin, but she knew now how to caress him, how to stroke him, how to drive him to the point and beyond. He had taught her that, and she was as bold in her lovemaking as he, demanding the responses he gave with ever-increasing passion.

She was wild as she'd never dared be wild, arching beneath

him as he blazed a trail down her body, removing the remainder of her clothing. He slipped his hands beneath her hips, lifting her up so he could bury his face in her feminine softness. When she felt his tongue flicking against her most intimate flesh, the tension inside her exploded, and she arched farther, sobbing out his name as more explosions shook her. She thought he would take her then, but she was wrong. He kept kissing her, slipping her legs over his shoulders so that he could deepen the love kiss.

His lips, tongue, and fingers tormented and delighted her, driving her from peak to peak, until she couldn't discern one from the other. Pleasure swamped her, and when she didn't think she could bear the exquisite sensations another moment, he raised himself above her. His hands were shaking as he gripped her hips, his eyes fever-bright as he gazed down at her. Slowly, deliberately, his gaze never leaving hers, he pressed inside her, filling her with the full power of his masculine hardness.

"Now you are mine," he said hoarsely, dipping his head to take her mouth in a sizzling kiss. "Mine."

She couldn't respond, too lost in passion to comprehend his possessive claim. She could only feel the fullness of him, moving in and out of her as he thrust against her. Crying out, she wrapped her arms and legs about him, closing her mind to everything but the wild storm engulfing her. He moved against her harder, faster, until the tempest broke over them, sweeping them both out of themselves and away.

His. Stephen gazed down at Cat's face, passion so recently sated still heating his blood. Her long black hair cascaded like satin about the creamy perfection of her shoulders, making her look like an exotic goddess. Bemused, he reached down and wrapped one of the midnight-dark strands about his fingers, raising it to his nose and inhaling deeply. The subtle scent of lilac enveloped him, and his body stirred to life.

He'd never forgotten that fragrance, he realized, rubbing the hair across his lips and tasting the sweetness of it. It had pervaded his dreams, haunting him until the thought of other women had left him cold. In Spain there had been many dark-haired señoritas, any of whom would have been more than delighted to warm his bed, but he'd never felt more than a flash of momentary desire for any of them. Beautiful they might have been; but they weren't Cat, and in the end resisting them had proved embarrassingly easy.

He knew his fellow officers had thought him quite mad for not indulging himself, but he hadn't cared. Granted, most of the time he'd been too busy fighting to keep himself and his men alive to dally with the ladies, but even when the opportunity presented itself, he'd always walked away. At the time he'd decided it was his own fastidious nature that was responsible, but now he wondered if it had been because Cat had bewitched him.

Because the thought stung his pride, he rejected it out of hand. He wasn't bewitched, he told himself quickly. The arrangement they had hammered out between them left no room for such fustian. What they had between them was revenge, duty, and simple lust, nothing more. He desired her, yes, but desire wasn't bewitchment. As if to verify his theory, his body hardened, and he bent his head to brush his mouth across her shoulder.

"Cat?"

"Mmmm?" She stirred beneath him, her lashes fluttering but not quite lifting.

He grinned and kissed her shoulder a second time. "How are you feeling, love?"

"Mmmm," she repeated, lazily stretching her arms above her head, and then draping them about his shoulders. "I'm fine."

He remembered she'd given that same response the first time they had lain together. She'd been sweetly shy then, he recalled, and completely dazzled by his lovemaking. He remembered feeling smugly pleased with himself, a feeling not unlike the emotions he was experiencing now.

"Are you ready to retire to our room, or is it your pleasure to remain down here for the rest of the day?" he asked, slipping his hand down her body to playfully cup a breast. "If so, I should be happy to oblige you. Although I'm not certain the servants will approve."

The teasing words brought her eyes popping open. "What?" she gasped, and then a hectic flush stained her cheeks. "Stephen!" She tried to sit up, only to bump into the solid wall of his chest. He took immediate advantage of the situation, wrapping his arms about her and holding her close while he reversed their positions. The look of surprise on her face as she blinked down at him had him roaring with laughter.

"It's not funny, you beast!" she protested, slapping his shoulder and blushing furiously. "Let me up! What if someone should come in and find us?"

"Then I daresay, ma'am, that they should stammer their most abject apologies and then back quickly out," he said, laughing as her blush grew even rosier.

"Stephen!" She began wriggling in earnest, her struggles delighting him even as they threatened to drive him mad.

"Cat, if you are trying to win your freedom, you're going about it the wrong way," he warned, groaning as she pressed intimately against his already inflamed manhood. "Move like that again, and we won't get off this settee until next week."

She froze, her eyes widening as she could feel him hardening beneath her. "So soon?" she asked, and then flushed a fiery red.

"So soon," he agreed, taking a conscious step back from the edge of passion. He had every intention of making love to her again, but he wanted the comfort of his bed when he did it. He loosened his grip and let her go, watching indulgently as she scrambled to her feet.

"You can leave that," he said when she bent to retrieve her gown from the floor.

She shot him an indignant scowl. "I can't just leave it here!" she protested, snatching at her discarded stockings and garters. "One of the servants might find it, and know that we—we—" She stuttered to a halt, glaring helplessly at him.

"That we made love," he concluded, amused by her shy modesty. "And what if they do know? We're married now, and 'tis our wedding night. It will be expected. Leave it."

She hesitated, chewing her lip uncertainly. "But—"

"Cat." He decided to take mercy on her. "When I said we would be alone, I meant *completely* alone. You needn't worry about anyone poking and prying in our things and snickering."

When it looked as if she meant to continue debating the matter, he silenced her by rising to his feet and scooping her up in his arms. Ignoring her shocked protests, he carried her up the short flight of stairs, giving her a quick kiss before depositing her on the bed.

The rest of the afternoon and evening spun away as he made lazy love to Cat. He satiated himself on the taste of her skin, and on the sweet, soft sounds she made as he brought her to climax again and again. Afterward they fell into an exhausted slumber, and he held her close, refusing to let her go, even in his sleep. It was twilight when he next awoke, and he felt a surge of panic when he realized he was alone.

"Cat?" He glanced frantically about the dim room. "Cat, where are you?"

"Down here." Her disembodied voice floated up from the lodge's main room. "I was just getting some water."

The tension knotting his gut unraveled, and Stephen relaxed against the pillows. For a moment he'd feared he'd been dreaming again. For years he would dream vividly of having Cat in his bed, only to awaken and find himself alone. Restless and unwilling to wait for his bride's return, he decided to go after her. As a concession to her sensibilities, he took a dressing gown from the wardrobe, shrugging into it before padding down the worn steps.

Cat was sitting at the small table, and she blushed a becoming shade of rose when she saw him.

"Are you hungry?" she asked, carefully avoiding his watchful gaze. "I've prepared a plate with some food I found in the cupboard. I can serve you something if you'd like."

He studied her before responding. "I'm not one of the children," he told her quietly. "You don't need to take care of me. If I'm hungry, I am more than capable of feeding myself."

Her flush deepened. "I'm sorry—"

He sighed. "No, Cat, 'tis I who am sorry," he said, joining

her at the table. "I didn't mean to twig you. Although you do have a habit of treating those about you like a pack of dirty-faced brats," he added, slanting her a teasing grin.

His efforts won a reluctant smile from her, and she finally raised her head to meet his gaze.

"If I treat you like a child, sir, 'tis because you so often behave as one," she retorted. "There are times, I vow, when you are as bad as Eddie."

Stephen thought of the pleasurable way they had wiled away the afternoon. "So you think me a little boy, do you?" he asked, moving his chair closer to hers.

"A very ill-mannered little boy," Cat said, entering into the spirit of the game by sending him a reproving look.

"And would a boy touch you like this?" he purred, slipping his hand inside her robe to stroke the soft skin above her knee.

"Stephen!" She grabbed his hand. "Behave yourself!"

He leaned forward to playfully nip her neck. "Oh, I am trying, love, I am trying."

She tilted her head to one side and sighed. "You're not succeeding very well," she said, her voice languorous with passion. "Miss Dicks was far too lenient with you."

"Who?" He slid his hand higher, rapidly losing interest in the conversation.

"M-Miss Dicks, your governess when you were a boy." Cat's eyes fluttered closed. "You told me she used to pinch you."

It took a moment for the memory of their long-ago conversation to filter through the sensual mists filling Stephen's head. "Oh, her," he said, delighted she'd remembered his offhand remark. "Yes, she was quite the terror of my childhood. But perhaps if I'd touched her like this"—he rubbed his finger across her thigh—"she'd have been less severe in her treatment of me. And if I'd touched her like this . . ."

Cat jumped as the tip of his finger breached her feminine softness. "Oh!"

Stephen chuckled, indulging himself for a few more moments before reluctantly withdrawing his hand and tugging her robe closed. He pressed a kiss against her cheek and then shifted away to help himself to a piece of the chicken piled on the plate in front of Cat.

"I thought we'd go up to London at the end of next week," he said casually, enjoying the dazed look in Cat's eyes. "Will that give you enough time to prepare?"

"What?" she blinked at him in hazy confusion.

"London," he repeated, taking a healthy bite of the crisp chicken. "I've been putting off going, but I see no reason why I should tarry any longer."

Cat gaped at him as if he'd just announced his intention to make a voyage to the stars. "I can't go to London!" she gasped, clearly appalled.

He paused. "Why not?" he asked, puzzled by her reaction.

"The children!"

Was that all that was worrying her? he thought, sending her a reassuring smile. He might have known. "What of them?" he asked, taking another bite of chicken. "We have servants aplenty, and I'm sure we may rely upon Nurse and Miss Blakely to keep a sharp eye on them while we're away.

"And you needn't look so horrified," he added as she continued staring at him. "We're not going to be gone that long. With the Season winding down, we should be home in a month or so."

"A month!" Cat was on her feet and glaring at him.

"Or so," he clarified, setting down his chicken as he realized she was genuinely upset. "After we quit London, I thought we might journey to some of my other properties. It's been years since I've seen most of them, and now that I am married, I'll need to—"

"I'm not going to London!" Cat interrupted, eyes flashing with indignation as she confronted him.

Stephen cautioned himself to tread carefully even as his temper began simmering. "Cat, I realize this may be something of a surprise for you, but it can't be completely unexpected. Surely you knew you'd be required to participate in Society as my wife. You're the countess of Rockholme now, and there are certain obligations to the title."

She lifted her chin another notch. "I am well aware of my

obligations to you, sir," she informed him in a voice dripping with ice. "But I do not see why I must leave my children alone in order to fulfill them. I know the ways of Society and know 'tis not uncommon for the wife to remain dutifully in the country while the husband comports himself in town."

Stephen's lips tightened in anger. He knew the sort of marriage she was referring to; it was the sort of marriage his parents and most of his friends had endured. A bloodless union where the man dallied with his mistresses in London, never coming home but to beget another brat when it was required. It was, in fact, precisely the sort of marriage he'd always assumed he'd enter into when it was his time to wed. But that didn't explain why now the very thought of such a match had his blood heating with fury. If he was going to London, then Cat was damn well going with him.

"Perhaps you weren't listening to the vicar as we made our vows," he said, advancing toward her. "But I was. You made a promise to love, honor, and obey your husband, and obey you shall. We're going to London, and that's the end of it."

For a moment he thought Cat would continue the argument, but instead a cold mask stole over her face. "Very well, *husband,*" she said, inclining her head with pride. "Now, if you'll pardon me, I wish to go to bed. I find I am quite weary."

Stephen watched her turn to go, and something in him roared to hungry life. He reached out and caught her, whirling her around in his arms. "Your husband, am I?" he asked, his voice a low purr as he pulled her against him.

She faced him bravely, her chin thrust out at a pugilistic angle. "You are."

"Then, wife, 'tis time you stopped nagging at your husband and come to bed," he said, and pressed a hot kiss to her mouth.

She resisted at first, her indignation plain, but he kept kissing her, his lips and tongue moving against hers in insistent demand. At last her mouth softened, and she was soon kissing him with the same urgent passion he lavished on her. Her hands tugged at the tie on his robe, slipping inside to caress his chest. He swept her up in his arms, carrying her up the steps once more to their waiting bed. There he laid her down on the rumpled sheets, closing his mind to everything but Cat and the wondrous feel of her moving beneath him as he made love to her with a wildness that bordered on desperation.

Ten

The next week passed quickly for Cat. Her duties as Lady Rockholme occupied most of her days, and additional duties kept her deliriously busy at night. Stephen proved an ardent lover, as insatiable as he was passionate, driving her to madness with his burning caresses. No matter how vexed she might become with him during the course of the day, she could never deny him once they were alone in her bedchamber. He had but to touch her, and her anger melted along with her resistance.

On the morning before they were to leave for London, she was in her room overseeing the last of the packing and dreaming over last night with Stephen. He'd coaxed her out onto the balcony, making wild love to her beneath the hazy light of the full moon.

"And you will buy me a bonnet, won't you, Mama?" Beth sat beside the opened trunk, one of Cat's newest bonnets perched on her dark curls. "A *real* London bonnet from Bond Street?"

Cat tore her mind away from her sensual memories and sent her eldest daughter a fond smile. "I might be persuaded to buy you something," she said, leaning down to press a kiss to Beth's cheek. "But only if Miss Blakely says you have completed all your lessons."

Beth gave a fulsome sigh and rolled her eyes. "Yes, Mama," she said, assuming her most put-upon expression.

Cat merely laughed, long accustomed to the girl's dramatic propensities. "Brat," she said affectionately. "But I do wish you wouldn't be in such a rush to grow up, my dear. You have several months yet before making your bows."

"*I* shan't ever grow up," Lydia announced, slipping one of Cat's gloves on her hand and examining it. "Not if it means I have to gush and sigh over something so tiresome as bonnets."

"You'd rather gush and sigh over horse gazettes, I suppose," Beth fired back in lofty tones. "You'd best have a care, Lydia, or you will become a complete hoyden, and no boy shall ever want to marry you."

"Good!" Lydia returned with obvious relish. "I wouldn't want to marry one of the pesky creatures, anyway. You won't make me marry some boy, will you, Papa?" She addressed her appeal to Stephen, who had appeared in the doorway and was watching them.

"Of course not, poppet," he assured her, pushing away from the door. "In fact, should some boy be so bold as to make an offer for you, I should set the dogs upon him."

Lydia's small face glowed with happiness. "You would?"

"After running him through with my sword," Stephen added, reaching down to run his hand over her rumpled hair.

"What about me?" Beth demanded, gazing up at Stephen with frank adoration.

"With you, sweetest, I shall have to arm the entire household to hold off the army of your suitors who will doubtlessly descend upon us to demand your hand in marriage."

Both girls laughed merrily, and Cat was once again struck by how at ease they were with Stephen. Once they had overcome their initial distrust of him, they had taken him into their hearts, and 'twas plain he had become an integral part of their lives. Part of Cat rejoiced her children were so happy, while another part couldn't help but feel piqued. She'd had all of their love for so long, it hurt to share even a portion of it.

"I encountered Miss Blakely on the stairs," Stephen was saying, bending a reproving frown on Beth and Lydia. "It seems you, Miss Brockton, owe her a page of French verbs, and you, Miss Lydia have yet to complete the watercolor she assigned you. Off with the both of you now."

Lydia made a face as she rose to her feet. "Watercolors are

boring," she grumbled. "Who wants to paint a bunch of flowers?"

"Then paint something you wish to paint," Stephen said, circumventing Cat, who was just about to suggest the same thing. "Take your easel and paints out to the stables and do a painting of Caliph, if you like."

The notion of painting Stephen's prize Arabian stallion evidently found favor with the young girl, for she dashed out of the room. Beth followed at a more dignified pace.

"If she continues to be this horse-mad, I shall have to buy a hunter for her," Stephen said, watching them go. "Everyone hereabout hunts, and it will do her good to participate."

Cat pictured the raptures Lydia would have at being given her own horse and felt a small prick of guilt. "She'd love that," she said quietly. "It is very good of you."

"Not at all. It is my pleasure to do so."

Cat's sense of guilt deepened, and she shook it off impatiently. "Is there something you wished, sir?" she asked, striving for an air of cool control.

He looked surprised, then slyly amused. "Must a man have some reason for entering his wife's bedchamber, other than the obvious, that is?" he drawled, walking toward her.

Cat willed herself not to blush. The many intimacies she'd shared with Stephen over the past week had almost broken her of the annoying habit of coloring up every time he said or did something outrageous, although there were times, like now, when it was exceedingly difficult.

"I merely meant you're usually not at home this time of day," she replied, pleased she hadn't succumbed. "I thought you and James were going to inspect the hay in the north field."

"We were, but while we were there a messenger from London arrived bearing this, and I thought I should bring it to you." He handed her a letter sealed with red wax.

Cat recognized the handwriting scrawled across the stiff paper, and her stomach sank to her toes.

"What is it?" Stephen's voice sharpened at her reaction.

"It is from Mr. Sedgewood," she said, staring at the letter as if it contained something vile, which, knowing Jeremey, it doubtlessly did.

Stephen tensed, a look of cold fury settling on his face. "Do you want me to open it?" he offered, stepping forward.

For a moment Cat was tempted to hand him the letter, but her pride quickly intervened. She'd been dealing with Jeremey for many years now with varying degrees of success, and she could see no reason why she shouldn't continue doing it now. Just because she was married didn't mean she could abdicate all of her responsibilities to Stephen, she told herself sternly.

"No," she said, breaking the wax seal with her thumb. "I will do it." She unfolded the stiff paper and began reading, her eyes widening at what she saw.

"Damn it, Cat, what has that devil written?" Stephen was at her side in a moment, murder gleaming in his dark eyes.

"What?" She stared up at him, and then shook her head. "Oh, it's nothing," she said, and then gazed back down at the letter.

" 'Nothing' wouldn't put that look on your face," he declared, holding his hand out imperiously. "Give it to me. I want to know what that bastard dared write to my wife."

Cat held the letter out of reach. "It is an apology," she said, still not believing what she had read. "He writes to beg our forgiveness for his actions the day he came to Larks Hall."

"Are you certain?" Stephen demanded, looking far from convinced. "He didn't insult or threaten you?"

Knowing there would be no peace until he knew everything, Cat relented and handed him the letter. He scanned it briefly, his lips tightening in obvious derision.

"Does he really think that by "humbly and penitently begging your most gracious pardon" he can atone for what he has done?" Stephen demanded, quoting the letter furiously. "He should count himself fortunate he's even alive to write the wretched note!"

"But he has never apologized before," Cat said, shaking her head. "Not even when his actions were far more objectionable."

Stephen's head shot up at that. *"How* objectionable?"

"Not so objectionable as you are thinking," she said, recognizing the violence in his deep voice. "He was merely drunk and greedy, and demanding he be allowed to move into the Hall. The servants and I tossed him out."

Stephen didn't seem mollified by her explanation. Instead he stalked over to the fireplace, crumpling the missive in his fist before consigning it to the flames. "Well, I mean to make it plain to him you have more than a few doddering old men and pink-cheeked boys guarding you now," he said, turning back to her, his jaw set with resolve. "And if he thinks he'll be received at Berkeley Square as he is hinting, he can damned well think again. If he dares step one foot inside, I'll boot him out myself."

Much as she agreed with his ruthless sentiments, Cat hesitated. "Are you certain?" she asked, nibbling her upper lip and regarding him worriedly. "However repellent Jeremey might be, he is still your cousin, and I fear it may cause talk if it becomes known there is an estrangement between you."

"I don't care if it causes the scandal of the Season, I'm not having that devil anywhere near you," Stephen said, crossing the room to her side. "He might be my cousin, but you are my wife."

Cat was unaccountably touched by his fierce declaration. "But what if—"

"Cat," he reached out and took her by the shoulders, his expression solemn as he gazed into her eyes. "I meant what I said. You are my wife, and I will protect you against anyone and anything that threatens you. I'll make certain Sedgewood understands that. I only wish you would understand it as well."

Cat wondered at the cryptic remark, and at the look of sadness in his dark eyes. She wanted to ask him for an explanation, but she couldn't seem to find the words. She regarded him for several moments, then reached out to gently cup his face between her hands.

"I do understand," she lied, reaching up to press her mouth against his. "And I thank you for the protection, Stephen. It means more to me than I can say." Then she kissed him again.

He seemed to hold himself back at first, and then his arms were stealing about her, holding her against him with the passionate strength she had come to crave. When she felt his hand graze the underside of her breast, she drew back to send him a provocative smile.

"About these obvious reasons why a man might enter his wife's bedchamber," she purred, her hands tugging at his loosely tied cravat. "Would you be so good as to explain them to me? I am not certain I take your meaning."

The bleak look was back, and then it was gone so fast she wasn't certain it had ever been there. Instead, his dark eyes danced with devilish laughter, and his lips curved in a slow smile of sensual delight.

"I should be more than happy to oblige, my lady," he said, his fingers going to the laces of her gown. "But first allow me to assist you to your bed. I fear the explanation you desire is somewhat complicated, and you may wish to get comfortable while I make it."

He gathered her into his arms, carrying her to the bed and laying her down on the clothes she had yet to pack. She started to protest, but when she felt his lips closing about the tip of her breast, she swallowed the words. What did a few wrinkled gowns matter? she thought, gasping as his mouth trailed across her flesh. Mayhap she didn't understand everything that lay between them; but it was plain he desired her, and for the moment she decided that would have to suffice. She closed her eyes, holding him close and surrendering to the magic of his touch.

What the devil was the matter with him? Stephen brooded, studying Cat as she snoozed across the carriage from him. Cat was his wife, generously warming his bed and carrying out her duties as his countess with perfection. With luck she would give him the son he so desperately craved, and perhaps even a few more sons after that. He had everything he wanted, and yet even as he was telling himself to be content with what he had, he knew he was still far from satisfied.

He wasn't even certain when his discontent had started. Perhaps it had been on their wedding night, when he'd had to resort to force to win her agreement to accompany him to London. Or perhaps it had been during the last week, when they had clashed over everything from Eddie's lessons to the correct way of disciplining servants. His wife, prim and proper as she might appear on the surface, was possessed of the devil's own will, and God knew he'd never been the retiring sort.

Given their forceful dispositions, he supposed disagreements between them were inevitable, and truth to tell, he'd enjoyed their spats. The passionate nature Cat showed in bed was revealed in the fiery way she held her ground, refusing to back down even when he was standing toe-to-toe with her and shouting. He'd never thought of defiance as a commendable feature in a woman, and yet he couldn't help but admire Cat for it. She was a woman of strength and determination, and the more he was around her, the more obvious that strength became.

Maybe *that* was the problem, he realized, shifting restlessly. Cat was strong and fiercely independent. She'd married him because he'd left her no other choice, but it was plain she'd yet to accept him as her husband. There was always that one part of her he could never touch, a part she held firmly out of his reach, and it was that part he realized he most needed. Until she gave it to him, he didn't think he could ever fully trust her.

The carriage hit a rut in the road, and the wild bump jostled Cat awake.

"What?" she grumbled, sitting up and blinking groggily about her. "Are we there yet?"

"Not yet, love," he said, tucking the robe back about her. "We're on the outskirts of London, so it will be some while before we are home. Lie back, and get some more rest."

"And miss my first glimpse of London?" she cried, shrugging aside the robe and leaning forward to press her nose against the glazed window like an eager child.

Stephen settled back to watch her, his dark thoughts forgotten. "Have you never been to London before?" he asked, amused by her enthusiasm.

"Never," she replied, wide-eyed as they were caught up in the flow of carts and carriages streaming into the city. "Edward disliked the place intensely, and of course, he was so ill travel was quite impossible."

"How about when you were a child?" he asked, realizing he

knew nothing of her life prior to her coming to Larks Hall. "Did your father never take you?"

She turned her head to give him a wry look. "My father was a simple country physician," she said. "There was little money for such luxuries as travel."

"Where did he practice?" Stephen leaned closer, anxious to learn more of his wife.

"In Levesham at first, and then we moved to Wendermere after my mother died. Father had family there, and he hoped they would take me in should anything happen to him."

"And did they?" He could tell from the sad note in her voice that something indeed had happened.

Cat shook her head. "No. That's how I came to be a governess. But it all turned out in the end," she added, flashing him a quick smile. "The third position I applied for was with Edward. So you see, we'd never have met if it hadn't been for that."

Stephen fell silent, the idea of never having met Cat leaving him suddenly hollow. London had changed in the years he'd been away, and he entertained himself pointing out various sights to Cat and laughing at her responses.

"No, love, the king is not kept locked in the Tower. However did you come by such a notion?"

"That is where all prisoners of the crown are kept," she retorted, scowling at him in indignation. "I hope I may know my history as well as the next Englishwoman."

"Yes, but in this case His Majesty is a prisoner of a diseased mind, and not the crown," Stephen pointed out. "He is kept locked safely away at Windsor."

Cat lifted her chin and glanced back out the window. "A rather poor way to treat one's king," she opined with a sniff.

He grinned. "I am sure His Majesty would agree with you, and really, when you consider the excesses of his profligate son, 'tis hard to say which of them is the madder, or if the lot of us are even madder still for tolerating them."

Cat spent the rest of the journey to Berkeley Square admonishing him for such treasonous talk. There was evidently still much of the governess left in her, and Stephen enjoyed listening to her ring a peal over him. Her hectoring continued until the carriage pulled to a halt before his town house, and then she fell silent, staring up at the elegant Palladian portico with an expression of horror.

"That is your house?"

"Yes," he replied, bristling in automatic defense. "Is there something wrong with it?"

She shook her head. "I . . . no, not at all. I just thought it would be smaller somehow."

Ah, so that was it, Stephen realized, his anger melting. She was nervous. "It won't seem so large once you get accustomed to it," he said, reaching out to take her hand. "And when we're having a ball, it will be so filled with people, you'll swear it's even smaller than the lodge at home."

She gave the towering stone edifice another anxious glance. "If you say so," she said, obviously far from convinced.

He would have liked to have reassured her more; but at that moment the front door opened, and a liveried footman hurried forward to greet them. Vowing to continue their discussion when they were alone, Stephen took her arm and led her into the house.

The next several minutes were taken up with the boring but necessary chore of introducing Cat to his staff. She seemed to have overcome her earlier nervousness, and was both gracious and efficient as she promised to meet with the housekeeper later in the day. A tour of the house followed, and then they retired to the drawing room for a much-needed cup of tea.

"Well done, my dear," he said, saluting her with his cup. "You shall soon have them all eating out of your hand."

"I am sure I wouldn't want that," she replied primly, tucking a stray curl back into her chignon. "But I think I will enjoy being mistress here." She sent him an approving smile. "You have an excellent staff here, sir. You are to be congratulated."

He didn't bother pointing out that most of the staff, the upper servants especially, were all relics from his father's day, or they had been hired by the butler and his man of business during his years away. Let her think he was an astute manager, he thought, leaning back in his chair. It would make for a pleasurable change of pace.

While they sat enjoying their tea and chatting like an old married couple, he went through his correspondence. His secretary had already leafed through it for him, and so the pile was only half of what he feared it would be. Still, it was the better part of an hour before he happened upon the note from his sister. Delighted, he picked it up and began reading it, chuckling at the acerbic tone.

"It's from my sister, Charlotte," he said, handing the letter to Cat. "As you see, she apologizes profusely for having missed our nuptials, and then in the same breath takes me to task for having the poor manners to schedule the wedding at the same time as the Edgecotts' tea. I told you she was a tartar."

"Who are the Edgecotts?" Cat was scanning the letter.

"Damned if I know, but I make no doubt we'll soon be finding out. You'll note she speaks of making certain you meet all the *proper* people. That's a veiled dig at me, by the way, for she never approved above half of most of my friends."

Instead of laughing as he expected, Cat tapped the letter against her hand and looked thoughtful. "Is it necessary that I meet anyone?" she asked, and then held up a hand before he could speak. "I know you said I should do my duty as your countess, and I'm sure you are right. But I've been thinking. What if someone recognizes me from the house party?"

Now it was Stephen's turn to stare. Good God, he realized, gaping at her in horror. She was right. Until this very moment he hadn't even considered such a possibility. But what if someone did recognize her and began gossiping? Reputations had been ruined on less, and he'd have to move fast if he hoped to circumvent any tattle. Who the hell was even there that weekend? he wondered frantically. Davinia was the only person he could recall, and he was fairly certain she wouldn't remember Cat. Davinia never paid attention to other women.

"Albert!" He leapt to his feet. "Albert would know!"

"Know what?" Cat was studying him worriedly.

"Who was there that weekend." Stephen crossed the room and tugged at the rope pull. "I'll just pop over to his house and have a word with him. Once we put a list of names together, I'll know better what is to be done."

A footman entered, and Stephen ordered his horse to be saddled and brought around front. It would mean calling upon his old friend in his travelling clothes, but it couldn't be helped.

"But what is there to be done?" Cat had risen to her feet and was ringing her hands. "What if someone who was there sees me again and recognizes me as Mrs. Frederick Thurston? What if they tell Jeremey, and he puts two and two together and learns Eddie is really your son?"

Stephen silenced her by placing his lips over hers in a swift kiss. "No one will tell Jeremey anything," he told her gently. "That much, I can promise you. As for recognizing you, once I learn who was there, I will call upon them and convince them to have a convenient lapse of memory. Or if they chose not to forget, then I shall persuade them they are mistaken."

"How will you do that?" Cat trailed him to the door.

He turned at the door to brush another kiss across her lips. "It's simple, my dear," he said, smiling benignly down at her. "I'll explain to them that it wasn't you at Exter's that weekend. And if they continue insisting it was, I will let them know I consider that as an affront to your name, and then I'll put a bullet through them. Once people understand that, I am sure we will have nothing left to fear."

Long after Stephen had taken his leave, Cat continued to pace and brood. He meant it, she realized dully. He truly meant he would kill someone for telling the truth. She supposed she should be appalled, and indeed she was; but at the same time she was also touched by this further evidence of his fiercely protective nature. She knew it was his own name and honor he was guarding as much as her own, but it still felt wonderful to know someone stood at her side ready to defend her. she'd had to fight so long and so hard on her own, she'd almost forgotten what it was like to have someone there to fight with her.

And not just with her, she thought, smiling. For her. Given Stephen's habit of shouldering responsibility for everyone and everything about him, she didn't doubt he would willingly battle on to victory alone. Not that she could let him, of course. This contretemps was far more her doing than it was his own, and it was up to her to resolve the matter. Although how she was to do that, she hadn't a clue.

She was still debating what was to be done when a footman entered the study and handed her a card.

"Lady Barton has arrived, my lady, and is asking if she might have a word with you. Are you at home?"

"Of course she is at home, you silly man!" An impatient voice sounded from the door, and a beautiful, dark-haired woman dressed in the first stare of fashion stepped into the room.

"You must be Catheryn," she said, striding briskly forward to smile at Cat. "I am Stephen's sister, Charlotte, but you may call me Lottie. Is that your best gown? If it is, I fear I shall have my work cut out bringing you up to snuff."

Cat rose from her chair, trying to decide if she was outraged or amused by the woman's disarming candor. "Lady Barton," she said, curtseying politely. "I'm pleased to meet you."

"Oh, dear, now I've set you on your high horse, haven't I?" the younger woman sighed, stripping off her gloves. "And I so did wish to make a good impression. You mustn't pay me any attention, my dear. David is forever telling me not everyone cares to have the truth thrown in their faces at first meeting, but really, since we are to be sisters, I didn't think you'd mind. You don't mind, do you? Not really?" She cast Cat an anxious look.

Cat's pique vanished in the face of such charm. "Of course not, my lady," she said, smiling. "But in defense of my modiste in Keswick, I do feel I must protest. Mrs. Pearsall is quite talented with the needle."

Stephen's sister gave a mock shudder as she gracefully lowered herself, onto one of the chairs facing the desk. "Please, Catheryn, I beg of you, *never* admit to wearing a gown from the provinces. It simply is not done, especially in the elevated society you will be moving in as Lady Rockholme. Now, David is forever telling me to begin as I mean to go, and so I will tell you that I have had a letter from James informing me of the true reasons for your marriage to my supercilious brother. I believe I'd like to hear your version of events before I decide whether or not we shall suit."

This was the fight Cat had been expecting, although she had hoped it wouldn't come quite this soon. "What did James tell you?" she asked, bracing herself for the worst.

"That you slept with Stephen to get a son from him so that you could stop Jeremey Sedgewood from inheriting."

The concise summation of the tangled events leading to her marriage made Cat blink. "That is the truth."

"It is?" Lottie sent her a beatific smile. "Oh, wonderful, then it's just as I'd hoped! I *knew* we would get along!"

"You're not shocked?" Cat stared at her in amazement.

"Shocked? Dearest, you forget I know Jeremey Sedgewood, and I consider him to be the vilest creature on the face of the earth! Also, I am a mother, and if it meant sleeping with the devil himself to keep that dreadful man away from my little one, I should do it in a thrice! You are to be commended, not condemned, for what you have done."

Such fierce support was almost Cat's undoing. "I wish your brother saw it that way," she muttered, thinking of James and the frozen courtesy he had shown her since her marriage.

"Well, what do you expect?" Lottie's shoulders lifted in a delicate shrug. "Stephen is a man, isn't he, and they're incapable of rational thought. And now that we have that behind us, it is time we turned our heads to something of real importance."

Cat smiled, understanding now that her sister-in-law's beauty and hen-witted chatter hid a determination every bit as strong as Stephen's. "My wardrobe?" she asked, settling back in her chair.

Lottie nodded, evidently pleased by Cat's perspicacity. "I know you won't take offense when I tell you there is a legion of my brother's cast off mistresses sharpening their claws in eager anticipation of shredding you," she said in her breezy manner. "The fact you are a beauty is certain to set more than one nose out of joint, but I am determined we shall give them even more reason to despise you. By the time I am done, you shall be the best-dressed woman in the whole of London!"

"The best-dressed woman in London after you, of course," Cat said, abandoning any hope of withstanding Lottie's warmth.

Lottie gave a tinkling laugh. "Of course! There, you see, didn't I say we should get along well together? Now ring for some tea that we might become better acquainted, and while we're waiting for it, I shall fill you in on all the latest *on-dits*. I'll begin first with Princess Caroline. Really, my dear, you won't believe it when I tell you what that foolish female has done this time . . ."

Eleven

"That's the last of them, I think," Lord Exter said, leaning back in his chair with a weary sigh. "I could ask Anne if you'd like, but I'm certain that's the name of everyone who was there that weekend. Everyone who is still alive, that is," he added, his lips thinning in a grim line.

Stephen said nothing, thinking as Albert obviously was of the friends who had fallen since that long-ago weekend. Sir Henry Fulwood, a classmate of theirs from Oxford, gunned down during the attack on Salmanaca, and William Merton, among the thousands killed in a single day's slaughter at Waterloo. "I see no reason why we should bother your lady wife," he said, shaking off his melancholy. "And in any case, the fewer who know Cat was at your home that weekend, the better."

Exter shrugged. "As you please, but I still say you're mad to think you can pull this off. Do you really believe you can intimidate the whole of the *ton* into doing as you wish?"

"Only the whole who matter," Stephen returned coolly.

Albert leaned forward, folding his hands on the desk as he studied Stephen. "Stephen, what difference does it make if people know you dallied with your wife before your marriage? Granted it might raise a few eyebrows, but it's not as if it would cause a scandal or some such thing."

"Would you be willing to let anyone gossip about your wife?" Stephen asked, then smiled at the dark look that settled on his friend's face. "Just so. Cat is my countess, and it is my duty to protect her. I'll do whatever is necessary to do just that."

"All right," Albert agreed cautiously. "I can see where you

feel you might be able to convince the men who were there to say nothing, but what of the women? Surely you don't mean to challenge a lady to a duel?"

Stephen thought of his sister and the power she wielded as one of London's premiere hostesses. "I'll find some way of dealing with them," he said. "Besides, given how many people were there, I doubt they'll even recall Cat."

"Even the Divine Davinia?"

"Especially Davinia. You know she never pays the slightest bit of attention to other women."

Albert looked thoughtful. "Perhaps, but I should tell you she was very put out with you for decamping that weekend. And the fact Mrs. Thurston left at about the same time made her that much more furious. She concluded the two of you had left together, and made several unpleasant remarks about it."

The information had Stephen's lips thinning in displeasure. He'd been hoping to avoid a private meeting with Davinia, but now it seemed it couldn't be avoided. "Leave Davinia to me," he said with cool confidence. "I will deal with her."

Albert shuddered delicately. "Better you than me, old fellow. I've never cared for that female above half. And I'd tread carefully were I you. Davinia is a widow now, and on the catch for a new husband, or so one hears."

"Well, she can't have me!" Stephen retorted, grimacing at the thought of being leg-shackled to the treacherous beauty he'd once gleefully bedded. "I'm already married to Cat."

"Yes, marriage does have its advantages, does it not? A mistress may demand many things of a married lover, but a wedding ring isn't one of them."

Stephen frowned at his friend's cryptic remark, sensing there was something Albert wanted to say, but wouldn't. "What is it?" he asked, and when Exter still hesitated, he added, "For God's sake, Albert! We have known each other since we were in leading strings. If you have something to say, say it!"

Albert drew in a deep breath and then puffed it out again. "Is it your intention to renew your affair with Davinia?"

Stephen stared at him in horror. "Of course not! I told you,

I'm only seeing her to make certain she doesn't say anything about Cat!"

"Then you intend keeping to your marriage vows?"

The blunt question made Stephen uneasy. "That's rather a personal question," he mumbled, running a hand through his thick hair. "What about you?" He shot Albert a resentful glare. "Do *you* keep *your* marriage vows?"

Albert folded his arms across his chest and regarded Stephen coolly. "Of course. Anne would stick a knife in me if she even thought I'd dallied with another woman. Don't let her sweet smiles and gentle ways fool you; when it comes to matters of fidelity, my wife is as fierce as a gypsy dancer. Not that she need worry, mind. I love her to distraction, and I'd never dream of deceiving her. Rather unfashionable of me, I grant you, but there you have it."

Stephen considered what his friend had said, and compared it to what he knew of the marriages of most people in his class. "And you've never been tempted, not in all the years you have been married?" he asked, curious despite himself.

"Tempted, as in looking at a pretty girl and wondering what it would be like to make love to her? Yes, I have, but that is as far as it has gone," Albert admitted, and then paused. "May I tell you something I have never confessed to another person?"

Stephen hesitated, and then nodded. "What is it?"

Albert remained quiet a long moment before speaking. "God's honest truth is that even if I were tempted to make love to another woman, I truly believe that when it came to the sticking point, so to speak, I could never become sufficiently aroused to go through with it. I love my wife so deeply, so passionately, that other women hold no appeal for me." He gave a self-deprecatory shrug and grinned at Stephen.

"And I would be most grateful, sir, if you keep that bit of intelligence to yourself. I should be laughed out of the House of Lords if it became known I had done something so *declasse* as fall in love with my own wife."

Stephen gave his oath at once, and the conversation swiftly changed to another topic. But even as he chatted with Albert about more pedestrian concerns, Stephen's thoughts kept returning to his friend's heartfelt confession.

To his shame he admitted that once he would have laughed himself silly at the thought of his boyhood friend hopelessly enamored of his own wife. He'd have thought it quite the joke, and would have wasted little time in spreading the tale to all who would listen. Privately he would have thought Albert a fool, a sentimental weakling caught up in his wife's apron strings. He also admitted he probably would have done his best to convince Albert to sleep with some pretty opera singer, just to prove his manhood, and the admission made him feel ill.

The rake he'd once been died years ago in the blood and horror of the Spanish peninsula, and until now he had mourned the loss of that carefree young man. Now he realized what a wastrel and a lout that man had been. The only good thing he'd ever done was to go into the army, and even though he'd almost died more times than he cared to remember, he knew that in the end it had been the making of him. He shuddered to think what might have become of him otherwise.

After leaving Albert's, Stephen made his way to Davinia's, deciding it might be wisest to put their confrontation behind him as quickly as possible. Luck was with him, and the viscountess was at home and receiving callers. He was ushered into a drawing room, and settled down with an impatient sigh to wait. One of the things he'd disliked most about Davinia during their brief involvement was her propensity for keeping her callers dangling while she sat primping. Cat would never resort to such feminine ploys, he thought with a flash of satisfaction.

When he'd waited over a quarter hour he rose to his feet, deciding he'd waited long enough. He was reaching for the rope pull to request pen and paper when the door opened and Davinia glided in, wearing a gold-and-cream-striped gown that showed her dark auburn hair and dark blue eyes to their best advantage.

"Stephen, darling!" she exclaimed, her face wreathed in smiles as she walked toward him. "How wonderful to see you again! When did you get back to London?"

"Only this afternoon, my lady," he replied, bowing over her

hand with the same cool courtesy he might have shown a complete stranger. The cut was discreet but effective, and Davinia's eyes narrowed in obvious displeasure.

"My lady?" she drawled, her painted mouth puckering in a small moue of disappointment. "My, how proper you have become. Your years in the army have made you dull, it would seem. Still, I am pleased that you should be calling upon me so soon after your return. I am quite flattered, I vow."

"You won't be, when you learn why I've called," Stephen returned, tiring of Davinia's airs. He was anxious to get home to Cat, and didn't want to spend the entire afternoon exchanging quips with his former mistress.

Davinia's eyebrows arched in mock alarm. "Oh, dear, that does sound ominous," she said, walking over to sit on the gold brocade settee Stephen had just vacated. "I do hope you haven't gambled away your fortune, and are come to beg a loan of me."

"No, I am come to tell you I am married."

To his surprise, Davinia took his blunt announcement without batting an eye. "I see," she said coolly. "Well, then, you must allow me to offer you and your bride my warmest felicitations. Who is she, by the by? Perhaps I know her."

"Her name is Catheryn, she was widow to my cousin, Brockton," Stephen said, equally cool. "And as for your knowing her, that is impossible. You've never met."

Davinia's smile grew speculative. "You sound rather positive of that, dearest. How can you be so certain? My circle of friends is rather extensive, you know."

"Cat has never left the Lake District," he told her, infusing a note of steel into his voice. "However, there is something I wish to clarify for you. Cat bears a passing resemblance to Mrs. Frederick Thurston. Do you remember her?"

Sharp speculation gleamed in Davinia's sapphire-colored eyes before she lowered them. "Ah yes, the pretty widow from the Exters' house party," she purred. "You were quite taken with her, as I recall. I should like to have furthered my acquaintance with her, but she left rather abruptly, without a word to anyone. Rather like you did, darling."

Stephen ignored her innuendo. "As I said, Cat bears some

resemblance to Mrs. Thurston. They are of a similar age and share the same coloring, but Cat is *not* Mrs. Thurston."

Davinia raised her eyes, the challenge in them unmistakable. "And if someone was to claim she is?"

"Then that someone would be wrong," Stephen said, dropping his mask of civility. "And if that someone should continue insisting such a thing, I would be forced to take action against them. A man I would call out. A woman," he hesitated, his smile like a knife as she studied her. "A woman I would ruin."

It was to Davinia's credit that he had no need to elaborate further. Other than paling she gave away nothing of what she was thinking, her expression cool as she rose to her feet.

"It was good of you to call upon me, my lord," she said, offering her hand along with a distant smile. "I shall look forward to meeting your wife. I am sure she is lovely."

Stephen gazed at her, thinking of Cat, and comparing the two women in his mind. "Yes," he said softly, "she is."

"Are you certain this is necessary, Lottie?" Cat asked, studying her reflection in the cheval glass. "This silk is terribly expensive."

Lottie gave a trill of laughter, glancing up from the pattern book she was examining to flash Cat an indulgent smile. "Don't be silly, dearest, Stephen's pockets are among the deepest in England! He shan't miss a few hundred pounds, I promise you. Besides, that color is just the thing to show off the family emeralds when you are introduced at the Aubervilles'."

Cat turned back to her reflection, biting her lip to quell the sudden attack of nerves that set her stomach to fluttering. By calling upon her powers as one of London's premiere hostesses, Lottie had managed to wrangle her an invitation to one of the Season's most prestigious events, and it was there she would be making her official debut as the countess of Rockholme.

Preparations for the event had occupied the better part of the past several days, but Cat felt no more ready now, than she had when they had begun. Until now the grandest event she'd attended had been the Exters' house party. Except according to

Stephen, she'd never been anywhere near Nottingham or Exter Manor.

"This one," Lottie said, indicating an illustration with her finger and handing the book back to the modiste. "Have it ready by next Tuesday, madame, if you please."

"Yes, Lady Barton," the modiste said, curtsying. "Shall I come to your house, my lady, or do you wish to come here?" she added, giving Cat a diffident look.

"We shall come here." As she'd done from the first, Lottie answered for Cat. "Now we must be on our way. We are expected at Countess Combey's, and we are already late. Come, Catheryn."

A bemused Cat allowed herself to be bear-led out to the waiting carriage. Much as she appreciated all her sister-in-law had done for her, she knew the time was rapidly approaching when she would have to put her foot down. Lottie meant well, and she always issued her commands with the sweetest of smiles, but it was always clear she intended ruling the roost. Until now Cat had been content to follow meekly behind, but she knew she could no longer continue doing so. She only hoped the gentle tyrant would not take mortal offense when she finally retook command.

"I should warn you about Penelope," Lottie began, with the authoritative air of a teacher giving instruction. "She is a sweet creature to be certain, but she is as blind as a mole. She won't wear her spectacles, and because of it she is forever calling people by the wrong name, mistaking them for other people, that sort of thing. Last year she mistook Sally Jersey for a maid, and asked her to pass the biscuits. Luckily Sal thought it a great joke, and spent the entire afternoon passing plates and curtsying."

Cat, who had already had the dubious honor of meeting the haughty beauty, could only wince in commiseration. "How awkward for her ladyship," she murmured, her heart going out to the hapless countess.

"Not as awkward as the time she mistook Lady Marlgate for the Divine Davinia, and asked her if she was still carrying on with the duke," Lottie said, chuckling. "You could hear Her Grace shrieking clear to Kensington Palace."

Cat laughed and then frowned. "Davinia," she repeated thoughtfully. "That name sounds familiar."

To her surprise, Lottie grew red-faced and apologetic. "Oh, drat, there I go again!" she said, sending Cat a penitent look. "I can't believe I had the poor manners to even mention her name. Pray forget all about it, I beg you."

"But who is she?" Cat insisted. "Is she one of the ladies who left me a card?"

Lottie hesitated, clearly uncertain what she should say. Finally she heaved a sigh and turned to meet Cat's puzzled gaze.

"She was, and mark you, I said *was,* Stephen's mistress, but that was years ago, before he went into the army, even. You mustn't concern yourself with her for a moment."

An image of a stunning redhead with a smug smile and a condescending manner flashed in Cat's mind. "She was at the Exters'," she said, recalling how the other woman had flirted shamelessly with Stephen at dinner.

"She was?" Lottie looked alarmed. "Oh, dear, that could be awkward, especially if she were to remember you. Well, we shall simply have to cross our fingers and pray the two of you never meet. Not that I think it likely. Since coming out of mourning Davinia has kept to her own crowd, so I doubt we shall see much of her. But if we should encounter her, you must pretend as if you've never met."

By biting her lip Cat was able to refrain from telling Lottie she wasn't a brainless child, but it was a very near thing. Lady Combey was every bit as sweet as Lottie had said she was, and obviously near-sighted as she peered up at Cat and pronounced her a "diamond of the first water." Twenty minutes later, Cat and Lottie were making their way about the countess's over-crowded drawing room when Lottie suddenly grabbed Cat's arm.

Oh, good heavens!"

"What is it?" Cat looked about to see if she could find what had distressed her sister-in-law, but there were too many people for her to see more than a few feet away from her.

Here's a special offer for
Romance Readers!
Get
4 FREE
Zebra
Splendor
Historical
Romance
Novels!
A
$19.96 value
absolutely
Free!
© ENNIS
Take a trip back in time and experience
the passion, adventure and excitement of a Splendor
Romance...delivered right to your doorstep!

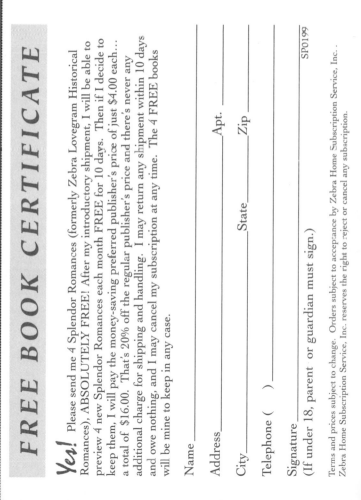

"Do you recall my saying it was unlikely we should see much of the Divine Davinia?" Lottie whispered, unfurling her fan to hide her face. "It seems I was overly optimistic. She is standing right over there."

Cat turned her head in the direction Lottie indicated, her stomach lurching when she saw a beautiful woman,—draped in shimmering gold silk, watching her with a look of smug amusement on her face. When she saw Cat staring at her, she set down her glass of sherry and began walking toward them.

"Oh, no!" Lottie wailed softly. "She's coming over here! The nerve of that creature! What Stephen ever saw in her, I am sure I do not—Lady Dewhurst!" She broke off, dropping a cool curtsey.

"Lady Barton," the beautiful redhead also curtseyed, her sharp blue eyes never leaving Cat's face. "But pray introduce me to this lady. I am sure we haven't been introduced as yet."

Clearly relieved by the other woman's failure to recognize Cat, Lottie clamped a hand on Cat's arm and dragged her forward. "My lady, I should like to make you known to my sister-in-law, Catheryn, countess of Rockholme. Catheryn, dearest, this is Davinia, the dowager viscountess of Dewhurst."

"So, you're Stephen's wife," Lady Dewhurst purred, regarding Cat with brazen speculation. "I'd heard he'd wed, but no one mentioned how charming you are. Country women have such glowing complexions, so tanned and robust."

"It is kind of you to say so, my lady," Cat replied, inclining her head warily. The viscountess reminded her of Edward's treacherous, immoral first wife, and Marie, she remembered, had liked nothing better than to stir up unhappiness and discord with her venom-tipped barbs.

Lady Dewhurst waited with palpable eagerness, but when Cat failed to respond, she tried again. "But how is that handsome husband of yours?" she asked, her voice dripping with sweetness. "We are old friends, you know, and I was so delighted when he called upon me last week. Do send him my regards." She drifted away, obviously much pleased with herself.

Lottie glared after her. "Odious cow, and foolish as well, to think you'd believe Stephen would take up with her again." She turned back to Cat, her expression earnest.

"You mustn't credit a single thing she says, Catheryn. She is as poisonous as an asp, and twice as deadly."

"I'd already decided as much," Cat replied, although she was privately troubled. Stephen had said nothing about calling upon his former mistress, and she refused to speculate what his omission might mean. They had never discussed the matter of fidelity, but she'd thought his sense of honor would prevent him from straying. Now she realized she'd been childishly optimistic. She'd known even before she'd met him that Stephen was a rake without equal, and she was too intelligent to believe the old saw about reformed rakes making the best of husbands.

Cat spent the afternoon brooding over her encounter with Lady Dewhurst. Much as she hated letting the viscountess's innuendoes overset her, she was unable to keep her suspicions at bay, and images of Stephen making love to the auburn-haired beauty tormented her. Telling herself she was being foolish did little to assuage the hurt, and by the time she returned to the house, her heart and her head were aching.

A footman was waiting to take her cloak and hat from her, and after surrendering them, Cat asked if Stephen had returned. The question was one she asked by rote, even knowing the answer was usually no. Stephen was seldom home these days, and he never left word where he went or when he would return.

"His lordship returned an hour ago, my lady." The footman's reply took Cat by surprise, a reaction she was quick to mask.

"Is he in his study?" she asked, wondering if Stephen would think her overly bold for seeking him out.

"No, my lady. He has retired to his bedchamber."

His bedchamber! Cat's gaze flew to the long-case clock in the hallway. It was scarce five o'clock, and the only time she could recall Stephen seeking his bed so early was when his leg was plaguing him. Alarmed, she hurried up to their rooms.

The drapes were drawn when she peeked into the room, but in the semidarkness she could see Stephen lying in the massive bed. She disliked the notion of disturbing him, but she knew she would never be at ease until she checked him. Closing the door behind her, she crept over to the bed. He seemed to be dozing, and she leaned down to study his face. He looked flushed, she fretted, and she laid her hand against his cheek.

In a flash he exploded off the mattress, grabbing her roughly by the arms and tossing her down onto the bed. Before she could scream he had pinned her down, one arm across her throat, and the other drawn back to administer a blow. She gazed up into the face of a warrior, his eyes glittering, and his face a cold, hard mask. Their gazes met, and the promise of death she saw in his ebony-flecked eyes faded into confusion and then horror.

"Cat?" He blinked down at her.

She stared back up at him, trying to gather her scattered wits enough to speak. "I-I was just seeing if you had a fever," she stammered, her heart hammering. "I didn't mean to waken you."

He gazed at her another moment, the muscle in his jaw clenching. Then he was gathering her against him, his arms holding her tight as he buried his face against her tumbled hair. "Oh God, Cat, I am sorry," he whispered, his hands trembling as he stroked her. "I am so sorry."

Worried, she raised her arms to circle his neck. "It's all right," she assured him, running her hands down his sweat-slicked back. "I must have startled you, that's all. I know you would never do anything to hurt me."

"Never," he vowed, holding her in a crushing embrace. "I would sooner die than harm you."

"I know," she murmured, soothing him as she would one of the children. "It's all right, Stephen. It's all right."

She continued holding him, stroking his tensed muscles, and whispering gentle words of comfort. At last his shoulders relaxed, and he raised his head to study her.

"I didn't hurt you, did I?" he asked, brushing back a curl from her cheek. "Be honest, Cat."

"No, you didn't hurt me," she said, smiling up at him. "Although I must admit you did give me a dreadful fright. What was wrong? Were you having a nightmare?"

"Not that I recall," he admitted, glancing away and looking

uncomfortable. "It is just habit, I suppose. In Spain some of the partisans worked for the French, and at night they'd steal into our camp and slit the throat of anyone they caught unawares. After I found my corporal dead outside my tent one morning, I learned never to drop my guard, even when sleeping."

Cat was horrified. "Oh, Stephen, how awful for you!"

He shrugged, his gaze fixed on something only he could see. "It was just one lad, one death. If you want to see true horror, you should see the aftermath of a battle, when thousands lay slaughtered all around you, and all you can hear is the screams of the wounded and the pleas of the dying."

There was no answer Cat could give him; and so she simply held him, her heart aching at the thought of all he had suffered. After a few moments he turned his attention back to her, his expression quizzical as he dropped a light kiss on her forehead.

"Why did you mean to waken me?" he asked, studying her. "Was there something you needed?"

"I did not mean to waken you," she denied, scowling. "The footman told me you'd retired, and I was but checking on you. I was worried your leg might be paining you."

"You were?" He looked boyishly pleased at the notion.

"Yes, and without cause, it would seem," she said with a sniff. "Evidently you were only malingering."

"I have never malingered in my life," he replied, feigning indignation. "Your bill from the modiste arrived, and trying to figure out how I was to pay for it gave me the headache."

She was instantly contrite. "Oh, Stephen, I am sorry! I told Lottie I was being too extravagant, but she—"

He silenced her with another kiss. "I was only funning, love," he said, smiling down at her. "You may buy as many gowns as you please, and not worry. I am rich enough."

"Then you didn't have a headache?"

"As it happens, I had a dreadful one, but your modiste bill had nothing to do with it. I am sometimes prone to them, and the only thing that relieves them is sleep. I'm recovered now."

"Are you certain?" She lifted her hand to his cheek once more. "You still feel flushed to me."

The wicked gleam in his eyes was her only warning. "Mayhap that is because there is another part of me that is aching," he drawled, catching her other hand and lowering it to his body. "But I don't think sleep will do it a wit of good."

The feel of his hard male flesh beneath her fingers had the breath catching in Cat's throat. The frenetic pace they had been keeping often had her falling asleep the moment she climbed into bed, and it had been several days since they had last made love. That Stephen seemed as hungry as she relieved her more than she cared admitting, and her fingers curled lovingly about him.

"Are you quite certain you shouldn't rest?" she asked, enjoying the way his eyes darkened as she stroked him in the way he loved best. "I wouldn't want you taking ill."

"I am positive," he said, his voice raspy with desire. "In fact, I fear sleeping might prove harmful . . . fatal even."

She grinned up at him. "Fatal?"

"Fatal to one of us," he replied, sliding his hands down her legs. When he slid them up again he brought her skirts up to her hips, leaving her stocking-clad legs to tangle with his.

"You always smell so sweet," he murmured, brushing the softest of kisses across her mouth. "You smell of spring and sunshine. You smell of home."

Her clothes melted away beneath his ardent caresses until she was as bare as he. His hands and lips moved over her body, leaving a trail of fire in their wake. She trembled, biting back a low moan of exquisite pleasure as his lips teased her most intimate flesh. From the first he had been the most considerate of lovers, driving her to the peak again and again before seeking his own release. Usually his ardent ministrations dazzled her, and they did now; but she found herself suddenly impatient. An inner hunger was driving her to seek more, and she writhed beneath him in urgent demand.

"Now, Stephen," she moaned, tangling her fingers in his dark hair. "Please now! I want you!"

"Soon, love," he promised, using his devilish fingers to tease her. "I only want to please you a little more."

Any more pleasing would be the death of her, Cat thought,

tossing her head restlessly on the pillow. The wildness was building in her to fever pitch, and she gave a keening cry as the passion exploded inside her. She thought then he would join with her, but even as she was trembling with the force of her release, he was ruthlessly pushing her toward another precipice.

"Stephen!" She gasped out his name with what remained of her breath. "What are you doing?"

"Making you wild," he returned, turning his head to lightly nip her thigh. "Hush, love, and let me pleasure you."

He did pleasure her, gloriously, and the more ardently he caressed her, the deeper and more insistent her hunger became. She tumbled over the edge again, and when she felt him thrusting inside her, she climaxed with a hoarse cry. Stephen drove into her, caught up in her passion that flamed ever higher. She wrapped her legs around his hips, clinging to him with desperate strength, and crying out in delight. Another time her wantonness would have horrified her, but she was too lost in sensation to care. She needed him, needed his strength and his essence with an urgency she'd never experienced.

Her wildness transferred to him, and he slipped his hands beneath her buttocks, lifting her into his ever-deepening thrusts. She clung even tighter, holding him and moving with him until they were both crying out from a pleasure that bordered on madness. Finally Stephen convulsed, his big body shaking with a powerful release that triggered her own. In the aftermath that followed, Cat cuddled Stephen to her breast, and in her heart she knew they had likely made the child he so desperately wanted.

Twelve

Two days following the passionate idyll in his bedchamber, Stephen walked into the private club where he was to meet Lord Exter. He'd barely taken a step into the staid parlor when he heard his name being called out.

"Rockholme! I say, Rockholme! Over here!"

He turned in the direction of the loud voice, his lips curving in a wry smile when he recognized the man hailing him. He ought to have known there was but one man audacious enough to shout across the parlor of Brooks as if he was in a posting inn. Ignoring the disapproving glares of his fellow members, he made his way to the side of the tall, blond man sprawled indolently in one of the club's plush leather chairs.

"Daintry," he said, acknowledging one of his oldest friends with a deep bow. "It is good to see you again."

"Now there is a plumper if ever I have heard one," Richard Balling, the fifth Marquess of Daintry, drawled, regarding Stephen mockingly. "You've been back in London for a fortnight, and you've not so much as sent me a card inviting me to call."

A tide of embarrassed color washed over Stephen's cheeks at the well-deserved reprimand. "I am sorry, Richard," he said, settling on one of the chairs facing Daintry. I meant to, I assure you, but between rigging out my wife and myself for her presentation, and assuming my seat in the House, I fear time simply got away from me."

In response, Daintry waved a well-shaped hand. "No apologies are necessary, I was but teasing you," he said, studying

Stephen before giving a heavy sigh. "Lud, Stephen, Albert is right. You are grown as stiff and proper as a country vicar!"

Stephen jerked back his head in shock. "Albert said that?" he demanded, stung at the unexpected attack. He thought Exter approved of what he was doing, and he couldn't help but be hurt to think otherwise.

"Indirectly." Daintry gave a casual shrug. "What he said was that you were finally behaving as befits your title, and that he was happy to see it. The interpretation is entirely my own."

Stephen gave brief consideration to planting the marquess a facer, and then shook his head with a reluctant laugh. "You are a complete rogue, Daintry, and from the sounds of it, in no danger of winning Albert's approval in the foreseeable future."

Daintry laid his hand over his heart. "I sincerely hope not," he intoned piously. "Both you and Exter used to be such jolly companions, ready to wench and riot at a moment's notice. Now look at the pair of you, prattling on about wives and duty. You'll be having brats soon, I don't wonder, and boring all around you with thrilling tales of their smallest accomplishments."

Stephen's smile faded at the mournful observation. He and Cat had been married for almost six weeks, and considering the many times they had made love, he knew she could well be with child. And what if she was? he brooded. What if some seven or eight months from now she presented him with the son and heir he had demanded? What would happen to them, and to the marriage he had forced upon her?

"Stephen? Did you not hear what I was saying?" Daintry was frowning at him.

"Yes, I heard you," Stephen said, shaking off his dark thoughts. "And I am afraid 'tis already too late. Cat and I are recently wed, but she has a small son and two stepdaughters I am rather fond of. The elder, Elizabeth, is a beauty, and you may be quite sure I mean to keep her far away from rakes like you when she makes her bows next year."

A look of comical dismay settled on Daintry's handsome features. "It's true, then," he said, looking mournful. "Wild bucks do make the severest of papas. I pray I may never marry and sire a daughter. Given my blackened past, the poor girl will count herself fortunate to be allowed out of the house!"

Stephen had to laugh at the image of a stern-faced Richard locking a weeping girl in her room. "It would serve you right," he agreed with a chuckle. "Considering the palpitations you've given any number of anxious papas over the years, 'tis only fitting you should be made to suffer their torment."

Daintry gave an indignant sniff. "What fustian! I have never been one to dangle after the debs. Like you, I considered the quarry too dangerous, and the objective not worth the sport. Accommodating wives and lively widows are much more to my liking, as evidently they are still yours."

Stephen's growing amusement faded. "What the devil do you mean by that?"

"Well, stands to reason, doesn't it?" Daintry didn't appear to notice he was treading on dangerous ground. "Your wife was your cousin's widow, wasn't she? And a beauty, if half the gossip one hears is true."

Fury shimmered in Stephen's eyes. "There has been gossip about my wife?" he demanded, his voice edged with violence.

"Only the usual." Daintry had finally noticed Stephen's annoyance, and was frowning at him. "Well, for God's sake, Stephen, what did you expect?" he exclaimed impatiently. "You're an earl, and a wealthy man in the bargain. Did you really think you could nip off and marry some little nobody no one had ever heard of, and not cause a seven-days wonder? Of course there is talk! It would be damned odd if there was not!"

Even knowing this was so did little to sooth Stephen's anger. "I won't have my countess made the object of common tattle," he said in his most repressive tones. "I thought I'd made that clear, but apparently I was mistaken."

Daintry gave another of his theatrical sighs. "Well, if you are going to behave like this, then I suppose I have no choice but to support you. You may rest assured I shall call to accounts the next person who dares to breathe your good lady's name in my hearing." He broke off with a sudden frown. "I wonder if that is why Albert insisted I meet you here. You must know I never step a foot in this place when I'm sober."

Before Stephen could reply, Lord Exter joined them, and the hard look on his face made it plain he had come for more than a comfortable chat with old friends.

"I've some news you should hear," he began without preamble. "Do you recall Henry Caldwell? He was with us at Oxford."

"Plump fellow with bad teeth and a stutter," Daintry supplied, tapping his chin and looking thoughtful. "He's a bit of a gamester, with more enthusiasm than skill; but he pays his vowels quickly enough, so he's allowed in most of the better clubs."

"Just so," Exter approved with a nod. "But he also plays in some of the less elegant establishments, and through them he has become privy to some gossip relating to your cousin, Sedgewood."

Stephen stiffened in immediate awareness, his hands clenching in a fist. "What about Sedgewood?" he asked, thinking if he discovered Jeremey had been wagging his foul tongue about Cat, he would put a bullet through him and be done with it.

"It seems hc has been engaging in some deep play of late," Exter replied, leaning forward. "Deep enough to be dangerous. Caldwell says he has been unable to redeem his vowels from several rather unsavory sorts, and that even the moneylenders have turned their backs on him."

Stephen digested what he had been told in silence. "Why should that concern me?" he asked after a few moments. "Sedgewood has been in trouble with the duns for as long as I can remember. I don't see why I need trouble myself with him now. Unless he is hinting that I mean to redeem his gaming debts," he added, frowning as the sudden thought occurred to him.

"No, but he is hinting he is soon to inherit the Brockton title and fortune."

The blood drained from Stephen's face. "What?"

"Caldwell informs me Sedgewood has been spinning a tale that Brockton's heir is a sick, feeble cub, prone to infections of the lungs, and that he is not expected to obtain his majority."

Cold terror washed through Stephen, followed by an even

colder fury. "I see," he said, his voice flat. "I thank you for the information, Exter. I shall attend to the matter at once."

"How? By killing Sedgewood?" Exter asked, correctly anticipating Stephen's reaction. "A most tempting solution, I grant you, but in the end, unfeasible. You can't murder a man for lying about a child, Stephen, and you know it."

"Lying about Eddie? He is threatening him, and you damn well know it!" Stephen rapped out, fighting to keep his voice low. "The lad is as lively and as healthy as they come, and if he doesn't live for several more decades, it will be because Sedgewood killed him! I'll see him in hell before I let him raise a hand to my son!"

"*Your* son?" Daintry gaped at him. "I thought you said the lad was your cousin's brat."

Stephen cursed the impetuous tongue that had him claiming Eddie. "When I married Cat her children became mine," he said gruffly. "And for your information, he is not a brat. He is a delightful child."

"I knew it." Daintry shook his head. "Didn't I say you would soon be bragging about your children?" He turned to Exter. "May I ask why I have been made privy to this discussion? I can see why you feel Rockholme should be informed of Sedgewood's perfidy, but I'm whipped if I can see how it concerns me."

"You move in his circles," Exter replied calmly. "More, you know his associates. We need someone keeping a watchful eye on him, and reporting back to us."

"I thought you had Caldwell for that."

"True," Exter conceded Daintry's point with a nod. "But Caldwell is a gambler, and a drunk with it as well. I trust him, but only so far. I want someone in place we can rely upon to give us the truth, someone I know will keep his wits about him."

Daintry studied the contents of his brandy glass. "So you desire I should seek out Sedgewood's company," he said after a thoughtful pause. "Really, Exter, you do expect a great deal from your friends, don't you? The man is a bore."

Exter's lips twitched slightly. "I know," he said in a dry tone.

"But I thought you would welcome the work. Things have been rather dull of late."

"That is so." Daintry's blue eyes took on a reminiscent gleam. "Say what you will of Napoleon, he did know how to keep a fellow on his toes."

Stephen cast both men a suspicious look. "What is that supposed to mean?" he demanded.

"Nothing," both men answered in unison. "That is, nothing that need concern you," Exter added, shooting Daintry a warning look. "It is a private matter between Daintry and myself."

"And a chosen few in the admiralty," Daintry added impishly.

"Daintry!"

"Oh, cut line, Albert," Daintry complained at Exter's howl of indignation. "Do you honestly expect Stephen to go about telling everyone I'm not quite the rake people would have me?"

"Of course not," Exter retorted, casting a cautious eye about him. "But I would remind you we are hardly private here. Lower your voice, curse it."

Stephen did his best not to stare as understanding dawned. The wild friend of his youth, the man he had dismissed in his mind as being little more than a fool, had been a spy for his country. The realization diverted him from his worry over Eddie, if only temporarily.

"I would appreciate any help you could give us," he said, his gaze meeting Daintry's. "I'll own this business with Sedgewood has me deeply troubled."

Daintry gave a mocking smile. "Always happy to oblige an old friend, which, if memory serves, is how I came to work for Exter in the first place. Very well, gentlemen, what's to be done?"

They spent the next half hour plotting their strategies with a diligence Stephen had only seen reserved for mapping out a battle. Nothing was left to chance, and he was impressed with the neat way Daintry's bravado meshed with Exter's more pragmatic caution. He could well have made use of such expertise on the Peninsula, he mused, content to sit in silence while the other two men laid their schemes.

"That should do it," Exter said, sitting back in his chair and looking pleased. "Daintry will let slip that rather than being a weakling, young Brockton is as healthy as may be. That should spike Sedgewood's guns, for the time being, at least."

"And I'll take note of Sedgewood's confederates as well," Daintry added, taking a sip of brandy. "If I suspect any of them are thinking of lending him the ready, I'll put a flea in their ear. It's best if we keep him contained.

"And not a word to your wife, mind," he warned, shooting Stephen a frown. "No need to worry the poor lady needlessly."

Stephen said nothing, although the idea of keeping something of this magnitude from Cat left him feeling vaguely guilty. He knew his bride well enough to know she wouldn't thank him for his silence. Indeed, she would likely box his ears and ring a peal over his head were she to learn of it. For all her ladylike demeanor, his wife was possessed of the devil's own temper.

"Speaking of Lady Rockholme, will you be meeting her at the Ellertons tonight?" Exter had settled back in his chair to enjoy his own glass of brandy.

Stephen gave a small start as he realized he hadn't a notion where Cat would be that evening. He'd assumed she and his pest of a sister would be off attending some function or another, but he'd made no plans to join them.

"Good lord, Rockholme, never say you have let your countess become tangled with that lot!" Daintry complained before Stephen could speak. "What could you have been thinking of?"

"Who are the Ellertons?" Stephen demanded, frowning at the notion of Cat becoming involved with anyone disreputable enough to shock a rake like Daintry.

"Francis Ellerton and his wife, Lady Heloise," Exter provided. "Ellerton is an essayist, and his wife is the Earl of Mayne's daughter. And they are perfectly respectable," he added, sending Daintry a reproving frown.

"For respectable read dull as ditch water," Daintry reprised. "All they ever speak of is politics, morality, and poetry. They actually read it, you know." He gave a delicate shudder.

Stephen relaxed, smiling at the memory of the first night he and Cat had met. "Cat has a fondness for Wordsworth."

"I shouldn't put that about if I were you," Daintry advised, taking another sip. "You wouldn't have Society saying you have wed a bluestocking, would you? Only consider the scandal."

"Where do the Ellertons reside?" Stephen asked Exter, ignoring Daintry with lordly indifference.

"Number Two Little Stanhope Street," Exter said, regarding Stephen with interest. "Will you be meeting your bride, then?"

Stephen didn't need to think before giving his answer. "Yes" he said firmly. "I believe I shall."

"And so you see, by reducing the tariff on imported grain we can better provide our poor with affordable bread," the earnest young man enthused, his brown eyes bright behind the smudged lenses of his spectacles. "Only think of what that shall mean!"

"But what of our farmers?" Cat argued back, enjoying herself to the hilt. "Prices are already dangerously low, and if we force the farmers to compete against imported grains as well, many will be ruined. What will happen then?"

"That is a concern, to be sure," the young man countered after a thoughtful pause. "But the needs of the poor must—"

"I beg pardon, Mr. Boothby," interrupted a handsome young man Cat had not seen before, smiling apologetically at Cat. "But our host was looking for you a minute ago. Something about a book he had promised you, I believe?"

"The volume of Shelley's?" Mr. Boothby asked, breaking into a wide smile. "I have been waiting all evening for a peek at it!" He hurried off without so much as a bow to Cat.

The intruder watched him depart, his smile of amusement still in place as he turned back to Cat. "I pray you will pardon the intrusion, ma'am," he said, the low, intimate tone of his voice making her instantly wary. "Boothby is a capital fellow from all accounts, but he tends to be prosy. I saw he had you cornered, and thought I would ride to your rescue."

Cat hadn't been in London a fortnight without learning something of Society from her sister-in-law, and one of the first things she learned was the fine art of how to give the cut direct.

She drew herself up, her eyes frosting over as she fixed her gaze on a point just beyond the stranger's shoulder.

"I am sure that is most noble of you, sir," she intoned, snapping open her fan. "But might I suggest that in the future you make quite sure the object you are attempting to rescue actually *requires* rescuing? As it happens I was enjoying Mr. Boothby's discourse, and I can not care for having it disrupted."

To her surprise the man actually flushed, a look of comic dismay stealing over his face. "Oh, dear, put my foot into it, didn't I?" he murmured contritely. "I beg pardon, Lady Rockholme, I truly meant no offense."

Cat's surprise gave way to caution. "You know my name, sir? If so, you have the advantage on me."

His look of dismay deepened. "Once again, I beg pardon. I fear I have been so long out of Polite Society, I've forgotten how to conduct myself. I am Captain Marcus Lacey, my lady, and I am most honored to make your acquaintance."

The name meant nothing to Cat, but his apologetic manner and the use of his rank had her softening toward him. "You are in the army, Captain?" she asked, thinking she recognized Stephen's proud carriage in the way he was standing.

"The Life Guards, ma'am," he replied, and then shrugged. "Or I was. I was cashiered out with the rest of my regiment when His Majesty concluded he had no further need of my services."

Cat's initial hostility vanished under a wave of sympathy. She had been reading in the papers of the thousands of soldiers cut loose by an ungrateful king and country, and her soft heart was warmed. "My husband was in the army as well," she told him, offering him a tentative smile. "Perhaps you have heard of him?"

Captain Lacey gave an eager nod. "Indeed, I have, ma'am, although I never had the pleasure of making the colonel's acquaintance. Different regiments, you know."

In truth Cat didn't know, but she supposed that given the sheer number of men in the army, it made sense the captain and Stephen had never met. "Were you at Waterloo?" she asked curiously, studying him beneath her lashes. She found it hard imagining the soft-looking younger man standing on a smoke-blackened battlefield, a sword in his hand as he called out orders to his men, an image of Stephen she could summon up with little or no effort on her part.

He shook his head. "No, my lady. My unit was stuck at home, awaiting a ship to take us to Belgium. By the time one was made ready, the battle was long over. More's the luck." He heaved a sigh of obvious disappointment.

Cat wasn't quite sure what to make of that. Stephen had never spoken of Waterloo, or indeed, any of the battles he had been through, but she knew he dreamed of them. He often had nightmares, tossing and turning in his sleep, and then waking up drenched in sweat and shaking from the memories. She somehow doubted he would have regretted missing such hell.

"I saw you at the lecture at the Royal Academy the other night," Lacey continued, his tone as warm as ever. "Have you an interest in science, ma'am?"

"A small one," Cat replied, deciding there was no real harm in the fellow. "Actually, it is my sister-in-law, Lady Barton, who is fascinated by science. She belongs to several societies, and she is forever dragging me to one lecture or another."

The captain's gaze flew to the corner where a diamond-bedecked Lottie was holding forth to her court of admirers. "Lady Barton is a bluestocking?" he asked, obviously amazed. "One could never tell as much by looking at her!"

Because that had been her initial reaction, Cat decided not to take offense at his observation. "I know," she said with a soft laugh. "When we first met she seemed devoted to nothing more than fashion and Society tattle. I was quite surprised when she began taking me to lectures and to soirees such as this."

"And why is it, I wonder, that I suspect you find the lectures and the soirees far more to your liking than fashion and Society tattle?" the captain remarked with an intimate smile. "In that regard we are much alike, you know. Two serious souls in a world populated by fribbles and fools."

Once Cat would have agreed with him, but since meeting so many of Lottie's friends, she now knew differently. "Not all fools," she said quietly, her gaze going to her host, who was locked in earnest debate with Mr. Wilberforce. Her gaze next fell on a dandy rigged out in yellow and crimson, and a rueful smile touched her lips. "I'm not so certain about the fribbles."

The captain gave a hearty laugh. "Ah, but at least fribbles have their uses, as do the fools, I am sure. They are necessary so that those with little claim to superiority can feel self-important, if only for a while."

The rather incisive remark took Cat aback, and she stole a quick look at the captain from beneath her lashes. Evidently there was more to him than she'd first supposed; she decided.

"Catheryn!" Lottie appeared at Cat's side, her pretty face set in a disapproving frown. "Why didn't you tell me he was coming? He will ruin everything!"

"Who?" Cat glanced around, trying to see who had set her sister-in-law's back up.

"Stephen, of course!" Lottie exclaimed, the dark brown eyes she shared with her brother snapping with annoyance. "He just came in and is making his bows to Lady Heloise."

"Stephen is here?" Cat forgot all about the captain in her pleasure at seeing Stephen. He hadn't said anything at breakfast about joining her tonight, and she was secretly delighted he had troubled to seek her out.

"Well, I shouldn't be so delighted if I were you," Lottie grumbled, her lips thrusting out in a decided pout. "The last time he attended a gathering such as this, he brought a soiled dove with him, and then he compounded his crime by trying to pass the creature off as a poetess. Stop laughing!" she added when Cat started chuckling. "I was mortified!"

"I am sorry." Cat struggled manfully to control herself. "It was shocking of him, to be sure."

"Hmph!" Lottie unfurled her fan with a snap, and then spoiled the effect by breaking into a sudden grin. "It was rather funny, now that I think on it. Especially when the 'poetess' began spouting words that had half the ladies swooning and the other half demanding explanations as to their precise meaning. And don't bother bowing to me, you wretch!" she added, when Stephen walked up to join them. "I am vexed with you!"

"Me? What have I done?" Stephen asked, carrying her hand

to his lips for a quick kiss before turning to Cat. "My lady." He bowed deeply before catching her hand and pressing a longer, more intimate kiss. "You are looking enchanting tonight," he said, his dark eyes warm as they caressed her.

"And stop making love to your wife in public," Lottie scolded with a shake of her head. "It's simply not the fashion."

Stephen merely grinned, repeating the process with Cat's other hand. "Then mayhap we should set a new one," he murmured, the gleam in his eyes challenging Cat. "What do you say, my sweet?"

The way Cat's heart was fluttering, she didn't think she could say anything. Fortunately with Lottie there, she knew her lack of speech wouldn't be so noticeable

"Behave, monster," Lottie was threatening Stephen, "or I shall tell your wife some other stories she may not find so amusing." Then apparently satisfied with her handiwork, she whirled back to face Catheryn and Captain Lacey.

"Now, Catheryn, do introduce me to this charming young man you were flirting with when I interrupted you," she ordered, thrusting out her gloved hand. "I'm certain we haven't met."

Bemused, Cat dutifully made the introductions, noting with amusement the cool way Stephen eyed the younger man. "Your regiment, Captain?" he asked, and Cat hid a smile at the unmistakable ring of command in his deep voice.

"The Life Guards, my lord," the captain replied, all but snapping to attention. "As I told your wife, I hadn't the good fortune to serve at Waterloo."

The bleak look Cat often saw darkened Stephen's eyes. "Some might say you were the one with the fortune," he said coolly. "We lost men by the thousands that day."

There was an uncomfortable silence Lottie was quick to fill. "Lacey, did you say?" she asked brightly. "Are you related to the Camberton Laceys? They are old friends of my husband."

"Only distantly, Lady Barton," Captain Lacey said, his manner smoothly polished. "My father is cousin to Lord Camberton."

"Is he?" That was all Lottie needed to chat on for the next

several minutes, discreetly dragging out each and every one of the captain's connections before she was satisfied.

"You must come to one of our informal little gatherings, Captain," she said, offering her hand, this time in dismissal. "Gallant young gentlemen are always a welcome addition, aren't they, Catheryn?" She sent Cat a speaking glance.

"Indeed," Cat agreed, wondering why Lottie seemed so determined to have the captain's company. "We should be most honored, Captain Lacey, if you would care to join us."

"I should be delighted, Lady Rockholme, Lady Barton," he returned, flushing with pleasure. He then bowed to Stephen, pronouncing himself honored, and then disappeared into the crowd. Lottie watched him go with a measuring look upon her face.

"An interesting man," she pronounced with a satisfied nod. "And a handsome one in the bargain. Just the sort to setup as your cicisbeo, Catheryn."

"*What?*" Cat and Stephen echoed the word together.

"My wife," Stephen continued frigidly when Cat lapsed into an appalled silence, "is most assuredly not in the market for a cicisbeo, so you may put that ridiculous notion out of your head this very minute! And how did it get there in the first place, I should very much like to know!"

Lottie gave a loud sigh and rolled her eyes "It is all the rage, Stephen," she said, using the same tone Cat had heard her use with her young son. "I know you have been away for a very long time, but you must know that all married ladies have at least one or two young men dancing attendance upon them. It means nothing, and it helps to keep other men well away."

Stephen's mouth had taken on the grim line Cat knew all too well. "Are you saying David lets you keep several of these young puppies nipping at your heels?" he asked, not bothering to hide his derision. "If so, he is a bigger fool than I took him for."

"Stephen!" Cat was aghast at her husband's lack of manners. "That was very unkind of you!"

"My husband is not a fool!" Lottie shot back, leaping to her lord's defense with the fierceness of a lioness. "And for your information, David understands these things far better than you ever shall. Now if you will pardon me, I must speak with Lady Heloise. I trust you will stay to see Catheryn home." She flounced off, her head held high.

"Stephen, you have hurt her feelings!" Cat scolded, feeling decidedly out of charity with her husband. "Go after her at once and apologize!"

"Damned if I will!" Stephen retorted, his chin set at a mutinous angle. "Deciding you should take a lover . . . who the devil does she think she is? I don't care what she says, Barton must be an imbecile to let her run loose as he does. If he can't control her any better than this, then I will have to do it for him. I'll not have my sister made the object of gossip any more than I would allow my wife's name to be dragged through the mud."

Cat couldn't help it; she burst into helpless laughter.

"What are you laughing at?" he demanded, looking even more incensed. She covered her lips with her hands, trying to muffle the giggles bubbling out of her. She knew others were looking at her, and doubtlessly whispering about her as well, but she couldn't stop chuckling. Stephen took her by the arm and led her out to the small garden in back of the Ellertons' town house. The moment they were alone he turned to face her, looking so much like an outraged papa, it nearly set her off again.

"Well, Madam Wife?" he inquired crossly, folding his arms across his chest and glaring at her. "Might I ask what you find so damned amusing? I hope you know you've just given the tabbies enough gossip to feed upon for a week!"

Cat managed to rein in her amusement, although it was far from easy. "I realize that, Stephen, and I am truly sorry," she said, trying her best to assume a penitent expression. "But Lottie had only just finished telling me about the lightskirt you'd brought to a soiree, and after hearing what a shocking rake you'd been, watching you act the stiff-necked papa was something of a shock. I was . . ." She paused, searching for the right word. "Overset," she decided, wisely hiding a gamine grin.

To her amusement a look akin to horror flashed across his

face. "Lottie told you about that?" he demanded, dropping his arms and taking a step forward.

"Yes." The imp of mischief Cat hadn't even suspected she possessed stirred to wicked life. "Was she pretty?"

"Who?" Stephen's look of bafflement deepened.

"The lightskirt, of course." She had to bite her lip to keep from laughing again. "Was she pretty?"

"What sort of question is that for a wife to ask her husband?" Stephen's bluster didn't quite hide his discomfiture.

"She was pretty." Cat nodded. "It was very wicked of you, Stephen, to do such a thing. Lottie said she was mortified."

A reminiscent smile stole across Stephen's features. "It was her fault. She was the one who forbade me to attend any of her tiresome salons. As if I wanted to do such a thing."

"I see." It was the sort of logic she imagined Eddie might employ to defend the undefendable, and she found it enchanting. "In that case, I'd best take care not to repeat the error. I'd not care to have you escort a lightskirt to one of my parties."

To her surprise, he gathered her into his arms. "Forbid me from seeing you whenever I please, my sweet, and my dangling a prostitute in front of you will be the least of your problems," he murmured, his tone as provocative as the hands he skimmed over her breasts. "And remember what I said; no cicisbeos."

Cat pretended to pout, even as her pulses raced. "Not even one?" she asked, feeling wonderfully decadent as she slid her arms about her husband's neck.

"Not even one." Stephen nipped her chin. "I mean it, Cat. You're my wife, and I share with no one. Remember that."

Knowing the words contained more tease than threat did little to ease the sudden sense of hurt that killed the pleasure building inside her. She drew a deep breath and stepped back.

"I gave you my word on the day we married, and despite what you may think, I have no intention of disgracing either you or our vows," she told him with quiet pride.

Stephen's head jerked back as if she'd struck him. "Cat, you can not believe I meant to imply . . ." his voice trailed off. "I was *joking,* damn it!"

She gave him a steady look. "Were you?" she asked. "How

many times, Stephen? How many times do you look at me and see Edward's unfaithful wife?"

There was no answer, but then, she hadn't expected one. Cat gave Stephen a final look, then turned and walked silently away.

Thirteen

Stephen stood in the center of the garden, staring after Cat indignantly. Since his arrival at the Ellertons', she'd taken him from desire to possessiveness, from masculine outrage to mind-whirling confusion, and all in the space of ten minutes! He could think of no other woman who could so effortlessly toss him into the center of an emotional maelstrom, and he wasn't certain he cared for the sensation.

Feeling greatly put-upon, he returned to the drawing room, determined to seek his wife. It didn't help his temper that when he succeeded in tracking her down, it was to find that damned puppy Lacey already cozying up to her. Presumptuous, parade-field dandy, he thought, his jaw clenching in anger. It seemed he would be forced to have words with the gentleman.

He paused scarce long enough to exchange pleasantries with his host and hostess before walking up in back of Cat and sliding his arm about her waist.

"Are you ready to leave, my dear?" he asked solicitously, his gaze cold as it rested on Lacey. "I hate to rush you, but you must know we are promised elsewhere."

In truth, they hadn't made any plans for the evening, but as he'd hoped, Cat demurred to his request without protest. "Very well, my lord," she said, turning to Lacey to offer him her hand. "Good-bye, Captain Lacey. I hope you enjoy your stay in London."

"Thank you, my lady." He bowed over her hand, keeping a wary eye on Stephen. "And, Colonel, it was an honor meeting you."

Stephen gave him a wintry smile. "You may call me Lord Rockholme, Lacey," he said coolly. "I've resigned my commission, and I find the use of military titles pretentious when one is no longer in uniform. Good evening." He led Cat away with a grim sense of satisfaction.

He expected her to ring a peal over his head the moment they were in the carriage, but to his disappointment she maintained a dignified silence for the duration of the journey to their house. It was scarce ten of the clock, early by London standards, but he wasn't in the least surprised when Cat bade him good night and turned to go up the stairs. It was evident she'd had enough of his company for one night.

"Just a moment," he said, ignoring the waiting footman as he started up the stairs after her. "I believe I will retire as well. It's been a long day."

She hesitated, one hand on the banister as she stared down at him. "I thought you would want to go out," she said, her tone cautious. "Aren't you expected at your club?"

"I've already been there," he replied, keeping his manner casual as he walked up the stairs beside her. "Exter sends his best, by the way. He and his lady are going to be at the ball tomorrow night, and he is hoping you will grant him a dance." This was an out-and-out fabrication, but he knew Albert could be relied upon to back him up.

They parted at their respective bedchambers, but Stephen had no intention of letting his wife sleep alone this night. After a hasty shave and a bath, he dismissed his valet and walked into Cat's room without knocking. Cat was standing in front of her cheval glass, her glorious body draped in oyster-colored silk, and she whirled around at the sound of the door closing.

"Oh, Stephen! I-I thought you were retiring for the night," she stammered, her eyes going wide as he took off his robe and casually dropped it on a chair.

"I am," he replied, strolling toward her in unselfconscious nudity. "In fact, I intend spending the rest of the night in bed. In *our* bed," he added, bending to brush a kiss across her trembling mouth.

Her hands fluttered to his lean waist. "I am vexed with you," she told him, even as she tipped back her head to bare her throat to his seeking lips.

"I know." He nipped at the tempting flesh. "That's why I am here. I've come crawling to beg your forgiveness."

She smiled at that, her eyes drifting shut. "Crawling?"

"In a manner of speaking," he said, his hands sliding up to cup her breasts. "I was a beast, a monster without equal, a—"

"A brainless ass?"

He jerked up his head at that, his plans for a playful seduction temporarily forgotten. "I wouldn't go that far," he muttered, his brows gathering in a frown.

She stood up on tiptoe to kiss his jaw. "I would. But it's all right. I've decided to forgive you."

Pride and practicality warred, and pride took a tumble. "Are you certain?" he asked, and resumed his task with renewed pleasure. "You don't require persuading?"

Cat gave a soft sigh as his skillful fingers teased her nipples. "Perhaps a touch of persuasion wouldn't go amiss," she sighed, her voice taking on the languorous purr that never failed to arouse him. "If you are truly sorry, that is."

Stephen ducked his head to take an already hardening nipple between his lips. "I am sorry, Cat," he murmured, gently suckling. "Tell me again I am forgiven."

He took her low moan of pleasure for consent, sweeping her up into his arms and carrying her to the bed. Keeping his mouth on her breast, he laid her down on the soft pillows, alternately licking and biting her sensitized flesh until she was writhing beneath him. She was so sweet, so wild, she made him half-mad, and he feared he would explode if he couldn't have her.

"Stephen!" Cat arched up to meet his ardent caresses.

"Yes, love," he groaned, dropping a line of fevered kisses down the slope of her breasts and across her stomach. "Whatever you want, Cat. Only tell me. Tell me what you want."

To his delight she did just that, the shyness she still showed in their bed dissolving beneath the heat of her passion. In a soft, breathless voice she begged for his touch, pleaded for his kisses, and demanded his most intimate loving. Stephen gave her all she wanted, losing himself in the wonder of their joining. He'd always taken pride in his skill as a lover, and he employed all of his art driving Cat and himself to madness.

She was coming down from the second peak when he thrust into her, clenching his teeth to hold back the guttural cry that rose from the depths of his soul. Cat cried out in pleasure, clinging to him with all of her strength.

"God, yes!" he ground out, timing his thrusts to the furious pounding of his heart. "Hold me, Cat! Hold me!"

She eagerly complied, wrapping her arms and legs about his straining body to hold him locked to her. But however tight she held him, it wasn't enough. In the most primitive and private part of him he accepted his need to bind Cat to him, by whatever means necessary. The fear of losing her was something he never allowed himself to consider, except at moments like this, when they were as intimately connected as two people could be.

Even after the shudders of completion shook them, he kept her locked against him, not wanting to let her go. She didn't seem to mind his possessive hold, drowsing contentedly with her head on his sweat-dampened shoulder.

"What are you thinking about?" he asked, sifting her hair through his fingers. He knew she grew sleepy after lovemaking, and he didn't want her to leave him, even in her dreams.

He felt her lips move in a satisfied smile. "I was thinking that you have a very nice way of apologizing," she murmured, pressing a kiss to his chest. "You have my permission to behave however ill you please, so long as you make amends like this."

He preened in masculine pleasure, even as he feigned indignation. "*I* was ill-behaved?" he said, giving her bottom a playful slap. "I am not the one who stood in the center of the Ellertons' drawing room braying like a donkey, if I may remind you. Don't you know the countesses of Rockholme are renowned for their dignity and somber mien?"

"Then one may only suppose I will make a very poor countess of Rockholme," Cat returned smugly. "And if you have complaint, you've only yourself to blame. You would marry me."

He tightened his hold. "Yes," he said, his voice fierce. "I would marry you."

Cat gave a delicate yawn and snuggled closer. "How much longer do you think we will need to stay in London?"

Stephen did some quick calculations. "Another month, perhaps. Why? Tiring of the *ton* already?" He dropped a teasing kiss on the top of her head.

"I was weary of it after the first week," she confessed with a chuckle. "And besides, I am missing the children. Eddie will have grown a foot or more before I see him again."

The mention of Eddie brought to mind his conversation with Exter and Daintry, and for a moment he considered telling her what he had learned. But in the end he decided against it, not wanting to spoil the comfortable peace between them. And as Daintry had observed, telling her could only cause her undue alarm, and would accomplish nothing. He shuddered to think what she might do. She already loathed Sedgewood, and she would tear him to bloody pieces if she suspected he'd threatened her son.

"Perhaps we might go home for a few days, if you'd like," he suggested after a few moments. "We'll need to be back in time for the Duke of Monkhouse's ball, but I—"

"Oh, Stephen! May we?" Cat raised her head from his shoulder and was beaming down at him with such delight, he would gladly have given her anything she pleased.

He reached up, idly tucking back an ebony-colored curl. "If you're certain you can bring yourself to miss a ball or two," he said, smiling and ignoring the lump in his throat.

"As if I cared for such things!" She dismissed the notion with a shrug that had the tips of her breasts brushing against his chest. "When can we leave? Tomorrow?"

He gave an indulgent laugh. "No, goose, not so soon as that. Tomorrow night is the ball at the Aubervilles', and it would be very poor manners to miss a ball being held in your honor."

"The day after, then," she wheedled, moving so that she lay completely over him, their legs intimately tangled. "Please, Stephen, say that we may go!"

Despite the passion so recently spent, his body responded at once to the feel of hers. "It depends," he said, sliding his hands down her back to cup her buttocks.

If she noticed the hard male flesh stirring against her, Cat didn't say, although she did give a sexy wriggle that had the breath lodging in his throat. "Depends on what?" she asked, her voice a throaty whisper.

Stephen lifted her, thrusting deep inside her moist folds. "On how well you apologize," he said, grinning up at her pleased, if startled, expression. "Your turn, love." He began moving, sending them soaring back into paradise.

"Oh, my lady, how beautiful you are!" exclaimed the young maid who acted as Cat's abigail, gazing up at her in wide-eyed approval. "You look a picture, indeed you do!"

"Thank you, Alice," Cat returned, gazing at the mirror and scarce recognizing herself in the stunning woman she saw reflected there. She'd worn many beautiful gowns since coming to London, but even the most exquisite of them paled when compared to the glorious creation now adorning her. Lottie was right, she decided, fighting panic. The sophisticated gown was just the thing to show the Rockholme emeralds to their best advantage.

Fashioned from brilliant green silk, shot through with shimmering gold threads, the sheer gown with its daring décolletage clung to every curve of her body with what Cat considered an immodest degree. Tiny puffs of sheerest silk decorated with gold and green satin ribbons served as sleeves, and more ribbons decorated the scalloped hem and train. It was a gown such as a princess might wear, and Cat had a difficult time believing it belonged to her.

"Will you be wanting anything else, my lady?" Alice rose to her feet, shaking out the folds of her own sensible black gown.

"No, Alice, that will be fine, and thank you for all your help." Cat reached inside a drawer and extracted a coin, handing it to the stuttering maid. She remembered her days as a governess, when she'd sometimes been required to help the lady of the house prepare for some grand occasion. It may have been many years since then; but she never forgot the hours of back-breaking work arranging and rearranging the folds of fabric to a demanding employer's exact specifications, and she never failed to reward those who assisted her.

After Alice scurried out, Cat spent the next several minutes fussing with her gloves and waiting for Stephen to join her with the necklace. She'd seen it shortly after her arrival in London, and she tried not to panic at the thought of wearing a fortune about her neck. The thought of losing it terrified her, and she wondered if she could convince Stephen to leave the jewels tucked in the safe. Probably not, she concluded with a sigh. He'd already told her it was custom for the countess of Rockholme to wear them at her first presentation, and she was determined not to disappoint him by failing in her duty.

"Here you are, my dear." The door connecting her room to Stephen's opened, and he stepped inside, a large, flat box cradled in his hand. "My apologies for keeping you waiting; but Nethers couldn't find the key to the safe, and we were forever in tracking it down. I was afraid for a moment we would—" He came to a halt, staring at her as if at a ghost.

"My God, Cat," he said, his voice raw as he studied her. "You're beautiful."

The stunned expression on his face made her flush with pleasure. "Fine feathers, sir," she said, turning back to the glass. "The plainest woman alive would look a goddess in a gown so lovely as this."

He walked slowly toward her, his eyes burning with desire. "No," he said, setting down the boxed jewels. "It's you. You're the most beautiful woman I've ever seen."

Cat's heart fluttered at his words. Stephen was always complimenting her, sometimes playfully, sometimes with heartfelt admiration, but she couldn't recall another time when he'd spoken so fiercely, looking at her as if he couldn't believe his eyes.

"You *do* look like a goddess," he whispered, cupping her face in his hands. "I'm not letting you step a foot outside this house."

"You're not?" She was foolishly touched by his declaration.

"No." He dragged his thumb across her mouth in an intimate caress. "I'm keeping you locked up here, so only I may see you. You're mine, Cat, and I'll kill the first man who so much as looks at you." He ducked his head, his lips demanding as he kissed her with a formidable mixture of passion and possession.

Cat responded eagerly, the taste and feel of him intoxicating her. "Mmmm," she murmured, smiling languorously up at him. "Perhaps we might send our regrets after all. I'm sure the Aubervilles will understand."

Stephen gave a husky laugh. "Hussy," he accused, kissing her hand and taking a deliberate step back from her. "You know Lottie would have both our heads if we did such a thing. Now turn around, so that I can fasten this about you."

Dutifully she did as she was told, swallowing nervously at the sight of the jewels being placed about her throat. The deep green fire of the emeralds was offset by the brilliant white flash of diamonds and the soft gleam of purest gold linking them together. A single stone, shaped into a perfect teardrop, hung suspended just above her breasts, and while she watched, Stephen reached down to stroke the stone.

"It's said the first earl of Rockholme won these as spoils of war when fighting the Spaniards in the Lowlands," he said, his gaze holding hers in the cheval glass. "Since then they've passed from father to son, but looking at you now, I think it was always intended you should wear them."

Tears burned Cat's eyes, and she turned away from the glass before Stephen could see them. She knew she should acknowledge the lavish compliment, but for the life of her, she couldn't think of a single word to say. Instead she gathered up her shawl and fan, keeping her face composed as she and Stephen walked out of the room and down the sweeping staircase.

She'd recovered her sensibilities by the time they reached the coach, and she kept up a smooth flow of inconsequential chatter. Despite her hope they would be able to leave for the country the next day, they had too many pressing obligations they couldn't cancel on so short a notice. Next week looked far more promising, and they made detailed plans for the brief visit as they made the short journey to Brook Street.

Lottie was waiting for them, and the moment they had paid

their respects to the duke and duchess, she swooped down on them and carried Cat off for a private coze.

"Is Stephen still in a temper?" she demanded, her lips set in a sulky frown. "If he is, you must tell me, and I shall have David speak with him. I won't have him ruining your debut."

Cat hid a smile at her sister-in-law's fierce tones. "Stephen is in the best of humors," she assured her, giving her hand a reassuring squeeze. "Relax, Lottie, do, else you will set my own nerves to quaking."

"I'm sorry." Lottie made a face. "This is the first time I've stood as a sponsor to anyone, and I must own I am more than a little overwhelmed at the responsibility. Now, let me look," she said briskly, grabbing Cat's hand and holding her at arm's length as she ran a critical eye over her.

"Perfect," she announced, giving a pleased nod. "You look every inch the countess of Rockholme. Now come, dearest, it was time we were introducing you to the *ton*."

The rest of the evening passed in a whirl for Cat. Following a seemingly endless dinner, she stood by Stephen's side and was formally introduced to Society. She'd already met many of the people to whom she was making her bows, so it seemed somewhat superfluous to her; but for Stephen's sake she kept such thoughts to herself. Instead she maintained a polite demeanor, smiling and curtseying until she felt certain she would scream.

Once that was done, Stephen led her into the ballroom for their first official dance as husband and wife. When she felt his arms close about her, she relaxed with a relieved sigh.

"Thank heavens that is over," she said, gazing up at him wryly. "If I had to say 'I am pleased to meet you,' one more time, I vow I should have swooned. Are you certain we must put poor Beth through this? It seems so cruel."

"I am afraid so, my love," he replied, using his hold on her waist to pull her closer. "And as for Beth, you know full well she will love every minute of it. It's Lydia I am worried about. We'll have our work cut out convincing the chit not to bolt."

His casual reference to the future overset her as much as his earlier remark, and again, Cat was at a loss. When he spoke like this, it almost made her forget the true reasons behind their marriage. Worse, she admitted with a sigh, it made her *want* to forget, and that made her very, very afraid.

"Cat?" Stephen frowned down at her. "Is something wrong?"

She shook her head even as she cursed his acuity. "No," she lied. "I was but thinking about what you said, and I fear you are right. Lydia will take a great deal of convincing if we expect her to participate in the social round."

"We'll promise her a fine hunter," Stephen decided with a laugh. "That should keep her in line."

Following her waltz with Stephen, Cat danced next with her host, Lord Barton, and a succession of Stephen's friends. She was considering retreating to the dowager's bench to rest her poor feet when yet another hopeful gentleman bowed in front of her. Swallowing her disappointment, she was trying to put a name to his face when he suddenly spoke.

"My lady, I am certain you do not remember me; that is, I pray that you do not remember me. I am Viscount Lester."

Cat studied him closer. He did look familiar, now that he mentioned it, but she still couldn't place him. Then it came to her, and she stiffened perceptibly.

"Ah yes, Lord Lester," she said, her voice chilling by several degrees. "I recall you now."

The viscount's plump face grew even rosier, and he shuffled his feet like a disgraced schoolboy. "Thought you might," he said glumly, his gaze dropping to the floor. "Your lord placed me soon enough. I could tell by the way he was looking at me, like he was measuring me for my shroud."

Cat had a sudden memory of Stephen growing unexpectedly cold and distant, offering a curt nod to the stammering man bowing before them—the man she now recognized as Jeremey's confederate that last time he'd visited Larks Hall.

"I can't tell you, ma'am, how bitterly I regret my behavior that day," Lester continued, addressing his remarks to the tips of his dancing slippers. "Lord Rockholme was right; I was too foxed and too stupid to admit it at the time, but he was right. We disgraced our names and our families with our actions, and

I am most heartily sorry for it. I know the words may not mean anything, but I am sorry." He raised his eyes then, his gaze meeting hers with surprising directness. "Pray forgive me."

Cat gazed at the viscount in amazement, her opinion of him undergoing a rapid adjustment. Her impressions of him the day they had met were blurry, and colored, no doubt, by her intense dislike of Jeremey. She had a vague memory of him leaning against the doorway, his cravat and jacket in disarray, and a knowing sneer on his face. Had he been alone his behavior would certainly have been objectionable enough, but the fact he'd been with Jeremey compounded his sin. Or did it? Despite the fawning letter Jeremey had written, she found it impossible to imagine her husband's villainous cousin making so genuine an apology.

"It means something that you say them now, my lord," she said quietly. "And it speaks well of you that you obviously mean them." She held out a slender hand to him. "You may consider yourself forgiven, Lord Lester."

He accepted her hand with a touching awkwardness. "I also want you to know that I've severed any connection to Sedgewood and his crowd," he said, his words tripping over themselves in his rush to get them out. "So has Derwood. We've decided they ain't really the right sort. Not like Lord Rockholme. *He* is a true gentleman," he added, then flushed even brighter.

Cat hid a quick smile at the admiration obvious in the young viscount's voice. "Yes," she agreed, thinking he couldn't have chosen a better pattern card. "He is."

Lester cleared his throat and shuffled his feet for a few more seconds before dropping her hand and taking a hasty step back. "Thank you again, my lady, You're most gracious. I-I shan't forget this." With that he turned and fled, and when she turned her head to watch him go she saw the reason for his abrupt departure. Stephen was stalking toward her, his expression thunderous.

"What did that young puppy want?" he demanded, scowling as he glared after Lester. "Was he bothering you? Because if he was, by God I'll—"

"You may sheath your sword, my lord," she interrupted, amused at his fierce protectiveness. The 'puppy,' as you call him, meant no harm. He was but apologizing, and very prettily, too."

Stephen's savage expression softened, although it by no means disappeared. "Well, in that case, perhaps I shall let him live. But he'd best keep his distance, else I won't answer for my actions," he muttered, then glanced down at her, the remaining tension fading into playful sensuality.

"I've come for another waltz," he said, capturing her hand and carrying it to his lips for a teasing kiss.

She smiled back, enjoying the pleasant rush of pleasure to her senses. "And if I have promised it to another?" she murmured, her tone deliberately provocative.

"Then I claim a husband's prerogative," he replied, his fingers tightening about hers. "You waltz with no one, Cat, save me. Now come, a new set is forming."

Two days before they were to leave for their visit to the country, Stephen spent the afternoon paying an impromptu visit to Marcus Crayhew, another old friend from his salad days. His encounter with Daintry had made him realize how callously he'd treated his friends, and he was anxious to make amends. Marcus had been one of the wilder of his acquaintances, with a reputation as a rake that had nearly exceeded his own, and it was obvious he hadn't mended his ways in the intervening years.

"You caught me at what might be called an awkward moment, old fellow," he said, covering a yawn with a fist and looking smug. "I just got out of bed, and I wasn't alone. If the lady should make so bold as to join us, you are to go deaf and dumb."

"As our old Latin don," Stephen promised, amused at his friend's words. "Your visitor is a married lady, I take it?"

"A widow," Marcus corrected, blue eyes bright with laughter. "And a former visitor of yours as well, if memory serves."

The trickle of unease that had saved his life more than once had Stephen stiffening warily. "Lady Dewhurst?"

"The Divine Davinia, and might I say, she is as divine in the bed as she is out of it. You must have been mad, Rockholme, to have given her up without a fight."

Discussing his former mistress with her current lover struck Stephen as decidedly unsavory. "She wasn't a widow then," he muttered, wondering if he'd erred in attempting to renew his friendship with the other man. He liked Marcus well enough, but he'd forgotten how malicious the man could be.

"That is so," Marcus replied in his cheerful manner. "And the old fool who was her husband wasn't nearly so old a fool as to let himself be cuckolded by a dashing young blade like you."

"I wasn't her first lover," Stephen grumbled, wincing at the guilt pricking his conscience. Back then he'd been too intent on bedding Davinia to give her husband's feelings any consideration, but now he felt an odd empathy with the long-dead viscount, and sent a silent apology winging heavenward.

"True enough," Marcus agreed with a laugh. "Nor the only one to enjoy her favors while you were her lover. I remember a story about her bedding Wynebrook in the morning, you in the afternoon, and her husband later that same night! A woman of great fortitude, would you not say?"

Stephen all but shuddered at the memory. It was that very rumor, along with the news her husband was willing to risk the scandal of divorce if she continued flaunting her lovers, that had convinced him to end their liaison. He may not have been foolish enough to expect faithfulness from his mistress, but he had expected a certain degree of discretion. The fact Davinia had lain with a notorious whore chaser like Wynebrook offended his fastidious nature, and he'd never touched her again.

The rattle of the door handle heralded Davinia's arrival, and she glided into Marcus's parlor as casually as if she was walking into her own drawing room at home.

"Ah, Stephen," she purred, her dark blue eyes moving daringly over him as she walked toward him with sinuous grace. "When I learned Marcus had a morning visitor, I was all prepared to slip quietly away, but when I was told it was you, I just had to come down and bid you good morning. I knew Marcus wouldn't mind, would you, love?" She slid the dark-haired man a knowing smile.

"It's nothing to do with me," Marcus said, shrugging as he poured out more brandy. "But if you're trying to catch his interest again, my dear, I fear you are wasting your time. I've seen his countess." He gave a dramatic sigh, clutching one hand to his heart in a manner that earned him glares from both Stephen and Davinia.

Davinia was first to recover, hiding her anger with a pretty pout. "Really, Marcus, you had best take care, else Stephen will call you to accounts," she warned, giving his arm a light slap. "He is said to be unfashionably protective of his pretty wife."

From the daggers she was casting him and the pointed words, Stephen knew she was alluding to the ruthless way he'd squashed any talk linking Cat to Exter's long-ago house party. He supposed she thought she was being clever, and wondered what she'd say if he told her she was being pathetically obvious.

"Yes," he said, meeting her challenging gaze with cold hauteur. "I am protective of my wife. I cherish her, and a man always guards fiercest the things he values most."

Stephen could tell by her expression that she'd missed the insult implicit in his words—the insinuation her late husband hadn't valued her at all, else he'd have had a better care of her. But Marcus was more discerning, and he gave a loud bark of laughter.

"Come, Stephen, you mustn't make impossible demands," he teased, casting Davinia an indulgent look. "It's enough our Davinia is a beauty without equal. You can't expect her to think as well; it is too unreasonable of you."

Davinia's pout grew more pronounced. "What is that supposed to mean?" she demanded truculently.

"Nothing, my dear, nothing at all." Marcus gave her cheek a pat. "Now, how about something to eat? I don't know about you, but I am famished. What say you, Stephen? Care to join us?"

Stephen looked at his one-time friend and former mistress

and felt his skin crawl. How could he ever have desired the one, and admired the other? he wondered, with a mental shake of his head. Gad, he must have been a bigger fool than he'd realized.

"I fear I must decline," he said, rising quickly to his feet. "Marcus, it was good seeing you. I hope we may encounter each other again before I retire to my country seat."

Marcus stared at Stephen a long moment, and then a bitter smile of understanding settled on his mouth. "As you wish," he said, inclining his head with an odd formality. "Good-bye then, Lord Rockholme. I wish you every happiness."

"And I you," Stephen responded, acknowledging it was unlikely he'd see the other man again, except briefly. He glanced next at Davinia, who was watching him with narrow-eyed intent.

"Good day, my lady," he said, good breeding preventing him from letting his distaste show. "I'm sure we shall see each other again."

Davinia's pout dissolved into a smile rife with the promise of revenge. "Oh, I'm sure we shall, my lord," she told him sweetly. "I'm sure we shall."

Stephen gave her a sharp look, refusing to respond to the scarcely veiled threat. Let her do her worst, he thought coldly, walking toward the door. They would see who triumphed in the end.

He was standing in the entry hall waiting for the butler to return with his hat and gloves when the door to the back hall flew open, and his own butler came rushing forward to meet him.

"My lord, thank heaven I have found you!" he exclaimed, wringing his hands in obvious distress. "You must return to the house at once! The most dreadful thing has occurred!"

For one agonizing moment Stephen felt his heart stop. "Cat." He whispered the word in terror, his own hands trembling as he grabbed the older man by the lapels. "What is it?" he demanded, fighting down the sick panic clawing at him. "Has something happened to my wife?

The butler shook his head with surprising vigor. "No, my lord," he said quickly. "It is her son, Lord Brockton. Your brother has sent word the child has taken gravely ill, and it is feared he won't last the night." Tears shone diamond-bright in his eyes as he added, "He is dying, my lord."

Fourteen

"I don't see why you insist upon returning to the country now," Lottie complained, pouting as Cat directed the last of the packing. "There's less than a month remaining before the Season ends. Can't you wait until then?"

"I want to see my children," Cat returned serenely, accustomed now to Lottie's pouts and complaints. "And we will be gone but four or five days. Should I bring Beth back with me, do you think? She'd love seeing London."

"How old did you say she is?" Lottie frowned in consideration.

"Seventeen, but soon to be eighteen." Cat smiled, thinking of how eagerly Beth was looking forward to the birthday that would put her childhood behind her.

"Leave her in the country," Lottie said after a moment. "A chit that age can't go out, at least not officially, and you'll be too busy to give her proper escort. But by all means bring her to town for the Petite Season. It will give her the chance to develop some polish before the start of the next Season."

Cat had already decided to do just that, but she knew it soothed Lottie's feelings to think she was in command. In all her days she'd never met a more determined tyrant, except, perhaps, the tyrant's own brother. He, the Lord knew, had no equal when it came to playing the despot.

The last of the portmanteaus was packed before Cat gave in to Lottie's entreaties and went downstairs to take tea. They had no sooner settled in the parlor when the butler entered, bowing in apology as he offered her a sealed note.

"A messenger from his lordship's estate has just arrived with this, my lady, and asks that you read it at once," he said, his formal manner forgotten. "He says it is an emergency."

"An emergency!" Cat almost knocked the tea cart over as she leapt to her feet, snatching the note from his hands. The children! Dear God, had something befallen the children? It was all she could think, and her fingers were shaking so badly she had to fumble to break the wax circlet sealing the letter. She spread the piece of paper open, and the hastily scrawled words she saw wrenched a cry of agony from her.

"Cat, dearest, what is it? What's wrong?" Lottie was at her side at once, draping a supportive arm about her waist.

"Eddie!" Cat forced the word out, trembling with shock and terror. "He's ill. I must go to him at once!"

"Of course you must!" Lottie said, ever practical. "But first you must wait for Stephen to return. He should be at his club this time of day. We can send a footman with a—"

"No!" Cat shook her head, panic clawing at her. She thought she'd known terror before, when Jeremey had forced his way into her room, or when Stephen had some storming back into her life, demanding a truth she dared not give. But overwhelming as that had been, it paled when compared to the weight and power of what she felt now. She closed her hand, crumbling the note, as if by destroying the words she could destroy the reality they conveyed.

> *"Edward has contracted fever. It is dangerously high, and can not be broken. The doctor fears the worst. Come at once."*
>
> *James*

"I must go," she said, stumbling forward on legs that threatened to fold beneath her. Her mind was racing like a mad thing, and she could think only of flight. She had to get to Eddie, to her son.

"Did the messenger come by horse or by carriage?" she asked, trying to think in a rational manner.

"Horse, my lady," the butler answered at once. "He rode straight through the night to get here."

Yes, a single horse could make a quicker journey of it, she thought with a distant calm. She considered calling for her own mount to be saddled and brought around, but common sense stilled her urgency. She'd never been a horsewoman, and knew a reckless ride could easily end in her being injured, if not killed.

"Have the carriage readied," she ordered. "I wish to leave at once."

The butler and Lady Barton exchanged shocked looks. "Without Stephen?" Lottie asked, a note of disbelief in her voice. "I know you're anxious to see your son, and I don't blame you, but you must be sensible. You can not set out for Rockholme alone."

Cat whirled around to face her sister-in-law. "I won't wait!" she said fiercely, tears burning her eyes. "Eddie is my son. *My son!* And I won't be kept from him by anyone!"

Lottie gave her a thoughtful look, then nodded at the anxious butler, who was hovering near the door and wringing his hands.

"Bring the carriage," she said coolly. "And have the maid bring her ladyship's cloak and portmanteau down."

"Yes, my lady." The butler bobbed a hasty bow and was gone, closing the door behind him. The moment they were alone, Lottie turned back to Cat, her expression surprisingly stern.

"Cat." For the first time since meeting her, Lottie used Stephen's diminutive form of her name. "I know you love your son, but what you are forgetting is that Stephen loves him as well. Eddie is his son, and if he is desperately ill, Stephen has the right to be with him. You can not deny him that."

Cat paled as Lottie's words struck home. She was right, Cat realized miserably. Stephen did love Eddie, that was the one thing she'd never doubted. But it didn't matter, couldn't matter. She wanted to see her son *now,* and she wouldn't wait if the king himself asked it of her.

"I'm denying Stephen nothing," she said, keeping her voice deliberately calm. "He can follow in his own carriage if he wishes, but I'm not waiting. I can not."

Lottie gave her another long look and then sighed. "All right, if that's what you wish, then by all means leave at once. But I can tell you this much," she added with a warning frown. "Stephen won't like your setting out without him."

Cat imagined her husband's possible reaction, and gave a soft laugh. "He'll be utterly furious, you mean. Well, let him be, then. I'm going to my son."

It took an agonizing hour to fight through the thick knot of traffic clogging the teeming streets of London, and it was all Cat could do to keep her impatience in check. She kept seeing Eddie lying pale and still, the unhealthy flush of fever on his cheeks still rounded with babyhood. Was he in pain? she fretted, twisting the strings of her reticule about her fingers. Did he pout and ask for her? Did he call for his mama, and wonder why she didn't come? Tears filled her eyes at the thought, and she blinked them back. She couldn't lose her son, she thought desolately. She would die if anything happened to Eddie.

Three hours after leaving London they reached an inn just outside of Chiddingstone. It was the same inn where she and Stephen had broken their journey on the trip to London. She knew there were fresh horses to be had, and she waited anxiously while the ostlers brought them out.

"Are you certain you won't stop for a rest, my lady?" Alice asked, eyeing her diffidently. "At least for a cup of tea?"

Cat started to say no, not wanting to delay her departure for as much as a second, but then she noticed the way Alice was shifting from one foot to the other, and changed her mind.

"I suppose a cup of tea wouldn't go amiss," she said, forcing herself to be patient. "And I am sure you and John Coachman must be thirsty as well. A quarter hour, then. No more."

Alice didn't waste time in thanks, but dashed immediately into the half-timbered building. Cat followed more leisurely and was greeted by the fawning innkeeper and led to a private parlor. After receiving assurances her maid and coachman would be fed, she forced herself to consume some of the tea and cakes the innkeeper had personally fetched for her. She wasn't hungry, but since she didn't plan on stopping again, she knew she'd best eat while she could. She'd do Eddie no good if she arrived half-dead from hunger.

She was hurriedly sipping her tea when the door to the private parlor was flung open, and Stephen came striding into the room. It took but one look at his hard face to discern he was in a dangerous temper.

"I might have preferred, madam wife, that you had the courtesy to wait for me," he ground out, tearing off his hat and sending it sailing

Cat said nothing. She'd known even before setting out from London that her actions would infuriate her husband, and while part of her acknowledged he had every right to his anger, the other part of her stirred in incipient rebellion.

"I was too worried to wait," she said, and then calmly poured out a cup of tea for him.

Judging by the anger glittering in his eyes, she half expected him to knock the cup from her hand. Instead he gave her a thoughtful look, some of the tension leaving his face as he joined her on the settee.

"Next time you will wait for me," he muttered, taking a thirsty sip of tea.

Would there be a next time? Cat wondered, then devoutly prayed there would not be. She didn't think her poor nerves could withstand a second such shock.

Soon they were back in the narrow confines of the travelling coach, racing southward toward Stephen's country house. With Alice in the carriage with them, there was little chance for private conversation, and in any case, Cat was in no mood for idle chatter. She kept thinking of the letter James had sent, and the more she thought of it, the more distraught she became.

James's letter, like the man himself, had been brief to the point of terseness, giving little in the way of details, and she felt she would go mad if she didn't know the whole of it. He wrote that Eddie had a fever, but what sort of fever was it? Was it some childish malady, easily overcome, or was it something more sinister? A fever that couldn't be broken was a dangerous thing; as the daughter of a physician she knew that. It drained the body of strength, leaving the sufferer vulnerable to other diseases. Her own mother had died of such a fever, and she remembered her father's anguish as he fought to save her.

Beside her, Stephen seemed to sense her distress. He reached out and took her hand in his. "Don't look so worried, Cat," he soothed, raising her hand to his lips. "Eddie is as strong as a young horse. He'll be fine, you'll see."

Because she desperately wished to believe him, Cat let herself be reassured. "I know," she said, accepting the comfort of his touch. "It's just he's so small, and he gets so terribly cross when he is not well."

Stephen smiled ruefully. "Then he is like me in that respect. I've always hated being ill, and I fear I wasn't the best of patients. I recall the time I was ten and broke my arm falling from my horse. . . ."

He spent the remainder of the journey regaling her with various exploits of his youth, and gently stroking her hair and arm. He even coaxed her into revealing a few of her own youthful misdeeds, chuckling at one particular episode.

"So you drowned the parson's wig in the punch, did you?" he teased, slipping a finger under her chin and tilting her face up to his. "I should like to have seen that."

"No, you wouldn't have." Cat smiled, recalling the chaotic scene that had followed. "Papa pretended to be outraged, but when we arrived home he patted me on the head and told me he was proud of me. And whatever you do, don't you repeat a word of this to Lydia! She is imp enough as it is."

"She is only high-spirited," Stephen said indulgently, defending the young girl with obvious fondness. "Now, tell me more of your childhood. I wish to know all."

Cat did as he requested, understanding he was distracting her to keep her from worrying overly much. And she had to admit talking helped wile away the hours and the miles separating her from her son. They stopped for another change of horses and for the bit of dinner Stephen insisted she take, and then set out again, reaching Rockholme Manor long after darkness had fallen. The carriage scarce had time to stop before Cat was leaping out, stumbling on the loose stones. She started forward, only to come to a halt at the sight of a house that seemed ablaze with lights.

"Something's wrong!" she cried, reaching blindly for Stephen. "Look at the house! Every window is lit!"

"It's all right, my love," Stephen said, stepping closer to wrap a comforting arm about her. "I sent a messenger ahead to let them know we were coming, that's all. The lights are for us."

Cat drew in a ragged breath, fighting to control her errant emotions. On the endless journey from London her one thought had been to get to her son as quickly as she could, but now that she was here, she was afraid to cross the threshold. So long as she remained outside she could pretend Eddie was fine; sick, yes, but *alive.* Once she went inside, there would be no avoiding the truth, no matter how horrifying that truth might be.

As if sensing her fear and the reasoning behind it, Stephen gave her a gentle nudge. "Come, my darling," he said, his voice gentle but firm, "let us go inside. It's time to see our son."

When Stephen and Cat entered the house, they found a scene of surprising domestic tranquility. James and the girls were waiting in the parlor in front of a cheerfully blazing fire, and when Cat burst in, they all glanced up in mild surprise.

"You've made good time, I must say." James smiled as he rose to his feet. "I wasn't expecting you for several hours yet."

"Eddie! How is Eddie?" Cat demanded, her eyes frantic as she sought out her daughters' gazes. "Where is he? Is he all right? I want to see him at once!"

The girls leapt to their feet and rushed forward, only to come skittering to a halt at a mild glance from James. Satisfied, he glanced back at Cat and took her hand in his. "He's fine, my lady," he said, his smile as gentle as his voice. "The fever broke early this afternoon, and he's sitting up in bed demanding the most disgusting selection of food. Nurse and Miss Blakely are with him now." He paused delicately, then added, "He has been asking for you."

Cat needed no further urging. She gave her daughters a quick smile and then turned and ran from the room as quickly as she could. Stephen made to follow, only to stop when James laid a restraining hand on his arm.

"Your daughters are in need of you," he said quietly, his voice pitched for Stephen's ears only. "When you have finished reassuring them, I need to speak with you as well. I will be in the study."

After he'd gone, Stephen spent the next quarter hour holding the girls and soothing their worry over their beloved baby brother. As he expected Beth was tearful, clinging to his hand and sobbing out her fears. Lydia was equally upset, her eyes wet with tears as she gazed up at him with touching faith.

"Uncle James and Miss Blakely said he would be fine," she said, rubbing at her nose with the back of her hand. "Will he? Will he truly, Papa?"

Stephen swallowed, an uncomfortable lump in his throat at the expression on her face. "I can not be completely certain until I have seen him," he told her, his voice somewhat gruff. "But I do know James would never lie about such a thing. If he says Edward has recovered from whatever ails him, then he has."

Lydia laid her head on his shoulder and sniffed again. "All right," she said in her truculent manner. "And I promise not to be cross with him ever again, no matter how much he plagues me."

Stephen had to chuckle at that. "Yes, you will, little one," he murmured, brushing a kiss across her forehead. "And plague you, he will. That is how it is between brothers and sisters."

Lydia considered that for a moment. "Then I promise to *try* not to become cross," she said, and snuggled closer. "I am glad you came home, Papa."

Now it was Stephen who found himself near to tears. "So am I, poppet," he said, giving her a gentle hug. "So am I."

When he was certain the girls were all right, Stephen went out into the hall. The grand staircase was to his right, and he cast it a longing glance. He wanted more than anything to go up to his wife and son, but he accepted he would have to wait. James's manner had been more than grim when he'd asked him to join him in the study. There had been an underlying hardness in his demeanor, and a cold, deadly fury Stephen had never seen before. James had always been hard-headed and hard-hearted, but he'd never been *hard.* Something was seriously amiss, and struggling to hide his impatience, he walked back to the study to learn what that something was.

James was standing in front of the fire, a snifter of brandy cradled in his hand, when Stephen walked into the room. After making sure the door was securely closed behind him, Stephen crossed the room to join his brother.

"Very well, I am here," he said, meeting James's hooded gaze. "What is it? What could you not tell me in front of the others?"

To his relief, James wasted no time with idle talk. "I have every reason to believe Eddie has been poisoned."

"What?" All the blood drained from Stephen's face.

"Your son was poisoned."

For a moment Stephen's mind froze. He could only stare at James, horror and rage clawing at him. Later he would take his revenge, for now he wanted only the truth.

"How can you be certain?" he asked, forcing himself to think with the calm that always served him so well in battle.

"He was fine that morning, bright, cheerful as a puppy," James began, his strained tone making it plain the memory hurt him. "He gave his maid the slip, and when she found him less than half an hour later, he was lying in the garden, sick near to death. A piece of cake lay beside him, a cake the cook insists did not come from our kitchen."

Rage flared, but Stephen fought it down, determined to be logical. He must know all before taking any sort of action. "Perhaps one of our tenants gave it to him," he said carefully.

James shook his head. "I asked. No one had seen the lad that morning."

"Could it have been an accident?" Stephen asked, his tone unnaturally calm. "Perhaps the cake had spoiled."

Again, James shook his head. "He was too ill, too quickly. Nurse says it takes time for spoiled food to make one so sick. It was she who first suggested the possibility of poison."

"Does she know what kind of poison was used?"

"She suspects oleander, although there is no way we can ever be certain," James replied tersely, and then hurled his snifter against thc bricks. "My God!" he said, his jaw clenching as fury darkened his eyes. "What sort of monster would poison a child?"

Stephen didn't have to think twice before answering. "Sedgewood," he said, balling his hand into a fist. "It was that bastard Sedgewood. And it is all my fault."

James raised a dark eyebrow. "Sedgewood?" he repeated, then nodded. "Yes, I suspected he might be involved. But I'd like to know why you think any of this might be your doing."

In a rush Stephen told him of the plan concocted by Exter, Daintry, and himself. "At the time I thought we were spiking his guns," he said, thrusting his hand through his hair and glaring down into the flames. "Now I realize that instead we forced his hand. The moneylenders might have considered helping him when they thought he had more than a passing chance of inheriting, but when they learned differently . . ." He gave a helpless shrug.

"What will you do?" James eyed him thoughtfully.

"I'd like to see him dangling from the gibbet," Stephen said savagely. "Or better still, skewered at the end of my sword, but without proof that may be difficult to accomplish."

"Do you mean you intend letting him get away unscathed?" James demanded, glaring at him incredulously.

"I said difficult, not impossible," Stephen corrected, his tone deceivingly gentle.

"Then what will you do? You intend doing something, I trust?" James added, with scarcely veiled sarcasm.

Stephen gave a weary sigh. He was exhausted, worried, and worn near to a frazzle, and the last thing he felt like doing was submitting to a dressing down by his younger brother. Unfortunately, he didn't think he had a choice. Were the circumstances reversed, he'd be making the same demand of James.

"He won't escape unscathed," he said heavily, shooting James a resentful look. "I have plans already in motion that if successful, will leave Sedgewood no other alternative but to flee the country. And you may be assured I intend letting him know that if anything should befall Eddie again, I will kill him."

"A threat I seem to have heard before," James muttered, looking far from pleased.

"And a threat I mean with every fiber of my being," Stephen returned, not caring to have his honor questioned. "Leave it, James. It is my family and my problem, and I will handle it as I see fit."

James's cheeks flushed with anger and hurt, and he drew himself up haughtily. "As you wish, my lord," he said, bowing coldly to Stephen. "See to your *problem*. But understand this; it is my family as well, and I will do what I must to see it safe." He stormed out of the room, slamming the door behind him.

Stephen watched him go, pride and irritation making him smile. It would seem his youngest brother had grown into quite a man, he decided. The knowledge was the one bright spot in what had been a hellish day.

"And I puked all over Uncle James's shoes, Papa," Eddie told Stephen, his childish voice piping with delight. "Twice."

"Did you, now? He must have found that a trifle disconcerting," Stephen said, gazing down at his son and taking in his delicately flushed cheeks and dancing bright eyes with a relief so profound it left him near to tears.

Eddie frowned, clearly confused at the unfamiliar word; then in the manner of children, he rushed gleefully on to finish his tale. "And the doctor came, and he had *leeches*. Nurse said he was going to put them on me, only Uncle James said he would shoot him if he did. I don't like leeches, Papa." This last statement was confided with an anxious look.

Stephen thought of his son enduring the horror of being bled, and felt his own stomach heave. "Neither do I," he said, his hand shaking as he laid it on the lad's head. "And you needn't ever worry about them again, I promise you." He meant it, too, he thought grimly. First thing tomorrow he'd seek out the physician and make it painfully clear what would happen if he ever dared attempt to bleed any of his children, or indeed, any of the children of his tenants, ever again.

The reassurance seemed to calm Eddie, and he continued prattling on, clearly regarding his illness as some grand sort of adventure. Stephen was heartily glad for that. He didn't think he'd ever want him to know how ill he had truly been.

Poisoned. The very word filled him with a black rage. Sedgewood had to be in worse shape than he thought to have attempted such a thing. On the one hand it rendered him vulnerable and therefore easily managed, but on the other hand it made him desperate. And desperate men, as Stephen had learned to his cost, were dangerously unpredictable.

Eddie was finally running out of words when Cat entered the room, a tray balanced in her hands. The sight of Stephen sitting at their son's bedside and holding his hand brought her to a halt, an expression Stephen couldn't name flickering across her face. It was gone so quickly he wondered if he might have imagined it, and then she was striding toward them, a frown of motherly displeasure drawing her brows together.

"I thought I told you to rest, Edward," she said, setting the tray on the table. "And you"—she flicked a glare at Stephen—"were supposed to be bathing."

"Papa came to see me, Mama," Eddie replied, assuming his most angelic mien. "I missed him."

"And I missed our son," Stephen replied, also doing his best to appear innocent.

Cat glowered at them for several seconds before giving a soft laugh. "Connivers, the pair of you," she said, ruefully shaking her head. "I don't know why I bother. Now, Eddie, Nurse has made you this special tea, and you are to drink every drop of it."

Eddie pulled an automatic face. "I don't like it."

"You haven't tasted it." Cat sat on the bed and held the cup to his lips. "Here you go, love. Sip carefully."

Eddie took a cautious sip; then his eyes widened in delight. "It's good!"

"Of course it's good, you wretch!" Cat replied with another laugh. "Did you think I was giving you hemlock? Now drink."

The mention of hemlock made Stephen grimace, and he glumly accepted he would have to tell her of his and James's suspicions. He thought of her likely response, and decided he'd rather face a brace of French cannon. At least with the cannon he stood some chance of surviving, he mused. He doubted his outraged wife would be as merciful once she knew the truth.

They lingered at Eddie's bedside, holding hands and watching until he fell into an easy sleep.

"How well he looks," Cat said softly, running a loving hand over the boy's soft curls. "Seeing him like this, it is hard to credit he was so ill but a few hours ago."

"I know," Stephen agreed, his own gaze feasting greedily upon his sleeping son. "But I have heard that is often the way it is with children."

Cat's mouth curved in a smile. "Yes, it is. I remember when one of the local children contracted the flux. He was terribly ill for two days, and when I went to visit him on the third day, it was to find him scampering about the cottage and terrorizing his sisters. Oh, Stephen," her voice broke, and she turned to bury her face against his shoulder, "I've never been so frightened in my entire life!"

Stephen slipped his arms about Cat and held her close. I know, my love, I know," he said gently. "I was scared, too."

They continued holding each other, taking strength and solace from their nearness. Finally Cat drew back, her beautiful green eyes bright with tears as she laid her hand on his cheek.

"I'm sorry I didn't wait for you," she said. "I know I should have, but I couldn't."

"I understand," he replied, bending to brush a quick kiss across her lips. "I don't like it, mind, but I understand."

When they were certain Eddie was safely asleep, they went arm in arm back to their rooms. Per his instructions a small table, laden with food, was set before the fire, and he gently bullied her into eating some of the meat and other delicacies. He also insisted she drink some of the warmed brandy, and she gave him a suspicious look over the rim of her glass.

"Are you by chance attempting to get me foxed?" she asked, her nose wrinkling at the strong bite of the fiery spirits.

"Why would I do that?" he asked, holding the brandy to her lips as she had held the cup of tea to their son's lips earlier. "Here, love, just another sip. There you are."

She gave a surprisingly girlish giggle, then promptly choked on the brandy he'd just tipped into her mouth. Stephen dutifully patted her on the back until she waved him off.

"Really, Stephen, are you trying to kill me?" she scolded, then spoiled the effect by giving another giggle. "You sounded just like a papa. If that is how I sounded to Eddie, I am amazed he finished his tea."

Stephen decided it was prudent not to mention that that was precisely how she sounded. Then he frowned as a sudden thought struck him. "What was in that tea, if I may ask? I know I distinctly smelled mint."

"To ease his stomach," Cat said, nodding. "And there were several other herbs as well. Nurse is well-skilled in their use, so you needn't fear she would inadvertently poison our son."

Her use of the word 'poison' made Stephen wince, and he knew he couldn't have asked for a better opening. He reached out and plucked the snifter from her fingers, his gaze holding hers as he covered her hand with his own.

"Cat," he said, his voice carefully even. "I want you to listen to me. There is something I need to tell you . . ."

Fifteen

"That monster!" Cat fumed, stalking up and down the length of the sitting room. "That hateful, loathsome, despicable monster! I am going to kill him!"

"Now, Cat—"

"Don't you 'Now, Cat' me, you beast!" Cat whirled around to face Stephen, green eyes flashing with outrage. "How dare you keep something like this from me! I am Eddie's mother; I had a right to know Jeremey threatened him! Why didn't you tell me what he had said? Didn't you think I would care?"

"Of course I knew you would care," Stephen replied, his soothing tone belied by the unmistakable laughter gleaming in his eyes. "I realize I should have told you at once, but I didn't want to upset you."

For a moment Cat was so furious, she fully expected to burst into a ball of flames. "Upset me?" she repeated in a strangled tone. "You didn't want to upset me? Well, I have news for you, your lordship; I am a great deal more than *upset*."

"Yes." Stephen's tone was wry. "I can tell."

"And don't laugh at me, either!" she snapped, her sense of indignation increasing at his obvious amusement. "My son almost dying is not a matter for jest!"

The expression of humor vanished from Stephen's face. "No," he agreed somberly. "It is not."

"Then why were you smiling?"

He was quiet a long moment before answering. "Because you are so fierce, my love," he said, his tone suspiciously light.

"And because I am glad that for once, that fury is directed at someone other than myself."

Cat wasn't certain she believed his smooth answer, but with so much on her mind, she didn't have time to dwell on it. "Well," she grumbled, crossing the room to stand in front of him, "what do you intend doing about this? You are going to do something, aren't you?" she added, when he remained silent.

He gave her another of those enigmatic looks. "James asked me much the same thing," he said, his voice growing cool, "and I will tell you what I told him; I am going to destroy Sedgewood. Plans are afoot that will insure he hasn't a friend left in the world, no place to turn to for money or support. Then when I have him grovelling in the dust, I will crush him. There, my fiery valkyrie, does that satisfy your blood lust?"

"No," she said decisively. "I want him dead as well."

"So do I."

The hard edge of fury she detected in his voice stilled most of her resentment, although she was still annoyed. "I wish you'd told me," she complained, joining him on the settee. "I would have come home at once if I'd known."

"I know," he said, slipping an arm about her shoulder and drawing her against him, "and mayhap that is why I didn't tell you. I am sorry, Cat."

She let herself be cuddled, accepting his touch for the apology she knew it to be. "We seem to spend a great deal of time apologizing to one another, don't we?" she mused, tilting her head back to send him a rueful smile.

He smiled in return, the distant look fading from his eyes. "So it would appear," he agreed softly. "Fortunately we also spend an equal amount of time forgiving one another. I *am* forgiven, aren't I?"

"I suppose," she said, unable to resist the urge to pout. "But really, Stephen, I am vexed with you. If you ever again hear such a thing, you must promise you'll tell me at once. I don't like it when you hide things from me."

"Agreed." He dipped his head and deposited a searing kiss on her mouth. "So long as you return the favor. I also dislike it when you keep things from me."

Cat winced inwardly, wondering if he was referring to Eddie, and the circumstances surrounding his conception and birth. When she'd first agreed to his demands for marriage, she had steeled herself to endure his scorn, but to her amazement he couldn't have been kinder. He'd never once taunted her about how cruelly she had used and deceived him, and he treated her with unfailing courtesy and respect.

It also made her think of the babe she suspected she might be carrying. It was too early to be certain, and yet she knew. Just as she had known she carried Eddie even before Nurse had confirmed it for her. She rested her hand on her stomach, a womanly smile softening her mouth. A few more weeks, she decided. If her flow did not come by then, she would share her hopes with Stephen. She didn't want to disappoint him.

They sat in contented silence for several minutes before Stephen glanced down at her. "Do you wish me to ring for hot water that you might bathe, or would you prefer retiring?" he asked, rubbing the back of her neck with a gentle hand. "It has been an eventful day."

The thought of bathing in front of the flickering fire was wonderfully appealing. "Mmmm, a bath sounds lovely."

He set her aside and rang for the maid. Soon a large copper tub was brought up, and while Alice helped her undress, other maids bustled in and out of the room, carrying container after container of steaming water. A short time later Cat was lounging in the fragrant water, eyes closed as the last of her cares soaked away. She was drifting contentedly when the brush of lips across her bare shoulder had her jolting awake.

"Stephen!" She sat up with a loud splash. "What are you doing in here?"

A wicked grin set his dark eyes to dancing. "I should think that obvious, my sweet. I am come to act as your lady's maid."

A rosy flush colored Cat's cheeks. "What about Alice?"

Stephen's hands slid down to cup her breasts. "She may get her own maid," he said, and playfully pinched her nipple.

The rest of the evening passed in a sensual haze as Stephen made love to her with tender hunger. He drove her wild with his touch, his soapy fingers sliding over her and teasing her into an almost unbearable state of arousal. He twice brought her to completion before lifting her out of the tub, laying her down in front of the fire and burying himself in her honeyed depths. Afterward he carefully dried her, and then carried her to the bed for another round of pleasure.

They were up early the next morning, and her eyes scarce had time to open before he was pulling her over him, thrusting into her with audacious demand. Later they went to visit their son, who was recovered enough to be a trial to both his nursemaid and Miss Blakely. Since the governess was beginning to look decidedly the worse for wear, Cat ordered her to spend the rest of the day recovering, and then settled down to reacquaint herself with her child.

That day set the tone for the days that were to follow, as Cat divided her time between Eddie and the girls, as well as seeing to her duties to the estate. It was the end of summer, and with harvest rapidly approaching, there was much to keep her occupied. On her third day home she was on her way to the kitchen to discuss a harvest ball for the tenants with the cook, when she heard what sounded like a child crying. Confused, she looked around and saw James walking toward her, a wriggling piglet tucked under his arm.

"Hello, James," she said, coming to a halt and smiling at him. "What is that you have there?"

James held up the loudly squealing piglet for her inspection. "A runt," he replied, giving the indignant animal's head a fond pat. "His brothers and sisters won't let him feed, and so I brought him to the house for milk and sops. I believe I shall call him Prinny," he added, looking up with a boyish grin. "He does look like our dear prince, doesn't he?"

Cat, who'd had the dubious honor of making the Prince Regent's acquaintance, gave the piglet a thoughtful look. "Indeed he does!" she agreed, then reached out to take the animal from him. "Don't let Eddie or the girls see him, else they will want to make a pet of him," she warned, ever the mother. "He is adorable now, but I doubt he will remain so."

"No." He retrieved the piglet and tucked it back under his arm with easy confidence. "When I was a lad I rescued a lamb from the slaughter and hid him in my room for almost a month. Lambs, I might add, grow to quarrelsome sheep appallingly fast."

Cat laughed, and then abruptly sobered as she realized she'd yet to thank him properly for all that he had done for her and her family. "James, I was wondering if I might have a word with you," she said, steeling herself to do what was right.

"All right," he said after a brief pause. "Just give me another ten minutes to take care of Prinny, and I will meet you in the library."

It was closer to twenty minutes before James finally arrived, an apologetic expression on his face. "Forgive me for keeping you waiting," he said, settling on one of the chairs. "But Mrs. Mallon was ringing a peal over my head for daring to bring livestock into her kitchen."

The notion of the short, plump cook tearing a strip off her formidable brother-in-law made Cat grin. "You seem to have survived," she drawled, teasing him for the first time.

"So did Prinny, although in his case it was a very near thing. Mrs. Mallon took one look at him and decided to put suckling pig on the menu. It took a great deal of persuading on my part to convince her otherwise. With any luck, he will survive for the fall butchering."

Cat had spent too many years in the country to be distressed by the wry observation. "That is good," she said, and then got down to the reason she had sought this meeting.

"We've not had much of an opportunity to speak, but I wanted to thank you for the excellent care you have taken of Eddie and the girls," she said, meeting his watchful gaze with quiet dignity. "I appreciate all you have done."

"Do you?" he asked, his lips twisting in a bitter smile. "Then you are too charitable by half, my lady. For my part, I consider that I've done a damn poor job of things."

"But why?" She gaped at him in honest bewilderment. "Eddie might have died if it hadn't been for you!"

"And he might never have been poisoned if I'd kept better watch over him," James said, sounding startlingly like his elder brother. "I knew how damned slippery the lad could be, and I did nothing to stop him. If he'd died . . ." He broke off, unable to continue. Cat saw the misery in his eyes, and rose from her chair to hurry to his side.

"But he didn't die," she said softly, laying a comforting hand on his arm as she knelt beside him. "As for keeping watch on Eddie, you forget I am his mother. Who better than I would know how inventive the imp can be when it comes to evading his nursemaids?"

"But if I'd been with him instead of in the fields—"

"The outcome would have been the same," she interrupted, her tone gentle. "Your being there would have made no difference whatsoever; any more than my being home would have prevented what happened." She paused delicately and then added, "Unless you are saying it is my fault for neglecting my children, that is."

As she expected his head jerked up, a look of horror on his face. "Cat! I should never even think such a thing!" he denied, clearly scandalized. "How can you say so?"

"And how can you say you are to blame for another's villainy?" Cat re-posed in a stern voice. "If Eddie was poisoned, it was due to that snake Jeremey Sedgewood. Hate him if you must, but not yourself. I won't allow it."

A slow smile touched his lips at her stout declaration. "You won't allow it?" he repeated, a wicked light dancing in his eyes.

"No." Then acting purely on impulse, she leaned forward and pressed a kiss on his tanned cheek. "Thank you for taking care of my children, James. I am in your debt."

Before he could respond the door to the library was flung open and Stephen came stalking in, coming to an abrupt halt when he saw his wife kneeling beside his brother's chair, her hand resting intimately on his arm. There was a charged silence, and then he reached behind him to push the door closed.

"Am I interrupting?" he asked, his voice dangerously polite.

"Yes," James said, not moving. "Now go away."

Instead of erupting into fury as she feared, Stephen merely looked cross. "Very funny, brother mine," he muttered, walking over to the cellaret to pour himself a glass of port. "I've spent the past half hour under that broiling sun waiting for you to keep our appointment. Or did you forget you were supposed to show me the new foals?"

"I forgot nothing," James said, still lolling negligently in his chair. "Your wife asked to meet with me, and it seemed ungentlemanly to refuse the invitation."

"Oh!" Cat struggled indignantly to her feet, furious with James and his odious sense of humor. "I did not ask you to meet me!" she denied vehemently. "Well, perhaps I did," she added when he cocked an eyebrow at her, "but not for the reason you are intimating! I wanted to thank you."

"You are welcome." In that instant James was the very image of the Stephen she'd met all those years ago, handsome, playful, and too devilish to be trusted above an inch. Cat adored him even as she longed to box his ears.

"Well, I am glad you are so amused, Mr. Wrexley," she said in her starchiest tones. "Now, if you will pardon me, I must go. I am sure you *gentlemen* must wish to be private." Nose in the air, she made to brush past her husband, only to be stopped when he stepped in front of her, blocking her retreat.

"Stay," he ordered, his dark eyes gleaming as he gazed down at her stormy countenance.

She raised her chin to meet his gaze. "And if I do not wish to?" she retorted, goaded beyond all endurance.

"Then I shall lock you in." Stephen ducked his head and brushed a light kiss over her mouth. "Take your seat, love. We have much we must discuss with my rapscallion of a brother."

Since Cat was as intrigued as she was annoyed, she decided she would remain. For that reason only, she assured herself, and not because he had "ordered" it. She walked back to her chair, resuming her seat with the dignity worthy of a princess.

"Well?" she asked coolly. "What is it you wish to say?"

Stephen's lips twitched, but he said nothing. He turned his head to James, his manner abruptly serious.

"I've thought about what we discussed this morning, and I've concluded you are right. Sedgewood clearly has a confederate in the household, and all that remains is deciding what is to be done about it."

Cat almost tumbled out of her chair in shock. She wasn't

certain what she had expected the brothers to discuss, but it certainly wasn't this. "What do you mean, what is to be done?" she demanded, glancing from man to man incredulously. "Find out whoever it is, and have them arrested!"

Both men looked at her, but it was Stephen who answered. "Whoever it is, he or she will be dealt with," he assured her. "But only after Sedgewood has been taken care of."

"You called Sedgewood a snake," James added, clasping his hands in front of him and leaning forward to study her. "And that is precisely how you must think of him. And everyone knows the best way of killing a snake is to lop off its head. If you chop off anything else, it will only slither away unscathed."

Cat considered the odd observation and then nodded. "You mean if we uncover the traitor and move too soon, Jeremey could escape. Yes, that makes sense."

"That's why I wrote Eddie had the fever," James continued. "If our communications are being monitored, I didn't dare risk tipping Sedgewood to the fact we know the truth. So long as he thinks we believe Eddie's illness to be just that, an illness, he'll think himself safe. He'll make another attempt, and that's when we'll have him."

Cat's hand fluttered to her throat. "You mean you want to use my son as *bait?"* she gasped, paling in horror.

"He'll be well guarded," James rushed to assure her. "In fact, since the moment we found him, he's been under constant observation. Sedgewood and whoever's helping him won't get within ten feet of him, I promise you!"

"But how can you be certain?" Cat cried, the thought of her son in any danger making her frantic. "You don't know Jeremey, don't know what he is capable of. He might have tried making Eddie's death look like an accident this time, but since it failed, what's to keep him from trying something more definite the next time?"

"Because he knows I would never rest if I suspected he had anything to do with Eddie's death," Stephen said, crossing the room to kneel by Cat's side. "Think about it, Cat," he added, silencing her when she would have protested. "A child might sicken and die and he could escape accusation, but if that same child were to meet with a more violent end, especially a child who stood between him and a fortune, he would find himself facing a magistrate. Sedgewood might be evil incarnate, but he is far from stupid. He'll move, but only so long as he believes there's a chance in Hades of his getting away with it."

Tears burned Cat's eyes as she gazed at him. "I don't want my son harmed."

Stephen gave her an intent look, and then rose to his feet. "No more than do I," he told her, his tone oddly formal. "But there is something you have failed to realize."

She frowned up at him, wondering what she'd said this time to put him on his high horse. "What do you mean?"

He studied her for several seconds before answering, a pensive, almost sad look in his dark eyes. "You keep saying Eddie is your son, but what you conveniently keep forgetting is that he is my son as well. *My son,* Cat," he added fiercely, striking his chest with a clenched hand. "And if you think for one moment I should allow any harm to befall him, then we have nothing left to say to each other."

"Are you all right?"

Stephen turned at the sound of his brother's voice. He might have known James would seek him out, even in this, his most private of refuges. "I am fine," he said, glancing back at his mother's tombstone.

After leaving the house he'd set out for his family tomb, located on the far end of the estate. Generations of Rockholmes lay interred here, and Stephen knew that when his time came, he would also be buried here. The notion should have depressed him, but instead he found it comforting. It was nice to know he truly belonged somewhere, he mused, a sad smile touching his lips.

"That was quite a scene back there," James said, joining Stephen on the stone bench. "I don't suppose you'd care to explain yourself, would you?"

Stephen thought about it for a moment. "No."

Instead of taking insult, James was amused. "Well," he drawled, scratching his ear, "that was succinct."

Stephen was instantly shamed. "James . . ."

"I know," his brother interrupted, holding up his hand. "It's none of my business, and believe it or not, I quite agree. Only know that I'm here should you ever change your mind."

Stephen said nothing, although he was deeply touched by his brother's show of support. He turned his attention back to his mother's grave, studying the intricately carved pedestal for several seconds before speaking. "Do you remember her?"

"Our mother?" James seemed taken aback by the question. "Vaguely. Impressions more than anything. The color of her hair, the sound of her voice. Lilies," he added, his eyes closing in memory, "I remember a distinct smell of lilies."

Stephen smiled sadly. "They were her favorite flowers," he murmured, thinking of the woman who had died over twenty years earlier. "She always wore the scent."

James was silent for several seconds before slanting Stephen a curious look. "Why do you mention her?" he asked, frowning in confusion. "Has this anything to do with Cat?"

In answer, Stephen said, "You knew she and Father had an arranged marriage, didn't you?"

James gave an uncertain shrug. "I suppose," he said, looking uncomfortable. "That's how it's done, isn't it?"

"For our class, most certainly," Stephen agreed, nodding absently. "But I can't but wonder if it would be better if one were to marry for love rather than expediency."

James kept his gaze fixed on the flower-decked grave in front of him. "Are you saying you are in love with Cat?"

Stephen wasn't certain how to answer. This was the very question he'd been pondering for many days, and he was no closer to an answer than when he'd started. "I don't know," he admitted painfully. "I care for her, deeply, but love . . ." He shook his head. "That was never part of the bargain I struck with her."

James shot him a teasing look. "Not that I would know, mind, but from what I've heard, love has its own reasons, and those reasons have little to do with any so-called bargains."

"Perhaps," Stephen conceded, thrusting a hand through his hair. "The only thing I do know with any certainty is that Cat doesn't love me."

"And that matters?" James' expression was thoughtful as he studied Stephen.

Stephen was quiet for several seconds, forcing himself to face emotions he'd never dared face before. "It matters," he said at last, his eyes hollow as he met his brother's gaze. "It matters very much."

James took his leave a short time later, leaving Stephen alone with his troubling thoughts. They weren't the most pleasant of companions. He was a man used to action, and he hated the feeling of helplessness that engulfed him whenever he thought of Cat. Her heart was a fortress that could not be stormed, and her mind a wall he couldn't breach, however hard he tried. How was he to win an objective so well defended? he mused. And how would he bear it if he never succeeded in his quest?

After spending another quarter hour wrestling with his inner demons, Stephen abandoned the effort and walked back to the house. He wasn't yet ready to face Cat and, on impulse, decided to pop into the nursery and check on his son. He was relieved to find the lad alone, save for the nursemaid who sat in a rocking chair, watching her young charge with an eagle eye.

"Papa!" Eddie gave a glad cry when he spied Stephen standing in the doorway. The tin soldiers he'd been playing with went flying as he leapt to his feet, racing toward Stephen with his small arms held wide in joyous welcome.

Stephen knelt down, catching his son and holding him in a fiercely protective embrace. He closed his eyes, a wave of sheer love overwhelming him as he cuddled the boy to his heart. In that moment he knew he would defy earth and heaven to keep him safe, and God help Sedgewood if his suspicions proved true. When he opened his eyes he saw the maid had scrambled to her feet and was bobbing a hasty curtsey.

"You may go about your other duties," he told the girl, softening the words with a smile. "I will watch my son."

A short time later Stephen was sprawled on the nursery floor, helping his son arrange his soldiers in battle formation.

"Always guard your infantry, lad," he advised, moving several mounted pieces to the front of the line. "They will serve you in good stead."

"Yes, Papa." Eddied nodded, his expression solemn. "I will."

They played in companionable silence for several more minutes, and as they waged their mock battle it occurred to Stephen now might be a good time to ask a few questions. Until now he hadn't permitted Eddie to be questioned for fear of upsetting him, but he was abruptly tired of waiting.

"Eddie," he began, striving to keep his manner casual, "do you recall the day you fell ill?"

"Uh huh." The lad continued arranging his tin soldiers.

"Do you remember the piece of cake you ate?"

Eddie's nose wrinkled in distaste. "It had almonds. I told the witch I didn't like almonds, but she said I had to eat it."

Stephen's hand froze as he was reaching for a soldier. "The witch?" he asked, his mind racing. "Do you mean an old lady?"

"Not old like Nurse," Eddie clarified. "Old like you, Papa."

Stephen's pride absorbed the insult, and he concentrated on gathering more intelligence. "Did you recognize this lady?" he pressed. "Is she known to you?"

Eddie started to shake his head and then paused, his brows meeting in a scowl of concentration. "In the village," he said at last. "She was at the inn when Miss Blakely took us there last week."

"Which inn?" Stephen demanded, making a mental note to set out for the village the moment he left the nursery.

Eddie shrugged, clearly indifferent. "It has tea cakes," he said. "And if you say please, they will take out the raisins."

That described every inn in the village, but since there were only four of them, Stephen didn't think it would take him above an hour to learn what he needed to know. "What did this lady look like?" he asked, abandoning any sign of indifference. "Describe her to me."

"She had a painted face, and a hat with lots of feathers," Eddie said, his frown deepening. "Miss Blakely said we mustn't acknowledge her. What is 'acknowledge,' Papa?"

"It means to recognize, Eddie," Stephen said, committing the woman's description to memory. She was obviously a doxy, which meant more than a few of the villagers would be certain to remember her. Then he thought about what Eddie had said, and his own brows gathered in a frown.

"Why did Miss Blakely not wish you to acknowledge the lady?" he asked. "Did she attempt to speak with you?"

Eddie shook his head vehemently, sending his dark curls tumbling across his forehead. "But she was *staring,* Papa, and when the man she was talking to pointed at me, she laughed."

Stephen pounced on this new bit of information. "Did you know the man? Was it Mr. Sedgewood?"

"No," Eddie responded stoutly. "I never saw him before. But Beth said she thought he was handsome, and she did this." He began sighing and fluttering his lashes in an absurd pantomime that won a reluctant smile from Stephen.

"It's not nice to mock your sister, Edward," he said, giving the boy an admonishing look. "Now, can you tell me more of this lady and the man with her? Did you see them again?"

"Just the day I was sick. She was by the garden, and she said she'd been waiting for me and that she had a gift for me."

"The cake?" Hatred welled up in Stephen, and for the first time in his life he honestly felt he could do a woman harm.

"She said it was a special present, and I was to eat it all."

"But it had almonds in it, so you wouldn't," Stephen said, thanking heaven for his son's fastidious appetite. There was no doubt in his mind that had Eddie eaten the entire cake, he would be dead by now.

Eddie gave a nod, and then as if noting his father's cold fury, he added, "I am sorry, Papa. I will eat it all next time."

"What?" The words jerked Stephen out of his dark thoughts, and he cast Eddie a horrified look. "No, Eddie, you mustn't do that," he said, gathering the lad close. "You are never again to take food from anyone but Nurse or one of the other servants, do you understand me? Never!"

Tears glimmered in Eddie's eyes at the fierceness in Stephen's voice. "I won't, Papa, I won't." Then he flung himself in Stephen's arms, great sobs wracking him as he clung to his father.

Stephen was stunned by the boy's tears, until he understood what they meant. He settled Eddie on his lap, gently brushing a kiss over his curls and holding him in a tender embrace.

"I'm not mad at you, Edward," he said, wiping a tear from the boy's flushed cheeks. "I am angry at the lady who gave you the cake. It must have been poorly made to have made you ill."

Eddie sniffed. "The cake made me sick?" he asked, obviously much struck by the notion.

Stephen hesitated before answering. "I think it may have," he said, choosing his words with care. "That's why it's never a good idea to accept food from people you do not know. There is always a chance it could make you ill."

Eddie rested his head on his father's shoulder as he struggled to make sense of what he had just been told. "What about the inn?" he asked. "Does this mean I can't ever have cream cakes when we go to the village?"

Stephen hid a smile at the note of horror in his son's voice. "Cream cakes are fine," he assured him, depositing another kiss on his forehead. "But only if Mama says you may have them."

"Mama says he may have them after he has had a nap." Cat's voice sounded from the doorway, and Stephen turned his head to see her standing just inside the room.

"Mama!" Eddie abandoned his father for his mother without so much as a backward glance. "I told Papa about the witch, and he said it was all right not to eat the cake!"

Cat gazed down at Eddie for several seconds before answering. "And who am I to argue with Papa?" she asked, ruffling his hair.

"May I go out?" Eddie pleaded, winding his arms about her waist and gazing up at her with hopeful eyes. "Please? I am all better now."

Cat's lips twitched at such obvious wheedling. "I am not certain," she said, then surprised Stephen by glancing over at him and smiling. "What do you say, Papa?" she asked. "Is our son well enough to be allowed outside, do you think?"

Stephen hid his astonishment at the easy way she sought his council. "So long as he stays to the garden and minds his nursemaid, I see no reason why he shouldn't be allowed outside for an hour or so," he said as he stood, adopting a serious mien. "But only for an hour, Edward, and not a moment longer."

Eddie beamed with delight. "Thank you, Papa! I will be very good, I promise!"

"See that you are, or I'll confine you to the stockade," Stephen threatened, then spoiled the effect by winking. "Off with you now, and wear a jacket!" he added, shouting the warning as Eddie raced from the room whooping in joy.

With Eddie's noisy departure an awkward silence fell between Cat and Stephen, and after an uncomfortable moment he cleared his throat. "Cat, there is something I—"

"Stephen, I want to apologize for—" she said, almost at the some time. They broke off, exchanging embarrassed looks. Encouraged because she had sought him out, Stephen crossed the room and reached out to gently touch her cheek.

"You first," he said, tucking a strand of hair back into place. "What is it you wanted to say?"

Her deep green eyes flicked for a moment, and then she drew a deep breath. "You're right," she said, her gaze holding his. "Eddie is your son as well as mine. I know you love him, and 'tis obvious he loves you. I promise I shall never deny you a part in his life again."

His life, Stephen noted bitterly; not hers. Never hers.

"And I promise not to exclude you from any future decisions regarding his safety," he said, masking his hurt behind a solemn look. "If you don't want to use Eddie to trap Sedgewood, then that's the end of it. I will abide by whatever you decide."

He expected her to insist he abandon his and James's plans for Sedgewood, but instead she continued gazing at him. "I want you to answer me truthfully," she said, covering his hand with her own. "If I do decide I don't wish it, will I be placing him in even greater danger?"

Because she demanded honesty, he gave it to her. "I believe that you will be," he said quietly. "So long as he lives he will be in danger of attack from Sedgewood. If we do this my way, we can be prepared, but if not, the attack could come at any time and from any quarter. Our best chance of protecting our son is to pretend ignorance, lay our trap, and then give Sedgewood time and rope enough to hang himself. Either that, or . . .

"Or what?" she prodded, when he failed to finish the thought.

"Or I can kill him and be done with it," he said, dropping all pretensions of gentility. "And I'll do it, Cat. I'll break his neck and not lose a moment's sleep over it."

She accepted his violent declaration in silence, and then gave a small nod. "All right," she said. "I agree to your plan. I'll just send a note to Lottie explaining I have decided to remain in the country, and—"

Stephen silenced her by laying a finger across her lips. "When I spoke of rope enough, I meant we will be returning to London as originally planned. If we stay, it could rouse Sedgewood's suspicions, or at least make him hesitant about taking action. For our plan to succeed, he must think Eddie to be alone and defenseless, save for James and the servants."

He saw the distress, and then the acceptance, in her emerald-colored eyes. "I see," she said softly. "Then by all means we must return at once."

"I've armed several of the senior servants," he added, not wanting her to think he'd leave their son in unnecessary danger. "And I intend having words with some of the tenants as well. They'll know to keep their eyes open, and their guns handy."

She nodded again, and then stood on tiptoe to brush her mouth over his. "Thank you, Stephen," she said, smiling up at him. "You are a very good father."

A few short days ago, the compliment would have meant everything to Stephen; now it slashed him to the very soul. "Yes," he agreed, a chilly bleakness settling in his soul. "I am."

Sixteen

Two days later a subdued Cat prepared for their return to London. Leaving Eddie and the girls was wrenching her apart, but she knew it was for the best. As Stephen said, the more ignorant they behaved, the more likely Sedgewood was to move. In fact, knowing Jeremey for the vicious coward that he was, she could almost guarantee that was precisely what he'd do. He only acted when he was certain he could do so without danger to himself.

Thinking of Jeremey made her remember the frustrating afternoon she and Stephen had spent tracking down Eddie's mysterious "witch." They spoke with both Miss Blakely and Beth, but their memories of the mysterious woman were little better than Eddie's. They went into the village to question the local innkeepers at length. The innkeeper at the second inn they visited remembered both the doxy and her protector, but could provide precious little in the way of useful information. They'd arrive by mailcoach and departed the same way, staying less than three days. When pressed for more detail the innkeeper replied that they'd paid their bill with good English gold and behaved themselves, so he'd seen no reason to pay them any mind.

But when Stephen threatened to withdraw his patronage, he suddenly recalled the woman had asked about renting a horse, although where she went or what she did, he could not say. The blacksmith provided the information the woman had asked for directions to Rockholme, and that she'd returned several hours later, the horse limping and covered with lather.

A few more discreet questions and they knew the protector was a well-heeled young man of some twenty-odd years, with dark hair and light-colored eyes. Neither the man nor the woman had ever referred to each other by name, which meant the name they had used to secure the room was doubtlessly a false one. It didn't seem like much to Cat, but Stephen appeared satisfied enough, nodding and handing out coins to all who helped them. He also swore those he spoke with to utmost secrecy, explaining to those brazen enough to ask that some silver had disappeared from the house and he suspected the doxy of taking it.

"Cat?" Stephen had entered the room and was regarding her quizzically. "Is everything ready? We leave within the hour."

Cat stirred, embarrassed at having been caught woolgathering. "Yes," she said, adding a scarf to the portmanteau and closing the lid. "I was just checking to see if I'd packed the accounts book. I mean to review them on the ride to London."

"James would see to that if you asked him," he said, his dark eyes watchful as he studied her.

"I know, but he's already done so much, I hate to impose. Besides"—she flashed him a smile—"I like doing the accounts."

He returned her smile, crossing the room to kneel beside her. "I'm glad to hear that," he said, brushing his finger down her cheek. "I never cared for it above half."

Cat studied him through her lashes before replying. "A good landowner should always see to such matters himself, else he runs the risk of being duped," she told him primly, enjoying the novelty of teasing her imperious husband.

"Not if he's clever enough to have a wife to do them for him," he said, sounding smugly pleased with himself. "I know you won't dupe me, my love. Now hurry. The staff and children are waiting for us to say our good-byes."

When she was alone again, Cat brooded over his lighthearted remarks. Did he trust her, she wondered, or was this another attempt on his part to close the distance between them? Since that uncomfortable scene in Eddie's room they had both made such attempts, and she was beginning to hope they might even succeed. They still hadn't made love; but he slept with her each night, and she took from that what comfort she could.

The good-byes took up the better part of the hour Stephen had granted her, and by the time the carriage was rolling down the long pathway leading to the main road, Cat was in tears.

"We'll be back in less than a month," Stephen soothed, patting Cat's arm. "And then I promise we won't have to leave for months, if that is what you wish."

"I know." She delicately blew her nose. "And I realize I'm being silly, but I can't help but worry."

"I worry, too," he said, his simple declaration taking her by surprise. "But it will be all right. I have to believe it will be all right."

The rest of the journey passed in comfortable companionship. In between chatting with Stephen and enjoying the scenery, Cat did her best to examine the accounts. Quarterly wages were coming due, and Cat was amazed at the huge number of servants required to operate a house like Rockholme Manor. She was noting down the names, positions, and amount of salary owed when a new name scrawled on the bottom of the page caught her attention.

"Stephen," she began, "are you aware a new footman was hired less than a month ago?"

"Mmm?" He glanced up from the book he was reading.

"A new footman, one . . ." She ran her finger under the man's name. "Thomas Bartlett. According to the estate manager's records, he was hired a few days after our wedding."

"That doesn't surprise me," Stephen said, stretching out his legs. "With four extra people in the household, there is more work to be done, and I am sure James would have instructed Mr. Hubert to take on additional staff. What name, did you say?"

"Thomas Bartlett."

"Bartlett . . ." Stephen tilted his head to one side. "The name doesn't sound familiar. We tend to hire our servants from amongst the families of the tenants, and I'm fairly certain we don't have anyone by that name in our employ."

Cat glanced back down at the name. "I'm sure it's nothing,"

she said, not wishing to cause a possibly innocent man any difficulties. "But if Jeremey does have a confederate inside, wouldn't it make more sense he would approach a new member of the staff, rather than someone who had been there for many years?"

Stephen looked startled, and then thoughtful. "Yes, it would. Bartlett might even have been in Sedgewood's employ before he came to work for us."

"What will you do?" Cat asked, not certain she cared for the dangerous look that turned Stephen's eyes to cold obsidian.

"Order him watched," Stephen said, his long fingers closing in a fist. "We'll find out what part of the house he works in and, if need be, have him assigned elsewhere, somewhere far from the nursery." He reached out and captured her hand, carrying it to his lips for an absentminded kiss. "Thank you for bringing it to my notice, my love."

The subject put a decided damper on the rest of the journey, and by the time they reached London, Cat's mounting anxiety had given her a headache. She hoped they would spend their first night back in town together, but less than an hour after their arrival, he was dressed and headed out the door. He didn't say where he was going, and she tried not to let it matter. She also thought about going out, but she was too tired and in too much pain to try. Tomorrow, she decided, and went wearily to bed.

Stephen was dressed and gone when she awoke the following morning. She remembered him slipping into bed beside her, murmuring gently as he settled her into his arms. He hadn't made love to her, and the continual withdrawal of his passion worried her even more. Could he have tired of her already? she fretted. Or was he still angry over her foolish refusal to include him in her and the children's lives?

Cat continued brooding over the precarious state of her marriage as she went downstairs to breakfast. Last night she'd noticed the mound of correspondence that had piled up during her absence, and she thought she'd spend a quiet morning answering letters and refusing invitations. She'd barely settled in the morning parlor, however, before Lottie came rushing in.

"My dear, I am so happy you are back!" she gushed, tossing her parasol and mitts down as she rushed to Cat's side. "I am afraid I have some rather unpleasant news to tell you."

Cat's stomach twisted, and then dropped to her toes with a sickening thud. "What is it?" she asked, and steeled herself to hear the very worst.

"Well, to begin, I want you to know that no one is giving the slightest credence to it," Lottie continued, untying the bow of her elaborate bonnet and setting it aside. "I mean, you are a *lady;* anyone can tell that at a glance, and despite my brother's rather unsavory past, he has shown himself to be a man of honor and impeccable pride. In fact, he—"

"Lottie!" Cat laid a hand to her pounding head. "Whatever are you talking about?"

"Well, the rumors, of course!" her sister-in-law exclaimed impatiently. "They are all over town!"

"What rumors?" Cat asked, although she had a grim notion what they might be.

"Rumors that Stephen is your son's father." Lottie's solemn words confirmed Cat's most secret fears. Sweat broke out on her forehead, and the nausea that had been plaguing her all morning became a presence she could no longer ignore. Terrified she was about to disgrace herself, she struggled to her feet, only to find her legs refused to hold her. Had it not been for Lottie, she'd have ended up face first on the floor.

"Cat!" Lottie caught her as she sagged in a boneless heap. "Here, let me help you to a chair. Oh, you poor dear! I'll just send for some tea, and you'll be fine."

Cat was too weak and ill to answer. She simply laid her head back against the pillows, eyes closed as she listened to Lottie barking out orders like a top sergeant.

"Some tea for her ladyship at once! And bring some cloths and a basin of water as well!"

She then hurried back to Cat, patting her hand and murmuring worriedly. "Are you going to be all right, dearest? I can send a footman for a doctor, if you'd like. I know that is what Stephen would insist you do."

That was all it took to snap Cat out of her lethargy. She

opened her eyes cautiously, and when she was certain her stomach would not betray her, she sat up carefully.

"No, I don't need a doctor," she said, and even managed a shaky smile. "Forgive me, this is so embarrassing. I've never fainted before, and I feel so foolish."

"Pish!" Lottie dismissed her apology with a wave of an elegant hand. "That hardly matters now. Just lie quietly, love, until the tea gets here."

Since the room was still dipping and swaying in an alarming fashion, Cat was only too happy to comply. She lay back against the plump cushions, keeping her eyes closed until the rattle of cups announced the arrival of the maids. A few moments later a cool, damp cloth was placed across her forehead, and the light floral scent of cologne water teased her senses.

"There," Lottie said, sounding satisfied. "You've a bit more color to you now. How are you feeling? You were so pale, I was terrified you would swoon, and then Stephen would have had me taken out and shot for daring to upset you."

Cat smiled at the mutinous note in the other woman's voice. "I'm fine," she said, opening her eyes to study Lottie. "It's just that between my social obligations here in the city and the worry over Eddie's illness, I haven't been sleeping well. I fear I was simply overwhelmed by everything."

"Speaking of your son, how is the little angel?" Lottie asked, a worried look on her face. "I meant to ask, but as usual, I let my tongue run away with me. David is forever lecturing me about it."

"Eddie is also fine. He's almost completely recovered, and back to making life a misery for his sisters," Cat assured her, fighting a stab of remorse. James and Stephen had convinced her, that for Eddie's sake no one but Nurse, Miss Blakely, and the three of them were to ever know the truth of his illness. She could see the sense of what they said, but that didn't lessen her guilt at having to deceive her sister-in-law.

"What was wrong with him?" Lottie asked, preparing a cup of tea for Cat and handing it to her. "Was it the fever?"

Cat shook her head. "Nurse thinks it was one of those childhood maladies that terrifies the parents, but leaves the patient unscathed. He was begging for a pony when we left."

"I know what you mean," Lottie gave a delicate shudder. "When he was eight months old, my Randolph came down with a fever and spots. I was certain it was the small pox, but it turned out to be nothing. Two days later, you could scarce tell he had been ill. Blast!" She broke off with an impatient exclamation.

"There I go again!" she cried, looking cross. "I vow, David is right; I can not keep my mind on one topic, no matter how hard I try! Now, back to the matter at hand, I am sorry if I have upset you; that was never my intention. I only thought you'd want to know what was going on, and I thought it would be better if you heard it from me rather than from a so-called friend."

Because she knew Lottie's frivolous manner hid a kind and loving heart, Cat believed her at once. "It's all right, Lottie," she said, sending the other woman a gentle smile. "I know you meant well, and you're correct; I do appreciate hearing it from you rather than from someone else. Only think of the scandal if I'd swooned in front of one of them."

Lottie gave another shudder. "I don't even want to contemplate it," she said darkly, and then took a restorative sip of tea. "Well, now that I've told you about the rumors, we must decide what's to be done about them. Have you any suggestions?"

Cat sipped her tea thoughtfully, trying to think as she thought Stephen might think. Clearly the first step he would take would be to determine the source of the rumors, she decided. Once they knew where they had originated, they would best know how to handle the matter.

"Do we know how the rumors got started?" she asked. "Was it Jeremey, or someone from the house party?"

"That's just it," Lottie said, scowling. "No one seems to know, or if they do know, they certainly aren't telling *me*."

"So that's the first thing we'll need to learn," Cat said, giving a decisive nod. "What are they saying?"

"That you and Stephen were lovers while you were still wed

to Edward, and that he is your babe's father," Lottie said, her lips thinning in anger.

"That's all?" Cat pressed, leaning forward. "No mention was made of Lord Exter's house party?"

"No, not that I've heard," Lottie said, then frowned at Cat's expression. "Why do you ask? Does it matter?"

"Jeremey never knew about the house party," Cat said slowly, her heart racing with excitement. "As far as he knows, I never left Cumbria. So, if the rumor is just that Stephen was my lover and no specific mention is made of Lord Exter's, then that would prove the source of the rumor—"

"Would be that wretched Jeremey Sedgewood!" Lottie exclaimed, clapping her hands in delight. "Congratulations, my dear! How very clever you are!"

Cat preened, even as she felt honor-bound to give credit where credit was due. "Thank you, although in all honesty, I was trying to think as Stephen would. Now that we know where the rumors started, it's time to decide how we'll settle the matter."

Lottie gave a disdainful sniff. "Tell Stephen. He will settle it with a bullet between the villain's eyes."

And he would, too, Cat thought, especially given the attack on Eddie. But not yet, not without the proof that would satisfy Stephen and the authorities should Stephen be forced to take final, decisive action against Jeremey.

"Has anyone directly accused Stephen of fathering Eddie, or is it all hints and smirks?" she asked, knowing that was usually the way rumors were spread amongst the *ton*.

"Hints and smirks, mostly," Lottie admitted. "Although a few people have been foolish enough to make more direct accusations."

Cat hesitated. Much as she loathed confrontations of any kind, she knew that would be the best way of dispelling the tattlers. Gossips tended to hold their tongues when met with a cold-eyed demand that they verify the lies they were spreading. She said, as much to Lottie, who nodded in agreement.

"You're right, my dear. Rumors do tend to wither and die

when placed under direct light. Which reminds me, you have a champion who has already done just that."

"Who?" Cat wondered if Lord Exter had been forced to defend her name and reputation.

"Captain Lacey!" Lottie provided, beaming in delight. "He came to see me yesterday afternoon. He'd heard the talk the night before, and he was positively passionate in your defense! You have obviously made a conquest in that quarter, my dear."

Cat felt her head beginning to throb. "Lottie . . ."

"Well, you have!" Lottie interrupted, tossing her head and pouting. "He was so upset; he kept saying he couldn't believe how anyone could speak so ill of a fine lady like yourself! He even said he meant to challenge the next person he heard uttering such falsehoods."

"He what?" Cat sat forward so quickly, the tea in her cup spilled over the rim, scalding her hand. She set it aside with an impatient mutter before turning to Lottie.

"Lottie, tell me you're joking!" she pleaded. "Please, tell me you are joking!

"I'm not!" Lottie insisted, staring at Cat in astonishment. "Really, Catheryn, calm yourself! He didn't mean it. It was just his hot blood speaking. For all he is a young buck, the captain is hardly a fool. I'm sure he's aware the honor of defending your name must fall to Stephen. He asked where you were," she added with a sly look.

"Stephen?" Cat rubbed her aching head wearily.

"Captain Lacey, silly!" Lottie gave a trill of laughter. "And he seemed most upset when I told him you'd left because your little son had taken ill. He asked that I convey his best wishes, and to tell you he is at your disposal should you have need of him. You see? He is the perfect gentleman."

"Yes, so he is," Cat said, vaguely surprised by the young officer's gallantry. They had met but the one time, after all, and afterward Stephen had been so rude to him, she wouldn't have blamed him had the captain cut them quite dead.

"I have always thought so," Lottie said, nibbling on a macaroon. "Although I daresay Stephen won't share that opinion."

Cat thought of Stephen's probable reaction, and hid a grin. "No," she said, picking up her cup, "I daresay he would not."

"Men are such hypocritical beasts," Lottie observed feelingly. "There is simply no accounting for their wretched sense of justice. Apparently it's fine if Stephen wishes to dance attendance on the Divine Davinia, but he flies up into the boughs at the very thought of a perfectly respectable gentleman like Captain Lacey honoring you with his friendship."

Cat's head jerked up at the artless observation. "What do you mean?" she asked, something deep inside her going cold.

"Catheryn! You remember that dreadful scene at the Ellertons' when you and Captain Lacey first met!" Lottie reminded her, shaking her head at Cat. "He was an absolute beast about it."

"No," Cat said, clutching her teacup in trembling fingers, "not that. I meant your remark about Lady Dewhurst. Are you implying Stephen is seeing her again?"

Lottie turned an alarming shade of red. "No!" she denied vehemently, then spoiled the repudiation by adding, "That is to say, he may have spoken with her upon occasion, but I am almost certain that is all there is to it. He would never do anything to disgrace you or his name!"

Cat wanted to believe that. She more than anyone knew what Stephen's pride and honor meant to him, and she found it impossible to believe he would jeopardize either by taking up with a former mistress. Then there was Eddie to be considered. With Jeremey posing such a real and deadly threat to their son, she couldn't imagine him setting aside his responsibilities and engaging in a frivolous affair. And yet. . . .

"No!" she said aloud, stilling the voice of uncertainty sounding in her head. "No, I won't believe it. I refuse to believe it. Stephen would never betray our vows."

"Bravo!" Lottie exclaimed, clapping her hands. "I can not tell you how relieved I am to see you being so eminently sensible about this. For a moment, I was afraid you were about to have a fit of the vapors like some tiresome wife in a French farce. I'm glad to see you are made of sterner stuff than that."

"Yes," Cat said, seeking to convince herself as well as Lottie. "I am."

"Good." Lottie nodded approval once more. "Not that I am suggesting you should let Stephen get away with even flirting with that she-devil. In fact, I have in mind the very thing to teach that arrogant wretch a lesson." She went on to outline a salacious scheme that had Cat's eyes going wide in disbelief.

"Poison." Lord Exter shook his head, his lips thinning in disgust. "My God, the man is a monster."

"It's my fault," Daintry added bitterly. "I shouldn't have suggested we put an end to his pretensions. So long as everyone thought he had a chance of inheriting, the lad was safe enough; I should have realized that." He raised his head to meet Stephen's gaze, his eyes dark with misery. "I'm sorry, Stephen."

"You're not to blame," Stephen said, touched by his friend's distress. They were sitting in Exter's study, hunched over plans like generals preparing for battle. And in a way it was a battle, he decided, his jaw hardening with resolve. The most important battle he'd ever waged: the battle for his son's life.

"So what's our next move?" Exter asked, tapping out an impatient tattoo on his leather-covered desk. "Do we continue or do we retrench? Your decision, Rockholme."

Stephen hesitated, forcing himself to view the situation from a purely tactical perspective. They had the enemy completely surrounded, he thought coolly. They had cut his lines of supply, and even had spies in his camp to monitor his every movement. Engaging him now would avail them nothing, and moreover, they would loose the vital element of surprise. As one of Wellington's officers, he'd learned well the value to be had in taking one's enemies unaware.

"We stand," he said at last. "Pressing Sedgewood further might make him react hastily, and in a way we can't anticipate. We'll let him stew, thinking himself the victor, and then when he moves, we'll take him." He smiled, a smile that had both Exter and Daintry shivering.

"I'd feel happier if we knew more of the doxy and her protector," Daintry spoke next. "If we manage to locate them and get them to swear they were acting at Sedgewood's behest, we'll be able to hand him over to the magistrate. There'll be talk, of course, especially if there is a trial, but it can't be avoided. And it's not as if there's not talk aplenty already."

Stephen sat up, his expression hardening. "What talk?"

Exter glared at Daintry. "Curse you, Richard! When will you learn to bridle that tongue of yours?"

"When you learn that not everyone appreciates being treated like a half-witted child," Daintry returned calmly. "It's his name and his honor, Albert. He has the right to know."

Stephen was on his feet, his hands balling into fists. "Know what?" he demanded, his voice raw with fury.

With a sigh, Exter told him of the talk that had been buzzing about London for the past week, leaving nothing out. By the time he was finished, Stephen was pacing the elegant confines of the study and cursing luridly.

"And you're certain none of your guests are to blame?" he demanded, coming to a halt beside Exter's chair.

The marquess raised an eyebrow in sardonic amusement. "After the way you terrorized them?" he drawled. "No, it wasn't one of them. I'd stake my reputation on that."

"It's not your reputation you'd be staking," Stephen reminded him, bitter hatred scalding his blood.

"It's certain Sedgewood is the source of the rumors, even if we can't prove it," Daintry said, nobly interposing himself between Stephen and Exter. "Almost since the moment of Edward Brockton's death, he's been telling anyone who would listen that young Brockton was not his father's son, but because of his own reputation no one ever listened."

"But they're listening now?"

"They're *talking* now," Exter answered, laying his hand on Stephen's arm. "There's a difference, Stephen."

Stephen met his friend's gaze coldly. "Is there?" he asked, withdrawing his arm. "I don't think so."

"Stephen . . ."

"Never mind, Albert," Stephen said, abruptly tired. "I'm not angry with you, I'm angry with Sedgewood. The man is like a blight, bringing misery and destruction wherever he goes."

"We'll have him," Daintry said quietly, all trace of his usual mockery quite gone. "My word to you, we'll have him."

Stephen studied the faces of his two friends, and felt a measure of peace steal over him. "Yes," he agreed. "We will."

Once his business with Exter and Daintry was completed, Stephen went directly home. The butler met him with the news her ladyship was in her study, and on a whim he decided to pop in and check on her. She'd been asleep when he'd left that morning, and he was suddenly anxious to see her again. Telling the butler to return to his duties, he made his way to the back of the house where Cat kept her study. He thought about knocking, but impulse had him carefully opening the door and sliding silently into the room and then shutting the door behind him.

Cat was sitting at her desk, her head bent as she studied the paper in her hand. She was dressed in a simple day dress of violet silk, a cambric cap set on her ebony curls. He leaned against the door, arms folded across his chest as he drank in his fill of her. Christ, she was beautiful, he thought, and was debating the best way of making her aware of him when she suddenly glanced up, starting when she saw him standing there.

"Oh, Stephen!" she exclaimed, laying her hand on her chest. "You startled me! How long have you been there?"

"Not long," he said, pushing away from the door and walking slowly toward her. "What are you doing?"

She turned back to the desk. "Answering invitations," she said, picking up a cream-colored card and frowning. "Or refusing them, to be more honest. Do you mind?"

He took the card and read it. "Mind missing some wretched female caterwauling in atrocious Italian? I should say not."

"Beast." She retrieved the card and added it to a pile on the desk. "I suppose you speak perfect Italian."

"Si, bellisima," he purred, brushing a teasing kiss across her neck. "I was in charge of interrogating Italian prisoners."

"I might have known." She pretended to pout, an effect quite ruined by the way she tilted her head to one side, granting him freer access. "What about this?" She handed him another card. "I believe the duke is a particular friend of yours?"

Stephen scanned the card and handed it back. "Not so particular I'm willing to rig myself out in some damned costume and go parading about like a fool," he muttered, cringing at the thought of a masquerade. "You may send our sincere regrets."

Cat turned in her chair. "Are you certain?" she asked, delighting Stephen by looping her arms about his neck. "I think I might enjoy seeing you in costume."

"You would?" Always willing to play and tease, he closed his own arms about her to draw her close. "How would you dress me?"

She cocked her head to one side, studying him through her lashes. "As a knight," she said after a moment. "In chain mail, with a tunic bearing your colors across your chest. Or perhaps as a Legionnaire. You'd make a most handsome Roman, I think."

He was ridiculously pleased by her observation. "And I see you as Cleopatra, dripping gold and arrogance," he said, sliding his hands up until they rested just below her breasts. "Or Isis, a goddess whose beauty drives mortal men to madness." He cupped her breasts, and took her mouth in a burning kiss.

She responded at once, burying her fingers in his hair and opening her lips to his questing tongue. They kissed deeply, the hunger in her more than answering the hunger raging inside of him. He wanted her more than he'd ever wanted her in the past, and he knew if he didn't have her that moment, he would die from the frustration. His hands pulled savagely at the bodice of her gown, baring her breasts to his hands and avid mouth.

"Stephen!" she gasped, blushing furiously as she pulled away from him. "Stop that! What if someone comes in?"

His body was throbbing with passion, but Stephen managed to rein himself in long enough to consider her objections. "The thought distresses you?"

"Of course it distresses me!" she exclaimed, hands shaking as she tugged her bodice back into place.

He thought about that for a moment. "Very well," he said, rising to his feet and walking purposefully toward the door.

Cat watched him through suspicious eyes. "What are you doing?"

"Locking the door," he said, sliding the bolt into place before turning around to grin at her. "I shouldn't wish you to be upset. There, am I not the most considerate of husbands?" he added, untying his cravat and walking back to where she was sitting.

She glanced up at him for several seconds before reaching up to unbutton his jacket. "Indeed you are," she agreed, a soft smile curving her lips. "The most considerate husband in the world." She went into his arms, giving him the passion he needed more than he needed his next breath.

Seventeen

"Good evening, Countess." Captain Lacey bowed before Cat, his light blue eyes gleaming with shy pleasure as he gazed at her. "It is good to see you again."

"Captain Lacey!" Cat replied, delighted at seeing the gallant officer again. She'd been hoping to encounter him so that she could thank him for his kindness, but this was the first time she'd seen him in the week since their return to London. "I wasn't aware you were acquainted with Lord Glendon," she added, smiling as she offered him her hand.

"I'm not," the captain admitted with a self-deprecatory shrug. "A mutual friend was kind enough to wrangle an invitation for me, and so here I am. May I ask how your son is faring? I trust he is recovered?"

The unexpectedness of the question took Cat aback, and it was several moments before she responded. "Yes, he is," she said, repeating the story she and Stephen had concocted. "It was nothing serious, thank heaven. Just a badly upset stomach. But dearest James is a bachelor with little experience of children, and I fear he flew into a panic."

"Are you certain?" Captain Lacey frowned worriedly. "I was made to understand the poor lad was near death."

"Well, he *was* dreadfully sick, poor lamb," she allowed delicately, "but once he'd rid his stomach of what was making him ill, he was fine. He is like his father in that respect. Edward was cursed with the most delicate of constitutions."

"I see." Now it was the captain who paused, shifting from one foot to another, and lowering his eyes. "My lady, forgive me," he said, keeping his gaze fixed firmly on his feet. "But there is something I believe you should know . . ."

Cat took his meaning at once. "You're referring to the rumors Edward is Stephen's son? You needn't look so embarrassed, sir," she said, when he raised his startled gaze to meet hers. "I had the tale from my sister-in-law my first day back in London, and as appalled as I am, I'm not surprised."

"You're not?" He gaped at her in astonishment.

Had it been anyone else, Cat would have held her tongue, but because of the way he'd championed her, she felt she owed him the courtesy of an explanation.

"It is old family business, I fear," she began reluctantly, "and as such, something I'd prefer not to discuss. I can only tell you there is a distant relation who is forever making mischief for me, and I am more than certain he is to blame for this latest tempest in a teacup. Speaking of which, Lottie also told me of your gallant defense, and I wish to thank you. It was very kind of you."

"It was my honor, ma'am!" he assured her, his words tumbling out in a rush. "You are a true lady, and as a gentleman, I couldn't stand by and allow such slander to go unchallenged."

"Nonetheless, I appreciate your efforts," Cat said firmly. "It is reassuring to know I have such a stalwart champion."

Before she could prevent it, he had grabbed her hand again and was carrying it to his lips. "Anything, Lady Rockholme!" he told her ardently, his eyes glowing with fervor. "You have but to name it, and I would do it for you!"

Cat could only stare at him, genuinely alarmed by his passionate declaration. She wondered if the captain had somehow formed an attachment for her, and then decided she was being foolish. Captain Lacey was obviously one of those romantic souls who enjoyed fancying themselves as knights of old, sworn to protect a lady's honor. It was touching, and rather sweet, but she didn't think he meant it in an improper way. Still, she thought a change of conversation mightn't go amiss.

"The Season will be winding down soon," she observed, turning slightly away. "Will you be remaining in the city, or shall you retire to the country with the rest of Society?"

At first she didn't think he would take the hint, but after a moment he politely followed her lead. "I haven't decided," he admitted, slipping his hand beneath her elbow and leading her about the ballroom. "I've family in Shropshire I've not seen in years, so I might go there. To be frank, it depends on my financial situation. I fear I am a trifle short of the ready at the moment."

Cat wasn't certain how to respond to so frank an admission. "I see," she said, deciding that sounded safest.

"But I am certain I will soon come about," he added swiftly. "I have some investments that are due to pay off any day now, and once they have, I shall lack for nothing."

Cat felt the conversation was becoming too personal and was trying to think of some polite way of ending it, when Lottie came bearing down on them, a scowl of displeasure on her face.

"Catheryn, why are you standing over here in the corner?" she scolded, slipping her arm through Cat's. "Lord Glendon is waiting for his dance with you!"

"Oh, that's right, I'd forgotten!" Cat exclaimed, grateful now for the demands of duty. She turned to the captain with an apologetic smile. "I'm sorry, Captain Lacey, but I fear I must be on my way," she said, making a proper show of regret. "I hope we might see each other soon."

"As do I, my lady," he said, and then bowed to Lottie. "Your servant, Lady Barton."

Instead of giving him his leave, Lottie sent him an encouraging smile. "Tell me, Captain Lacey, have you any plans for tomorrow afternoon?" she asked, fluttering her lashes with practiced coquetry. "If not, I should like to invite you to the small soiree I am giving, just an informal gathering of friends, you understand."

From the expression on his face, Cat mused one would think he'd just been granted entry into the holiest of the holies. "I should be delighted, ma'am," he said, bowing again. "Thank you."

"You're most welcome, sir," Lottie replied with a pleased nod. "We'll expect you at three o'clock, then. Good night, Captain."

"What the devil was all that about?" Cat demanded in an angry whisper as she and Lottie walked away. "You know perfectly well you aren't having a soiree tomorrow!"

"I am now," Lottie returned, brown eyes dancing with laughter. "And stop scowling at me. I know what I'm doing."

"Yes, making mischief," Cat muttered feelingly, shooting her sister-in-law an aggrieved look. "Really, Lottie, I told you I have no desire to encourage the captain's attentions!"

"Oh, don't be so stuffy!" Lottie admonished with a trill of amusement. "It's all for the best, you'll see. Ah, there's our host now," she said, pulling Cat to a halt and eyeing the plump, pasty-skinned man waiting hopefully by the dais.

"Oh, dear," she murmured, hiding a smile behind her fan, "one might wish he hadn't paired a green jacket with a yellow waistcoat. He looks more like a frog than ever, doesn't he? Oh well, it can't be helped. Off you go, my dear, and remember to flirt. His lordship's vanity is easily pricked."

For the next hour Cat danced with several gentlemen, smiling and making idle conversation until she thought she would go mad. Despite her trepidations, she even waltzed with Captain Lacey, trying not to stiffen when he held her a trifle closer than propriety allowed. When the dance ended she escaped with a babbled apology, fleeing to the formal parlor in search of refuge. She was relaxing with a cooling glass of champagne when a familiar pair of arms stole about her waist from behind her.

"My lady," Stephen murmured, kissing the curve of her neck. "I have been looking for you."

Cat shut her eyes, briefly savoring the feel of his warm body against hers. It reminded her of the passionate idyll in her study, and her own body softened with desire. "Then it would seem you have found me, my lord," she replied, turning to smile up at him. He was dressed in a tight jacket of black velvet, his cravat arranged in simple folds beneath his chin. He wasn't the finest dressed man present, she decided with a flash of wifely pride, but in her eyes he was the most handsome.

"You're wearing the family's emeralds," he observed, flicking his finger against the center stone. "They look well on you."

Cat's cheeks warmed with pleasure at his words. "Lottie insisted," she said, recalling her sister-in-law's dogged demands she wear the costly jewels. "She says Lord Glendon once tried to buy them from your grandfather, and that seeing them on me would be certain to put his nose out of joint."

Stephen's mouth curved in a reminiscent smile. "Lottie has always been one to hold a grudge. The earl debated her husband last year, and called him a knave."

"Ah, that explains it," Cat said, thinking of the other woman's scathing remarks about the earl's coat. Then she thought of something else, and sent her husband a reproving frown. "You're late," she told him in a stern tone. "The waltz has already been played, and 'tis your fault I was forced to seek another partner."

"Then I shall bribe the orchestra to play another," he said with a casual shrug. "Who did you give my waltz to, by the by? I'll have to call him out."

"I gave it to Captain Lacey," Cat told him, "and you're not to call him out after he has been so kind to me."

"Insolent puppy," Stephen muttered, albeit with little heat. "I am getting tired of finding him making up to my countess every time I turn around. It shall be pistols at ten paces if this continues, mark me."

They returned to the ballroom, and Stephen briefly abandoned her to have a word with the orchestra's conductor. She wasn't in the least surprised to hear the delicate strains of a waltz following him as he made his way back to her.

"You are a rascal, sir," she said, shaking her head at him. "This was supposed to be a contradance."

"I don't see anyone looking disappointed," he replied with the arrogance that once set her teeth on edge, but now delighted her. "Besides, I want to waltz with you."

He twirled her expertly about the dance floor, controlling her with the same mastery he showed in their bed. Thinking of Stephen in their bed made Cat think of the secret she had been hugging to her heart, and she knew she could no longer keep the truth from him. She was certain she was with child, and she was suddenly eager to share her news with him. Tonight, she decided, her heart pounding with happiness. I'll tell him tonight.

She peeked up at him from beneath her lashes, pleased to find he was watching her with scarcely veiled passion. "Are you promised elsewhere this evening, my lord, or might your countess hope you will be available to escort her home?" she purred, sliding her fingers up to tease the back of his neck.

He gave her a slow, sensual smile and drew her against him. "She might reasonably hope such a thing," he drawled, pressing his hardened body to hers. "So long as she remembers that like any good coachman, I too expect payment."

Thrilling at the teasing game they were playing, she sent him an imperious look. "Do you? How awkward. I left my reticule in my bedchamber. If you wish to receive payment, I fear you shall have to meet me there. Only mind you don't tell my husband," she warned with a sultry look. "You wouldn't believe how possessive the devil is."

"So long as you believe it, my lady, there shouldn't be any problem," he returned wryly. "And I shall be delighted to meet you in your bedchamber. I have a few thoughts on what sort of coin I should like to receive, should you be interested." He ducked his head, whispering audacious suggestions in her ear that had her blushing and laughing by turns.

He all but dragged her off the floor, impervious to the stares and knowing sniggers that followed them. They were standing in the hallway waiting for Cat's wrap to be fetched, when a footman handed Stephen a sealed note. He read it quickly, and when he raised his eyes, all signs of the playful lover were gone.

"I'm sorry, my love, but I'm afraid something has come up and I shan't be able to keep our appointment," he said, his tone coolly remote. "Will you mind waiting for Lottie?"

Cat felt like bursting into petulant tears, so great was her disappointment. She was also wildly curious as to what sort of emergency could summon Stephen at this hour of the night, but she managed to hold her emotions in check. "I'll be fine," she told him, proud of her cool control. "You may go."

Instead of leaving, Stephen lingered at her side. "Hopefully this shouldn't take very long," he said, his gaze resting on her face. "Will you go directly to bed when you get home, or will you wait up for me?"

Cat understood what he was really asking, and the realization he was still eager to make love to her did much to soothe her injured feelings. "I am very sleepy," she replied, pouting just a little. "But I suppose I might be persuaded to stay up, for a little while, at least."

He carried her gloved hands to his lips and kissed them. "You're too good to your coachman," he murmured, his dark eyes incandescent. "Give my impossible sister my regards, and tell her I expect her to take my wife home at a decent hour." With that he walked away, leaving Cat alone in the entryway.

"Well, I'm here," Stephen groused, scowling at Exter as he faced him across the desk in Lord Farringdale's private study. "What's so important you had to summon me here, and why couldn't it wait until tomorrow?"

Exter leaned back in his chair, meeting Stephen's gaze coldly. "I've some news for you. It isn't pleasant, so I shall be blunt. Daintry has been shot."

Stephen staggered back in horror. "What?"

"Daintry has been shot," Exter repeated. "He was found earlier this evening not quite three blocks from a gaming hell frequented by Sedgewood. He'd been shot through the chest."

Stephen closed his eyes, his years on the battlefield making it all too easy for him to envision the horrific scene Albert described so dispassionately. "Is he alive?" he managed, his hands balling into fists as he opened his eyes.

"Barely. One of the urchins I sometimes use was following him, and saw some of what happened. He was able to get Richard into a cart and had him brought to my home; otherwise God only knows what might have happened to him."

Stephen lowered himself onto a chair facing the desk. "Did he see the man who shot him?" he asked, thinking with icy calm. "Was it Sedgewood?"

"No," Exter answered firmly. "The light in the alley was poor, but Dickie saw enough to know that the man was younger than Sedgewood. The man he described was "a smartly dressed cove," tall, with dark hair. Sound familiar?"

Stephen thought for a moment. "The man at the inn," he said, and nodded. He started to ask another question then stopped, shooting Exter an outraged glare.

"If Richard is lying wounded at your house, then what the devil are you doing here? Why aren't you with him?"

"Because I didn't want to tip our hand to Sedgewood and whoever's helping him," Exter returned, not seeming the least offended by Stephen's furious demand. "And as for Richard, I've one of my most trusted men sitting with him. He's receiving the best of care, that much I can assure you."

It helped, but Stephen was far from mollified. "Where is Sedgewood now?"

"At home," Exter said, leaning forward, "and if you're thinking of confronting him, don't."

"Damn it, Albert!" Stephen's fist slammed onto the desk, sending a porcelain figurine skittering. "This bastard has slandered and threatened my wife, attacked my son, and now he's shot one of my oldest friends! And you expect me to do nothing?"

"I've just told you it wasn't Sedgewood who shot Richard."

"Sedgewood may not have pulled the trigger, but you and I both know he damned well aimed the pistol," Stephen returned, then drew a deep breath, taking a deliberate step back from the edge of anger. "What was Daintry doing when he was shot?" he asked, studying Exter closely. "Was he following Sedgewood?"

"No." Exter shook his head. "As I said, Sedgewood is at home. Richard was following someone else. He developed intelligence that Sedgewood was deeply in debt to someone to the tune of nearly twenty thousand pounds, and I believe that's who he was following when he was attacked."

Twenty thousand pounds! Stephen's eyebrows arched in astonishment. That was rather deep play, even for a notorious gambler like Sedgewood, and perhaps it explained his attack on Eddie. A debt of that magnitude was like to drive anyone to desperation. "What is the gentleman's name?" he asked, thinking it might be prudent to call upon the man himself.

"He didn't tell me," Exter said, sounding frustrated. "We

were supposed to meet tomorrow to discuss the matter. He did say the man was in Society and is a known gamester, but that's all."

"You just described half of Society," Stephen grumbled, trying to think of any man who specifically met that description and that of the man at the inn. Unfortunately he'd been too long from London, and not a single name came to mind. There was no hope for it, he decided glumly. He'd have to ask Lottie. If the man was indeed in the *ton,* she was certain to know who he was.

"What do we do now?" he asked, rubbing the back of his neck.

"I'm not certain," Exter admitted, looking grim. "If this was an affair I was handling for the Home Office, I would suggest waiting for a bit and then send in another operative when it was safe. But this . . ." He shook his head.

"I still think killing Sedgewood would simplify everything," Stephen said, his jaw hardening with hatred. "I much doubt anyone would complain."

"No," Exter agreed, "but killing Sedgewood won't give you the man who shot Richard and arranged for your son to be poisoned. That's the man you should fear every bit as much as Sedgewood. He's the more cunning of the pair, and far more dangerous."

That brought Stephen's head jerking up. "What do you mean?"

"Merely that until recently Sedgewood has confined himself to blustering threats and slanderous accusations against your wife. Now he is actively seeking to remove the one barrier between himself and a fortune. Is this all his doing, or is he acting at someone else's behest? Because if it is the latter, removing Sedgewood may not be the answer you think it is.

"Think about what I've said," Exter added, rising to his feet and laying his hand on Stephen's shoulder. "We'll meet again tomorrow, and perhaps by then we'll have some answers."

Stephen also rose, his mind whirling at what Exter had said. "I'll be at your house after lunch, then." He started to go, then turned at the door. "You'll let me know if anything happens, won't you?" he asked, forcing out the painful words.

Exter nodded, understanding he was talking about Richard. "I will," he said quietly. "And, Stephen?" He smiled sadly. "I know I'm probably wasting my time, but this isn't your fault. Richard has been an operative for years. He knew what the dangers were, and he accepted them. You must remember that."

"Those were risks he took for king and country," Stephen corrected, bitterness welling up inside of him. "But this was for me. I won't forget that."

After leaving the study, Stephen pushed his way through the crowds. The viscount of Farringdale was notorious for his crushes, which was why Stephen had refused his invitation in the first place, and the presence of so many laughing, gossiping people blocking his path made him long to rage in fury. They were useless, pathetic parasites, the whole lot of them not worth a valiant man like Daintry, he thought hotly. The knowledge he'd once been exactly the same added to his feelings of distaste, and his anger all but choked him.

He bypassed the ballroom and the card room, and was almost to the stairs when he felt the touch of a hand on his arm. He turned and found himself looking into Davinia's mocking eyes.

"My lord, we meet again," she purred, smiling up at him.

"Lady Dewhurst." He bowed stiffly, silently cursing his bad luck in encountering the one person he most wanted to avoid.

"Are you here alone?" Davinia stroked her fan down his arm. "Never say your charming wife has let you slip the leash? One hears she keeps you tethered closely to her side."

"My wife is at home, where I am now bound," he said, not bothering to mask his displeasure. "Good evening, my lady."

She gave a throaty laugh and moved to block him with her supple body. "Oh, don't be so high in the instep, Stephen," she chided. "I was only funning. Surely I am entitled to that much, after all we once meant to one another."

He eyed her with deliberate insult. "Did we mean anything to each other? I thought I was nothing more than one of your conquests . . . as you were one of mine. Good night."

Her dark blue eyes flared with anger, and she took a step

toward him, her hand raised. Expecting a slap he was honest enough to admit he deserved, Stephen was unprepared when instead of striking him, she threw her arms about his neck. She clung with the tenacity of a leech, the cloying smell of her perfume all but choking him. Outraged, he pushed her aside and stalked away, so intent on making his escape he missed the satisfied smile curving her painted lips.

It was nearing two of the morning before he reached his house, and he was relieved to hear Cat had arrived ahead of him and had already retired for the night. He went up to his dressing room, dismissing his valet with an impatient flick of his wrist. He supposed he should disrobe first, but he was too anxious to see Cat. Pushing open the door, he peered into the bedchamber, his heart pounding with pleasure when he saw the candle flickering at her bedside. She'd waited up for him, just as she'd promised.

Closing the door behind him, he walked silently over to the bed, his lips curving in a rueful smile as he saw that whatever her intentions, his Cat was sound asleep. Unaccountably moved, he bent and brushed his lips across her cheek. Light as the touch was, she moved at once, her lashes fluttering as she gave a sleepy smile.

"Stephen? Is that you?" she asked, keeping her eyes closed.

"For the sake of our marriage, it had better be," he teased, bending lower to nip the curve of her neck. "Were you expecting someone else, mayhap?"

"Mmmm . . ." She smiled wantonly, winding her arms about his shoulders, drawing him down to her. "Now that you mention it, a rather handsome coachman I met this evening hinted he might be paying me a visit. I trust you don't object?"

"Strenuously." He leaned down to lick the top of her breast. "If the fellow does have the temerity to appear, I must insist you send him packing. I share my countess with no one."

"Then I suppose I—" Cat's voice broke off, and her entire body went rigid as a board.

Ever sensitive to her every move, he drew back at once. "What is it?" he asked worriedly.

"I . . . it's nothing," Cat stammered, shifting away from him. "I suppose I'm still half-asleep. I've had rather a busy day."

Stephen hesitated, noting her sudden pallor with resignation. "Go back to sleep, love," he said gently, ignoring the screaming protest of his aroused body as he covered her with the sheets. "I just need to change, and then I'll join you."

"Very well." Her voice was soft. "Good night, Stephen."

He studied her for several seconds before moving back. He was almost desperate for the sweetness of release, but there was no way he could importune Cat when she was so clearly exhausted. He could wait . . . he hoped. For the moment, it was more important that Cat get the rest she needed.

He peeled off his tight jacket with frustrated impatience, brooding over all that had happened that night. He'd been careful to give Sedgewood a wide berth, but perhaps it was time for a change of strategy. He didn't have to make the bastard his bosom beau, but that didn't mean he couldn't pay him a cousinly visit. With Daintry out of commission, they would need someone else to keep an eye on him, and Stephen could think of no one better suited for the task than himself.

Satisfied at the way he'd worked things out, Stephen picked up his jacket from the floor and was about to toss it on the wardrobe chair when he noted the shoulders were decidedly damp. What the devil? He lifted the jacket for a cautious sniff and was engulfed in the overpowering stench of violets.

In a flash, he realized Davinia must have dumped some of her perfume on him when she'd embraced him. It had been a trick of hers when they had been lovers; a way of marking a man as hers, she'd purred, looking smug. He whirled around and cast Cat a frantic look. Had she noticed? he wondered, studying the figure lying peacefully in the bed. God, he hoped not.

He finished undressing, taking care to toss the ruined jacket into his dressing room. He'd give it to his valet, he decided, knowing he'd never feel comfortable wearing it again. Devil take Davinia! What had the witch been trying to prove?

Naked, he padded over to the bed and slipped under the covers beside Cat. Her breathing was deep and even, and he assumed she'd fallen asleep, a small mercy that had him sending a small prayer of gratitude heavenward. He slipped his arms around her, cuddling her against him and savoring the feel of her in his arms. His mind was racing, but as he'd learned to do while a soldier, he simply shut the thoughts off, falling dreamlessly into sleep with his wife held tightly in his arms.

Eighteen

Another woman. Cat lay staring up at the ceiling, dry-eyed and dead inside as she struggled to accept the painful truth. Stephen had come to their bed reeking of another woman. The knowledge was agonizing, but more agonizing still was the realization that followed. She was in love with him.

She bit her lip to hold back a cry of pain. Love. It hadn't been something she'd wanted, something she'd ever envisioned for herself, and yet there it was. She loved Stephen, and the mere possibility he'd been unfaithful to her was almost more than she could bear.

There had to be some explanation, she thought, forcing herself to think past her turbulent emotions. Stephen was a man of impeccable integrity, a man who took his obligations with the utmost seriousness. Indeed, it had been those qualities, so unexpected in the wild rake he'd once been, that had attracted her first. It wasn't hard to love a man who was the very embodiment of strength and honor, she mused, her eyes welling with tears. And given that strength and honor, how could she suspect him of disgracing himself and her?

It didn't make sense, she brooded, sleep as elusive as a chimera. None of it did. Not his odd behavior these past few days, or the mysterious note that had sent him rushing from her side earlier this evening. Something was clearly amiss, and she wondered if that something involved Jeremey. The thought made her freeze, and she rolled over to face Stephen.

"Stephen?" She gently elbowed him. "Stephen?"

His answer was to tighten his arm about her and snuggle her

even closer. "Go to sleep, Cat," he mumbled, nuzzling against her. "We'll make love tomorrow morning."

Cat gaped at him, fighting back the sudden urge to giggle. Here she wanted to discuss Jeremey, and he thought she was waking him up to make love. If she didn't adore him so much, she'd have boxed his ears. Instead she settled against the pillows, her lips curving in an indulgent smile. She wondered what he'd do if she leaned over and whispered he was about to become a father.

That would wake him up soon enough, she thought, imagining the stunned expression on his handsome face giving way to incredible joy. For a moment she was tempted to do just that, but common sense had her holding back. The news she was carrying his child was something too special, too wondrous, to share as a lark. It had to be done at the right time, in the right way, and perhaps, if she managed to find the courage, she'd even tell him she loved him.

Oddly, once she'd decided that, the exhaustion she'd been holding at bay overwhelmed her, and she was asleep almost at once. She was awakened several hours later by the brush of Stephen's lips on hers, and she forced open her eyes to find him bending over her.

"Stephen?" She blinked up at him, puzzled to see he was already dressed. "Are you going out?"

"A friend of mine has been injured," he said, his voice coolly controlled. "I must go at once. I want you to stay in bed for the rest of the day. You've been driving yourself too hard, and I won't have you making yourself ill."

Cat thought of the conversation she'd wanted to have with him last night, and tried to force herself out of the mires of sleep. "But, Stephen—"

"Later, my love." He kissed her again, harder this time. "Just mind you do as you are bid. I'll check on you when I return. Good-bye." He was gone before she could stop him.

To her annoyance she fell back asleep, not awakening until much later in the morning. The dragging exhaustion was something she remembered from Eddie's pregnancy, but that didn't make her like it any more. She rang for the maid, and when

Alice appeared with her morning chocolate, the powerful nausea that hit her was another uncomfortable reminder of the changes her body would be undergoing over the next few months.

"Blast!" She barely got the word out before she lost control of her stomach and was dreadfully ill.

"My lady!" Alice was at her side at once, all cooing concern as she held the slop jar for Cat.

"There, there," she said, patting Cat's cheeks with a damp towel and settling her back against the pillows. "You just lie back and rest a wee bit. You ought to have told me you was increasing, ma'am."

"I wasn't certain until now," Cat muttered, fighting back nausea with grim determination. "I'll be fine in a few moments."

"Hmmph! Fine in six months, more like!" Alice grumbled, picking up the tray and stomping from the room.

From experience Cat knew if she remained quiet for at least an hour the sickness would leave, and she was much cheered when this proved to be the case. This time Alice brought a pot of weak tea with her, hovering over Cat until she'd drained it and eaten the toast that accompanied it.

"And mind you stay in bed, just as his lordship ordered," Alice scolded, waggling her finger at Cat.

"Nonsense, Alice," Cat said sternly, her pride returning with her strength. "I'm fine now, and I'm promised at Lady Barton's."

"But his lordship—"

"His lordship has never borne a child," Cat interrupted. "I have. And I know well what I can and can not do. Believe me," she added, laying her hand on her stomach, "I would never do anything to harm my babe."

That seemed to mollify Alice, although she muttered and complained through Cat's bath and toilette. Because she'd slept in so late, it was nearing three of the clock when Cat left the house, and nearer to three-thirty by the time she was greeting her irate sister-in-law.

"You're late!" Lottie reproved, a rigid smile in place as she embraced Cat. "There's something I must tell you!"

"And there's something I must tell you," Cat said with an indulgent laugh. "I'll explain later. After I've told Stephen."

Lottie gave her a sharp look, but with so many other guests to tend to, there was little she could do but turn away. Cat wasn't naive enough to think her sister-in-law would allow her remark to go by without demanding all the details, and knew she probably had less than half an hour before Lottie cornered her. In the meanwhile, she was human enough to take sadistic glee in knowing Lottie was probably suffering the torments of the damned trying to guess what she meant.

Since she was well-acquainted with most of Lottie's friends, Cat moved easily about the salon, smiling and greeting everyone with serene confidence. She thought a few people looked at her strangely or seemed uneasy in her presence, but she was too happy to care. She was chatting with Mrs. Ellerton when she saw Captain Lacey enter through the garden door. Before she could raise her hand in acknowledgement, he was at her side, his expression anxious as he studied her.

"Good afternoon, Captain Lacey!" she said brightly, smiling up at him. "How are you this glorious day?"

In answer he took her hand in his, using his firm grip to draw her slightly away from the others.

"My lady, I am surprised to see you here!" he said, his voice pitched at an intimate level. "When you were so late in coming, I thought, that is, naturally I assumed . . ."

"Assumed what?" Cat asked, wondering what on earth could be ailing him. He seemed almost nervous, darting furtive glances over his shoulder, and drawing her farther away from the others.

He grew decidedly more uneasy at her question. "I'm sorry, this is so embarrassing. I thought you knew, but evidently you don't. I'm sorry," he repeated, and then turned and fled as if pursued by demons straight from the bowels of hell.

Cat gazed after him in a mixture of confusion and impatience. Something was clearly afoot, she decided, her lips thinning in annoyance, and clearly there was only one way she would learn what that something was. She set out after the captain, grabbing him unceremoniously by the arm and dragging him over to a corner.

"Captain Lacey," she began, fixing him with her sternest look, "I must tell you I have little use for mendacity. If there is something you wish to say, then be so good as to say it! What was it you'd thought I'd heard?"

"The gossip about your husband and . . . and Lady Dewhurst. They were seen together last night at Viscount Farringdale's ball, and they . . . they were embracing," he stammered, looking everywhere but at her. "I am very sorry. I thought you knew."

Cat's fingers slid from his sleeve. All of last night's pain and uncertainty returned a hundredfold, and for a brief moment she couldn't seem to breathe. It was so easy, so terribly easy to envision Stephen holding the beautiful redhead in his arms, kissing her, making love to her. And then she remembered last night's other revelation, and felt relief flooding through her. She was so relieved, in fact, that not knowing how else to respond, she burst into laughter.

"But it's the truth!" the captain exclaimed, obviously taken aback by her reaction. "A friend of mine was standing not ten feet from them, and he saw everything! He said—forgive me, ma'am—he said there was no mistaking the nature of the embrace."

"If he was standing ten feet from them, then it is obvious he did more than mistake the nature of the embrace; he mistook the very nature of what he saw! Heavens, is this what everyone is in such an uproar over?" She gave another trill of laughter. "Talk about something being a great deal of sound and fury, signifying nothing!" She shook her head in amusement.

He stared at her as if she'd run mad. "Do you mean to say you do not mind?" he demanded incredulously.

"Of course I mind!" Cat responded, taking care to keep her tone light. "I mind very much, indeed! And if that hussy dares to lay her hands on my husband again, I shall scratch her eyes out. But I certainly am not going to go into the swoons because my husband was allegedly seen embracing his former mistress at the Farringdales' ball! It is too ridiculous by half!"

"But, my lady—"

"Captain"—she laid her hand back on his arm—"I am sure you mean well, and I am going to credit your actions in repeating such slander to me as being purely altruistic, but in future, I would much appreciate if you would keep such tiresome tattle to yourself. Whatever Society chooses to say or believe about my husband and myself is of very little interest to me, and I have no desire to hear it. Is that quite clear?"

A mutinous anger flashed in his blue eyes, then was quickly gone. "Yes, Lady Rockholme," he said, sketching a stiff bow. "And I apologize if I have given offense."

"You haven't offended me," Cat assured him, unbending enough to offer him a smile. "But I do mean what I say. No more gossip, or discussion about gossip, ever again. All right?"

"All right." He nodded, a look of profound relief on his face. "Thank you, my lady, you're very kind."

She smiled again and moved away, making a mental note to keep as far from the captain as she could. His motives might be innocent enough, but she was wearying of his incessant tattling. Heavens, he was as bad as some of her former pupils, forever carrying tales of each other's misbehavior to whoever would listen, she thought, wisely hiding a smile. She was willing to wager he was a perfect pest as a child.

The rest of the afternoon passed quickly. To her amusement Lottie's duties as hostess prevented her from carrying her off for a private coze, a situation the other woman clearly found intolerable. She kept catching Cat's eye and jerking her head like someone in a fit, but Cat mischievously paid her no mind. Given the way Lottie had bear-led her about London, she found it refreshing to have her sister-in-law in her power.

She was starting to weaken when one of the other young ladies, a Miss Amelia Montgomery, sidled up to her and laid a trembling hand on her arm.

"I beg pardon, Lady Rockholme," she said, affecting the die-away accents Cat had always decried, "but I was wondering if I might ask a favor of you?"

"Certainly, Miss Montgomery, what is it?" Cat asked, wondering if the young woman had overindulged in the champagne punch Lottie had served. Her cheeks were brightly pink, and there was a decided sparkle to her otherwise dull eyes.

"I am feeling unwell . . . yes, most unwell." The girl's lively speech and the dramatic way she laid her hand on her forehead confirmed Cat's suspicions. "I was hoping you would be so good as to take me home in your carriage. I-I fear I shall swoon." She started swaying like a sapling in a strong breeze.

Deciding she'd lecture the girl later on the evils of strong spirits, Cat swiftly slipped her arm about her waist and guided her from the room. The moment they were out in the hall she ordered their cloaks and bonnets, and requested her carriage be brought around at once. Miss Montgomery continued swaying and moaning in a manner that was beginning to grate on Cat's nerves. She only prayed the foolish chit didn't cast up her accounts in the carriage. The prospect wasn't one a pregnant woman could imagine with any degree of comfort.

A hovering footman opened the door, and another ran ahead to open the door of the waiting carriage. Cat had already put one foot on the step of the carriage before she realized the error.

"Wait a moment," she said, coming to a puzzled halt. "There's been a mistake. This isn't my carriage." She turned to inform Hiss Montgomery, when she was suddenly shoved forcefully from behind. The shove was so strong it sent her flying onto the floor of the carriage, and then someone was climbing in after her and slamming the door behind them.

Cat struggled to sit upright, her initial confusion turning to blood-chilling terror as she whirled around to face whoever had climbed in after her. Seeing Captain Lacey sitting there had her breathing a sigh of relief, until she saw the man sitting opposite from him.

"Not one sound, you bitch," Jeremey Sedgewood drawled, pulling a pistol from his greatcoat and calmly pointing it at Cat. "Not one damned sound, or I'll kill you where you are."

"Lacey," Stephen enunciated through clenched teeth, raw fury making him shake. "You're certain it was Lacey?"

"Quite sure," Daintry responded weakly, his pale lips twisting in a ghastly smile. "Fellow's not likely to forget the man who walked up to him, calm as you please, and put a bullet in his gut. The bastard was even *smiling* as he did it."

"But why?" Stephen demanded, struggling to make sense of everything he'd learned in the past several hours. Richard had regained consciousness shortly after sunrise, and the moment he'd opened his eyes, the words of the sordid tale of Lacey's involvement with Sedgewood had come spilling out.

"I told you, the money," he said, stirring restlessly on the bed. "Sedgewood had lost heavily to him, but Lacey had withheld demanding payment, believing Sedgewood's promise he'd soon be the viscount. When it became plain Sedgewood had lied, Lacey knew he had to do something or face financial ruin."

"He tried slandering Lady Rockholme first." Exter picked up the threads of the story. "He'd learned, somehow, that young Brockton was your natural son, something you never saw fit to disclose to me," he added, sending Stephen an injured look.

Stephen thrust a weary hand through his hair, remembering that day by the standing stones, when the jingle of a horse's bridle had alerted him to the fact he and Cat were being watched. If only he'd followed through on his instincts, instead of allowing himself to be distracted, he thought bitterly. If he had, only think of what all might have been avoided.

"I couldn't tell you, Albert," he said heavily, meeting his friend's gaze without apology. "It would have meant branding my son a bastard, and I couldn't do that."

"All right"—Albert accepted Stephen's explanation with a curt nod—"I can understand that. But after the attack on Eddie, why the devil weren't you more forthcoming? Didn't you think we'd need to know everything if we were to defeat Sedgewood?"

"Soldiers," Daintry said, giving a weak chuckle. "They're too used to taking or giving commands to understand the concept of working in double harness, eh, Rockholme?"

"That may be," Exter continued doggedly, "but in this case, Stephen's compunction could well have cost his son his life. You ought to have trusted us, old boy."

A knock at the door prevented Stephen from responding, and

a young man Stephen had never seen slipped in to hand Exter a note. He studied it briefly, and then crossed to the cellaret, opening it up to reveal an incredible cache of arms. He selected two pistols and carried them to Stephen.

"The moment I learned of Lacey's involvement with Sedgewood, I set a man to watching him," he said, meeting Stephen's gaze with a steady look. "He just reported back. Lacey and Sedgewood have kidnapped your wife."

Everything in Stephen stopped. His heart, his breath, his ability to think, all ground to a halt at Exter's imperturbable words. His chest ached so fiercely he thought it would burst, and he forced himself to draw in a deep breath of air. "Where have they taken her?" he asked, the calm he'd experienced so many times in battle stealing over him.

He doesn't know," Exter answered, keeping his voice at the same even level. "They were heading north on the Great Road, and we have two more men following them; but we can't be certain of their final destination. They may be making a break for the border, but there's no way to know at this point."

"Waltham Abbey!" Daintry exclaimed, struggling to sit up. "Lacey has a hunting lodge there, not far off the road. It's isolated, but near to town. They'll need to be near town, if-if they mean to hold her to ransom," he stammered, sending Stephen an apologetic look.

Stephen didn't bother replying, knowing that their greatest hope, their only hope of Cat remaining alive, was if the kidnappers were holding her for money. He refused to contemplate what might happen if they were holding her for any other reason.

"How many men can you muster?" he asked, calmly tucking the pistols in his pockets.

"Give me an hour and I can have thirty, all armed and ready to move," Exter replied bluntly. "But you're not going to wait, are you?"

"No." Stephen shook his head, his mind already on the ride ahead and what had to be done. "Follow when you're able, and be sure the men understand Cat's safety is their first priority. Make certain they understand that, Albert."

"I will," Albert promised solemnly. "Is there anything else you need?"

Stephen forced himself to be practical, even as he was longing to be on his horse and away. "Ammunition," he said, thinking carefully. "More pistols, a knife, and as much gold as you can spare. It may be necessary to barter with the men holding my wife, and I'd as lief have something to offer them."

"You may have whatever you need," Albert said, crossing back to the cellaret. "You do know this may be a trap," he added, meeting Stephen's dark gaze. "You could well be riding to your death."

"I know." Stephen's voice was calm as he faced the magnitude of what he was feeling and all that it meant. "But it doesn't really matter, because if anything happens to Cat, I'm already as good as dead. I love her."

"So you see, my dear, it's really quite simple," Jeremey said, simpering at Cat from across the confines of the carriage. "Sign this piece of paper admitting you're a whore, and that your precious son is nothing more than a bastard with no claim to the Brockton name or estate, and you may go free."

Cat met Jeremey's gaze, doing her best not to let her revulsion show. "And if I do not?" she asked, biding desperately for time. "What will you do then?"

"Why, kill you, of course, and then forge your name to the papers," Jeremey responded with an indifferent shrug. "That was my original idea, but Marcus here persuaded me it would not serve. There is always a small chance, you see, that the forgery would be detected, and I should likely swing. I've no desire to hang, you know. I'd much rather live as a viscount in the very lap of luxury."

Cat stole a look at Lacey, who was sitting across from them, regarding her and Jeremey with a smug smile on his face. She'd always regarded Jeremey as a monster without equal, but here, she realized, was the true monster.

"Something displeases you, my lady?" he mocked, using the same solicitous tones he'd always used when addressing her.

Cat gave him a cold look, raising her chin with pride. "You displease me," she said, refusing to glance away.

"Do I?" His smirk grew marked. "Pity, and after I went to such length to put myself in your good graces. Certainly your hen-witted sister-in-law was convinced of my sincerity, as was that tiresome Miss Montgomery. She was only too happy to lure you out to the carriage so that I could steal a few brief moments with my beloved." He gave a nasty laugh that had Cat longing to box his ears. At least she now understood the younger woman's role in all this, she thought, and then turned back to Jeremey.

"You've said you'll release me if I sign the papers," She told him. "How do I know you'll keep your word?"

"Why, because I am a gentleman, of course," Jeremey laughed. "And because I don't wish to have that murderous beast you're married to coming after me."

Cat bit her tongue, keeping back the words that Stephen would come after him anyway, and that he wouldn't stop until both he and Lacey were dead. She knew that as certainly as she knew that even now he was searching for her, and that somehow he would find her. All she had to do was remain calm and remain alive, a prospect that grew increasingly dim the farther they travelled from London.

"All right," she said, deciding she had nothing to lose by meeting his demands. "Give me the papers. I'll sign them now."

"Oh, I haven't them with me." Jeremey chortled, his laugh making her stomach twist. "They're at Marcus's hunting lodge. We thought it might be amusing to spend a few hours in your company, my lady. Then we'll release you."

They meant to rape her. Cat accepted the knowledge coolly, knowing by the gleam in Jeremey's eyes that he was waiting for her to plead and cry for mercy. Well, he could wait forever, she decided with a calm sense of pride. She would never beg.

The rest of the journey passed in agonizing slowness for Cat. Jeremey kept trying to goad her into speech, telling her in nauseating detail the things he meant to do to her, the things they would demand she do for them, but Cat remained silent. Had it just been her, she knew she would fight them to the death before allowing them to make good their disgusting boasts. But it wasn't just her, and the thought of her babe made her determined to survive anything . . . even rape.

Her lack of response finally silenced Jeremey, and he fell into a petulant state, contenting himself with pointed glares, and fortifying himself with sips from a silver flask. Cat had vivid memories of the night he had forced his way into her room when in his cups, and tried not to shudder. She had escaped that time because of Edward, she thought. She would survive this time because of herself.

All too soon they were pulling to a halt before a tumbled-down ruin of a lodge. Jeremey pulled her out of the carriage, shoving her into the house ahead of them.

"The only servants here work for me," he told her, the hot, sick look she remembered dancing in his eyes. "You can scream if you wish, but they'll not lift a finger to help you."

Cat merely lifted her eyebrow, crossing the room to sit at the simple table in front of the fire. "I'm ready to sign the papers," she said calmly. "Bring them."

She could tell her behavior both angered and confused Jeremey. He was accustomed to hurting things weaker than he, and her implacable calm was starting to unnerve him.

"Don't you want some brandy first?" he asked, grabbing a decanter from a shelf and spilling the contents into a glass. "Here." He thrust the glass at her. "Take it. I said take it, damn you, or by God I'll pour it down you!"

"That's enough," Marcus said, speaking for the first time since entering the house. "Let her sign the papers first, Sedgewood; then you may have your fun."

Jeremey whirled on him, his face twisting with frustrated rage. "Don't you tell me what to do, you damned Cit!" he roared, taking a threatening step forward. "Mind your manners, or else I'll teach you more!"

Marcus smiled. "Will you? I much doubt that."

Cat watched them avidly, trying to gauge how best to make use of their discord to her advantage. If she could keep them at each other's throats, there was a small chance she could escape. All she had to do was watch and wait.

Tension filled the small room of the lodge as Jeremey and Captain Lacey faced each other. In the end, it was Jeremey who backed down, hurling the glass against the soot-blackened stones of the fireplace.

"Have it your way, curse you," he muttered, stalking over to a secretary set against the far wall. "But once this damned bitch signs these papers, *I'll* be the viscount; then we'll just see what's what!"

Instead of being cowed, Lacey seemed coolly amused. "I'm sure we shall, my lord. I'm sure we shall."

"My lord." Jeremey brightened at that. "Aye, that's what I'll soon be. Mayhap then you won't mind spreading your legs for me, eh, Lady Rockholme?" He laughed at what he viewed as a fine witticism.

Cat ignored him, although it was growing increasingly difficult to do so. She looked around her, and this time she noted the fruit and cheese board sitting on the side table. Her stomach rolled at the thought of food, but the knife she saw lying in readiness had her heart pounding with hope. It wouldn't do for her to ask for food just yet, she decided. But later, after she'd signed the papers and Jeremey was feeling smugly in control, she would politely ask for a bit of cheese. One moment, one small moment, that's all she needed.

"Here." Jeremey tossed the sheaf of official-looking documents in front of her. "Hurry up and sign 'em. There's not many hours left in the day, and I intend using everyone of them teaching you how to please a man. Like as not your fine husband will even thank me for it. You can't give a man much of a ride if your husband's already sniffing around his former mistress, eh, Lacey?" He turned to wink at the captain.

Understanding dawned, and Cat gave him a cool look. "That was all your doing, was it?" she asked quietly. "I wondered."

"It seemed your husband had wounded the lady's delicate sensibilities, and she was more than willing to get a little of her own back," he said, looking bored. "She will be devastated to learn that rather than putting a wedge between you as I'd hoped to do, you merely seemed amused by it all."

So Davinia was involved as well; Cat filed the information

away for future use. "I love my husband," she said, hating that she was saying the words aloud for the first time to the two of them. "I know he would never deceive me."

"No, but it's you who will deceive him, just as you deceived your first husband with him," Lacey said with a laugh. "That's rather ironic, isn't it? And really, it couldn't have worked out more for the better, now that I think of it."

"Eh?" Jeremey shot him a confused look. "What's that mean?"

"Nothing."

"There is still one thing I do not understand, and that is how you formed the impression Stephen is Edward's father," Cat said, hedging for information. "Did Lady Dewhurst tell you some dreadful lie about me?"

In answer, Captain Lacey gave a mocking laugh. "How indignant you sound, my lady. You almost convince me of your innocence. But in answer to your question, other than attempting to seduce your husband, Lady Dewhurst has naught to do with this. I myself heard you and Lord Rockholme discussing the matter that day by the standing stones. And my thanks, my lady, for persuading him not to fire," he added with a sneering smile. "I would have found it most disagreeable to be shot."

Cat remembered the noise that had caught Stephen's notice that day, and wished now she had held her tongue. Had she let him shoot, she would not now find herself in such danger. She spent the next several minutes pretending to read the papers, poring over the unfamiliar Latin phrases as if she understood their meaning. "These are very good," she said, feigning admiration. "One could almost believe them to be genuine."

"They are genuine!" Jeremey took instant umbrage to her remark. "A fat lot of good a bunch of forged papers would do me! I paid a damned solicitor in Lincoln's Commons good gold for these, and they'll hold up in the highest court in the land."

"I'm sure they shall," she turned back to the papers, continuing to study them despite Jeremey's repeated demands that she sign the documents and be done with it.

"One moment," she said, pausing at one particular paragraph. "This grants you full authority over Elizabeth and Lydia. You must know I can not allow that."

Jeremey threw back his head in raucous laughter. "I'd like to know how you intend stopping me. Once you sign those papers, you'll be an admitted adulteress. You'll have no rights where those sweet chits are concerned. They'll be all mine."

Cold terror made Cat sway on her chair. "Stephen would never allow it," she said, reaching for the calm she thought she'd mastered. "He'll kill you before he'd let you hurt the girls."

"Oh, devil take it, then!" Jeremey snatched up the papers and, to her amazement, drew a large X through the offending paragraph. "There! I never wanted the stupid chits, anyway. You can keep them for all of me! Now will you sign the papers!"

Now that the direct threat to her daughters had been removed, Cat could breathe easy, and she resumed her study of the papers. "Everything seems to be in order," she said, picking up the quill. "There's just one more thing."

"Now what?" Jeremey howled. "You're as bad as a damned solicitor, haggling over every word and paragraph!"

"I want your word you will leave Eddie alone," she said, forcing herself to meet Jeremey's gaze. "There are to be no more 'illnesses,' no accidents of any sort. Do I make myself plain?"

"Of course," Jeremey soothed, beaming like a benevolent uncle. "Never meant the lad any real harm. And really, you've only yourself to blame. If you'd given me what was mine instead of stealing it, I'd have had no cause to hurt the boy."

Such childlike reasoning made Cat long to bash him over the head. "So long as it's understood Eddie is not to be harmed in any way," she said, glancing back at the document. She knew she'd prevaricated as long as she dared, and that the time had come to sign the papers and be done with it. She only prayed Stephen arrived soon, or that she'd have the strength to endure whatever came next. She signed the document.

"At last!" She'd scarce set the quill down before Jeremey snatched up the papers, carrying them over to the secretary and sprinkling sand on them. "I've waited half my life for this, but I'll soon have what's mine!"

"As will I," Lacey said coolly. "Remember our agreement, Sedgewood. Twenty thousand pounds, plus interest."

"Certainly, certainly." Jeremey was all smiles and charm as he locked the papers away. "A gentleman always pays his debts."

"Don't believe him, Captain," Cat said, realizing the opportunity she'd just been handed. "Mr. Sedgewood has never paid an honest debt in his life. I was forever settling the accounts he'd run up at the local merchants."

"Tradesmen!" Jeremey dismissed the subject with a contemptuous snort. "As if a bunch of dirty Cits with a fistful of my vowels mattered! They ought to have been grateful for my custom."

"He called *you* a Cit," she reminded Lacey, quick to press the advantage. "What's to stop him from dismissing you as well?"

While Jeremey howled in indignation, Cat rose from the table and walked over to the sideboard. She picked at the cheese, nibbled on a bit of bread, and when she was certain no one was watching, she grabbed the knife. She had a weapon now, she thought gratefully. All she needed was the opportunity to use it, and the fortitude to plunge it into a man when the time came.

Nineteen

"I'll ask you one last time, lad," Stephen said silkily, pressing the barrel of the gun to the terrified groom's head. "How many men are inside the lodge besides Captain Lacey and Sedgewood? You've precisely five seconds to tell me."

"But-but, sir, ye don't understand!" the lad babbled, sweat rolling down his filthy face. " 'E'll kill me if I tell!"

"One." Stephen cocked the pistol.

"Please, me lord, that one's the devil 'imself!"

"Two." He placed the barrel against the man's forehead.

"It's just the two of them, and the lady!" The groom cried, shaking in his terror. "They sent everyone else away!"

Satisfied the lad was too frightened to be less than truthful, Stephen calmly hit him with the pistol. He wasted a few precious seconds tying him up and dumping him in one of the empty stalls before moving around to the front of the house. One down, he thought, the coldness sliding once more over him. Now there was only Sedgewood and Lacey to be dealt with.

The door to the lodge was closed, and through the thick wood he could hear the indistinct sound of raised voices. Praying they had been too distracted to bar the door, he closed one hand around the handle and the other against the door, pushing carefully. When it opened, he closed his eyes in sweet relief.

"The devil if I'll sign Larks Hall over to you!" He heard Sedgewood snap, and through the narrow crack he could see the other man confronting Lacey across the width of a crude table. "You've my word as a gentleman you'll get your damned money! If that's not enough for you, then may the plague take you!"

"Your word!" Lacey sneered. "The word of the lowest born cutpurse is worth more than that!"

The argument continued, and while the men shouted insults at each other, Stephen searched desperately for some sign of Cat. He was debating whether or not he should risk opening the door even farther, when a flash of movement to his right caught his notice. It was Cat, and to his overwhelming relief, she seemed unhurt. She was also moving stealthily away from the men, and he realized that in a few seconds she would be between him and them, placing herself in the line of fire. It was now or never.

"Eh? What's this?" Before Stephen could move Sedgewood had noticed Cat's furtive movement and was leaping toward her, grabbing her roughly by the arm. Stephen didn't wait another moment; he shoved open the door, firing his pistol into the air as he burst into the room.

"Let her go, Sedgewood, or you're a dead man!" he said, leveling his other pistol at the stunned man.

"Rockholme!" Sedgewood gaped at him as if he'd sprung up from the floorboards. "What the devil . . ."

"Ah, the noble colonel, riding bravely to the rescue," Lacey drawled with a mocking sneer. "I was wondering when you would make your appearance." He pulled out a pistol from his coat and levelled it at Cat. "As you can see," he added at Stephen's narrow-eyed glare. "I was prepared for any eventuality. Drop your weapons, sir, or I shall be forced to shoot your lovely wife. And it would be such a shame to kill her before Sedgewood and I have the pleasure of bedding her."

Rage and fear erupted in Stephen, but he forced himself to remain cool. "I could still shoot Sedgewood," he said, keeping his weapon trained on the other man. "And then I'd kill you."

"What are you doing, you dolt?" Sedgewood wailed, gazing at Lacey as if he feared the other man had taken leave of his senses. "You're going to get the pair of us killed!"

"Perhaps." Lacey shrugged as if the possibility was of little interest to him. "But what you fail to realize, Sedgewood, is that we're dead men already. Or did you really expect his lordship to simply let us walk away unscathed? You've come for our lives, haven't you?"

"Let my wife go, Sedgewood," Stephen said, not letting the captain distract him. "That will satisfy me."

He saw Sedgewood hesitate, and then in a flash Stephen whirled, bringing his pistol to bear on Lacey, who he now realized presented the greatest threat. The roar of the pistol echoed deafeningly in the small room, followed by a cry of pain. He turned back to see Sedgewood writhing on the floor, the handle of a knife sticking out of his thigh.

Cat stood blinking at him, and to his horror, a stain of dark red blood was spreading across her shoulder. "I knew you would come," she said softly, swaying slightly. "I love you."

"Cat!" He roared out her name in agony, leaping forward to catch her as she crumpled to the floor. He cradled her against him, rocking back and forth as sobs tore through him. "Cat! God, no! No! No! No!"

"I'm wounded!" Sedgewood was crying, clasping his leg. "Help me! For the love of heaven, help me!"

"Heaven will be of no help to the likes of you," Exter said, stepping through the door with a brace of pistols. Several other men crowded in behind him, all of them carrying pistols and the cold, deadly air of seasoned warriors. Stephen paid them no mind, his attention completely wrapped up in Cat.

She was so pale, he thought, hands shaking as he tore open the front of her gown. Lacey's bullet had struck her just beneath her shoulder, and a torrent of blood was flowing from the wound.

"I've a doctor with us." Exter laid a gentle hand on Stephen's arm. "Step back, old fellow, and let him tend her."

"I know how to treat a gunshot wound," Stephen said, his voice devoid of emotion. He couldn't think, he realized dully. He didn't dare let himself think, or he would fall to pieces.

"So does Dr. Hamilton." Exter gently helped Stephen to his feet. "Let him help your lady wife, Stephen. Come now."

Sedgewood was still blubbering for help, but none of the men paid him the slightest mind. Lacey lay sprawled in the corner, and Stephen had seen enough of death to know his bullet had struck home. Noting the direction of his stare, Exter gave a curt nod.

"Dead," he said, sounding grimly pleased. "Good shot, my lord. You put the round right between his eyes."

"I wasn't fast enough," Stephen said, closing his eyes and seeing again the cold way Lacey had taken aim at Cat. "Another second, if I would just have fired another second before I did, I could have killed him before he shot Cat."

"Or he might have shot her anyway," Exter pointed out calmly. "You can't blame yourself for fate, Stephen. It's foolish."

"A doctor! A doctor!" Sedgewood was calling. "Someone send for a doctor before I bleed to death!"

Stephen looked at him, the man who had authored the deadly sequence of events, and he started to walk toward him. Sedgewood saw his expression and began crying out in panic.

"It was Lacey's idea!" he cried, trying to crawl away. "He was the one who thought up the idea of kidnapping her and forcing her to sign the papers! I haven't done anything but take back what was mine!"

Stephen didn't answer; he simply took a pistol from one of the other men and pointed it at Sedgewood. He cocked it, closing his ears to the wounded man's pathetic pleas. No one made a move to stop him, and his finger tightened slowly on the trigger.

"No," he said, lowering the gun. "No, I'm not giving you an easy death after all you've done. You'll live. You'll live and spend the rest of your life rotting in the foulest prison I can find." He turned and walked away.

"The doctor believes it might be best to remove her ladyship to London," Exter said, taking the pistol from Stephen's nerveless fingers. "You ride ahead with them, and I will see to everything here."

Stephen nodded, having lost any interest in Sedgewood. Only Cat mattered, and with that thought in mind he walked over to where she was lying. A sturdy-looking man was stepping forward to lift her, but at one look from Stephen he moved back.

"I will carry my wife," he said, bending to gently gather her in his arms. Then cradling her to his heart, he turned and walked out the door.

The next several hours passed in a haze for Stephen. The ride back to London was a blur he couldn't clearly recall. He could only remember holding Cat on his lap, brushing kisses over her hair and whispering ardently of his love. The thick bandage the doctor had tied over the wound had helped stop the bleeding, but she was still too pale for Stephen's liking. At first he'd fought the doctor's suggestion Cat be given laudanum, but when she roused and began to moan from the pain, he changed his mind. He could bear anything but for his poor wife to he in pain.

He wanted to remain in the bedroom while the bullet was removed, but the doctor wisely had him barred. Instead he passed the time pacing and cursing, demanding news from the harried staff and making himself ill with worry. Lottie and her husband, David, arrived at some point during the vigil, and Lottie wasted little time before flinging herself in his arms.

"It's my fault, all my fault!" she sobbed, dabbing at her eyes with a crumpled handkerchief. "I encouraged his attentions to her! I even invited him to my soirée after Cat made it plain she wanted nothing to do with him. I'm sorry, Stephen."

"Charlotte." David moved forward to pry her away from Stephen. "Later there will be more than enough time for recriminations. For now, we must concentrate on Cat, and what we might do to be of assistance." He raised his solemn gray eyes to meet Stephen's gaze. "What can we do to help you, my lord?" he asked quietly. "You have only to name it."

Stephen studied the younger man silently, realizing there was far more bottom to him than he'd first supposed. "The children will need to be informed," he said, giving Lord Barton the courtesy of accepting his offer of help. "I would be most grateful if you and Lottie went down to Rockholme and brought them here. I-I know Cat would want to see them."

"We'll leave at once," Lord Barton said firmly. "Come, Charlotte, we must be away," he said, and guided his protesting wife from the room.

They had scarce left before Lord Exter and his pretty wife, Anne, arrived to bear him company. The marchioness bullied him into taking some tea and a bit of a sandwich, and her sweet, practical manner made him think of Cat. The two ladies were much alike, be thought, tears burning his eyes. God, how could he bear it if he lost Cat?

"Dr. Hamilton is the man who treated Daintry," Exter said, correctly guessing Stephen's bleak thoughts. "He is a marvel. If anyone can help your wife, it is he."

"The bullet entered below her shoulder," Stephen answered, trying to maintain control over his wildly vacillating emotions. "I don't think any vital organs were hit. If the infection and fever aren't too bad, she should be all right."

"There shouldn't be any infection," Exter assured him. "Dr. Hamilton has trained in Edinburgh, and he is careful to keep his instruments cleaned. Daintry is showing no signs of fever, and his injury was far more serious."

Another hour passed, and still no word came from the doctor. Stephen was growing increasingly agitated, certain Cat had died and the doctor was too afraid to tell him. Exter tried distracting him by telling him about the papers he'd found and then destroyed, but Stephen was too distraught to care. Unable to bear it another moment, he stormed to the door and jerked it open, nearly knocking over the young man who stood there.

"Doctor!" Stephen grabbed him roughly by his lapels and pulled into the room. "How is my wife? Will she he all right? Did you get the ball out? When may I see her?"

Dr. Hamilton's dark blue eyes danced at the flood of questions pouring out of Stephen. "Your wife is fine, my lord," he said, peeling Stephen's fingers from his jacket. "With rest and proper care, there is every reason to expect she will make a full recovery. I was able to extract the ball with very little effort, and you may see her ladyship as soon as you please."

Stephen almost knocked him down, dashing out of the room and taking the stairs two at a time. The room was lit bright as day by several braces of candles, and in their brilliant light he could see Cat lying unmoving in their bed.

"Oh, love," he whispered brokenly, lifting her hand and

pressing it to his mouth. "I love you so very much. Please be all right. I can not live without you."

"She is sleeping, my lord," Dr. Hamilton said, walking up behind him. "She can't hear you."

"I know," Stephen said, his gaze fixed on Cat's face. Some of the color was coming back into her cheeks, and he was relieved to see it wasn't the hectic flush that would have indicated the presence of a fever. To be certain, he laid the back of his hand on her cheeks, reassured by the warm feel of her flesh.

"Now that we are private, my lord, there is something we must discuss."

The relief washing through Stephen turned to ice at the doctor's words. He turned to face him, his heart pounding with fear. "What is it?" he asked, steeling himself for a mortal blow.

"Your wife's maid, Alice, I believe she is called, informed me her ladyship is likely with child. Were you aware of this?"

Stephen felt as if Lacey's ball had entered his own chest. He could only stare at the doctor in blank astonishment. "No," he said, glancing back at Cat and fighting tears. "I wasn't."

"I see." Dr. Hamilton cleared his throat at Stephen's stark tone. "Well, there is a danger, a small one, I grant you, that your wife's injury, compounded as it is with her pregnancy, might prove too much for her system. The human body is a most delicate instrument, and it is easily overset. I just want you to be prepared for—"

"Take the child!" Stephen interrupted, tears streaming down his face as he confronted the doctor. His joy at learning Cat was carrying his babe was cancelled by the terror that the babe could also cost Cat her life.

"I beg pardon, my lord?" Dr. Hamilton said, blinking at him.

"You heard me," Stephen said desperately. "Take the child. I won't have my wife's life endangered."

"But, Lord Rockholme, what you are suggesting is dangerous, to say nothing of illegal!" the doctor protested in shock.

"Don't tell me that!" Stephen grabbed at the doctor's coat again, shaking him like a rat. "I know there are potions you can give her. Do it at once, do you hear me?"

"Your lordship, I told you the risk to your wife is a small

one," Dr. Hamilton answered, trying to make Stephen see sense. "There is no reason to assume the worst. With rest and care—"

"Any risk is too much!" Stephen exclaimed, fear making him wild. "If it comes to a matter of choosing between Cat and the babe, I chose Cat. Don't you understand? She is my life."

"Sir, I cannot do what you ask! I—"

"Stephen?" Cat's soft voice brought Stephen's head snapping around, and he saw her staring up at him in dazed pain.

"It's all right, my sweetest." He dropped to his knees beside the bed. "Rest now, darling. You're safe."

Cat's lips moved in a weak smile. "I know," she said, gazing up at him. "I love you, Stephen."

He could feel the tears on his face, and he didn't care. "And I love you," he said, ardently kissing her hand. "I love you more than I have ever loved anyone."

"I think I loved you from the moment I first met you," she said, her gaze holding his. "I pretended not to, but I did."

"I loved you even before then," Stephen replied, stunned to realize it was nothing less than the truth. "I saw you at Exter's, and all other women ceased to matter for me. There's been no one else for me, Cat. Not since that first night."

To his alarm, Cat's eyes flooded with tears. "What is wrong?" he demanded in panic. "Are you in pain? Doctor, she is in pain, do something!"

"No, it's not that," Cat protested, raising her hand for Stephen's. "It's the babe. Have I lost it? Have I lost our child?"

"No, you're fine, my lady, as is your babe," Dr. Hamilton said reassuringly. "Rest now, ma'am. All will be fine."

"Your son, Stephen." Cat closed her eyes again, and her fingers slipped from Stephen's. "I carry your son."

"There, she is asleep again, thank heavens." Dr. Hamilton said with a heartfelt sigh. "You must take care not to upset her again, my lord. It could be disastrous."

"I won't upset her," Stephen promised. "But understand I meant what I said. Cat's life is all that matters to me. Now kindly go. I want to be alone with my wife."

* * *

Images and voices drifted in and out of Cat's consciousness over the long hours of the night. Sometimes she would think she was back in that horrid lodge with Jeremey and Captain Lacey. Other times she thought she was in the lodge where she and Stephen had spent their wedding night, and he was making tender love to her. She even imagined she saw Edward again, and that he was smiling and nodding at her in approval. That made her cry, and she felt the cool touch of a washcloth on her forehead.

"It's all right, sweetheart," she heard Stephen whisper softly. "Rest now, you'll be fine."

"Stephen?" She gazed up into his haggard face. "What time is it?"

"Ten of the morning," he answered, lifting her head up and giving her a small sip of tea. "Go back to sleep."

But Cat had had enough of sleep. Another memory, this one hazy and yet heartbreakingly real, kept teasing her, and she knew she had to know if it was real, or a dream.

"I love you," she said, reveling in the chance to say the words aloud and free of any restraint. "I meant to tell you before all this happened, but I couldn't."

"I love you," he said, bending to kiss her lips. "I've told you that half a dozen times through the night, and I'll go on saying it to you for the rest of our lives."

She returned his kiss with as much energy as she could muster. "I heard you," she said softly, her eyes aglow with emotions. "I heard you every time you said it."

"I prayed that you would. That's why I said it. I wanted you to know that you mean everything to me."

Cat felt a lump of emotion forming in her throat. "Did I tell you about the baby?" she asked, taking his hand and laying it over her stomach.

"Yes," to her confusion he withdrew his hand, his gaze not meeting hers.

"I—aren't you pleased?" she asked, puzzled by his reaction. "I thought you would be delighted."

"I am," he said with a singular lack of conviction. "But Dr.

Hamilton fears that because of your wound the baby might prove too much for you. I—I told him to take it."

"What?"

"Don't you see, Cat?" He grabbed her hand, his fingers crushing hers in a desperate grip. "I can't risk something happening to you! I won't!"

"But I am carrying your heir!" Cat said, gazing up at him in horror. "I know I am! How can you think to destroy it?"

"Because I love you!" Stephen cried, his voice ragged with the force of his emotions. "I don't want to lose you, Cat. I would rather lose my own life than that."

She believed him. It was obvious by the way he spoke, by the anguish in his dark eyes. The force of his love overwhelmed her, and she found herself blinking back tears.

"You're not going to lose me," she said, pressing their joined fingers to her cheeks. "And we're not going to lose our child. I'll be fine, Stephen. So long as I know I have your love, I'll be fine."

"Then you'll be fine for the whole of eternity," he murmured, bending to kiss her. "Because that's how long I shall love you."

They continued holding each other and kissing, sharing their love and their joy in their child. He told her Lacey was dead and Sedgewood was in prison awaiting trial on charges of kidnapping, attempted murder, and attempted fraud.

"Exter destroyed the papers," he added, feeding her another sip of tea. "Even if he pursues his claims, he'll have no proof to back them up. Although if you want my opinion, he'll let the matter drop. Pressing it now would avail him nothing."

"So it's ended," she murmured, feeling a great wave of relief washing over her. "Eddie is safe."

"Yes, he's safe," Stephen said with a chuckle. "Or as safe as an imp like that can ever be."

Cat hesitated, and then she asked the question she had been longing to ask since seeing him at Larks Hall. "Does it bother you knowing that you can never claim him as your son?" she asked, gazing up at him. "Answer me honestly."

"Yes, it bothers me," he said without preamble. "But only because I love him, and because he is so fine a son. We made a wonderful child between us, Cat, and I am certain this babe will be every bit as unique."

They kissed again, and Cat settled against his chest with a troubled sigh. "I wish there was a way we could tell him the truth," she brooded. "He deserves to know you are his father."

"I am already the only father he remembers, the only father he will love, let that be enough. And speaking of Eddie, there is something I think you should know . . ."

"Mama!" The door was thrown open as if by magic, and Eddie came dashing into the room, followed by Elizabeth, Lydia, and Miss Blakely. Eddie made a beeline for the bed, and would have leapt on top of it if Stephen hadn't snatched him out of midair.

"Have a care for her shoulder!" he warned sternly. "I won't have you jostling her."

Eddie was instantly contrite. "Yes, Papa," he said in solemn tones, and then leaned down from Stephen's arms to place a smacking kiss on Cat's cheek.

"I am sorry you are hurted, Mama," he said, his dark eyes tearful. "Are you better now?"

"Oh, yes, love, I am fine," Cat said, laughing and crying as she cuddled him to her uninjured side. "But what are you doing here? I thought you were all in Kent!"

"Aunt Lottie and Uncle David came to get us." Lydia sidled forward to touch Cat's dark hair. "He has two pairs of matched grays to pull his coach."

"And Aunt Lottie says I might come to London with you for the petite season," Beth said, torn between eagerness and worry over Cat. "May I, Mama? May I please?"

Then everyone was talking at once, and hugs and tears were exchanged with equal abandon. Even Miss Blakely slipped forward to give Cat a quick kiss, delicately blowing her nose as she admonished Cat for taking such foolish risks.

More tea was brought, and the bedroom was soon ringing with the noisy sound of family. Cat reveled in the sheer joy of it, and she could tell by the wide grin on Stephen's face that he was also enjoying himself. Beth and Lydia were waging a fierce battle over the last macaroon, which Stephen settled by cutting it in half and handing a piece to each girl. When he caught Cat, watching him, he gave her an audacious wink.

"This one might be a son," he murmured, laying a hand on her stomach and giving her a burning kiss. "But I want a daughter as well. Perhaps even two."

Lydia and Beth had devoured their sweets and were now arguing over who got to pour the next cup of tea. "Are you quite certain of that, Lord Stephen?" she teased, her heart brimming with love as she met his gaze once more.

"Aye, Lady Cat," he said, and kissed her once more. "I am certain."

Epilogue

Rockholme Manor, Kent, England 1816

"Mama! It's my turn to hold the baby! Let me hold the baby!" Eddie danced around Cat, holding up his arms in impatient demand. "Give me my brother!"

"In a moment, Edward," Stephen said, smiling indulgently down at Cat and their newest son. "Young Stephen isn't done taking his supper as yet."

"Yes, he is." Cat handed the baby to him, and closed up the front of her gown. She knew she shocked the servants by not using a wet nurse; but she'd nursed Eddie, and she didn't want to miss the same glorious experience with Stephen.

"Here." Stephen was placing the baby in Eddie's arms. "Put your arm just there, under his head. Mind you support him."

"Papa, I know how to hold a baby," Eddie informed him with a patient sigh. "*I* am a big boy now."

Stephen's lips twitched in amusement, and he ruffled Eddie's hair. "My mistake, son. I meant no offense."

Eddie paid them no mind, his attention caught as it always was by his younger brother. He'd adored the babe with a fierce devotion almost from the moment of his birth, and Cat was secretly touched by his love for his brother.

The girls were equally devoted, and between them, Miss Blakely, and a besotted James, both Cat and Stephen had to fight for the privilege of holding their own child. Thinking of Miss Blakely and James made Cat give the younger couple a pleased smile. They had announced their engagement a few weeks before Stephen's birth, and their wedding would take place before Beth left for London to make her bows.

"What are you thinking?" Stephen asked a short time later as he led her out into the garden. It was late June, and the air was filled with the seductive smell of roses.

"Oh, I was remembering another garden, another time," she replied, slipping her arm into his, and sighing with contentment.

"The one at Exter's?" he asked, then grinned at her telling blush. "I was remembering it as well. I seduced you amongst the pinks, as I recall."

"You did not seduce me!" Cat denied, turning to face him with a scowl of mock indignation.

"Very well." His arms closed about her waist. "It was you who seduced me."

"That's better," Cat said, sliding her arms about her husband's neck and pressing close to him. "What do you think are the chances I shall be able to seduce you again?"

He gave her the rake's grin that had enchanted her from the first. "What do you think?" he drawled, picking her up and carrying her to a nearby arbor.

Cat gave a joyous laugh, her heart overflowing with love and happiness as she gave herself to the man she adored with all her soul.

"You're still a rake without equal," she sighed, helping him push off his tight-fitting jacket.

"And you're still my Lady Cat," he returned, undoing the front of her dress. "Now hush, love. Your husband wants to make love to you."

Cat's emerald green eyes danced with amusement. "Very well, my lord," she said demurely, and then gave herself up to the pleasure they had found together.